THE IDEAL, GENUINE MAN

DON ROBERTSON

THE IDEAL, GENUINE MAN

With a forenote by Stephen King

Bangor, Maine
PHILTRUM PRESS
1987

A Philtrum Publication

Distributed by
The Putnam Publishing Group
200 Madison Avenue
New York, NY 10016

Published simultaneously in Canada.

ISBN 0-399-19993-4

Printed in the United States of America

For Irving Gitlin and N. R. Howard II

THE IDEAL, GENUINE WRITER:
A FORENOTE

NOTE: *I want to thank my wife, Tabitha King, for her careful reading and diplomatic criticism of the essay which follows—what I mean is that I had everything bass-ackwards, and she managed to set me straight without making me mad. Well . . . too mad. The fact is, I did not even manage to find a way into the subject of Don Robertson and his work until the fourth try, which was the bass-ackwards one. Well, it's always better to have an ackwards bass, sez I, than no bass at all. That's one you'll never find in Bartlett's.*

More seriously, it was extremely difficult for me to write about Don Robertson, because his work has been so important to me. To find critical distance is impossible, which is why there is very little concrete criticism of the novel which follows in the essay. To do the job at all is hard enough, when you feel so strongly about the work a living man has made. In a way, writing such an essay as this is very like playing in the World Series: if you're a pro and your team gets there, you are expected to play, nerves or not, and play well—you are, after all, a pro, and pros are paid, and playing well under pressure is what they are paid for.

But pros are human, too. Under pressure, a great shortstop may boot an easy grounder; an ordinarily steady outfielder may throw wild to the backstop; a good hitter may choke at the plate and bat .127 in a six-game Series.

In the case of pro writers, the equivalent of a wild cut at a bad ball for strike three is a piece of incoherent writing. I am grateful to my wife, for Don's sake as well as my own, for saving this piece . . . but then: if not

*for me, she might never have read a Don Robertson novel. So maybe turn-
about's fair play.*

Either way, thanks, Tabby, and lots of love—Steve

1

This is a forenote to Don Robertson's novel *The Ideal, Genuine Man*.
It is not an introduction. The idea of writing an introduction to a
Don Robertson novel is ridiculous because it is impossible. This is
a topic to which we will return once we have set our feet firmly on
the ground . . . something which is not always easy to do when
discussing Robertson and his work.

2

Don Robertson was and is one of the three writers who influenced
me as a young man who was trying to "become" a novelist (the
other two being Richard Matheson and John D. MacDonald). I
might have "become" without one of the three, possibly without
any of them (I somehow doubt it, though), but making writers is a
little like making bread: it's best not to frig too much with the
recipe or the conditions that recipe calls for. If the yeast is old, if
the water is too cold, if there's a draft where you've placed your
dough, the stuff will not rise; it will simply sit there in the bowl, a
dead thing.

This is not a way of saying "You owe this guy a vote of thanks
for producing such a great writer as you." I have an ego, but I hope
I have it under better control than that. I am quite capable of doing
my own thanking, and that's just what I have done here. Because
when thanks are owed, thanks must be given. "Else the devil shall
knock on your door and take you for an ingrate," the Irish say (or
so Charles Maturin *says* they say in *Melmoth the Wanderer*).

Thanks owed or no thanks owed, I would not publish a piece of
shit. There are people who love the industry, but I am not one of

them. Philtrum Press's spring /summer list consists of one book—
the one you hold in your hands—and our backlist consists of a
second book, the original edition of *The Eyes of the Dragon*, of which
I sold 1000 copies so I could afford to give away 250. We have a
staff of five, although I (as president) and Stephanie Leonard (trea-
surer and my sister-in-law) are contemplating adding a temp to
deal with mail-orders.

We are, in other words, a very humble storefront in a world
dominated by a few great glassy shopping malls.

So I would not publish a bad book, nor even a good one (please
do not infer any personal opinion of the worth of *The Eyes of the
Dragon* from that; defendants who serve as their own legal coun-
sellors and publishers who issue their own fiction both have fools
for clients, and the opinions of fools must be disregarded). I am,
after all, a writer, and I must be about the work I can do, since I'm
not much good at any other . . . although I make good omelettes,
when allowed to concentrate. But *The Ideal, Genuine Man* is not
just good. I think it's a brilliant novel of American life and American attitudes in these waning years of the century. Robertson,
always very good and sometimes even brilliant, has transcended
himself. Publishing this book is no thank-you note, but a simple
necessity. To not publish when I have the means to do so would
be an irresponsible act.

3

I began by saying an introduction in this case was simply not possible. This is because the quality and flavor of Robertson's fiction
is unlike that of anyone else's fiction; his work defeats metaphor
and comparison. You can't "introduce" anchovies or caviar; all
you can do is pass them around and let people try them if they
will. And if I may take caviar as an example, let me explain a little
more fully.

There are three groups of people in the world in the matter of caviar. They are:

1.) People who *love* caviar and can't help pigging out when it's served and think people who don't like it must be either unsophisticated or simply crazy.

2.) People who *hate* caviar and think people low enough to eat raw fish-eggs that leave a slimy sludge on the plate when the stuff is gone would probably geek chickens without the slightest hesitation.

3.) People who have never *tried* caviar.

You can say only one thing about this third group of people, but it is an incredibly *satisfying* thing to say, because of all the world's truisms, it must be one of those with the fewest exceptions: give a person from Group Three some caviar and he will immediately cease to become a Three and will *at once* become a Group One or Group Two person for the rest of his or her life.

With stuff like Don Robertson and fresh Beluga, there is simply no middle ground.

It would be a great relief to *do* an introduction. Like most writers, I am a fundamentally lazy person, and introductions are always easier than essays. The former is like climbing a stepladder; the latter like shinnying up a firepole coated with axle grease. If I could introduce the man, I think I'd opt for the Vegas sort: "Thank you very much, ladies-an-germs, ha-ha, now lemme innerduce to yez all a man who *needs* no innerduction, fresh from his latest stint onna *Hollywood Squares*, pleeze give a great big hand to . . ."

Et cetera.

4

The most unfortunate thing about Don Robertson is that he *does* need an introduction: he may be one of the best unknown publishing novelists in the United States. This is not to say he does not have a coterie of fans and admirers, because he does. One of his novels, *Praise the Human Season* (1974), was a best-seller. *Paradise Falls* (1968), a mammoth work about an Ohio town in the years between the end of the Civil War and the turn of the century, was a main selection of the Literary Guild (published in two volumes), and remains one of the Guild's most successful "mains," in terms of overall sales to club-members, of all time. His trilogy about Morris Bird III, *The Greatest Thing Since Sliced Bread, The Sum and Total of Now*, and *The Greatest Thing that Almost Happened*, has been read and loved by millions (the last was a made-for-TV movie on CBS).

Yet in an age when New York publishers have become more and more savagely focused on best-selling genre novels and highly-praised "prestige" novelists (Roth, Bellow, Beattie, Crewes, *et al.*), guys like Don Robertson have become expendable. There are no rocketships in Robertson novels, you see; no hard-boiled private dicks; no double, triple, and quadruple agents trying to get hold of the plans for the super-secret Zen Bomb which will blow up the whole world if it !!!FALLS INTO THE WRONG HANDS!!!! You will find no one who demands their martinis shaken, not stirred (most Robertson characters drink domestic beer) and has a licence to kill (people *do* kill other people in Robertson novels from time to time, but they don't bother with a licence; shit, they don't even bother with a learner's permit); no one with paranormal powers; no one who goes from rags to riches !!!BY DINT OF HARD WORK AND AMAZING SEXUAL PROWESS!!! No one ever has long, languorous sex in a Beverly Hills hot-tub, approaching climax and then putting it off to drink a little French wine or do a joint or snort a line. There are no tanned guys with whipcord muscles in ebony tuxes helping beautiful women in Dior

[xi]

originals (*sans* panties beneath, of course, although you could feed a family of four hungry Haitians a year or more for the price of the garter-belt holding up the Mlle Hose. In Robertson novels, the guys are apt to be fat slobs in loud sports shirts who drive Chevvies with blown mufflers, the women waitresses with varicose veins and tired faces.

There is sex in Robertson's novels; lots of it. But you never saw people like Robertson's in one of those steamy lap-dissolve scenes Hollywood so loves; Robertson is an ardent film fan, but when he writes, the romantic goes out for coffee and the man punching the keys is a flinty realist . . . but one whose best work is not unmarked by compassion and love for his fellow humans. The people who fuck in Robertson's books puff and pant and snort; sometimes they're fat, sometimes they're old, sometimes they drool when they achieve orgasm, and sometimes they are not able to complete the act at all, let alone have an orgasm.

They are the sort of people New York publishers dismiss as—o kiss of death—*ordinary*. Publishers want either ordinary people in extraordinary situations (King, Ludlum, Follett, Sheldon, *et al.*) or extraordinary people in ordinary situations (Murdoch, Irving, Thomas, Naipaul, Morris, *et al.*), but ordinary people in ordinary situations?

The accountants frown on such things. They frown even though such TV programs as *All in the Family* and *The Cosby Show* were and are huge successes depicting just such people and milieu; they frown in spite of Harper Lee's *To Kill a Mockingbird* or Judith Guest's book, which bore that exact title, *Ordinary People*, or Robertson's own poignant (and popular) *Praise the Human Season*.

Accountants like hired killers out to steal the Zen-Bomb.

Accountants like $1,000 a night call-girls who ram handfuls of ice-cubes up some rich guy's ass at the proper moment, a technique which !!!INCREASES HIS PLEASURE A THOUSANDFOLD!!!

[xii]

Can I introduce a man who renders the phrase "ordinary people" as meaningless as it really is? I cannot. But I can thank God for him and for the chance to publish this book. And I do.

5

I can't introduce him, but I can perhaps give you a hazy idea of what you are in for. There is, for instance, the case of Michael Alpert, the man who designed and executed the book you now hold in your hands. Michael is a small, neat man who speaks in a low voice—not so low you have to strain to hear him, but low enough to compel attention. I went to college with Michael Alpert, attended poetry seminars with him, and can attest to both his intelligence and creative ability not just as a book-designer but as a writer. Some of his poetry approaches brilliance.

And he really *does* know all there is about making books—he's not the kind of guy who takes bets on the ponies in a back room, you understand, but a man who is deeply in love not just with the words *in* books but with the books themselves. My wife has left this on a sticky-note on this page of my rough draft, and it's a true thing: "Books are such commonplaces," she writes, "[that] we rarely appreciate them as objects. Michael does." The making of books as a subject of conversation is one most people would consider as being right up there with the mating habits of Brazilian macaws. But in the hands of a man like Stephen Jay Gould, the mating habits of Brazilian macaws becomes fascinating and wonderful. Similarly, when Michael discusses creating books, one finds oneself listening eagerly. Part of your interest comes from his comprehensive knowledge, but comprehensive knowledge itself isn't much of a hedge against boredom, or they'd sell the Encyclopedia Britannica with a sticker reading "You won't be able to put it down until you reach the end of Volume W-Z, breathless and exalted."

[xiii]

But Michael's knowledge is seasoned, as is Gould's, with his clear love of the combined art and craft of his chosen occupation . . . and, of course, as with Gould, much comes from his innate skill as a communicator.

He's well-read, but like thousands of intelligent, well-read men and women, he had never heard of Don Robertson before, let alone read anything by him before I put the manuscript of this novel in his hands and asked if he would help me publish it as he had *The Eyes of the Dragon*. He agreed to read the book . . . but no more. If you think of book-design as nothing more than craftsmanship, like plumbing or house-wiring, you may think Alpert's implicit attitude of I'll-get-involved-if-I-think-the-book-warrants-it a snooty one. If you understand the occupation is as much art as craft (Michael will open a well-made book, plunge his face into it and breathe deeply, as if smelling roses), an occupation demanding both talent and the commitment of *prodigious* amounts of energy, I think you'll sympathize. I would have been surprised—and disappointed—if Michael had agreed to prepare the work in question for publication without first examining the contents.

Man, I'll never forget the afternoon he brought the manuscript back. He looked like a man who has pulled the lever on his F-111 ejection seat and realizes a split-second before the charge goes off that he neglected to first jettison the canopy.

"This," Michael said in his soft voice, "This is . . . is . . ." He stopped and looked at me rather hopelessly. "This is simply incredible," he finished.

"Yes," I said. "I know."

Then he said the only thing that *ever* convinces me that the guy who's talking to me isn't bullshitting. "Have you got anything else by this guy?"

"All of it," I said, smiling.

[xiv]

In a very real sense, Michael *still* hasn't recovered from the shock of *The Ideal Genuine Man.*

One's first encounter with Don Robertson often has that effect.

6

I read *The River and the Wilderness* (1962) the year I started high school. In it was a use of onomatopoeia which struck me as forcibly as a slap in the face. Twenty-four years later, the thought of it still leaves me kind of dazed and flabbergasted, but nodding and grinning like a good rockabilly song with just the right guitar-boogie-shuffle beat. You can't communicate something like that to other people by telling them about it any more than you can tell them how great caviar is . . . or explaining a joke the listener didn't get, for that matter. But you *can* report.

I was reading a passage about wounded soldiers being taken away from a Civil War battle-site. They were on a train, crowded in there like sardines. And there's one guy playing a banjo. The sound the banjo makes, Robertson says, is BLUNK! BLUNK!

I sat there in period four study-hall, transfixed.

Holy God! I thought. *Yeah. You're goddam right! Fuckin-A! That really is the sound a banjo makes!*

This mattered a great deal to me, and that I *can* explain. It mattered because it was more than just close to right; it mattered because it was more than *right*. It mattered because it was *perfect*, like that Dale Hawkins lick on *Suzy Q.* that rock and roll guitarists have been trying to duplicate since 1957. It wasn't like reading. It was as if Robertson had slipped a magic little tape-player into that book, one which was activated not by voice but by something as delicate as the pressure of the eye falling upon it.

There are two technical terms for what I am speaking of: one is epiphany; the other is *frisson*. Call it whatever you want to, it is a talent God gives to only a handful of writers, and many of them can only do it in one book. Robertson does it again and again. If you read a lot—and I do—most of what you read comes up into the forefront of your mind while you're reading the book, then simply falls back into this big anonymous hopper of words—the literary equivalent of a cement mixer—when you're done.

Robertson is different. He has written things in his previous books, and he has written things here, that you will never forget. He may sometimes stumble, he may sometimes over-write, he occasionally falls into sentimentality (that, Gentle Reader, is not the case in this book—again, you have been warned). But my own memory can serve up so many phrases, sentences, and passages whole and complete that I know how often he is simply . . . perfect.

I have no intention of belaboring you with Don Robertson's Greatest Hits (Operators Are Standing By to Take Your Order, Dial the 800 Number at the Bottom of Your Screen Except in Maryland and Wyoming), although I *could*. Two or three examples of Robertson's odd and unique view should serve.

There is, for example, Virgil T. Light, a character in *Paradise Falls* (one of Virgil T. Light's descendents appears in *The Talisman*, courtesy of Don, and he also loaned me his wonderfully named little Ohio town for *Christine*—a minor character hails from there). Virgil T. Light is described as being "a large bald man with a large bald voice." Light's mistress, Nancy, is the wife of the protagonist of *Paradise Falls* (one cannot by any stretch call this slimebucket, Charles Palmer Wells by name, a "hero"). Years earlier, on one giddy adolescent occasion back in their Indiana hometown, Nancy and Charley came very close to making love during a tornado, in a barn. They are kept from consummating the act by a grade-school teacher who has gone mad—a *Minnesota Gothic* situation Robertson handles with dry and deadly force. Charley runs away instead of protecting Nancy, thus losing the woman Providence (one is never quite sure if there *is* such a thing in the world of Don Robertson, but he never quite says there *isn't*) perhaps meant for him to have. Nancy eventually marries Charley, but for a time she takes up with Virgil T. Light, the large bald man with the large bald voice, and for the remaining eight or nine hundred pages of this American epic, a sullen Charley thinks of Nancy as The Precious Pussy Long Withheld. He also thinks a great deal about her tiddies. Note: *tiddies*. Not breasts, jugs, bazooms, or knockers. No other word but that exquisite seventh-grade-hayseed word will do. Many writers would not know it; those who did might stick at using it; Robertson, however, sticks at nothing (for the third and last time, Reader, you have been warned). So for C. P. Wells, the first gyspy moth of capitalism arising from the cocoon of the late 19th century, it is tiddies she has and always *will* have, hallelujah, amen.

Ah, friends! Is stuff like this important? Absolutely not. It's just all there is. Like breathing, you only notice it when it stops being there.

Capable of paragraphs which sometimes glide gaily on for twenty pages or more, Robertson is also capable of startling acts of compression—compression so complete it is nearly poetry. One chapter in *Paradise Falls* describes a funeral, and it ends with this sentence: "There were that day o Lord squadrons of birds." It is enough.

In *Miss Margaret Ridpath and the Dismantling of the Universe* (1977), Robertson depicts one of the most horrifying bands of thugs ever to exist on paper (although, when one reflects upon such friendly folks as the Manson family, one dismisses the excessive evil of Robertson's fictional band as black romanticism at one's own peril). We are fascinated by them . . . yet Robertson is able to equally fascinate us in that novel by narrating a game of bridge. How can a game of bridge and the depredations of a gang which makes Ma

Barker and her boys look like the Mouseketeers command equal attention and fascination in the reader's mind? Although only God and Don may know how it's done (and Don, at least, would be happy to expound on the subject, but it would be like trying to teach a potato to play *Trivial Persuit*), the remarkably similar emotional effects Robertson achieves with such disparate plot elements not just in this novel but in almost *all* of them suggests a simple explanation: he possesses the rare and remarkable talent of being able to turn microcosm into macrocosm and macrocosm into microcosm. Beneath his powerful (but compassionate) microscope, every bacterium becomes Godzilla-sized, and when Robertson swings his telescope around to look through the far end (as he often and deliberately does), giants such as C. P. Wells become squeaking mice. In a Robertson novel, somehow *everything* is happening even when *nothing* is happening. Thus, in *The Greatest Thing Since Sliced Bread*, the trip a boy and his little sister make across Cleveland, Ohio, just before a gas-works explosion becomes as magnificent as *The Odyssey*. Do you think I'm twisting your tit? Pulling your leg? Jerking your joint? Maybe you do. *Probably* you do (that soft *whissshhh* sound you hear isn't imagination or the wind in the eaves but academic snoots turning imperiously upward all over America, but it does not hurt to remember that a university English professor is usually a man who has sold his birthright—not to mention his brains—for a plot of message). If you *do* think I'm jerking your joint, you have never read Don Robertson . . . and that first encounter always *is* a little like blowing your ejection seat without remembering to first jettison the canopy.

7

Let me finish with reiteration: Ordinary people do not exist in Robertson's world, which are systemic, seeming to revolve around

[xviii]

the central point of Paradise Falls, Ohio. In his books, "ordinary people" become creatures of mystery, both light and dark. I will not dissect *The Ideal Genuine Man* for you, any more than I would chew your food for you if you had any working teeth left in your head (or even a good set of what the old folks used to call "Roebuckers").

There are no ordinary people and, thank God, there are no Beautiful People. Have you ever read one of those book-flaps (the cover of books such as those to which I now refer usually show photographs of blonde women on black leather couches with their cakes falling out of their evening dresses and at least three rings on each hand, the stone set in each roughly the size of a Clydesdale's asshole) where it says "the action moves with dizzying rapidity from the decadent, glamorous world of Palm Beach to the ski-slopes of Gstaad to the opulent casinos of Monte Carlo"? No such flap copy exists or could exist here. Here there is only the brooding avatar of Houston, Texas, a cheesy Xanadu which exists in its own flat and grainy yellow light. Here in the enervating heat and the Texas sprawls and drawls are the rednecks, the oil-rich (only in Houston town you say that *ohl*, sonny, like that thang you use to punch holes in leather . . . or maybe in the neck of that ole boy who just kep on playing G-3 on the jukebox even after you done told him *twicet* to lay off'n it on account of that song *always* reminds you of Luanne), the drunks . . . and the old.

It is upon the old that Robertson fixes his eye with the most force and understanding and compassion. These are not the sweet old codgers of sitcom TV but the forgotten old, sour and confused people who sit in dark bars and brood in the unreal colors thrown by badly tuned TV sets showing afternoon soap operas. Instead of streaking from Palm Beach to Gstaad to the opulent casinos of Monte Carlo, these people creep in the Chevrolets with the blown mufflers from the banks where they stand in line to cash welfare checks to the local bar for a few bottles of Lone Star, and finally home to a house which may be empty or where a spouse may be dying by lonely inches. Robertson's people are not jet-setters but lonely people rolling creakily from the unglamorous world of bewilderment to the slopes of terror and finally to the not-very-opulent casinos of fury and random violence. Here are men with prostate trouble and women with sagging, wrinkled breasts.

I see no part in a film version for either John Forsythe or Joan Collins. A Robertson heroine would look more like Ruth Gordon; a hero more like the late Strother Martin.

If all this sounds depressing, I have misled you. There is enough vigor and exuberance in Robertson's work to offset his often grim themes. His vision of the world is dark, but the horrifying darkness of that vision could not be glimpsed without the sparkles of humor that illuminate what he writes like a gala fireworks show over a blasted and sterile landscape. All of which makes him the latest—but not the last, or at least so one hopes—in a brawny bunch of American story-tellers who wrote naturalistic fiction . . . tales not of the four hundred but of what O. Henry called the four *million*. That line descends to Robertson from Mark Twain to Stephen Crane to Frank Norris to Theodore Dreiser to James Jones and Hubert Selby, Jr. He has written as brilliantly as any of these men, and in *The Ideal, Genuine Man* I believe he has outwritten all of them as well as himself. This is, quite simply, a great book by an ideal, genuine writer.

Have I said why? Can it be that, in all of this sound and fury, I have neglected to say *why*? Indeed I have. I *can't*. All I can do is offer you this novel and tell you that by page fifty you will have joined Group One, those who think Robertson is like the title of one of his novels—the greatest thing since sliced bread—or Group

Two, who think he is a nasty man writing in a nasty way about nasty people who don't matter and are too ugly to look at anyway . . . particularly as closely as Don Robertson insists on looking at things. But I do know one thing: Most of you who've never read Robertson before are going to end up looking a lot like Michael Alpert did on the day he returned the manuscript. I envy you the experience, although I must tell you that you may never again be entirely satisfied with a book purporting to depict "real" American life. And the effect of Robertson is a little like the effect of going a fast five rounds with Cassius Clay about two decades ago: it takes quite awhile to wear off.

I repeat: win, lose, or draw, you have never read anything quite like the novel which follows.

Never.

Never.

Stephen King
Bangor, Maine
January 27–28, 1987

Passions are not natural to mankind; they are always exceptions or excrescences. The ideal, genuine man is calm in joy and calm in pain and sorrow. Passions must quickly pass or else they must be driven out.

BRAHMS

CHAPTER ONE

HERMAN MARSHALL SQUINTED at the rain. He told himself he needed to get clean. He told himself he needed to run out into the street and soak his toes. He swallowed. He coughed. He rubbed his cheeks. He told himself he was thinking like a damn fool. He glanced across the room. Edna lay in the brass bed. It had come down from Hope, Arkansas. It had been a wedding gift from Herman Marshall's parents. Again he squinted at the rain. He was trying to picture his parents' faces. He closed his eyes for a moment. It did no good. He could not really picture his parents' faces. Oh, they had been thin faces, but the thinness was all he could summon. Raw bones. Wet, tough eyes. That sort of thing. He opened his eyes. He blinked toward his wife. She never had been thin. She always had had places to grab holt of. Herman Marshall began rubbing his eyes. He dug his knuckles against his eyes. His eyes began to hurt. Well, so what? Who cared? He wept. The sound of it was full of sand and torn things. He sucked snot. He jerked his hands away from his eyes. He opened his eyes, but his vision was blurred and full of dancing dots. He jammed his thumbs against his nostrils to keep the snot from leaking. He leaned forward. He pressed his forehead against the windowpane. He sucked snot and tears.

"Hey," said Edna from the bed.

The rain tapped and splattered. It gathered itself in oily lumps. Herman Marshall said nothing.

"You're mad at me, ain't you?" said Edna.

Herman Marshall shuddered.

[1]

"Well, you got a right," said Edna.

Herman Marshall's forehead moved from side to side against the windowpane, and the windowpane squeaked. He groaned. He hugged himself. He was seventyfour, and he had made his living driving a truck, and he was not used to weeping. He was just an old boy from Hope, Arkansas, and his sort never had looked kindly on weeping. If you wept, chances were you got your pants pulled down. Or you got throwed in somebody's cistern. For Herman Marshall, his tears were an alien embarrassment. He'd had three brothers (they all were dead now), and they would have laughed at him because of his tears. He wondered whether they were laughing at him right now. Maybe, come to think of it, they were laughing at him from up in Paradise. (Did he believe in Paradise? Well, why not? He'd thought about it a whole lot, yessir. It was the sort of thing that often occupied a man's attention at night when he sat alone in the cab of his truck, and headlights tore at his eyes, and the pavement bounced the hell out of his kidneys, and finally the sun came green and inevitable in the east, and early scrub cattle rubbed at fenceposts and trailed stale straw from their languid foolish mouths.)

Edna moved her legs. "Ow," she said.

Herman Marshall leaned back from the windowpane and rubbed his eyes with the heels of his hands. This time he rubbed them gently. He was sitting in a narrow chair that had a leather seat. He leaned a little toward the brass bed, and the seat made a silly soprano sound that almost was like a tight fart. "I been thinkin . . ." he said, hesitating.

"I *hurt*," said Edna.

"I know," said Herman Marshall.

Edna moistened her lips. She always was moistening her lips. But it wasn't because she was particularly thirsty. It was something to do, she'd told Herman. Something to *do*, and it didn't *hurt* anybody, did it? "Thinkin?" she said.

"Yes ma'am," said Herman Marshall to his wife. "Bout how quick it's all been. I mean, I feel like yesterday I was fifty, an Billy was alive, an air was chicken on the table an a new car in the garage."

"You shouldn't ought to think at way," said Edna.

"I expect not," said Herman Marshall.

"I'm sorry," said Edna.

"You don't have to keep sayin at," said Herman Marshall. His voice was passionless. It shrugged and scuffed; it was dusty, exhausted.

Edna didn't say anything, but her head moved from side to side. She still was fat, was old Edna. Never mind the cancer. (If it was possible for fat people to starve, as Herman Marshall had read one time in the *Chronicle*, he supposed it was possible for fat people to have cancer.)

"You want another of em pills?" said Herman Marshall.

"No," said Edna. "Em pills, all they do is make me fall asleep. If I keep fallin asleep, I expect I might as well be dead an be done with it. I mean, the plot is all paid for an all."

"What?"

"I wish Houston had hills, though."

"Oh," said Herman Marshall.

"I wouldn't mind bein planted on a hill. A hill with a nice little old view."

"But the plot's all paid for."

"I know," said Edna. "I *know*."

Herman Marshall grunted. "An you picked it out," he said to Edna. He was telling her something she already knew, but he didn't suppose it mattered. "An we'll be next to Billy. You was all fussy an particular when you picked out the plot. You could of been Miss Ima Hogg pickin out a new big one of her mansions . . ." Herman Marshall hesitated. Billy had been their son and their only child. He had died at seventeen of spinal meningitis. He had been damn near a Change of Life baby for Edna, and he had been something of a surprise. Years earlier, she and Herman Marshall had agreed that having kids would be nice, but they'd just about given up. Now, abruptly, Herman Marshall resumed speaking. "It's a whole big wonderful life," he said.

"Ha," said Edna.

"What with one thing an another," said Herman Marshall.

"Shoot," said Edna.

"All I keep thinkin, over an over, is how *fast* it's all been," said Herman Marshall. "I keep tellin myself hell, Herman, you ain't *you* at all; you're still young, an your old man's body's a flabby god-damn *joke*, an one day you'll—"

"Ow," said Edna, and she wrapped her head in her arms. Her arms were bluish. She squeezed her skull. She was seventy, and every last wisp of her hair was gone. That was good old chemotherapy for you. She and Herman Marshall had been warned about the chemotherapy, but what choice had they had? (He had deflowered her in a vacant lot behind a movie house in Shreveport in 1934, and the movie had been a good one—*Manhattan Melodrama*, the same movie old John Dillinger had seen the night Melvin Purvis and the FBI had pulled off their dirty little ambush in that Chicago alley. Edna had been Edna Stillman in those days, and Herman Marshall had told her God damn but what she wasn't prettier than a speckled trout, ha ha, just a little joke air, and a whole lot of nice sweet meat sat warmly on her pretty bones, and Edna had told him to stop that *you*, stop it *right now*, and a yarden-gine hooted over at the Kansas City Southern yards, and Herman

[4]

Marshall breathed creosote, and his fists dug at the lumpy and littered earth, and a thin sound of Gable and William Powell and ittybitty Mickey Rooney wormed and inched through the movie house's walls, and Edna jerked and snickered, and her fragrant fatgirl's flesh wobbled and slapped, and finally she shrugged a little and tugged down her cotton drawers and said she didn't suppose air was much sense savin It any longer, and so she gave way, and she welcomed him with laughter and warm maneuverings, and Herman Marshall humped and groaned and listened to his breath and said to himself: Hot *damn*. And that had been forever ago. A forever of days. A forever of betrayals, beer, trucks, waitresses, prayer meetings, rodeos, guitars, bleats, guilts, death.)

Herman Marshall stood up. He leaned against the chair for a moment. He breathed with his mouth open. Then he walked to the bed. Outside, a car shushed past. The rain had made Herman Marshall feel clammy, especially in his armpits and his crotch. At his age, he often felt clammy in those places. And he frequently pissed. Sometimes he couldn't hold in his piss until he reached the bathroom, and a reluctant few drops would stain his underwear and cause him to stink. Which was why there were times he had to breathe with his mouth open. Sighing, he knelt next to the brass bed. He reached for Edna's arms and gently pulled them away from her head. There was no strength in them, no resistance. Her hands fluttered. Her fingers were fatly pink. He kissed her forehead. "You need a nice pill," he said.

". . . ain't no such a thing as a nice pill," said Edna, wheezing a little.

"You're bein brave. Maybe too brave."

"Ain't at for me to be the judge?"

". . . maybe," said Herman Marshall.

"Maybe other things hurt more," said Edna.

"Never mind bout it."

"You fixin to go up to the attic?"

Herman Marshall released his wife's arms. He looked directly at her eyes, which were gray. He did not like to look at her skull. The chemotherapy had taken away too much and then some. He said to her: "Maybe. Soon as you're sleepin real good."

"An you'll come down with a story?"

"Could be," said Herman Marshall.

"You're good with a story," said Edna. "You should of been a writer or somethin."

Herman Marshall tried to smile. Maybe he succeeded. Maybe he didn't. He still was kneeling, and his joints were beginning to hurt. He rested his elbows on the bedspread. It was a cheneille bedspread. Green. It dated back to 1946 or so, as closely as he could remember. "A writer," he said. "At would of been the day." He still was trying to smile. Maybe, in the Sweet Bye & Bye, God would give him credit for trying to smile. It wasn't easy, trying to smile at an old woman who sure as shit would have been better off dead.

"Go on an go up air," said Edna. "I'll be all right. I ain't goin noplace. Go find a good story for me. Make it 1931 or even 1942. A laugh maybe. Or a tear. I don't care, long as it takes me away from all . . . well, you know, all this . . ."

Herman Marshall stood up. He rubbed his knees. He listened to the rain.

Edna spoke quickly. "You're mad at me, ain't you?"

"*No*," said Herman Marshall. "I'm an *old man*. My *joints hurt*. I'm too old to be mad. An listen here . . . in order to be mad, a man's got to be able to *do* somethin bout it, give somebody a whippin or whatever . . . an me, I'm too old to cut the mustard, you expect you can follow at?"

". . . yes."

"I been too old too long to think bout it," said Herman Marshall. "I can't hardly remember it."

"Remember what?"

"Billy."

"I don't believe at," said Edna, and she winced. Maybe she should have been wearing a kerchief on her head. She surely would have looked better. Herman Marshall had to look away from her. Not even her eyes held him. "You're just bein nice to me," she said. "You're *sparin* me. At's the way we all was when Uncle Floyd died back up in St Louis when I was a little girl. We *spared* him. Him an his brain tumor an all. We all of us behaved like oh shoot, Uncle Floyd, all you got is a headache, an maybe you ought to lay off the home brew . . ." Again Edna winced, and this time she touched her head with the fingertips of her right hand. Both her hands were knobbed with arthritis. Knobbed and brown. She tried to smile at Herman Marshall. "Go on upstairs," she said. "I ain't fixin to run round the block or nothin like at. The rain'll sound nice on the roof, an you'll find me a story. Maybe you'll find his trains or somethin."

"I found his trains last month," said Herman Marshall. He nodded toward the chair at the window. He was leaning a little from side to side. "I set them up over air," he said, "an I fixed the transformer an all, an I fixed the crossin gate that had the little man who came out an waved the lantern, an it all made you smile. Don't you remember at?"

". . . maybe," said Edna, frowning. She folded her arms across her chest. She was wearing a pink wrapper that had had lace cuffs. It had been a Christmas present from old Jobeth Stephenson across the street. Jobeth Stephenson, who was eighty if she was a day and watched dirty movies on cable TV. She always was inviting Herman Marshall over to see the dirty movies. She always laughed and asked him what harm would it do. *Old folks surely are comical*, she had told him once. *Like your barrel of monkeys, only more so.* And then she had cackled, and she had pounded her palms together, and the sound had been dusty and helpless.

Herman Marshall wanted to give way to more weeping. He stared at the floor. He linked his fingers together in front of his crotch. "The trains," he said. "Yes. They ran real good. I done a little wirin . . . at an a little oil here an air . . . an em trains went scootin round an round, good as the day they was new. Member how he used to go choo choo choo in time with the wheels?"

"No," said Edna. Then: "Yes." She poked at a corner of her mouth and rubbed her dentures with a misshapen finger. She spoke around the finger. "I member, all ight. I ain't altogether eeble in the head, not ight et . . ."

"It was a secret thing with him," said Herman Marshall.

Edna pulled the finger from her mouth. "We all got secret things," she said. "I ain't the only one."

"I never said you was."

"But you was good to him."

"I *loved* him," said Herman Marshall.

"Maybe this here what I got is a Judgment," said Edna. She glanced at the finger. Then she wiped it on the covers.

"You're always sayin at," said Herman Marshall. "Maybe you say it too much."

"It was at hash this mornin," said Edna. "At corned beef hash you fixed for me. A little piece of it got wedged next to my gum, you know. A thing like at can drive a person crazy. An me, ha, I'm crazy enough already."

"Crazy like a fox," said Herman Marshall.

"Not true," said Edna.

"How long we been married?"

[8]

"Too long, ha ha."

"Close on to fifty years, correct?"

"I expect," said Edna.

Herman Marshall still was swaying. "Now you just listen here," he said. "You always been the family bookkeeper, right? I can't add a column of figures to save my soul, an we both know it. An you're the best cook I've ever knowed. You can fix barbecuc like it's—"

"I *was* the best cook you've ever knowed," said Edna. "I ain't *nothin* no *more*."

"Don't say at."

"I ain't sayin nothin but the truth. I'd be better off dead, an we both know it. I mean dead an in the grave, not dead but breathin an talkin here in this old bed an talkin bout *corned beef hash* . . ."

Herman Marshall leaned down and touched his wife's forehead. "Hush up," he said. His voice was soft. Perhaps it was a whisper. It nearly was erased by the sound of the rain against the windowpanes and the splashy rattlings of the downspouts. He rubbed his eyes, and rubbing his eyes was the last thing he wanted to do. He backed away from the bed. He walked to the window and leaned against the chair. Now his back was to the bed. When he spoke again, he didn't know whether he was speaking to Edna or God or the rain or what. His voice remained soft. He said: "We always have talked. I'll give us at. Come what may, air's been plenty of the old blabber, ain't air? I'd come home, an my ass'd be all sore an hurty from bouncin in the rig, an you'd laugh an tell me my ass was all sore an hurty on account of some woman, an we'd drink Shiner out air in the kitchen, an you'd tell me you'd missed me, an it was like I'd been gone a million years, an we'd go upstairs, an it didn't matter none whether we awaked the neighbors, an em times would make it all seem worth the trouble, you know what I'm sayin? An sometimes you'd wear hairribbons for me, on account of hairribbons made you look so *young*. An I was a *goat*, wasn't I? Herman Eugene Marshall, goat of goats. I wonder when all at stopped. I can't quite get it straight in my mind. It was long bout 1950, wasn't it? Billy wasn't much more than a *bitty baby*, was he? An the hairribbons got put away. Where'd you put em, Edna? You throw em out with the trash? You had blue ones an green ones an red ones an yellow ones an maybe you even had striped ones, for all I can remember. It all stops, don't it? Everthin. An how come I'm talkin this way? I ought to be cheerin you up. I ought to go up to the attic an find maybe a baseball glove or some-thin. *At's* what I ought to do." Herman Marshall turned and faced the brass bed and his dying wife. His voice was fragile. Maybe it wasn't even audible. "Please," he said. "*Please.*"

Edna blinked at him. "What?" she said. "Please what?"

"The thing about Billy . . ." said Herman Marshall, choking.

". . . what?"

"Please don't take it with you. Please don't talk bout no Judg-ment." Herman Marshall spoke quickly. His words capered and jostled. He could have been a child delivering a memorized recita-tion. "Billy *died*, at's all."

"I'm not talkin bout the *dyin* of him," said Edna, speaking flatly, like maybe one of those Information operators on the tele-phone. "I'm talkin bout how it came to be he got *borned.*"

Herman Marshall tried to shrug. "Well, I needed help . . ." He smiled a little, and the smile was death.

Edna inhaled. "Shame on you," she said.

Herman Marshall leaned against the windowsill. He was begin-ning to feel the urge to piss. It was necessary that his halfassed fucking smile be removed, and so he rubbed his mouth. He rubbed it fiercely, as though he were scraping it with steel wool. He had enough troubles; he didn't need to carry death stamped on his lips.

[10]

"*Shame* on *Herman*," said Edna. "Don't make fun of yourself. Air's more *to* you an at. You an me, we didn't never set the world to burstin into flames, like they say, an we ain't exactly got much money, an our boy's layin out air in at *place*, an we don't even no more get hardly no *Christmas cards*, an maybe Santa Claus has keeled over dead, for all *we* know, but you an me, we had our days, didn't we? *Didn't we?*"

". . . surely," said Herman Marshall. "At's what I been *tellin* you. The Shiner an the hairribbons an all. God damn. A good beer an a good woman. An hairribbons. God *damn*."

"Correct," said Edna. "An you was the best."

"The best except for one."

"The *best*," said Edna. "The *best*. The *best*. The *best*."

"All right," said Herman Marshall.

"Believe it," said Edna.

"All right," said Herman Marshall.

"You say you don't want me to take it with me. Fine an dandy. Then you got to believe me. He wasn't nothin. I was alone, an en he dropped by, an he told me I was pretty, an I knowed all the hairribbons in the world wouldn't never make me pretty no more, an—"

"You don't have to tell me the details," said Herman Marshall. "I know all bout the goddamn *details*."

"Don't be mad," said Edna, and she tugged up the covers until they touched her throat. Her terrible hands were smeared with liverspots.

"I ain't *mad*," said Herman Marshall.

". . . don't hurt me."

"Hurt you? I ain't never hurt you." And Herman Marshall sucked air, and the rain's dampness had filled the room with a stink of brass. His bladder hurt.

"I'm oh God so sorry," said Edna.

[11]

"Stop sayin at."

"I mean, you was gone all the time in your truck."

"All the time?"

"Well, maybe not *all* the time . . ."

"Yeah," said Herman Marshall.

"An I didn't know but what you was layin up with who knows what," said Edna. "Waitresses. Whores. Preachers' wives. You know what they say about preachers' wives, an I was alone, an I didn't think I was pretty no more, an at's a bad thing for a woman to be—"

"*Yes,*" said Herman Marshall. "All *right.* Yes *ma'am. I understand.* We been *over* it. I mean, it's like *I* could recite it to *you* by *heart.* It don't *matter* no more. It's a big old *joke,* is what it is."

"Billy always thought of you as his daddy," said Edna, and her eyes were leaking.

"I know at," said Herman Marshall. He went to the bed. He knelt. He kissed Edna's hands. "In my mind, I mean, I know it real good—I think of him as my son. I still miss him. I want to kiss his grave. Way down where my mind's got its roots, he's *my* son. He ain't nobody else's son. I mean, he lived *here* an died *here.* He was part of *us.* What the hell."

". . . you . . . um, you fixin to go to the attic?"

"Yes ma'am," said Herman Marshall. He glanced back toward the Houston window and the Houston street and the Houston rain. Cicadas screamed. The sound rolled and dipped and coruscated. He adjusted the covers on his wife's bed. "We'll find somethin real nice," he said. He stroked Edna's sad bald head. The thing was, what the hell.

CHAPTER TWO

HE ALMOST MADE IT UPSTAIRS to the toilet. Almost. Which was fine, as the fellow said, as long as you were pitching horseshoes, ha ha. It was funny, real funny, the wisdom a man could pick up. But almost wasn't good enough when he wanted to avoid wetting his pants. And Herman Marshall had wet his pants. At least a little. Which was enough. If the toilet seat hadn't been down, he might have been all right. But he'd had to lift the toilet seat, and that had been enough of a delay so that a brief hot little stream had issued from his weary old wrinkled prick. Maybe it all had to do with the rain. Over the past five years or so, the sound of rain—in fact, the sound of *any* sort of running water—had made him want to piss. He'd had a girlfriend oncet, and her name had been Helen Burnside (a grinning fat girl, every bit as fat as Edna and then some), and the sound of running water had driven her *crazy*. Her word. *Crazy*. And she had said to him something like: *Honeybunch, it honest to God HURTS. An it comes on me so QUICK. An I'm lucky if I can make it to the bathroom on time. An I'm tuggin at my drawers all the while, you know? Whoo. An I'm tellin you, sometimes all I need is the sound of thunder, an I'm just like a little old downhome SIEVE. An the sound can be away off in the distance, but it don't make no matter.* And Herman Marshall had laughed. Good old Helen Burnside. She always had made more out of a thing than it had been worth. But she surely had been a sport. He'd once seen her eat seven burgers at a sitting. And seven helpings of fries. In the Spot Café, located right smack in the middle of the rumpus and the clamor of downtown Hope, Arkansas. With himself and a fry

[13]

cook named Sam Logan as the official witnesses. And then Helen had taken Herman Marshall home, and her mama and her daddy and her three little brothers had been off at the picture show, and she had permitted him to fuck her on the parlor carpet, and she had jiggled, and she had shuddered, and then she had insisted on jamming his prick in her mouth, and she had been seventeen, and later she had said: *I'm a real whole load of fun on a dry day, ha ha.* And now, climbing the narrow and no doubt mildewed stairs that led to the attic of his little home in Houston, Texas, Herman Marshall smiled broadly. The memory of Helen Burnside—an abrupt memory, unheralded and splendid, scooped from a dark forlorn corner of his mind and held up to some sort of sweet faded light—had caused him really to smile for the first time in he didn't know how long. It maybe even was worth his wetting of his pants. Herman Marshall snorted. He shook his head. He breathed with his mouth open. He hadn't bothered to change his pants and his undershorts. He already smelled so bad he didn't really suppose the piss mattered. That was Houston for you, with its rain and its humidity. He'd once heard a fellow compare Houston to a whore, and the fellow had said: *Shit, an it's like Houston's a whore who's real POPULAR, you know? A whore who's workin all the time, humpin an suckin all the time. It's like Houston's the best piece of ass between here an Judgment Day. Which means she ain't even got the time to wipe off her sweat. So she sort of . . . STINKS. You hear what I'm sayin? I mean, air she is, with the sweat rollin down her belly, an she's rubbin her tongue on her lips an tellin you COME AWN, COME AWN; yall don't want to make me fall behind, do you?* And the fellow's words . . . delivered, best as Herman Marshall could remember, in a little old fleabag honkytonk a friend of his named Harry Munger owned down in old redneck Pasadena, shouted over music and laughter and a heavy stomping sound of dancing (mothers danced alone with their babies, and the mothers hugged the babies to their chests, and back in the sweet old days Edna had hugged little Billy to *her* chest) . . . oh, the fellow's words had caused Herman Marshall, belly full of Shiner and balls about to burst from horniness, to pound the bar and say: *Yessir! Ain't at the truth though!* And he had looked around for Edna, who had gone stumbling off to the ladies' room. And then he had pulled the fellow close to him (he didn't want eavesdroppers sticking their nosy noses into his business) and he had said to the fellow: *Buddy, I'm gettin all worked up, you know at? Which means my old woman's just goin to RISE UP tonight, RISE UP an SHOUT HALLELUJAH, if you follow my drift. An the sparks will fly upward, like they say.* And the fellow . . . thick of chest and neck, with teeth that were heavy and horsy . . . had brayed in the general direction of the honkytonk's rusted corrugated ceiling, and he and Herman Marshall had feinted and jabbed, and surely the world would last forever, as long as the beer held out. You got drunk. You feinted and jabbed with a stranger, and then you clapped him on his back, and he clapped you on yours. And everyone looked at you and grinned and applauded. And for a moment you *were* somebody. The webbed and crazed texture of your days almost indicated a benevolence. But then, shit, the beer wore off, and your fingers tightened, and your wrists began to hurt, and you bounced along US 90 in an eighteenwheeler, and some sort of busy enemy was scraping your skull with a straight razor that was nicked and rusty, and steam issued from the morning earth, and you kept pinching the bridge of your nose, and so maybe you knew a waitress or two, a cashier in a Woolworth's, the urgent and stringy wife of an undertaker. Yessir. All right. You weren't perfect. Fact of the matter was you'd fuck a snake, long as it wasn't no nigger snake. And Herman Marshall suddenly spoke aloud. "Shit," he said. He was at the top of the narrow stairs. He pushed open the

[15]

door to the attic. A stink of mildew came at him in palpable and knotted clouds. The stink was all wooly, hairy; it poked at his lips; it made him want to clean out his ears. Herman Marshall wondered whether he would be able to breathe. He spent a great deal of time up here in the attic. Edna always had been a pack rat, and she had saved everything, and what did it matter that the awful mildew had defeated just about everything up here in this damp and airless place? Oh, there was *air*, all right. There couldn't be rot without air. But *this* air was all mossy and final; it took away more than it gave; it curled and drenched; it had tongues, and the tongues spread rust and mold. Herman Marshall stood in a crouch. He was too tall for the attic. There was an unshaded bulb attached to a ceiling connection. Herman Marshall switched on the bulb, and its brightness made him blink. He looked around at boxes and packages and scattered books. He saw abandoned wicker porch furniture, several floor lamps (they all had broken shades, and one of the broken shades showed a procession of headless green and brown ducks), an old television set from perhaps 1949 (a Zenith, with a round screen that was like a porthole), and he and Edna and Billy had watched *Perry Mason* and *Rawhide* and *Twilight Zone* on that sorry old set, and at the end Billy had screamed, but he had insisted that the television set be on through all his screaming, telling Herman Marshall and Edna the sounds from the television set—especially the sounds of canned laughter—took his mind off his pain, even though he *did* scream, even though he *did* writhe and twitch, even though he *did* plead with Herman Marshall and Edna to chop him apart with an ax, please, *please*, I can't stand it; I'm dyin, so let me die, oh you fuckers, you cocksuckers; you *like* watchin what you're watchin? (This from a boy who at the end was only seventeen, and at the end the pain was too much for his heart, and at the end his heart burst, and Herman Marshall was with him, and Billy

[16]

rose up as though the mattress were a wet soiled noxious terrible trampoline, and briefly he glared a red vexed hot astonished glare at Herman Marshall, and then he fell back, and he was as dead as he ever would be, and no one was deader.) Herman Marshall looked away from the television set. He stumbled across the attic to a place where the floor was relatively clear. He flopped down. He coughed. He sneezed. He dug at a nostril with a forefinger. He licked the forefinger. Hell with it. No one was looking. He listened to the rain slap at the roof. This was some rain. Maybe there would be a big old flood. Houston was a great place for big old floods. Houston, Mother of Floods. Ha. Real funny. Herman Marshall gnawed on the forefinger. His tongue had discovered a loose cuticle. He told himself he was like a little kid setting in the dirt and sucking a finger. And then he told himself he didn't give a fuck. Grunting, he forced his legs (they were stiff, what with all the dampness) into the Brave Little Tailor position. He worked on the cuticle. He looked around. He saw the boxes Billy's trains were in. The boxes said *LIONEL*. They were all lumpy with mildew. Herman Marshall really had done a job of work on those trains. He had needed a week to scrape the rust off the engines and the cars and the track, not to mention the crossing gate that had the amusing little man who waved the lantern. He had told Edna the job had required only a little oil and a little new wiring, but that had been a goddamn hoot. He'd not spoken to her of all the rust he'd had to scrape away. What would have been the sense in it? Where would have been the kindness? Herman Marshall believed in kindness; he believed in kindness as much as he believed in Paradise, and maybe more. Kindness came from *inside* him, and *he* was responsible for it, and no faith was required. No prayers. No bowing and scraping. No belief that virgins could pop babies. Herman Marshall jerked the finger from his mouth and sighed. He had been bringing things

[17]

down to Edna and making up stories about them. A week ago Sunday he had brought down her wedding dress, and he had held it in front of himself, and he had danced and sashayed next to her bed, and he had told her a story about the beautiful Princess of Texarkana who had married a handsome prince, and the handsome prince had spirited her away. On eighteen wheels, you understand. And the beautiful Princess of Texarkana had lived forever with the handsome prince, and he never once had turned into a frog when she had kissed him, and she told him he was a *super* prince, and he said aw shucks, ma'am, it ain't nothin really for a man to be braggin on. (He had tried to make his voice all quavery and bashful, like the voice of Johnny Cash.) And Edna had rewarded him with the necessary smiles and chucklings, and maybe she'd been remembering times in bed when the two of them had gotten to humping real fine and proud, like maybe they'd just discovered what humping was. There were times—and Herman Marshall knew this for a pure and certain fact, by God—when married people were able to carry themselves beyond routine gropings, when the familiar was redefined and ancient courtship strategies were renewed, and a quick happy groan of memory caused the husband and the wife to link, clot, wriggle and shout. They jammed shut their eyes, and it was 1934 again, and ittybitty Mickey Rooney was up there on the screen, and the FBI had murdered old John Dillinger, and the fat girl tugged down her drawers, and no one died. Herman Marshall had had such times with his Edna . . . at least back in the days before Billy had come along. But the seventeen years of Billy had sort of wrung out Herman Marshall and Edna. Billy and his pain. Billy and his bedsores and his spine. Billy Marshall. You looked at him and you said to yourself: It's like he's a human comma. In those days, Herman Marshall often had crept up to this attic and had crouched in a corner and had sipped from a pint of muscatel. And sometimes he had closed his eyes, and he had held his breath, and he had crossed his fingers, and he had prayed to his God, his God of Paradise, for a miracle . . . some grand and perfect event that would change Billy into nothing less than an exclamation point. But nothing had happened. Oh, the *muscatel* had happened, and it often had made him puke and shudder, but he had supposed that was what muscatel was *for*. Otherwise, it wouldn't have tasted so goddamn awful. Herman Marshall rubbed his ankles. He grimaced. He was familiar with this attic, and he wasn't familiar with it. Every so often he would say to himself: Shit, air ain't nothin up here I don't already know bout. Nothin I ain't pawed through more times an is worth the tellin. But Herman Marshall always was being fooled. Something . . . a towel, a doily, an old cracked dish, the sad bland head of a wrecked teddy-bear . . . would set him off, and a screen would be knocked down, and forgotten things would dust themselves off and come prancing forward for his inspection, forming a parade of trivial and precious events. Now . . . for no reason that made sense . . . he remembered a day the three of them had gone downtown (he had washed the car, a '49 Chevy, and he had waxed it) and had eaten Thanksgiving dinner in the dining room of the Rice Hotel, and Edna had said grace, and the turkey had surrendered its wishbone to Billy, and Edna had told Billy oh, it surely was a fine life, and the Rice Hotel was fine (look at the fine ceiling! the fine chandeliers! feel the fine carpeting! touch these fine napkins! stroke all the fine cutlery and china!), and the three of them had spoken in tight whispered exclamations, and they had nudged one another, and the nigger waiter had had heavy lips and he had said *yassuh* and *no ma'am* just like in the old movies on TV, and Edna had taken home a menu. *She had taken home a menu.* Herman Marshall rubbed his cheeks. He just bet the menu's eventual destination had been this attic. He leaned for-

ward and reached for a carton. No doubt he already had opened
that particular carton, and more than once, but he couldn't quite
remember. He shook his head. He was pouring sweat. The menu—
maybe it had rotted, but this day he would search for it. Oh, there
was no *maybe* about it. The humidity *surely* had destroyed the
menu. But Herman Marshall didn't care. Maybe he would be able
to gather together a few torn and musty fragments. They would be
all he'd need. He'd go downstairs and strew them around the room
where Edna was dying and speak to her of banquets and honors;
he'd paint a stupid picture of Billy sitting there in a tux and telling
his parents of all the oil money he was making, and yes, yes, yes,
Daddy and Mommy, I'm so *proud* I'm your son, an I couldn't of
done it without you, an you'll never again have to fuss yourselves
bout money, long as you live. And an arm is raised. And a nigger
waiter approaches. And the nigger waiter is grinning a purple
nigger grin. And the nigger waiter is carrying high a silver tray.
And a bottle of champagne stands on the silver tray. And Billy
touches his parents' hands and tells them nothin but the best; Top
Ticket all the way, an don't you forget it. And this surely would
have been Billy, had he lived. He would have been the King of the
Rice Hotel, Lord & Master of All He Surveyed. Cigars and parks
and office buildings would have been named after him, and college
presidents would have petitioned him for funds. Herman Marshall
smiled for a moment. He tugged open the carton. It gave off a
plump stink of moldy paper. Herman Marshall was wearing spec-
tacles. The humidity had fogged them. He wiped them with a
handkerchief. (He remembered the banisters at the Rice Hotel. The
memory came in a bright explosion. The banisters had gleamed.
They had carried a thin and prissy odor of polish. Herman Marshall
had rubbed a palm against one of them, and he had created a
squeaky sound that had caused a tall and stately woman to stare at

him for a moment. The woman's hair had been in a feather bob, and she had been young, and her lipstick had glistened, and she had carried herself as though she could have bought and sold Houston ten times over, with maybe enough change left for Galveston and Texas City. Herman Marshall never really had forgotten her. One night a few years later, while lying in a motel bed just the other side of Sulphur, Louisiana, he had summoned her image while masturbating. She had stripped herself naked right in front of everyone in the lobby of the Rice Hotel, and she had rolled on the carpeting, and she had told him she would give him all of Waco and Wichita Falls and Corpus Christi for just one honest and uncompromising fuck. And her glistening mouth had been sort of spittled and urgent. All in all, he'd had himself a great old jackoff, and he'd damn near sprained his wrist, truth to tell. But dear Jesus, why had that single glance by that woman caused her to keep hanging around his memory? He supposed there was a lot he had missed. He supposed there was a lot he never would know. And he supposed there was a lot he had misunderstood.) Herman Marshall rubbed his glasses and rubbed them. Then he adjusted them on the bridge of his nose. He began poking through the contents of the box. A copy of *Family Circle* for July 1952. The cover had been torn off. The pages were full of recipes and shit like that. Fuck it. A Sundayschool book, faded and split, something having to do with cows and sheep and the Lord's Kingdom. The cows and the sheep appeared to be smiling. Since when did cows and sheep smile? Herman Marshall never had seen a cow smile, let alone a dumb dirty old *sheep*. He told himself it was no wonder so many people didn't go to church. Oh, not that he didn't believe in God. After all, if you believed in Paradise, surely you had to believe in God, right? But what did smiling cows and smiling sheep have to do with the good old Man Upstairs? Herman Marshall snorted. He

[21]

tossed the Sundayschool book aside. Poor Billy probably had been made to read that stupid thing. Poor Billy. God *damn*. And Herman Marshall removed a packet of letters from the box. The packet was wrapped in red paper and held together with a green ribbon. It was like a Christmas package. He frowned. The contents of this box all were new to him. How could that be, what with all the trips he'd made up here? He squeezed the packet. Maybe he shouldn't open it. Maybe it contained letters from Edna's goddamned . . . friend. Edna, the pack rat. Edna, who would save snot and cat shit if you let her. If there'd been any letters from that Romero asshole, she would have saved them. Christ's sake, it was a wonder she hadn't had them framed. Romero. Romero the Mex. Romero the asshole, for fair and for sure. Romero, who had fucked another man's wife probably because it had been a better way of spending the afternoon than playing cards with his Mex pals. Oh, how Herman Marshall ever did remember that Romero. The backstabbing sonofabitch. If Herman Marshall knew where Romero's grave was, he'd go empty his leaky bladder on it. (How could he find out where it was? How many Mex graveyards were there in Houston anyway?) Herman Marshall exhaled. He was dripping sweat from his forehead and his chin. His tongue rested against his lower lip, which was extended. He was a tall and bony man with sparse gray hair and large hands and feet, and he seemed all of a piece—except for his lips. They were sausages. They were nigger lips. All his life his world had seen fit to razz him because of his lips. In his working days, the other truckers had nicknamed him Nig. *Good old Nig Marshall*, they had said. *The best colored man between here an New Orleans*, they had said. *A hard worker, for a nigger*, they had said. And these truckers had exploded with urgent guffawings, and they had sprayed spit, and their teeth had gleamed. Yeah, the old razz, all right. And he had become used to it, Lord knows. But

[22]

why *him*? It wasn't as though he *was* a nigger. His *folks* hadn't had nigger lips, and his three *brothers* hadn't had nigger lips (they'd all had *proper* lips, pink and narrow and drawn thinly taut), and so how come he carried such heavy embarrassments under his nose? Not since his boyhood and young manhood had he been much for talking, and maybe his lips were the reason. After all, talking called attention to them. Shit. Right—and double shit. Again Herman Marshall exhaled. He made a fist and pressed it against his awful lips. Then he undid the ribbon on the packet. He said to himself: Well, maybe she fucked him because she was sick of my lips. But his lips were just as fat as mine are. After all, they were *Mex* lips, so how could they have been an improvement? Herman Marshall shrugged. He should march downstairs and *ask* her. But he'd not asked her. He'd not found a way to be that much of a man. (Billy hadn't looked a bit like a Mex, though. Maybe Billy's father hadn't been Romero at all. Maybe Edna had lied to Herman Marshall because it had been safer that way, what with Romero having been dead and all. Maybe Edna had fucked the butcher or the baker or the candlestick maker. Or maybe she'd fucked the goddamn Marx Brothers. Or the Texas A&M football team. Ha. What a lot of horse cock everything was. Billy had been sturdy and fair—before the meningitis. Billy had not been in the least bit greazzy, and he had not been in the least bit lazy. He had been a *good* boy, the light of Herman Marshall's life . . . and sometimes, while standing over the crapper and relieving himself, Herman Marshall had spoken affectionately to his prick, rubbing it and milking it and saying to it: *You done good, old buddy. You made a fine boy. Your aim was good, an you hit the mark, an GRUNT!!! GROAN!!! she worked hard and after a bit she popped him an much was the rejoicin thereof, ha ha.*) Herman Marshall fumbled with one of the envelopes. Maybe it once had been open, but it had been resealed by the humidity. He chewed at his enormous lips. He glanced at the postmark, and it said *CLEVELAND OHIO*, and the date was July 1950. And the envelope was addressed to one *HERMAN E. MARSHALL*. And Herman Marshall flinched. He groaned a little, and his shoulders shifted. That was the summer Edna had taken little Billy up to Cleveland for a visit to her sister Corinne. Her only sister and her only kin. Corinne Coffee, the woman's name had been, and her husband had been a bigdeal real estate salesman, and they'd reared a fat son named Alexander. (For some reason, this Alexander eventually dropped his first name and adopted his middle name— Eugene—as his new first name. He grew up to be some sort of college professor up there in Cleveland, but anymore he didn't even send Herman Marshall and Edna a card at Christmastime, and no doubt he believed his shit smelled like a field full of petunias, and he could kiss Herman Marshall's withered old ass.) Now Herman Marshall was tearing at the envelope, and his groans came from his chest. Then the envelope was open, and a note fell out—together with a snapshot. The note was in Edna's spidery and imprecise hand, and some of the words had blurred, but he was able to read them: *We went to a plais calt Euclid Beech & rode the roleycoasters & I screamed but little Billy had hemsef a fine time & dint even so mutch as wet hemsef. Eugene tagged along & he is a fine boy altho a little "fat"!!! (JOKE!!!) Were eatin good, & theres lots of nice picsher shows & the niggers ain't no bother. I love you. Look at the picsher here. Aint Billy growin tho? Lots of xxxxx & ooooo. YOUR ONE & ONLY EDNA.* Herman Marshall looked at the snapshot. It also was blurred, but Herman Marshall was able to make out Edna and Billy just fine. They were sitting on a porch glider, and Billy was plump (he was one year of age in July 1950), and he sat erectly next to his mother (erectly! erectly! *erectly!* this was before the meningitis and before the pain and before any of it! this was when Billy's future had been as sweet as any other kid's!

[24]

oh, shit! oh, God!). Herman Marshall bent forward. He closed his
eyes. He wanted to wad up the snapshot and throw it away. He
was so goddamn tired of taking things down to Edna and making
up stories about them. He opened his eyes and spoke aloud. "The
Princess of Texarkana, my ass," he said. "I should of gone out to
the Panhandle an been a cowboy. At's what I wanted to do. I
wanted to set tall in the saddle like Tom Mix or whoever, an
maybe chew on a matchstick, an maybe squint at the sky, an
maybe whisper real calm to my horse if it got nervous. You know,
at sort of thing. It would of been—" Then Herman Marshall
abruptly cut off his words. What sort of man was a man who
talked to himself in a hot littered attic while clutching an old snapshot that came from so far in the past it might as well have come
from the goddamn moon? A boy and his mother on a porch glider,
and they had taken a ride on the roleycoaster. Herman Marshall
looked around. Had anything been listening? A mouse? a cockroach? a tired and foolish moth? Herman Marshall straightened.
Holding the snapshot, he pulled himself to his feet. He winced
from the pain in his joints. It was an electrical sort of pain, and it
skittered up and down his bones. The hell with it. He would take
the snapshot down to his wife. A woman who had written: *xxxxx*.
And: *ooooo*. Terms of endearment from a loving and faithful wife.
He would give her the snapshot, and no doubt she would weep,
and he would sit next to the brass bed and tell her the little boy in
the snapshot actually is President Ronald Reagan, an he is a nice
man, an never you mind all the bad things the Democrats say
bout him, an look at the way he's smilin, an is it any wonder the
people chose him to be air President? A little boy an his mother.
Mama an baby. Yes ma'am. Right. And Herman Marshall made
his way downstairs, and the first thing Edna said to him was: "You
find somethin?" And Herman Marshall said: "You betcha. An

you're goin to like it." And he handed her the snapshot. And Edna wept. And Herman Marshall's eyes idly followed the pattern of veins that lay across her skull. After a time he began speaking to her of Ronald Reagan and Ronald Reagan's smile and all the rest of it. And then he was done, and a weakly smiling Edna kissed the snapshot and wept a little more and said to him: "Thank you."

CHAPTER THREE

IN THE AUTUMN OF 1949, shortly after they were married, a
young couple named Harry and Beth Munger saw a gangster
movie called *White Heat*, starring James Cagney as a crazy killer
who had a mother fixation. The movie ended with the trapped
Cagney climbing atop a huge gasoline storage tank and blowing
up the tank and himself after shouting: *"Top of the world, Ma!"*

Harry and Beth figured *White Heat* was the best movie they'd
ever seen, and the ending had been like a regular goddamn one of
em atom bomb explosions. They saw the movie seven times, and
years later they watched it whenever it was on television, even if
this meant getting up at three in the morning or whenever. Beth
would fix popcorn (even at three in the morning), and she and
Harry would sit close together on the davenport while they watched
the movie. And Beth, a perky little blonde with high tits and a
gentle squirrely overbite, always asked Harry whether he thought
she resembled Virginia Mayo, who played Cagney's girlfriend in
the movie. And he always told her sure; at's a fact; you an her
could be twins, you little sweetmeat *devil* you, ha ha. And Harry
and Beth would cuddle, and they would hiss that dirty rat of an
FBI stooge of an Edmond O'Brien, and more than once did Harry
and Beth Munger make quick solemn love on the floor in the dark,
with their faces and bodies smeared by the nervous and imprecise
light from the television set.

In 1951 a number of gas wells came in on a farm Harry Munger
had inherited from an uncle. The farm was up toward Waco, and
Harry's royalties from the wells enabled him to quit his job as a

mail carrier in Houston's Montrose area. He became a genuine entrepeneur, by God, and he opened a little honkytonk out in the suburb of Pasadena, a tough place full of refineries and pecker-woods. And the peckerwoods were belligerent bastards who drove pickup trucks and kicked their dawgs and would as leave shoot you as say howdo. But Harry and Beth were peckerwoods themselves, and Harry often would say: *We're so iggerant it's like we invented it.* And he laughed. And so did Beth, exposing her overbite in an abrupt flash that just about made a person blink. The honkytonk was a flat little building made of sheet metal, and it was right on the Stevens Highway, and so it received a lot of trade. It was named, of course, the Top of the World. Harry and Beth poured an honest drink, and there always was plenty of beer, and on Friday and Saturday nights you could dance to the music of such outfits as Slim Eaves & His Dixie Dudes, or the Bayou Bums, or Tabby Queen's Delta Dumplings, or Big Billy Lord & The Texas Blasters. Harry and Beth raised four kids on his gas royalties and the profits from the Top of the World—even after 1977, when a windstorm tore off the place's roof and destroyed the dance floor. Harry and Beth, who were getting up there in the old years department, de-cided not to rebuild the dance floor. He told her he was tired of all the goddamn fights that had taken place just about every Friday and Saturday night. The kids all were out of the nest, and this meant his expenses had declined, an so what the hell, sweetmeat, let's just have us a nice little bar operation an forget the rest, all right? And Beth nodded. She was fortysix there in 1977, and she was wearing remedial braces on her remarkable teeth, and she sel-dom spoke. Harry had taken to calling her his little sourpuss, but he'd always been quick to tell her whoo*ee* but she surely would be beautiful after the braces had done their work. He saw himself as a friendly and kindly man, and this assessment was more or less correct. Certainly as far as Beth and the kids were concerned. And certainly as far as his friends were concerned. (Herman Marshall was one of them.) But it also must be pointed out that twice—first in 1956, then in 1973—Harry Munger had killed people. Both of them had been wouldbe holdup men. The first was an unemployed spot welder named Amos LaGrange, and Harry drilled him with three shots to the head. The second was a colored fellow named Something or Other Jackson, or maybe Johnson, and Harry had taken care of *that* fucker with two shots to the chest cavity, one to the belly and one to the balls. And that nigger had been torn open like an exhibit on a medical school slab. That had been some dumb nigger, all right, trying to rob a saloon in good old peckerwood Pasadena. Well, maybe he'd had an incurable disease and he'd wanted to check out in a hurry. You just never knew, by God. And after all, if you could predict everyone's behavior right down to the last cross of a T and dot of an I, what fun would there be, right? And so Something or Other Jackson, or Johnson, was scooped up, and the floor was mopped, and then Harry Munger sprung to have it painted, and clocks ticked, and babies hollered, and drunks wept, and life went on. (The floor was painted red. You just never knew.)

Every other year or so Harry and Beth visited the farm up toward Waco. It was dotted with gas storage tanks, and Harry and Beth had several photographs showing Harry standing atop one or another of the tanks. They called these their Top of the World photographs, and they had been framed, and the photographs hung on the wall behind the cash register. Harry was grimacing in the photographs, and he was raising clenched fists to the sky. He was too large and heavy to be a James Cagney, but it was the *idea* of the thing that counted, and never mind physical dissimilarity. He and Beth had a sort of dream having to do with all this. The dream was

[29]

that James Cagney, who now was such a very old man it was absolutely indecent, would come into the Top of the World some fine day and say to them: *You're my greatest fans, you dirty rats*. And then James Cagney would laugh a crisp bark of a laugh, and the drinks would be on the house, and he would reminisce about Bogart and Pat O'Brien and all the rest of those good old Warner Brothers boys.

Herman Marshall liked Harry and Beth. Edna never had quite approved of them (they were a little tacky for her taste, and they surely did *drink* a whole lot), but she tolerated them, and she didn't really mind when Herman Marshall drove down to Pasadena and visited the Top of the World. She told Herman Marshall she was his *wife* and not his *boss*, and if he wanted to rub elbows with all that sorry trash down there in Pasadena, well, she hoped the Lord kept a careful eye on him. And then, likely as not, Edna would smile. And she would tell him to give her regards to Harry and Beth. And Herman Marshall would kiss her and thank her. And she'd tell him oh, *shoot*.

Herman Marshall and Harry Munger had known one another ever since an incident that had taken place in the Greyhound bus depot in Houston in early 1955. And the incident almost had resulted in a fistfight. Herman Marshall and Edna and little Billy had gone to Texarkana to visit a woman named Ethel Mae Kelleher, who had been Edna's best chum in high school. This Ethel Mae Kelleher's name had been Ethel Mae Snodgrass in those days, and she had gone pregnant in her junior year, and an older man (twentyfive, if he was a day) named Harold Kelleher had been forced to marry Ethel Mae. This Harold Kelleher had been a foreman in a box factory, and he had been considered quite a catch. And he would have been—except that two weeks to the day after the wedding he became drunk and drove his pickup truck into a stone wall at a cemetery. No one knew why he had gone to that cemetery, especially since it had been a nigger cemetery. Maybe he had been too drunk to know where he had been. At least this was what most people had believed, and anyway, what difference had it made? Dead was dead. Period. But, at any rate, Ethel Mae Snodgrass had required a decent name, and people no longer would laugh at her and call her Snotass and Stinkass, and this was important. She had explained all of it in careful detail to Edna, and Edna had said there, *there*, and Edna and Ethel Mae had embraced, and something had moved in Ethel Mae's belly, and Edna had permitted herself a girlish squeal. And she and Ethel Mae had kept in touch after she had moved down to Houston with Herman Marshall, and Ethel Mae had given birth to two more kids (without benefit of clergy), and oh yes, Ethel Mae was a scandal, all right, and Edna freely admitted to Herman Marshall she didn't know what would *become* of Ethel Mae, but Ethel Mae had a good heart, you know? And Ethel Mae was not a bad person, you know? And Herman Marshall always nodded when Edna spoke of Ethel Mae. And sometimes he thought of Ethel Mae, who was tall and redhaired, with small breasts and slender legs (more or less the opposite of plump Edna), in bed with him, and he just bet Ethel Mae had a fierce clenched way of fucking that would be real choice. There wasn't much honor or loyalty attached to that sort of thinking, but Herman Marshall told himself he was nothing if he wasn't human, and what sort of man was it who didn't from time to time think on such a subject? It was a way of knowing you had blood in your veins. Or something in your something, ha ha. And maybe Herman Marshall had been preoccupied with salacious thoughts of Ethel Mae Kelleher that day in the Greyhound bus depot in 1955. Whatever the reason, he did a stupid thing. When the driver opened the baggage compartment under the bus, Herman Marshall took the wrong suitcase. It was a big leather job with the initials *HM*, and those were *his* initials, correct? Well . . . yes . . . but they also were the initials of another passenger, a fellow named Harry Munger. And this Harry Munger came blundering up to Herman Marshall and told him to hold on air, feller; you got my suitcase air. And Herman Marshall, who was tired (Billy hadn't liked riding in a bus, and the little fellow had puked into some wadded Kleenex a grimacing Edna had held to his mouth), told the man to go to hell; the suitcase was *his*, and it even had *his* initials on it, and *he* knew *his* own suitcase when *he* saw it. But the man's head moved from side to side. The man was carrying another suitcase, and it was a trifle bigger than the one Herman Marshall was holding, and its leather was a trifle darker, and it had the same initials: *HM*. Herman Marshall's head hurt, and all he wanted was to go home and have Edna put the kid to bed so there would be a little peace and quiet, and just who the hell was this man who was having at him because of a couple of fucking suitcases? So words were exchanged, and the man advanced on Herman Marshall, and Herman Marshall tried to give the man a push. Whereupon the man made a fist. Edna was hugging Billy, and Billy was whooping, and Edna was trying to tell Herman Marshall stop it, stop it; you got the wrong suitcase, but Herman Marshall wasn't hearing much of anything, and then the bus driver seized him by the arms and said hey now, slow down, buddy; it's been a hot day an we don't want to make it no hotter. And Herman Marshall, who hadn't even wanted to go up to Texarkana to visit goddamn roundheeled Ethel Mae Kelleher in the first place, who could have caught a run to Baton Rouge that would have earned him time and a half for two days (and he could have stopped for a quick one with a nervous widowed schoolteacher he knew in Beaumont, a fragile and tintinnabulating woman who would do anything for him as long as he didn't mind shoving a finger up her ass) . . . oh, this Herman Marshall finally shrugged, set down the suitcase, squeezed his skull, winced and then tried to listen to what was being said. And eventually it all was worked out, and the suitcases were exchanged, and Herman Marshall and the other fellow, this Harry Munger, paid a quick visit to the men's room, and the man was carrying a pint of Old Crow, and he and Herman Marshall drank from it, and Herman Marshall told the man shit, I acted like a goddamn asshole out air, an I sure enough apologize to you. And Harry Munger allowed as how tiredness made assholes of us all. And then both men grinned. And that more or less marked the beginning of their friendship. Harry Munger gave Herman Marshall a card on which the name and address and telephone number of the Top of the World were printed. *A topdrawer honkytonk*, said Harry Munger, softly punching one of Herman Marshall's shoulders, *is a joy upon the face of the earth. With real music on the weekends. None of at jukebox stuff on the weekends. No SIR.* And Harry Munger and Herman Marshall—after putting away three swigs apiece from the pint of Old Crow—were grinning and scratching and in general behaving like asshole buddies when they emerged from that men's room. So began their friendship. Edna accompanied Herman Marshall to the Top of the World the first few times he visited the place, and they met Beth, and Beth bestowed her brilliant grin on them, but Edna never really enjoyed the Top of the World the way Herman Marshall did. *Now don't get me wrong, though*, said Edna. *Your Harry an your Beth, air fine people, the salt of the earth an all at, but at honkytonk of airs . . . well, air's noise an air's NOISE, you know what I mean? Me, I expect maybe I got ears at are too, um, delicate for all the uproar an commotion. At's me. Delicate Edna. Ho ho.* And then Edna shook her head and chuckled fatly, chins flabbing. She told Herman Marshall she would accompany him to the Top of the World every once in awhile, but she really didn't mind staying home when he went out there alone. It saved hiring a babysitter for Billy . . . and, well, to be real honest about it, she favored the peace and quiet. She could watch a little TV. She could knit. She could crochet. She could bake a cake or can a mess of tomatoes. There always were quiet things to do, correct? And Herman Marshall nodded. *The only thing is*, he said, *I don't want you to think I'm tryin to shut you out of nothin*. Edna grinned. *I think I know you better an at*, she said. Her grin flickered for a moment. She appeared to be remembering something she really didn't want to remember. Or maybe looking ahead to something she really didn't want to contemplate. She wiped her mouth with the back of a hand. She shrugged. *It's just . . . fine an dandy*, she said, blinking. She held that afternoon's edition of the *Chronicle* in her lap. She had folded the paper open to the comic section. She loved the comic section. Other people could study the world; Edna Stillman Marshall preferred to study the doings of people and animals that spoke in balloons. This made a lot of sense to her, and Herman Marshall couldn't really argue with her about it. Maybe her addiction to the comic page was something like his trips to the Top of the World. So once a week or so he drove down to Pasadena and did some serious drinking and tried not to worry about Edna. The visits originally took place in the evening, but later—after he had retired—he got to driving down there in the daytime. The place was quieter in the daytime; it was patronized by only a few regulars, most of them gentle rummies whose best days (if they'd ever had any) were so far behind them they no longer gave much of a shit. Herman Marshall figured he understood them. By that time, Billy was long dead of the meningitis, and the dying cancerous Edna had confessed to Herman Marshall that he wasn't Billy's father, that the late Phil Romero had been Billy's father, that she was *so* sorry, that she . . . well, never mind. Yeah. *Never mind*. Yessir you betcha. Herman Marshall always spoke quietly with the gentle rummies who patronized the Top of the World in those motionless afternoons of his retirement. Somehow they had managed to master the various techniques having to do with no longer giving much of a shit. It had to do with staring at the veins that spread all ropy and tough across their hands. It had to do with the pain that was created when dentures rubbed against gums. It had to do with hot quick unexpected pissings. It had to do with remembering Alf Landon in a world that didn't know Alf Landon from a stuffed goose. It had to do with remembering the 1950 Nash with its back seat that could be changed into a bed, and no wonder folks had called it the Sexmobile. It had to do with the thoughtful and deprecatory laughter that came from memories of failed ambitions. Such gentle rummies indeed. They were the best gentle rummies in the world. Herman Marshall wouldn't have exchanged them for the world's weight in gold. He wouldn't even have exchanged them for a night of unbuttoned abandon with the Elizabeth Taylor of, say, 1953 . . . before she gave way to the bloat, or whatever was the matter with her. And he'd not been bashful about telling them they were his buddies. And the gentle rummies smiled. And they nodded. And they touched the brims of their caps. They wore caps that said *GILLEY'S*. They wore caps that said *CAT*. They wore caps that said *COORS* and *PURINA*. They seldom took off their caps. It didn't matter whether they were indoors or where they were—their caps remained on their old gray heads. Herman Marshall had a cap. It said *ASTROS*. It was yellow and orange, with a sort of maroon thrown in. A million years earlier, back in Hope, Arkansas, when he'd been young and strong and his pecker had had the capacity to fuck polecats, paste jars, pine stumps and library books, he had played first base for a semipro team, and God save the pitcher who served him a fast ball. When

[35]

it came to the fast ball, Herman Marshall had had the power to slug the goddamn thing halfway to Baton Rouge, Louisiana. (The curve ball had been another matter, though, and to hell with remembering the curve ball.) But he never had followed through on his baseball ambitions. He met a chunky and friendly girl named Edna Stillman, and he told her she was his one and only true love, and one night a year and a half later they drove to Shreveport to see *Manhattan Melodrama*. Which they enjoyed. And then they visited the vacant lot behind the theater. Which they enjoyed even more. Down came her drawers, and she was jolly about it, and how could a feller *not* love her? Sure, marriage to her put the kibosh on his baseball ambitions, but where was it written that he could have *everything* he wanted? So he went to work as a trucker (and in those days he was damned lucky to get the job; all three of his brothers fucking good and well envied him), and Edna often wore hairribbons for him, and it more or less some of the time was a good life, even though she couldn't get pregnant to save her ass. Until sometime in the summer of 1948, when Herman Marshall had just about given up on her, and—

No.

Never mind.

That sort of stuff needed to be pushed out of his skull. It no longer mattered doodly doo what had happened in the summer of 1948. And it wasn't as though he, Herman Marshall, known to his trucker buddies as Nig, hadn't been messing around with all sorts of women. Some of his trucking buddies had called him Nig the Lover, and—

No.

No!

Such pain, such thinking and remembering were absolute goddamn death. They were enough to make him fumble at his *AS-*

TROS cap and scratch his scalp. Still, he and his friend Harry Munger occasionally touched at the edges of . . . well, whatever it was. One afternoon in the spring of 1984, Herman Marshall said: "Did you go to church when you was a boy?"

Harry was standing behind the bar and trying to work the crossword puzzle from the *Post*. He was bent forward, and he was sucking a pencil, and he was frowning. No one else was in the Top of the World at that particular moment. Shadows from a *Miller Lite* neon sign streaked Harry's face yellow and pink. Traffic clacked and slammed outside on the Stevens Highway. Harry looked up at Herman Marshall and said: "How's at again, old buddy?"

"Church," said Herman Marshall. "I want to know did you go to church when you was a boy, an I want to know what they told you, an I want to know whether you *listened* to any of it."

"I don't member," said Harry, shrugging.

"If you don't member, it means you didn't listen."

"Well," said Harry, "maybe I *did* listen *at the time*."

Herman Marshall smiled. Softly he snorted. A Shiner longneck was on the bar in front of him. He drank from the longneck. The beer was so cold it made his gums ache. He grimaced.

"How can you drink at stuff?" said Harry.

"You always ask me at," said Herman Marshall.

"Well, maybe so, but I keep forgettin what your answer is."

"All right. I'll tell you again. I drink this here Shiner on account of I'm from Arkansas an I don't know no better."

Harry shook his head. "I swear, you got your brains where your asshole ought to be."

"Right," said Herman Marshall. He set down the longneck. He hesitated. Then: "I surely am sorry, an I don't mean to fuss at you, but didn't they tell you *nothin* in church—nothin at you *member*?"

"Why do you care? What the hell difference does it make? If

[37]

you're askin me do I believe in God, sure I believe in God. An me an Beth, well, we go to church four, five times a year regular as clockwork, ha ha."

"It hep you?"

". . . a little, I guess."

"It hep your conscience?" said Herman Marshall.

"It hep yours?" said Harry.

"I asked you first," said Herman Marshall. "An if you want to know, I ain't gone to no church since the day of Billy's funeral. Ain't I never told you at?"

Harry sucked the pencil. "Maybe. I'm not real sure."

"Your conscience," said Herman Marshall. "Tell me bout your conscience. Tell me bout church. I mean, what do you do when you feel bad bout somethin?"

Harry removed the pencil from his mouth and gave Herman Marshall the benefit of a snicker. "I'm too old to have a conscience," said Harry, shaking a little with amusement. "The thing is, what bad thing could *I* do, at *my* age, to have a conscience *about*? Same goes for you too, you old fart. I wish air *was* somethin, an at's a fact. I'd be off *doin* the bad thing, whatever it was, rather an standin here an gruntin over a crossword puzzle an talkin with the likes of *you*."

"But how was it at the beginnin?" said Herman Marshall.

"How was *what*?" said Harry. "An at *what* beginnin?"

"When you was a boy," said Herman Marshall. "When some preacher stood in front of everbody an got to yellin an whoopin bout retribution an the Wrath of God an Love Thy Neighbor an keep your fuckin hands to yourself when it comes to Thy Neighbor's Wife. You know what I mean. All at hard stuff. Hard stuff to live up to, I mean. You're from up by Waco, right? Didn't the preachers preach at sort of stuff up by Waco?"

[38]

"Yessir," said Harry. "They sure enough did. They made the walls rattle. Or at least the good ones did. The ones who passed the plate an the people *paid*. On account of they didn't want to roast in the dark place."

"Did you believe what the preachers said?"

"I don't know. I wasn't nothin but a boy. Maybe I did."

"Don't you think back on it?" said Herman Marshall. "I know *I* do. I think back on all at sort of thing. I can't seem to hep it. An I keep askin how come it's all gone past so . . . *fast*. An I think bout Edna, an how she's just layin air an waitin to die, an how the biggest thing in her life is when I go up to the attic an fetch her some . . . some . . . some forgotten thing an make up a story bout it . . . an she always loves the story . . . loves it to death."

"Okay," said Harry. He looked away from Herman Marshall.

"What?"

"Enough."

"Enough of what?"

"These here words," said Harry. His voice was without inflection. "You're whippin yourself with em, an you're whippin *me* with em. I expect maybe I don't care what you do to yourself, but leave *me* out of it, you hear?"

"I didn't mean no—"

"*Enough*," said Harry.

Herman Marshall nodded. He was silent. His belly and chest were shrieking, but he was silent. He sucked his Shiner. He was alone, and he would remain alone, because everyone remained alone. He sucked more of his Shiner. He belched . . . but gently, so as not to aggravate good old Harry.

CHAPTER FOUR

THE OLD MEN WITH THEIR CAPS, their *GILLEY'S* caps and
their *COORS* caps and their *PURINA* caps, such *old* old men
they were, older than God and the sky, and they were the first to
admit they were older than God and the sky. They hung around
the Top of the World most every afternoon and they actually *made
jokes* about how old they were. Or at least most of them did. Those
who weren't deaf. Those whose eyes didn't cloud over with the
sort of intense puzzlement reserved for old men who didn't quite
know where the hell they were and what the hell they were doing
there. But the other old men, the ones who still had some sort of
grip (however shaky and tentative) on their senses and their ability
to know what day it was, didn't particularly mind participating in
the jokes having to do with their age. The jokes of course were dry
and tired. They were jokes that had been retold again and again for
decades. A rich old man has a girlfriend he keeps in a big apartment, and she insists she loves him. Unfortunately, the old man
can't get it up. Still, this is all right, since he is able to achieve
satisfaction by spreading her naked on the bathroom floor, dropping his britches and shitting in her face. But one night he is con-
stipated. Try as he might, he is unable to shit in the woman's face.
Finally she begins to weep. She's down there on the bathroom
floor, and she's looking straight up his asshole, and she's weeping
like a baby that's misplaced its pacifier. Concerned and alarmed,
the old man says: *Honey, what's wrong?* And, sniffling and choking,
the woman says: *You don't love me no more, do you?* And this was
precisely the sort of joke that caused the old men in the Top of the

World to snigger and nudge. And they would say: *Lordamighty*. And: *Shit*. And: *I swear*. And the old men rested their elbows on the pocked and lacerated bar there in the Top of the World, and Harry Munger quietly moved from one old man to another (and he never really razzed them; after all, he was just as old as they were), and beer flowed, and the old men trekked and lurched to and from the men's room, and not even their bladders were safe from their empty little jokes, and a fellow named Frank Lee Doubleday (who once had been an English teacher at Pasadena High School and therefore had a fondness for fancy words) said one afternoon: "Air is an inverse proportion at work here, gents."

"What?" said a large man named Milt Willis, staggering back from the men's room and still fussing with his fly. "You got words of schoolteacher wisdom for us, Frank Lee?" And then Milt Willis collided with the bar. "Shit," he said, and he clucked disapprovingly at himself. He braced himself against the bar and carefully slumped down on a barstool that had a ragged imitation leather seat.

"You're really gettin air, ain't you?" said Harry to Milt Willis.

"No problem," said Milt Willis. "I'm just doin fine."

"I expect you *are*," said Harry.

Milt Willis glanced down and tugged for a moment at his fly. Then, after apparently doing it up to his satisfaction, he turned his attention from Harry. He blinked at Frank Lee Doubleday and said: "What's a reverse proportion?"

"*Inverse*," said Frank Lee.

"Oh," said Milt. "It got to do with . . . um, cocksuckers?"

"No," said Frank Lee. "It's got to do with . . . well, one thing goin up while the other thing goes down."

". . . oh," said Milt.

There was a general snickering. Herman Marshall, who was

sitting at the other end of the bar, shifted his weight from one cheek of his ass to the other.

"Like in pissin," said Frank Lee.

"Pissin?" said Milt.

"Yessir," said Frank Lee. "Pissin's half of it. The other half is fuckin. You see, the older a man gets, the more he pisses an the less he fucks. An at's your inverse proportion for you. The one goes up, an the other goes down."

More snickering, but Herman Marshall winced. He didn't like to be reminded of his bladder. He didn't like to be reminded of the times he couldn't hold his piss and had to wet his pants and then walk around smelling like a fucking dead pig. He wondered whether any of the other daytime patrons of the Top of the World shared his problem. He'd always meant to ask one or two of them, but he'd never gotten up the nerve. And that was stupid. After all, they were nothing more than gentle rummies, and what would they have done? Would they have tossed him out onto the Stevens Highway, there to be squashed by a bus or a Cadillac or an oil truck? Hell, *no*. They probably would have understood, and maybe they would have been able to help him. But Herman Marshall could be real timid, and this was one of those times . . .

Milt and Frank Lee continued their discussion, and Milt took exception to what Frank Lee had said. "I don't know bout at," said Milt to Frank Lee. "Me, I'm a good old sixtyseven goin on sixtyeight, an yessir, I'll admit it . . . I do seem to piss a whole lot more often an I used to . . . but at don't mean I ain't gettin no nooky . . ." And Milt grinned.

If you counted in Harry Munger, there were eleven men in the Top of the World that afternoon. Nine of them stared at Milt. The only one who didn't stare at Milt was a codger named Rollie Beecham, who was hard of hearing.

[43]

A fresh and sweating Shiner longneck was on the bar in front of Herman Marshall. He moved the longneck to his mouth. He tongued the longneck, and the beer was so cold it just about made his tongue shiver and curl. God, he loved Shiner. To Herman Marshall, Shiner was what holy water was to the Pope of Rome. He tried to concentrate on it. He hoped Milt and Harry Lee wouldn't say anything more about pissing. They could talk about fucking if they wanted to . . . fucking was a fine and proper subject, and it interested the shit out of Herman Marshall, even now, with so much water under the dam, or over the bridge, or however the saying went.

Milt cleared his throat. His particular cap said *PEPSI*. He rubbed its bill with the back of a hand. "I been settin on the news for more an a week now, an I'm just bout fixin to blow up."

"Slow up?" said Rollie Beecham, the old codger who was hard of hearing.

"*Blow* up," said Milt. "Why don't you stick a blowtorch up your ears an clean em out?"

"Hush now," said Harry to Milt. "At ain't a decent thing to say. You ought to be ashamed of yourself. I mean, what with all the beers he's bought you over the years."

"Ears?" said Rollie Beecham. "You talkin to me?"

"Never you mind, buddy," said Harry to Rollie Beecham. "It's all fine now. Don't get yourself in a stew. You're doin real good, Rollie. You're my friend, an you're doin fine as fine can be."

Rollie Beecham blinked, stared down at his hands. He'd once been a brakeman for the old T&NO, and he was a good eightyfive if he was a day, and maybe his ears had been damaged by the loudness of too many trains. Still, he did try to keep up with whatever was going on there in the Top of the World. He really did take a good hard determined shot at concentrating. Not that this was par-

[44]

ticularly strange. After all, he had little else to do. He had three dead wives, four dead children and six dead grandchildren. The wives all had died of cancer. Two of the children had died of strokes. Another had died of an embolism. The fourth—together with the six grandchildren—had died in a bus crash in 1971 on a narrow rainswept highway not far from Tupelo, Mississippi. Oh, seven other grandchildren still were alive, and several of them had children of their own, but Rollie seldom was able to put straight in his mind just who was dead and who was alive. The effort always seemed to tire him and make him cranky, and often he breathed through clenched dentures and glared at the world (and maybe at his past and all the afflictions and deaths that had punctuated and perhaps ultimately had governed it), and often he made feeble wrinkled fists and softly thudded those fists against the bar. The other old rummies in the Top of the World seldom anymore asked him about his past. The questions got him all bollixed up. It was better if he was just left alone with his confusions and his sad deaf speculations.

Milt Willis nodded toward Rollie Beecham and said: "*I sure am sorry, Rollie! Can you hear me?*"

"I can hear you fine," said Rollie, still staring down at his hands. "You don't have to holler. I ain't stupid, you know."

(Herman Marshall sighed. He'd seen a mess of movie shows that had had scenes like this, and you were supposed to laugh at the person who was deaf. Well, he for one didn't see anything funny about any of it.)

Milt resumed his conversation with Harry. Milt grinned and moistened his lips. He had a substantial belly, and he had one chin too many, but much of his hair still was dark . . . and naturally so, not because of Grecian Formula Whatever It Was. Now he briefly brushed at it with the heel of a hand. He adjusted his cap. "Listen," he said to Harry, "let's get back to what I'm just about fixin to blow up about."

"Oh?" said Harry. "You got to go piss again, you old asshole? How come? I mean, wasn't you just in the bathroom?"

"No," said Milt. "*No*, you sonofabitch. I ain't talkin about no *pissin*. Oh sure, I'll be the first to admit I piss a lot. Ten times a day. A dozen times a day. Maybe more." And Milt patted his crotch. "I mean, I give old Roscoe here a workout." Now Milt was more than grinning; he was smirking. He was wearing Army fatigues, and its sleeves were rolled up, and his arms were tattooed with hearts and roses and forkedtongued snakes. He hugged himself. He rubbed his arms. "But," he said, "old Roscoe needs him a little bath ever now an again. In cunt juice, you know?" A hesitation. His eyes glittered, and he had to wipe spittle from a corner of his mouth.

The old rummies all leaned forward. Even Rollie Beecham, although perhaps he didn't quite know why.

"I got your attention, ain't I?" said Milt.

"Get on with it," said a man named Ralph Danielson, a retired Pasadena policeman.

Milt snickered. "Well," he said, "one day last week I stopped at the Plymouth Rock over by the Gulf Freeway. I stopped air an got real lucky." Another pause. Milt had been a newspaper advertising salesman, and so he knew all about when to pause. Then: "A Plymouth Rock. I got lucky in a *Plymouth Rock*. Honest to shit. I wouldn't lie to you."

"Fuck you wouldn't," said Ralph Danielson. "Everbody lies. Includin you, Milt. *Especially* includin you, I expect."

"No," said Milt. "Maybe air've been other times when I've lied a little. To make a point or whatever. But I ain't lyin *this* time. God strike me down deader an a doornail."

[46]

Several of the men in the Top of the World glanced sharply up at the ceiling.

Milt grinned. "Ah," he said, "you boys ain't got no faith in me."

"Well told we ain't," said Ralph Danielson. His cap displayed the insignia of the Fraternal Order of Police.

"Let him talk," said Harry to Ralph Danielson. "I expect we're gettin to the good part."

Ralph Danielson had large shoulders. He moved them. "All right," he said. "I ain't standin in nobody's way."

Milt quickly resumed. "Wasn't nothin to it," he said. "Like the kids say, it was a piece of cake. I walked into at Plymouth Rock with my laundry an some suits to be cleaned an pressed. An this woman is standin behind the counter, an she smiles at me, an first thing I notice is well maybe she ain't the youngest chicken in the barnyard, but she's more or less still got her figure, an—"

"More or less," said Frank Lee Doubleday, rubbing his mouth.

"Don't interrupt," said Milt to Frank Lee. "We sure enough are gettin to the good part, just like old Harry here done said. So, anyway, this woman asks me my name an fills out this little piece of paper, an en she asks me what my telephone number is. An me, bein so fresh an all, *I* ask *her* what *hers* is. An she gives it to me. She writes it down on another of em little pieces of paper an gives it to me an *squeezes* my *hand*. Right air in front of God an the world, an it ain't but bout ten o'clock in the mornin, so help me Gussie. An she tells me her name is Diana. A pretty name, Diana; it's always sort of gave me a hardon, you know? Diana. Whoo*ee*. She's wearin one of em white Plymouth Rock uniforms, an it's open at the neck, an she leans forward on the counter an gives me a good flash of the top part of her tits, an they ain't hardly wrinkled none a *tall*. An she says to me I seem like a happy an positive sort of old boy, an she bets me I'm just ready an willin an able for whatever comes along, ho ho, do I get what she means? An I say yesm, I do believe I do. An old Roscoe is standin up. An this here Diana comes out from behind the counter an walks to the door an *locks* it. Boom, bam, she slams shut the bolt. An me, I'm standin air with my mouth open an good old Roscoe real interested. An air's one of em cardboard signs hangin on the door, an she turns the sign over, changin it from *OPEN* to *CLOSED*. An she turns to me an tells me she don't care if she gets fired; she wants to take me into the back so we can do . . . well, whatever we figure out we *need* to do. An me, I'm sayin to myself: Hell's bells, Milt, you wake up in the mornin, an your laundry's dirty, an so you take it to the Plymouth Rock, an look what's bout to happen to you. So her an me, we go to the back of the place, an we pick our way round carts of laundry and whatnot, an by God en allofasudden she says to me: We might as well be comfortable, honey. An she tips over one of em carts, an all the laundry an whatnot comes spillin out, an she grins at me, an she pulls up her skirt quick as a flash, an you want to know somethin? *She ain't wearin no drawers! Air it is! Her bush! An air ain't a gray hair in it!* An she flops down on the pile of laundry an tells me hurry, hurry, ain't no time like the present, now is air? So *I* flop down an I get workin on the buttons at hold the front of her uniform together, an she tells me careful, lover, we don't want to rip nothin; this here uniform is the property of the Plymouth Rock company. An I grunt an maybe even sort of slobber, truth be known, an she is wearin a brassière . . . I'll give her at much . . . an she helps me with the goddamn catch . . . an she tells me she's drownin . . . she's all wet an ready . . . yessir . . . ready for Freddie, like we used to say . . . an so, to make a long story soft, ha ha, I throw a good old fuck into her . . . an en, when it's over, you know what she does? She . . . well, God as my Witness, she tells me I'm terrific, an she *licks my balls*. Honest to shit. I can't hardly member when the last time was a woman licked my balls. Maybe when Eisenhower was President. Or maybe Lincoln. Ha ha. Oh. Ah. Just the memberin of it . . . well, you know . . ." And Milt subsided. He plucked at his fly for a moment, then blushed a little.

". . . an?" said Harry.

"An what?" said Milt.

"You seen her since?"

"Surely. Ever mornin."

"*Ever* mornin?" said Harry. "At *your* age?"

"Yessir," said Milt. "An I don't care if it kills me. She'll think I'm comin, but I'll be goin, an we'll both be happy. I mean, I don't know what it is she sees in me, but I ain't askin no questions, you know? I just haul my old bones over air to at Plymouth Rock at ten o'clock ever mornin an do my holy duty like a man."

"*Holy* duty?" said Harry.

"Yessir," said Milt. "Miracle of God duty. She's only fiftyeight, is this Diana of mine, an she tells me I remind her of her second husband, whose name was Alvin an who she says was a *stud*, who she says would fuck a dump truck if he was of a mind. She says my pecker is even like his. Long an slick, you know. Long an slick . . ."

"Wonderful," said Harry.

"Outstandin," said Ralph Danielson.

"Thanks, boys," said Milt, and he gave them both a slow and thoughtful finger. "An fuck you an the horses you rode in on."

"I think *he* thinks we don't believe him," said Ralph Danielson to Harry.

"If pigs had wings, they'd fly," said Harry. "At'll be the day we believe him."

Milt shifted his weight. His barstool squeaked. "Why would I lie about a thing like at? I mean, it ain't a thing a man lies about. It's a . . . well, it's a *sacred* thing . . ."

[49]

Herman Marshall spoke up. He hadn't really felt the words coming, but suddenly they were there, and he said: "Air's a woman acrost the street from me, an she keeps askin me over to watch dirty movies on her cable TV."

"The ones at are on late at night?" said Frank Lee Doubleday.

"Yessir," said Herman Marshall. "Her name's Jobeth Stephenson, an she ain't hardly old a tall, an she's *beautiful*. An she can't be but fiftyfive, if she's at. Tall, with a whole lot of blond in her hair, an I think maybe it's real . . . " Christ's sake, why was Herman Marshall saying all these things? Jobeth Stephenson was a goddamn *crone*, and she liked to cackle, and it was a wonder she didn't have goddamn warts on her chinny chin chin. *Shit.*

"You mean the really depraved ones?" said Frank Lee Doubleday, showing off again just because he'd been a schoolteacher. Showing off all his words.

"The really what?" said Herman Marshall. "I don't know what you're sayin. You an your big old . . . vocation."

"Vocabulary," said Frank Lee.

"How's at?" said Herman Marshall.

"You were makin reference to my *vocabulary*," said Frank Lee, "an not to my *vocation*. I have no vocation any longer. I am too old to have a vocation, remember? I live alone in a little frame house, remember? An ever day I breathe the refineries. Good old Pasadena, where all the peckerwoods in Texas have come to roost. An I sit air in at little house, an I know all bout the dirty movies. Air on the cable at midnight, one in the mornin, *two* in the mornin, whenever, an many's the night I set the alarm so I can watch em."

"I seen em oncet or twicet," said a nervous bald little fellow named Ike Sage. "They show cunts, an they even show jism juice."

"At is correct," said Frank Lee, sighing.

"Old boys jackin off," said Ike Sage, "an they come all over some little old gal's tits."

[50]

"Well, Ike," said Frank Lee, "air's nothin wrong with your eyesight."

"I earned Sharpshooter on the rifle range in basic trainin," said Ike Sage. "It was 19 an 42, an we all laid on the ground, an if you missed the target altogether, you got a red flag waved at you, an it was called Maggie's Drawers. An if you got two Maggie's Drawers, they gave you KP for a goddamn month, seven days a week, no excuses, no sick call, no fuckin off. Fort Bennin, Georgia, not exactly your garden spot of your universe."

Milt Willis cleared his throat. "I been workin somethin in my mind."

"Congratulations," said Harry.

"If yall don't believe me, yall want to come to the Plymouth Rock tomorrow mornin an *watch?*" said Milt. "I'll ask her to let you in. She won't mind. She's too horny to mind. She wants my pecker too much."

"Yessir," said Ralph Danielson. "On account of it's long an slick. Maybe from now on we ought to call you Slick Willis, like you was some sort of fiddleplayer or somethin."

"Well, *I* ain't goin to *watch*," said Harry.

" . . . why not?" said Milt.

"Watch a sorry old fart try to fuck a sorry old bag?" said Harry. "No way. If I want to do at, I can nail a mirror on my bedroom ceilin an watch me an Beth when we try to go at it."

There was a general wheeze of laughter from the old rummies. All except Rollie Beecham, who was blinking at his fingers and working his lips. Maybe he was trying to count his fingers. It probably was reasonable to believe he would come up with eleven. Ike Sage had a few more things to say about jism. He told of a time, in 1950 maybe, when he'd shot a wad a good ten feet, and it had smeared a windowpane in an Alabama Street whorehouse. And the whore had said: *My God an Sweet Jesus, what was AT?*

[51]

One of the Lone Ranger's silver bullets? More laughter, and then Milt Willis asked the boys if they wanted to hear anything more about his hot Diana of the Plymouth Rock. Someone told him to go shit in his hat and pull it all down over his ears and tell the world he had sprouted a fine fresh set of brown curls. Herman Marshall made a face and looked away. But he was as disgusted with himself as he was with the other old rummies. Making up all that stuff about Jobeth. Why had such a thing been necessary? Did he think he was fooling anyone? *He was seventyfour years of age*, and at seventyfour a man has few ways to fool people. But give him three or four Shiners, plant him here in this ramshackle place with his buddies, permit a beery warmth to float into his brain and his belly, watch his face as he listens to descriptions of cunts and jism, and for a little while he almost can believe he is an intruder into this place of decrepitude and pathetic exaggerations; he almost can believe he'll suddenly stand up and tug loose the flaccid flesh of his face and reveal himself to be, oh, a young and energetic *forty*, and he says to the old rummies: *Ha! Ha! Ha! The joke's on you! I been in disguise all this time, an yall was took in, am I right or am I right?* And Herman Marshall picked at a patch of loose skin on a knuckle. The rummies told dirty stories. The rummies laughed. Harry came to Herman Marshall and told him yessir, all right, we all of us got reason to be down in the dumps, an you maybe got more reason an a whole lot of us got, but come on, my friend, the bartender is buyin you a Shiner. And Herman Marshall managed a smile. One more Shiner was all he had time for. He had to drive home. There was a Mrs Quealy who sat with Edna when Herman Marshall made his excursions to the Top of the World, but at five o'clock in the afternoon Mrs Quealy turned into a pumpkin, Mr Marshall, hee hee, pardon my little joke air, but I *do* got to fix my husband's supper for him, you know. So he won't beat me with a strap, hee hee. But, by God, strap or no strap, Herman Marshall drank his last Shiner slowly. The bottle sweated. He licked it. He said to himself: *This here is the Top of the World.* Milt Willis edged toward him and spoke of Diana and the truth. Herman Marshall nodded. Yesterday Herman Marshall had been fifty or forty or twenty or whatever, and he couldn't remember much of what had happened since then. He wanted to ask Milt about that, but he didn't. He simply adjusted his *ASTROS* cap and sat there and allowed the Shiner to do whatever it was supposed to do. What the hell, he had managed to sneak through another day.

CHAPTER FIVE

Edna's hair had been dark, now black and now a sort of reddish brown, depending on how the light had organized itself. She had taken straightforward pride in her hair, and this was why she had gathered unto herself so many hairribbons. Her hair by Jesus had *flowed*, and so she'd never cared for bobs and perms and all that *tight* and *arranged* stuff. *Hair ought to be natural*, she'd said back in those days, *an it's a sin for a person to try to fuss with curlin irons an things like at air.* And she would nod with her words. Sitting in front of the bedroom mirror (it was curved and ornate, inlaid with a design of palm fronds and studded with ridged glass knobs), she always had combed her hair slowly, lovingly, even after it had whitened. For it still had been beautiful, even then. In its final days (the final days of her magnificent hair, before it had been murdered by chemotherapy), she had worn it in a mighty topknot . . . and, hell, she could have been some sort of fine old empress straight out of an old movie that featured people such as Tyrone Power and old nasty Basil Rathbone and was full of costumes and jewels and horses and galleons in full sail. And Herman Marshall had told Edna this, and abruptly she had wept. The words had come the day Dr Moomaw had told Edna she had the cancer. Dr Homer Moomaw, whose initials were the same as Herman Marshall's and Harry Munger's. Who was young and curlyhaired. Who had a thin and precise voice. Who always wore glasses and who sometimes wore Adidas jogging shoes while talking with a patient and the patient's spouse. *I'm your typical young man in a hurry*, he liked to say. *I don't know what I'm hurryin FOR, but this is Houston, an I*

*think it's expected of people like me. So I jog whenever I get the chance,
an I believe you folks can forgive me at little weakness, can't you? Ah.
I thank you. I thank you very much. An my heart thanks you. I come
from a long line of coronary thrombosi, to coin a phrase, an I want to
break the losin streak.* And then—inevitably—Dr Moomaw would
deliver more bad news about the cancer, and it was as though he
were telling Edna *her* losing streak still was *flourishing*, and sometimes Herman Marshall wanted to crawl over that bespectacled
little fucker's desk and knock him to the floor and twist off his balls
and stuff those jogging shoes up his pink little thrombosi ass, whatever a thrombosi was. What the hell did Dr Moomaw think he was
talking about? a cockroach with a toothache? a billygoat with a hair
in its nose? a rattlesnake with lockjaw? God damn that little shithead sonofabitch, he was talking about *Edna Stillman Marshall*, who
was *Mrs Herman E. Marshall*, and she was *important*. Or at least she
should have been. She had been so chunky and jolly, and she had
had the capacity to make off with Herman Marshall's goddamned
breath, and *that* had been the exact and final truth of *that*. To kiss
the corners of her mouth. To kiss them gently, barely brushing
them with his awkward nigger lips. To say to her: *You know, when
I ain't with you, it's like my belly hurts so bad I feel like I've swallowed
the bell of the First Baptist Church*. To touch the curve of her breasts
and think of those breasts in terms of benevolence and generosity.
To listen to her, and *really* listen to her, when she said: *I'll give you
a hunnert years with me, an en you can run off with some chorus girl or
whatever*. To touch her hairribbons. To kiss them. To suck her
tongue. To laugh with her over Laurel & Hardy. To hold hands
and drive down to Texarkana and suck on ice cream cones and
watch the trains come waddling and swaying into the depot and
make up stories about the people who were sitting in the daycoaches and the Pullmans: *At one air—see the fat one with the straw*

[56]

hat? He owns the railroad, an he's on his way to see his girlfriend, an her
name is Jean Harlot, ha ha, an she'll milk him for every last penny he's
worth, sure as my name is Franklin D. Rosyfelt, ha ha. An at old lady in
the black hat . . . see her? Yes ma' am, at one. Third window from the left.
Second daycoach. Her cat died last week, an she's goin to Austin to see her
daughter on account of she misses the cat an she don't know what to do.
All she does is mope around the house an TOUCH things . . . things
the cat liked . . . its bowl maybe, or a davenport where it took naps all
the time an air was plenty of sunlight. Oh, in those days the world was
larger than vision and death, and Herman Marshall and his Edna
perhaps even believed they could comprehend it. After all, what
was such a big thing? You loved, and every now and again the
loving became so delicious, so candied with gropings and hot
breathy eloquence, that you believed your flesh would balloon and
rip open and your love would spill all golden and silly (they found
haystacks and barns; once they found a tourist court, and a chicken
strutted into the place just at the wrong time, ha ha, or the *right*
time, ha ha, poking through a hole in the screen and clucking away
in a tone of prissy and astonished outrage), and you told yourself
hey, hot shit, her an me are puttin together a time at ain't never
happened to nobody, least not *quite*, and you laughed, and maybe
your teeth were larger than hailstorms and the sun, and where was
the book that really told you there was anything the matter with
that sort of thing? And Herman Marshall wasn't thinking of Holy
Scripture. He was thinking of a book that was *real*, that could be
understood, that a human being had a chance of living up to. No
virgins popping babies. No Lazarus rising from no grave. No
handwriting on no wall. No loaves. No fishes. All his life Herman
Marshall had sought a book that would address itself to Hope,
Arkansas, and Houston, Texas, to old boys with guns and hats and
enormous beltbuckles. The older he became, the more he figured

he needed that book. He'd never spoken to Edna of the book. He'd never spoken to anyone of the book—not even Harry Munger. But that didn't mean it had leaked from his mind. Not fucking likely. No sir. The fact was, a lot of shit had been dropped on his life, and he had done a good sight of the dropping. Edna had done a little of it (fucking Romero or maybe somebody else or maybe ten or twenty somebody elses), but most of it had come from Herman Marshall, which gave him a really outstanding feeling . . . oh you betcha . . . when he shuffled around the house while he and Edna waited for her to die. (Dr Moomaw had held out no hope. Dr Moomaw then had excused himself and had skedaddled outside for a brisk jog.) And one morning Herman Marshall came to a point where he just about was ready to press a pillow over Edna's face and send her across. Because that, by God, was her wish, and it was a decent and proper wish, at least as far as he was concerned. (But where was the book that would back him up? He'd never found it.) The thing began that morning when Edna got to weeping over the loss of her hair. Herman Marshall was sitting on the edge of the brass bed. He'd just emptied and washed out Edna's bedpan. It was July, and the airconditioning was on fullblast, but he was sweating. And maybe he smelled like piss. He wasn't quite sure. He touched one of Edna's shoulders after she got to weeping. She told him she was ugly. She told him no one was uglier. She told him she wished he would send her across. And he said: "No. You don't mean at. You ain't talkin sense."

Edna's weeping was quiet. Maybe it even was dignified. It consisted mostly of dry snifflings, and she managed to keep her mouth from giving way. "I'm ugly now," she said. "I'm ugly *now* . . . an I'll be ugly *forever* . . . an after I die I'll be uglier an *at* . . . an you wouldn't argue with me about any of it, would you?"

"Hush up," said Herman Marshall. "I love you."

"At ain't got nothin to do with nothin . . . the time for at sort of talk is gone . . ."

"No," said Herman Marshall. He squeezed her shoulder ever such a little bit. He didn't want to hurt her. "Just because we're old don't mean we—"

"*You* hush up," said Edna, and her head moved from side to side. She closed her eyes. She was breathing with her mouth open. She opened her eyes. She rubbed them with the heels of her hands. "I got no *hair*," she said. "I'm all *tore up*. I got one foot in the undertakin place an the other foot in the grave, an it's all a Judgment, likely as not, an you'd be doin me a real big favor if . . . well, you know . . ."

"*No*," said Herman Marshall. "*Never*."

". . . never?"

"Yes ma'am," said Herman Marshall.

". . . which is a long time," said Edna. She had been hunched forward, but now she slumped back, and she twisted her shoulder free of Herman Marshall's hand.

Herman Marshall stared at the hand. He rubbed it across his belly. He did not know why. He stared at one of Edna's wrists. He did not know why. The wrist was too plump. It didn't fall in line with his notion of a cancer person's wrist. After all, a cancer person's wrist should have been nothing but toothpicks and broken—

"You're dumb," said Edna.

"What?"

"You ain't got the sense the Lord gave a boiled egg," said Edna, "an at's a fact. I'm *old*, an I'm *ugly*, an I'm *bald*, an oh yessir, I'll admit it . . . I surely do appreciate your kind words, but they ain't takin away none of the oldness an the ugliness, an they ain't growin me no new hair, an I ain't nothin but *hurt* an *sorrow*, an so why don't you do me a favor an send me acrost an be done with it? An

[59]

en air won't be no more of you *comfortin* me, layin the sweet words on me like you was spreadin, um, well, like you was spreadin peanut butter with a paddle . . ."

"But . . . but I ain't talkin *peanut butter*. I'm talkin the *truth* . . "

"Truth?" said Edna. "Since when have we had at much truth?"

" . . . what?"

Edna cleared her throat. Her tears were gone. They were so far gone maybe they'd never been there at all. Again she cleared her throat. She moistened her lips. Her tongue was gray. "Billy," she said. "You want to talk bout Billy? You want to talk bout me an Phil Romero? You want me to tell you at it was right here in this room, right over air by the window where the old flowered davenport used to be, at him an me, at . . . at . . . *you want truth?*"

Herman Marshall spoke quickly. "I'll go upstairs to the attic. I'll find somethin an I'll bring it down, an I'll talk to you bout whatever it is . . . "

"Take a pillow. Press it on my face."

" . . . no."

"Phil told me I was pretty. An he came deep an hot in me."

"No," said Herman Marshall.

"I was a slut. Kill me. At's what ought to be done to sluts. They ought to be kilt."

"Oh, Jesus Christ," said Herman Marshall.

Edna pulled a pillow out from behind her shoulders. The pillow-case was pink and lacy. Maybe Edna had sewn it. She'd always been good at sewing.

"The trains?" said Herman Marshall. "Billy's trains? You want me to bring em back down? It won't take but bout half an hour, an they'll be all set up."

Edna held out the pillow. "Here," she said. "This would do me. I ain't got no strength to fight you off. I'm a sinner, an you'd be doin me a favor."

Herman Marshall opened his mouth and roared, but there was no sound. Only he heard any sort of sound, and it was like a dog lost in a cave. He reached for the pillow. "Sure enough?" he said. His arms were outstretched, but he wasn't quite touching the pillow.

" . . . yessir," said Edna, nodding.

"He was *deep* an *hot*, was he?"

" . . . yes *sir*," said Edna, and she still was nodding. And her eyes had enlarged. They were green eyes, and they appeared to be floating on eggs. "Listen," she said. "You remember what Dr Moomaw told us, don't you? Him an his funny shoes. You remember how he said it wasn't goin to get no better? He was bendin over an gruntin an *tyin* em shoes, remember? An at was all right, wasn't it? I mean, would it of made a speck of difference if he'd been settin air in a black suit with a tie an a white shirt an patentleather shoes? Would it of made a speck of difference if he would of rolled around on the rug an tore at his face with, um, with his fingernails, like maybe I was the first person in the world who was fixin to die of cancer, an nobody'd had cancer before I'd got it, an it was like the worst thing that'd ever happened since the world came together? Here. Take this here pillow. Don't just reach for it. Take it."

Herman Marshall wrapped his arms around his chest.

" . . . shoot," said Edna. She dropped the pillow on her knees.

Herman Marshall's voice came as a croak. "I . . . the thing is . . . I can't do nothin like at . . . "

" . . . all right," said Edna.

"I don't care bout Phil Romero . . . "

"I don't believe at . . . "

"It was *19* an *48*," said Herman Marshall. "I . . . Jesus . . . I want to *go upstairs*. I want to *find* somethin . . ."

"What did we do with at old flowered davenport anyway? It upstairs?"

"No," said Herman Marshall. "I seem to recollect we gave it to the Salvation Army."

"Or maybe we threw it out with the trash," said Edna. "At would of been better. Please. Please kill me. Please do at."

Herman Marshall flinched.

Edna's face was without expression. Everything was in order, and she was blinking and breathing, and her hairless skull was a trifle damp, but her face was like a wrinkled blot of pudding; it was a face reserved for bus passengers and people at supermarket checkout counters. "Please," she said. You peckerwood sonofabitch. *Please.*"

He closed his eyes.

"You miserable shitface," said Edna.

". . . no," said Herman Marshall.

"I sucked his thing," said Edna. "I never told you *at*, did I? At part of it. He was a big Mex, with a big Mex thing. All purple it was, an I took it in my mouth an he squeezed my head, an my ears got to hurtin, an I looked up at him like maybe I was a cow or somethin . . ."

Herman Marshall shuddered. He opened his eyes and tried to stand up, but his joints hurt too much. Again he roared, and this time there was a sound to it. And this time there was blood to it.

"Yes," said Edna, and she nearly smiled. "Right. Fine. Do it."

Herman Marshall leaned forward and seized the pillow. He roared and roared.

"Won't be nothin to it," said Edna, nodding. "It's the human thing to do . . ."

Herman Marshall leaned over his wife and wadded the pillow. He still was roaring.

"*Do* it . . ." said Edna. She nearly had to shout.

Herman Marshall's bile rose. He needed to piss. He roared. He dropped the pillow. He turned away. He roared. He vomited down the front of his shirt, and he roared through the vomit. He wet his pants. He roared and choked.

Behind him, Edna said: "Oh, wonderful . . ."

Herman Marshall's legs gave way, and he knelt in his vomit. He kept pissing and pissing, and he felt his piss trail into his socks. His throat had been blowtorched, and it abounded with hot wet fragments of he didn't know the fuck what. His roaring faded away. Edna said nothing more. It was a good five minutes before Herman Marshall was able to stand up and clean away his mess. He went upstairs and took a tub bath. Lying spent and gasping in the tub, he remembered how it had been with Billy, all the pain and screaming. Billy, who hadn't looked like a Mex at all. Billy, who probably would have been better off choking to death in his mother's womb. His mother, the cocksucker. Herman Marshall beat at the bathwater with his naked legs, and he roared over the splashings. (He wanted to go to the attic. Maybe he would find a windup monkey in the attic. Or whatever remained of an Erector set. Or an unopened box of old *Liberty* magazines. Or maybe even a checkerboard with all its checkers. As a boy, Herman Marshall had been a fine player, and everyone agreed on that. *He can think ahead*, people said, *an he don't let nothin much rattle him.* He had been every bit as good a checker player as he had been a baseball player, and right now he would have given five years out of his sorry demolished life to have been sitting in Leo's Barber Shop in Hope, Arkansas, on maybe a summer afternoon, hot and golden, in maybe 1928 and breathing bay rum and hair clippings and soft thick barbersoap while bending over a checkerboard and whipping the ass off some shitkicking sonofabitch who'd walked into a checkerplaying buzzsaw without knowing it, ha ha, and fuck him.) Herman Marshall's head jerked from side to side. Blood came from his throat. Residual puke came from his throat. His hair was matted, scummy, foul. His body moved in spasms from side to side, and gray bathwater sprayed over the sides of the tub. His wife, the cocksucker. For thirty years and more he'd tried to get her to suck *his* cock, but she'd always said no, no; that was something a man had bestowed on him by a dirty whore or a waitress or a woman who was outright crazy in the head and full of evil thoughts. So Herman Marshall every so often had *found* a whore or a waitress or a crazy woman who would suck his cock. And the nervous tintinnabulating widowed schoolteacher in Beaumont had sucked his cock. And she actually had given signs of *enjoying* it—as long as he had been generous enough to jam a finger up her ass. And now Herman Marshall's teeth . . . dentures, rather . . . were clacking. Abruptly he stood up. He was colder than bear shit. The bathwater was mildly pink and yellow from blood and puke. No, his wife was no cocksucker. She had lied. Herman Marshall stepped out of the tub and began more or less briskly toweling himself. She had lied because she had wanted to make him so angry with her he would send her across. With a fucking pink pillow. Herman Marshall took care as he wiped his belly and his crotch. His balls were tight, and his cock was tiny, retracted, stupid. (He said to himself: I ain't never really have liked gettin my cock sucked. At least not too much. I mean, a *little*, all right, but not *too* much. An she tells me she looked up at the Mex like she was a cow. I don't believe it. I don't believe none of it. I don't believe he fucked her. She wouldn't fuck no *Mex*. An Billy didn't look like no Mex. It was another man altogether, an she ain't never goin to tell me who at old boy was; his goddamn name'll go to the grave with her. The plot she's already picked out. How can I believe in Paradise? Answer me at. I mean, maybe at the beginnin, all right: Paradise was tall an settin up air in real fine sharp focus, an the angels was all of them lined up an playin air harps like it all *meant* somethin, an I could drive my rig an not be bothered by nobody an tell myself hey, you sad sack of shit you, it's all in the *believin*, an you believe. But at's all gone. I don't believe in nothin except piss, an the only reason I believe in piss is on account of it's always with me an so what choice I got, ha ha, you know?) Herman Marshall's legs were wobbling. He fought to keep his balance. He flapped like a crippled goose. He slammed against the washbasin. He moaned. He surely did wish he knew of a book that would explain this sort of situation. He dropped the towel and leaned against the washbasin. After a time he walked naked to his bedroom. It had been *their* bedroom—his and Edna's—from the time they'd bought this place back in 1946 right up until her cancer had sent her downstairs, there to groan and shriek in the old brass bed, there to beg Herman Marshall to bring things down from the attic and tell sweet stories about those things . . . sweet *tall* stories, silly and loving. And there in that old brass bed she had told him Phil Romero had been Billy's father. And she had spoken of a Judgment. And this day, in order to flummox Herman Marshall into killing her, she had told him she had sucked Phil Romero's cock. Did she really expect him to believe that? She, who always had spoken of cocksucking in a voice all bloated with horror and disgust? Jesus Christ, maybe there was a sucker born every minute, but Herman Marshall wasn't such a sucker that he believed his wife's *cock*sucker story, ha ha, ho ho. No *sir*. No *way*. He put on a clean pair of shorts. He grunted. He put on a faded blue workshirt and an old wrinkled pair of khaki britches. He didn't bother with shoes and socks. The hell with shoes and socks. He wasn't leaving the house, was he? He touched his crotch before he zipped up the britches. Everything seemed all right. He felt no need to piss. He returned to the bathroom and brushed his teeth. He gargled with Listerine, and it stung his throat, but then that was to be expected, wasn't it? He went downstairs, and he walked in a splayed waddle. His mouth sang with the sting of the Listerine. He wondered how many goddamn whoop de do millions of germs had been killed by the good old vigilant Listerine. Maybe billions. Maybe zillions. He didn't know. Edna's eyes were closed when he came into the front room. Her hands gripped her belly, and she had kicked back the covers. Her legs were exposed, and they were pale, flabby, spidered with aimless wandering veins. Herman Marshall went to the bed and pulled up the covers. Edna opened her eyes and said to him: "You was bawlin up air in the bathroom. I heard you."

"Yes ma'am," said Herman Marshall, adjusting Edna's pillows. He made fists and pounded the pillows, plumping them up real good for her. He was leaning over her, and he was smiling, or at least he believed he was smiling. There was a faint odor of his puke, but he'd really done quite a competent job of cleaning up his mess. He straightened. He was proud that he'd been so efficient. He seated himself on a straightbacked chair next to the bed. He still felt a little cold, but not as cold as he'd been up in the bathroom. Old age really did take the heat out of a person's bones, and that was no shit.

Edna spoke. "Herman?"

". . . ma'am?"

"I didn't do like I said I done. I didn't take him in my mouth."

"All right."

"You believe me?"

"Yes ma'am," said Herman Marshall.

"I only said at so maybe you'd kill me."

"Yes ma'am," said Herman Marshall. He touched one of Edna's cheeks.

"At sounds funny, don't it?"

"I expect it does . . ."

"I mean, just sayin a thing *out* like at air. Makin myself out to be a slut. I ain't been no slut. Not no *real* slut. I done it with Phil on account of I was lonely, an I wasn't gettin no prettier, an—"

"I know all at," said Herman Marshall.

"Sayin a thing like at air on account of you want your husband to kill you. Now *at's* what *I* call *funny*." Edna's eyes had turned all glittery, and various smiles touched her face. Toothy smiles. Quick skittery smiles. Soft abashed smiles. She plucked at one of her lacy pillowcases. "Makin myself all dirty like at," she said. "It's so awful an dumb it's iggerant."

"It don't matter none," said Herman Marshall, patting Edna's cheek.

"I sure enough am sorry I made you sick."

"Don't matter none."

"You still love me?" said Edna.

"Surely," said Herman Marshall. He looked away from her and listened to the airconditioner. He breathed with his mouth open, and the Listerine went at his gums with razorblades and high bright fire.

CHAPTER SIX

As a boy, HERMAN MARSHALL had a hero, and his hero's name was Tom Mix. Herman Marshall went to all the Tom Mix movies. He went to most of the showings of all the Tom Mix movies. He mowed lawns to earn the admission price. He wheelbarrowed bricks. He cleaned cisterns. He beat rugs for old women. He loved it when Tom Mix shot dead all the dirty outlaws and badmen. He loved Tom Mix's horse, which was named Tony. He told himself he'd give anything to be just like Tom Mix. Maybe it was Tom Mix's eyes. Maybe it was Tom Mix's speed in drawing a revolver. Maybe it was the fact that Tom Mix was *there*, and you *knew* he was there, and his thereness told you the affairs of men held a possibility of honor, not to mention bravery. As a boy, Herman Marshall often sneaked away to secret places where he would try to squint the way Tom Mix squinted. The Tom Mix squint was not a *squint* squint. Rather, it was a simple and subtle show of tension at the corners of the eyes. The sort of squint that spoke quietly, but it said dangerous things to you. It said: *No sense hollerin at me, pard. At sort of thing won't do a stitch of good. You might as well try to draw on me an be done with it, an en we can go bout the business of findin a proper preacher to say the proper words over your open grave on Boot Hill, you polecat you.* There were times when Herman Marshall squatted at the edge of the Red River (it ran, heavy and hot, across a corner of his Uncle Jack's farm in good old Hempstead County, Arkansas), and Herman Marshall used the riverwater as a mirror so he could practice imitating Tom Mix's squint in a place where none of his brothers . . . or anyone else . . . would catch him at it and laugh at him. He didn't like being laughed at, especially when it came to such a serious matter as Tom Mix and the squint of Tom Mix, the thereness of Tom Mix. Maybe Herman Marshall didn't have all that much of a sense of humor. Maybe he never would amount to a hill of beans. But by God he wanted to give her a try, this Success thing, and he wanted to give Bravery a try, and he figured he probably wanted to be another Tom Mix right down to his very tough smooth *balls*, and so the *last* thing he wanted was to be ridiculed. (Later, he would remember himself as having been competitive and full of The Old Nick, and maybe the memory was accurate, what with his skill at checkers and baseball. He surely did like to think so. And maybe the thought even blurred a little of the pain that came later.) He was the youngest of four sons of a man named Eldred Marshall, who was a plumber and had a small truck farm down on the Texarkana road. This Eldred Marshall had a narrow bony frame, and so did his wife, whose name was Hannah Marshall and who had given birth to the four boys in six years. Herman Marshall's three brothers were named Eldred Junior, Lute and Jackson. They were big fellows, and they liked to caper and bray, and they liked to tease girls and shoot rabbits, and they liked to rag their little brother because of his quiet ways, his feelings for Tom Mix—and, of course, his nigger lips. He never quite decided whether he ever had given much of a damn about Eldred Junior and Lute and Jackson. Oh, he went hunting with them (he became an excellent shot, and he could bag a bird at a hundred yards without even thinking much about it), and he tried to suck in his nigger lips so his brothers wouldn't be reminded of them, and most of the time his brothers more or less took it easy on him. But there were occasions when they let themselves, like the man said, get carried away a little too much. One time they stripped him naked in a woods, chained him loosely to a tree and

[70]

left a watermelon for him in case he became *hongry*, hwa, hwa. *Don't forget to spit out the seeds, little nigger*, said Eldred Junior. *We wouldn't want no watermelon vines pokin out of your sweet pretty asshole.* And then Eldred Junior and Lute and Jackson went crashing and stumbling away, and they took his clothes with them, and the chains were cold against his flesh. He was just twelve years of age at the time. He needed more than an hour before he was able to work himself free of the goddamn chains. He kicked the watermelon, and his toes stung. He picked up a rock and squashed the watermelon. He kept hitting it and hitting it. Seeds shot out in a black and slippery spray. He wanted to weep, but he did not weep. He had not wept when his brothers had chained him to that tree, and he was not about to weep now that he was free. A week later, he went walking along the river with Eldred Junior's coon hound, Elsie. He held Elsie's head under the water until she drowned. He didn't let her float away, though. He did what he figured maybe was the decent thing. He fetched a shovel from Uncle Jack's barn and buried old Elsie, and he buried her deep, so the buzzards and the wild pigs wouldn't dig her up and tear her apart and feast on her like maybe she was Fourth of July barbecue. He couldn't remember exactly who'd told him the buzzards and the wild pigs were fond of digging up dead things, and maybe it wasn't true at all, but he wanted to be on the safe side. Eldred Junior actually broke down and wept at the suppertable after two weeks of searching for Elsie. He was eighteen years of age, was Eldred Junior, and his mouth became cavernous, and his face was shadowed by pale shoots of light coming in wavy blots from the coaloil lanterns that illuminated the room (there would be no electricity in that place until 1937 or so). Eldred Junior made fists and more or less beat his cheeks and his jaw with those fists. His mother tried to touch one of his shoulders, but he jerked the shoulder free of her thin tentative

[71]

hand. Everyone else sort of looked away. Herman Marshall briefly covered his mouth and cleared his throat. Eldred Junior finally lurched out of the room, and he knocked a plate of baked beans to the floor when he stood up. His footsteps were uneven and altogether too heavy, like the footsteps of a feebleminded person who didn't know which end was up, you might say. The rest of the family sat silently at the table. The front door slammed. A moment later Eldred Junior began to call and whistle. He was somewhere out in the fields, but the sounds carried easily. It was a calm and starry summer night, and the sounds carried like blades. Sitting at the suppertable, Herman Marshall linked his fingers and cracked his knuckles. No one spoke. Everyone simply listened to Eldred Junior calling and whistling—for Elsie, of course. Herman Marshall glanced at his other two brothers. Lute was chewing on his lips (they were *thin* lips; they were *a white person's* lips; they were not *nigger* lips). Jackson was poking at his plate of beans with a bent spoon. Steam rose from the beans. They were plump. No one made a move to clean up the beans Eldred Junior had knocked to the floor. Eldred Junior was gone most of the night, and the next morning his father made him clean up the bean mess. He did so without fussing about it. He squatted in his BVDs and scraped up the dried and scummy beans with a spatula. Herman Marshall sat at the table and watched his oldest brother. He noticed that Eldred Junior's lips appeared to be cracked—maybe from too much whistling. He told himself he had an obligation to enjoy what he was watching. He was bright enough to know he wouldn't be able to punish Lute and Jackson like this. If he did, then the three of them would know he was responsible, since who else had reason to hate them so much? The disappearance of Elsie was taken as . . . well, a disappearance . . . but anything further would have made even Herman Marshall's clumsy thickheaded lummoxing brothers altogether too suspicious. He had no trouble understanding this, which maybe had something to do with why he played checkers so well. You always had to *anticipate*, by God. If Lute's baseball glove had vanished, and if Jackson's best Sunday britches had been torn to sad foolish pious shreds, surely Herman Marshall would have been exposed and punished. Which meant his revenge against Eldred Junior also would have to serve as his revenge against Lute and Jackson. This wasn't altogether satisfactory, but it would have to do . . . unless he wanted his ass nailed to the barn wall, ha ha. He didn't suppose Tom Mix would have approved of all this. Tom Mix probably would have called him a sneaky little sidewinder. And honest to God, Herman Marshall was sorry about all that stuff. And did this mean a little fellow had no way to punish bigger people? Probably so. Which was unfair. Which meant Elsie had had to die. Herman Marshall never forgot any of it. The thing had taken place in the summer of the year 1922, and heat waggled up from the earth, and flivvers choked and loomed, dust curling around them, and old women sipped lemonade and deplored the behavior of the idolatrous Papists, and folks sat at their kitchen tables and ate cucumbers with vinegar and told one another hell yes, President Harding was (as the rumor had it) a nigger; why, he even *looked* like a nigger, wasn't that so? (Or at least a little.) That was a summer of cornfields and the river, of piling into Herman Marshall's daddy's 1913 Chevrolet and driving up to Arkadelphia to a prayer meeting at the Baptist college, and always there was a hope of Paradise, but it was knocked down and buried by a promise of Hell, and Herman Marshall sometimes didn't know *what* to think. But the drive to Arkadelphia was nice (everyone bounced and grinned, and Daddy said oh yes, yes indeed; one of these days he surely would have to buy a new machine, on account of *one of these days this here 19 an 13 Chevvy's goin to blow up, don't you ex-*

[73]

pect?), and Daddy bought ice cream cones for everyone, and Eldred Junior and Lute and Jackson were on their best bowtied and goose-greased behavior, just in case one of em air college girls would give one or tuther of em a smile (it was widely held that college girls, even Baptist college girls, liked to kiss and pet and sometimes maybe even go all the way down a certain sweet road, hwa hwa). Oh great God, the prayer meetings. Herman Marshall figured they just eventually may have caused him to believe in Paradise, even though the preachers . . . men preachers and women preachers, and the women wore golden robes, and there even were boy preachers and girl preachers, and the eyes of the boy preachers were enormous, and the flesh of the girl preachers actually appeared to glow, mystical and profound, in the goddamn holyrolling dark . . . paid more attention to Hell than they did to Paradise. But Hell was more *exciting* than Paradise was, correct? What would the average person rather watch, naked women chained in the Abyss and writhing in eternal torment or angels mildly plucking their harps with everywhere fucking lions laying down with fucking lambs? All right, it all was understandable, but it was no way to look at the situation with a clear eye, at least as far as Herman Marshall was concerned. Even as a boy, he figured that sooner or later he'd need to slow down and take himself a nice rest. This maybe was his checkerplaying mind at work—figuring the right future move to make as his days rolled along. And he figured it was better to ascend to Paradise than descend to Hell. *He* didn't want to be chained in no Abyss, and it didn't matter *how* many naked women would be down there with him. (And anyway, who was to say that there weren't naked *angel* women? Yes *sir*. With their sweet angeltits peeking through the harpstrings.) All these thoughts (and others, having to do with stars and death and virgin birth and the Handwriting on the Wall) crept and jostled through Herman Mar-

[74]

shall's mind when he was a boy—and, for that matter, they stayed with him all his life. You had to think about *something* when you drove a truck. Something besides, as the fellow said, booze and cooze. And why *not* speculate on the existence of Paradise? It diverted a man's attention from the real world as he knew it. So maybe Herman Marshall actually was more than a little religious. The thought always made him snort and shake his head and call himself a goddamn moron of a biblebanger, but maybe there was something to it. And surely Tom Mix would have approved of *that*. Tom Mix of that particular miraculous and righteous squint. And Tom Mix no doubt would have said to Herman Marshall: *You're my pard, all right, an it don't matter at you ain't perfect.* Now then, that last part, the part about Herman Marshall not being perfect, was more of a hope than it was an imagined reality. After all, what was there in Tom Mix's face that showed such understanding? Oh, well. Hoping wasn't so bad. It didn't break anyone's legs or cause barns to burn or make trains jump the tracks. So Herman Marshall endured. The largest event in his boyhood probably was his murder of old Elsie (and he called it by its rightful name; he called it murder), and he was sorry he'd had to get rid of her, but at the same time the getting rid of her had been necessary. She had threshed a little, but she really hadn't put up much resistance. Maybe she'd believed he'd just been teasing her, and any second he would pull her out of the water and laugh and give her a good old hug and tell her she was a real sport to be taking a joke so good. Well, the thing didn't shake down that way, and the world bade Elsie an abrupt farewell, courtesy of one Herman E. Marshall, and it all really was a goddamn shame, wasn't it? But Eldred Junior had been made to pay, and Eldred Junior's punishment balanced out the death of an old coon hound bitch, didn't it? Herman Marshall, squatting alone in a dusty alley, breathing horse manure and hot

[75]

fresh garbage and the exhaust from someone's Model T, listening to the reluctant whisk and murmur of willowtrees and the anxious whine of a sawmill, touching his belly and the straps of his faded bib overalls, sucking a sliver of straw and whistling something tuneless and distracted through the openings between his teeth, grimacing at the naked Arkansas sun and trying to squint the Tom Mix squint . . . well, this Herman Marshall told himself yessir, the Lord giveth, but badness an evil taketh away. He had liked old Elsie, and so he hadn't exactly passed through any sort of joy when he'd murdered her, and he'd expected to feel an assault on his conscience because of what he'd done. But it never really came. After all, had Eldred Junior and Lute and Jackson felt an assault on *their* consciences because of what *they'd* done? Not so you could notice —and that was for damn sure. None of them had taken Herman Marshall aside in order to apologize. None of them had told him his nigger lips weren't all *that* ugly. Looking back on this entire fucking mess, and especially his murder of Elsie, Herman Marshall often asked himself how a boy who had believed in Paradise could have behaved that way. And the answer was easy. Herman Marshall had been good and god damn well told *raped*, and his brothers simply had brayed; they simply had gone blundering off after leaving him with that . . . that *watermelon*. That . . . that *nigger food*. Oh, not that he had anything against niggers, you understand, but there were limits to how seriously a fellow could be humiliated before he decided to go to work on his enemies. Or at least he had decided to go to work on Eldred Junior, who would have to do. Maybe later, when the disappearance of Elsie was forgotten, Herman Marshall would punish Lute and Jackson, but he didn't believe so. Later would be too late. He figured his anger would wear off. Again, he was thinking ahead, and no wonder the checkerplayers in Leo's Barber Shop were so respectful of him. So he settled for the murder

[76]

of Elsie. He settled for listening to Eldred Junior call and whistle for her. He settled for cracking his knuckles and glancing down at the plump beans on the floor. He settled for Eldred Junior's tears and howlings, and yes *sir*, the whole thing was real good, maybe even better than naked women chained in the Abyss and writhing in eternal torment. You took what you could. You inflicted what you could. These things were better than nothing. You plucked at the straps of your bib overalls and told yourself hell, you had done all right, all things considered. Oh, every so often Herman Marshall winced when he thought of Tom Mix and what Tom Mix's reaction no doubt would have been, but doesn't a fellow have to do what he has to do? Herman Marshall lived in a world punctuated by *NEHI* signs and *MAIL POUCH* signs and the quiet shuffle of mules and cattle and timid sheep; sometimes he worked for his Uncle Jack, and he washed bugs and caterpillars off his Uncle Jack's corn, and sometimes the wind came hard and hot from across the river, and other times there was nothing except a tight silence and the thoughtful shadowed presence of the good old Ouachitas up to the north. Which meant he could think and plan, and most of the time no one came along to interrupt him. He simply washed the corn and let his mind go skittering off wherever it liked. Maybe he would become the checker champion of the whole entire world. Maybe he would shoulder aside old Babe Ruth and hit home runs as easily as a goddamn spider laid down its eggs. What was the name of that place? Yankee Stadium? Yes. Yankee Stadium, and it was in New York, and people said New York was full of dirty whatchucallums, dirty *Semites*, and old men shook their heads and spat lumpy brown gobs of Mail Pouch or Red Man or whatever, and they allowed as how the Semites was worse than the Papists, on account of the Semites had nailed Jesus to the Cross back in the Bye & Bye when the New Testament had taken place.

A town called Washington was the county seat in those days, and the old men would lounge on the courthouse steps and scratch their balls and dig dirt from their nostrils, and the old men spoke slowly of how it was a damn shame all the wealth of the country had been grabbed up by the Semites, and the Semites had turned New York into hell on earth, what with their greed and their oily ways, and the thing was . . . oh, the laughable and dumb *thing* of the matter *was* . . . the way those old men talked, they made being a Semite sound mighty damn much like a whole lot of fun. And sometimes Herman Marshall would sort of laugh up his sleeve at the old men, and he kept wanting to ask them how much it would cost if a young fellow wanted to buy his way into being a Semite. And so, what with one thing and the tuther, he had a nimble and reasonably easy boyhood, and most everyone applauded him because he played checkers so well, and a lot of older folks told him he must have a mind like a bear trap. Oh, sometimes other boys would rag him because of his nigger lips, but he grew to a good size, which meant the ragging sort of faded away. Before that happened, though, he tried not to cause a lot of fuss because of the ragging. Sometimes he would assume an oldtimey boxer's stance and say to his tormentors: *Come on, you boys. Come on. Come AWN. I'll beat you to death with my lips.* And he would flinch comically, like prize-fighters he had seen in the movies. And he would exhale, flapping his mighty lips. And then his tormentors usually would guffaw and tell him he sure as shit knew how to take a joke. And he would dance among them, jabbing and sniggering, and it was like he was putting on a *show*, like maybe an act from the vaudeville theater he and his family had visited a few times down in Shreveport, and every so often his tormentors would stand aside and actually *clap* for him, while at the same time bending forward and whinnying like spindly new colts. In those days, he really enjoyed whooping

[78]

and capering and playing the fool and even making up stories. You could show him a pile of sticks, and he would make up a story about that pile of sticks. You could mention the mayor's wife's left tit, and he would make up a story about *that*. Abandoned cabooses, old guitars, babies sunning in their perambulators, clouds skipping across a bland bathwater sky . . . Herman Marshall was able to draw *something* from them, and most of the time his little stories made people smile. And his mother shook her head. And she said: *Lord, I don't know where you get it FROM, but maybe it'll be your fame an fortune. At'd be be real nice now, wouldn't it?* And Hannah Marshall's voice hesitated, then lowered itself to a comfortable mutter, and he couldn't make out the words. Hannah Marshall always had been much given to comfortable mutterings. She knew this habit was enough to drive a listener crazy, but she defended it by saying: *I got a right to my thoughts, ain't I? An the thing is, I need my mouth to hep me long with my thoughts, sort of lay em out, you know. I mean, I always move my lips when I read the paper, don't I? Well, I expect at's the same thing.* And then . . . thinly, quietly, so as not to disturb the bugs in the fields and the paper on the walls . . . Hannah Marshall delivered herself of a tight little cackle. She and Herman were sitting in the kitchen, and they were shelling corn. She touched one of his hands. She was so goddamn *skinny*, and she couldn't have been much more than, oh, thirtyfive years of age at the time, and her neck was all strings and knots, and her aproned bosom barely had a curve to it (he was noticing bosoms; his mind had assembled a treasured catalogue of them), and her wrists were a dead flopped fishbelly blue and white. *Whatever you do*, she said to Herman Marshall, *I'd admire it if you didn't hold back.* And she blinked at Herman Marshall. *The rest of us*, she said, *well, we ain't got no . . . spark. Not anyways like YOU got a spark. You an your little stories, your checkers an your baseball an all. A lot of boys would give the world an all to have*

[79]

got what you got. The world an all. So don't hold back. Whatever you got, USE it. And Hannah Marshall's fingers again were busy with the corn. And Hannah Marshall's fingers squirmed. She smiled. *I am YOUR MOTHER*, she said, *an I am PROUD*. Her teeth were yellow and nubby. She told Herman Marshall his father felt the same as she did. She told Herman Marshall his father was too shy to say anything about it, but the feeling was *there*, and he could wager his bottom dollar on it. *I know your daddy good enough*, said Hannah Marshall. *I know him SO good air's times I know what he's thinkin before he gets round to thinkin it*. And then Hannah Marshall unleashed another of her tight little cackles on an unsuspecting planet. And corn rattled in a tin pot. Herman Marshall smiled at his mother. He wanted to kiss her, but maybe that would have been too soft a thing to do. Hell, he was too tough for it. He had shot rabbits, squirrels, and once he had shot a fawn. Straight through the skull. Ear to ear. And he had murdered his oldest brother's dog, and maybe the worst thing you can do is murder a fellow's dog. You cause the fellow to wander the fields, to call, to whistle. But all this was good . . . or at least it was what was expected. And Herman Marshall moved through his boyhood with that notion rattling around inside his belly. And he dreamed of tits and home runs and triple jumps. The Great War had come and had gone, and the recruiting posters had been torn off the postoffice walls, and the years of the 1920s were the large ones of Herman Marshall's boyhood. He was chained to the tree in 1922. He murdered Elsie in 1922. A girl named Georgette Deaver showed him her snatch in 1923, and she let him penetrate it with the little finger of his left hand. He played first base for Hope High School in 1924, and he was only fourteen (he hit sixteen home runs; his batting average was .560). The Hope Chamber of Commerce sponsored a checker tournament in 1925, and he won it. He fucked three whores in one night in a Texarkana whorehouse in 1926 (two of the whores were white and the third was colored, and the colored one wore a red wig and had a cluster of what appeared to be carbuncles on her ass; his batting average that year at Hope High School was .778). He stopped attending prayer meetings in 1927, but he told himself he would hang onto his belief in Paradise. He began playing checkers for money in 1928, and he kept fastidious records, and by year's end he had won nearly nine hundred of the old smackeroos. He went to work in a sawmill in 1929, and he played first base for the sawmill's semipro team, and everything was just fine and dandy as long as no one tossed him any goddamn curve balls. Then came the Depression, but he kept his job at the sawmill. He was too good a first baseman, and the owner of the sawmill . . . a Mr W. E. Omarr, who drank English gin and smoked Chesterfield cigarettes and nine days out of ten wore pale blue seersucker suits on his thin and jaunty little body . . . told Herman Marshall *shoot, boy, the day old Hoover takes away my baseball team is the day this here old world of ours goes bellyup altogether, you hear me? We're doin all right, boy, an we're fixin to do better, an in the meantime we're goin to whip the ass off Hughson Brickyard an Arkadelphia Savins & Loan, you got at?* And Mr W. E. Omarr waved his cigarette at Herman Marshall, who grinned and nodded. *Oh yes SIR*, said Herman Marshall, and Mr W. E. Omarr clapped Herman Marshall on the back and told him *yes sir yourself*. And that was Herman Marshall's boyhood . . . quiet, dusty, prayerful, punctuated with *NEHI* signs and *MAIL POUCH* signs, Tom Mix movies, a certain famous squint, the murder of a dog, the rage of a young fellow who had nigger lips. It spread itself slowly, and every so often there was the passionless flat click of checkers hopping across a checkerboard, and you had to think ahead; you had to figure and scheme. Mr W. E. Omarr's sawmill went bankrupt in February of 1933, and so Mr W. E. Omarr killed

[81]

himself, and that was the month Herman Marshall met a rounded and cheerful little old virgin named Edna Stillman. And in five minutes . . . ten at the most . . . he fell smack in love with her. It was as though he had been pounded on the head with mountains.

CHAPTER SEVEN

IT TOOK HERMAN MARSHALL damn near a year and a half before he popped old Edna in that vacant lot behind the movie theater in Shreveport. It took thousands of reassurances that he loved her. It took hands, breath, laughter, ice cream cones, imagined stories about passengers in railroad trains. And he did love Edna. And he figured he always would. And he was more or less right on that score. And she never once . . . not in all the years they knew one another . . . spoke to him of his nigger lips. She simply said she loved him. And she smiled a bright chunky smile, all lips and jawbone and threaded spittle. And she was a virgin, all right. A fellow had to have a virgin. Oh, there was nothing wrong with messing around with whores, even nigger whores whose hind ends were decorated with carbuncles, but no old boy in his right mind *married* one of them. Not unless he was studying to raise some little baby carbuncles of his own, ha ha. Edna and her folks came to Hope, Arkansas, from Missouri in December of 1932. Her daddy had been a druggist up in St. Louis, but a bank had foreclosed him, and so he'd had to come down to Hope, where he worked in the Domino Pharmacy. The owner of the Domino Pharmacy was a man named H. K. Heving, and this H. K. Heving and Edna's daddy had gone to school together and had belonged to the same fraternity. Apparently that meant a whole lot of old collegeboy loyalty was involved, seeing as how jobs were so scarce and the Domino Pharmacy didn't exactly appear to be making H. K. Heving too awful rich. Great God, the only prosperous people in Hope, Arkansas, in 1932 and 1933 and all the

[83]

rest of those arid and silent years were the people who painted the signs that advertised all the homes and farms and business being sold off by the sheriff. All of the late Mr W. E. Omarr's possessions were sold off, for example. Even his blue seersucker suits were sold off. An autopsy revealed he had been drunk at the time of his death. An empty Gordon's gin bottle was on the floor next to his body. He had blown off his head with a blast from a shotgun that had a fancy butt decorated with an ivory inlay. The shotgun brought in four dollars at the sheriff's sale. It was purchased by a banker named G. D. Gilbert, who had a substantial collection of rifles and shotguns. A large crowd turned out for Mr W. E. Omarr's funeral. The coffin was cheap. It appeared to be nothing more than a sort of laminated pine. The coffin remained closed, and the talk was there wasn't enough of Mr W. E. Omarr's skull remaining to glue a postage stamp to an envelope. Herman Marshall had liked Mr W. E. Omarr, and he had liked working at Mr W. E. Omarr's sawmill, and he had liked playing first base for Mr W. E. Omarr's baseball team and squaring off against such despised enemies as Hughson Brickyard and Arkadelphia Savings & Loan. But then Mr Omarr and his sawmill and his baseball team and all the rest of it vanished, and Herman Marshall was out of a job, and he didn't know whether to leave town or rob banks or go on poor relief or what. And it didn't help matters that he had to go and cross paths with plump little Edna Stillman. He met her one brisk February afternoon when her daddy's old Buick stalled and died on the Texarkana road just a few dozen yards from the little Marshall truck farm. (He lived alone there with his parents in 1933; all three of his brothers had married and had moved away, and Eldred Junior never had learned what had happened to Elsie.) Herman Marshall used his father's *ELDRED MARSHALL PLUMBING CO* truck to tow the Stillmans' ancient car to town. Most of the Stillman family—father, mother, Edna and the family cocker, whose name was Rusty—was in the car, and everyone giggled and whooped as the car bounced along behind that *ELDRED MARSHALL PLUMBING CO* truck, which wheezed a bit and every so often gave off a flatulent backfire that sounded too loud and too tight in the clouded and belligerent February air. The Stillmans lived in the south end of town in what was little more than a shack. They invited Herman Marshall inside, and the place was dark, and Mr Stillman said: *You'll have to excuse this place, Mr Marshall. We are in straitened circumstances, you see, courtesy of Mr Hoover an I don't know who all else.* It was clear that Mr Stillman once had been damn close to corpulent, but most of the fat had been taken away from him, and all that remained of it were slabs of empty bluish flesh that wattled his face and his neck. He led Herman Marshall and the others into a rear room, and at least there were windows in that rear room, and the windows captured whatever reluctant light there was that day. Everyone sat down at a chipped round table. There was a rash on Mr Stillman's hands. He folded them on the table. *Welcome,* he said to Herman Marshall. *You are our first guest, an I apologize for the condition of this . . . hovel. An all I can do is blame it on the times.* A smile from Mr Stillman. It was an astringent smile, a difficult smile for a man who carried so much useless flesh on his face and his neck. He shrugged. *You know,* he said, *these times are good times for people who never would of amounted to a hill of beans no matter what. Nowadays they have the best excuse in the world. They blame everthin on Hoover. Air . . . well, air like me.* And then Mr Stillman loosed a barrage of coughs, bending forward, and his terrible facial flesh flabbed and clapped and rearranged itself. Edna was sitting next to him, and she slapped him on the back. She was wearing a dark skirt and a white blouse, and the cold had hardened her nipples. They were large nipples, and Herman Marshall couldn't help but notice them, and he figured he was in love with her, and he figured her nipples were as good a reason as any for his love . . . and probably better than most. Mr Stillman spoke for quite a time, and Mrs Stillman fixed a pot of coffee. Mr Stillman spoke of an older daughter, and the older daughter's name was Corinne, and Corinne was married to an insurance man and living up in Cleveland, and she recently had had a baby. *I'm now officially a grandfather*, said Mr Stillman, shaking his head, *an I ask you—where have the days gone?* And Herman Marshall, who wasn't particularly listening, who was concentrating on this Edna's nipples and her mouth and her belly and her sweet plump wrists and fingers, who didn't really care what had happened to Mr Stillman's goddamn *days*, whose balls were warm and painful, nonetheless managed to shrug and say something to the effect that time was time, and beyond that he didn't really know. And that was how he met Edna, who was a senior that year at Hope High School, who became his steady girl before the week was out, who almost immediately told him yes, yes, *of course* she loved him, but there was no sense rushing anything, what with all the fun she wanted to have before she settled down and had babies and did all the other things that were expected of her . . . well, this Edna led him what was known in those days as a merry chase, and sometimes she said to him: *Ohhh, I am such a BAD girl, aren't I? An I expect you'd just like to spank an SPANK me!* And then came a sassy succession of giggles and wet inhalings, and she likely as not would tickle him with her plump fingers, or muss his hair, or give his galluses a hearty snap. But he did finally marry her. He made up enough stories about railroad passengers. First he deflowered her, and then he married her, and his folks gave the young couple a brass bed for a wedding present, and everyone

[86]

laughed. Corinne and her husband and their kid came down from Cleveland for the wedding, and the kid whooped and gulped throughout the ceremony. Corinne didn't carry the little brat out of the church. It was a boy, and its name was Alexander, and this Alexander was two years of age, and Herman Marshall wanted to string up the shitfaced little bastard with a rope. The ceremony was performed by a spidery little Baptist preacher named Amos L. Haynes, and this Amos L. Haynes had to holler to make himself heard above the baby's shrieks. And some of the wedding guests shifted their feet and giggled. Herman Marshall never forgot Corinne's rotten fucking kid, and neither did Edna. Maybe they should have laughed about Corinne's rotten fucking kid, but they never really did. Even Edna, laughing Edna, a good old girl who took most everything in her stride, including Hoover and her daddy's awful cough and the fact that she barely had made it through Hope High School, what with her inability really to concentrate on such dumb old froufrou things as English and algebra and the order of the Presidents of the United States since Ulysses S. Grant. But that didn't mean she was stupid. Rather, it meant she was more interested in ice cream cones and necking and laughter. Her father died exactly two weeks after her wedding. Fluids had leaked into his lungs, and he was just fifty years of age. Herman Marshall was a pallbearer. It was an autumn afternoon, and the graveyard was fragrant with dry things. Mrs Stillman kept telling everyone she had no idea how she would be able to buy a headstone for her husband. Herman Marshall's mother embraced Mrs Stillman and told her *air, air, it'll all work out when times get better*. The words reminded Herman Marshall of what Mr Stillman had said that first day at the chipped round table. And Herman Marshall said to himself: I expect air'll always be excuses—for whatever, from wars an death to the end of the world. And Herman Marshall tried to inhale the fragrant graveyard air and not think of things that were beyond him. He and Edna lived in a tworoom flat over the Spot Café (the site of Helen Burnside's magnificent victory over the seven burgers and the seven helpings of fries), and they took in Mrs Stillman plus fucking Rusty the fucking cocker, and this probably was a principal reason Herman Marshall turned to truckdriving as his life's calling or whatever. He'd gone to school with an old boy named Elroy Catchings (tall, slow of speech, with an adamsapple like old Slim Summerville of the movies), and Elroy Catchings had been a pretty fair southpaw pitcher for the Hope High School team . . . wild sometimes, but the possessor of a curve ball that dropped off the old table like a sack of stones. Elroy had no particular baseball ambitions, though, and he married a girl named Olive Pearson less than a month after the two of them were graduated from Hope High. And they moved to Houston, where Olive had an uncle who was a dispatcher for an outfit called the Gulfway Trucking Lines. Elroy began there as little more than an officeboy and janitor, but within a year he was driving for Gulfway on the route from Houston to New Orleans. And every so often he had a run to Little Rock, and he would stop in Hope and visit with his parents and sit in the Spot Café and drink coffee with Herman Marshall. And one night Elroy Catchings said: *Hell, I wouldn't shit you . . . drivin a truck ain't exactly no one's idea of heaven on this here earth, but it sure beats standin around an playin with your balls on account of your pockets ain't got nothin in them but maybe fuzz an lint.* And Elroy permitted himself a dry chuckle. *Olive likes it better at way, too,* he said. *Keeps food on the table. Keeps me from playin with myself, hee hee. You ought to keep it in mind, son. Whenever your life slows down for you here in good old, um, madcap Hope, Arkansas, you just fetch yourself down to Houston, an maybe me an my fatherinlaw will be able to do you some good. I mean, the thing is, it ain't who you know;*

it's who you blow. Somethin like at, you hear what I'm sayin? And Elroy lightly jabbed Herman Marshall in the chest. *Think on it. Houston is hotter an cat turds on a tin roof, but air's money to be made, you know?* This chat with Elroy Catchings took place in the summer of 1929, and there hadn't been any Depression in the summer of 1929, and Herman Marshall had been doing just fine and dandy, thank you kindly, working for Mr W. E. Omarr and playing first base for Mr W. E. Omarr's baseball team. But then came the Depression, and Mr W. E. Omarr did himself in with the shotgun that had the butt with the ivory inlay and brought in the four dollars at the sheriff's sale, and in 1934 Herman Marshall was ready—more than ready—to take up old Elroy on the offer. And it wasn't only the Depression that made Herman Marshall so hot to make his living driving trucks. It was his goddamned shitfaced mother-inlaw, Mrs Stillman. For one thing, she had a voice that was like a splintered plank, and she never felt the need to give it a rest. She had large bones, heavy feet, a dark and peevish face. For some reason, she almost always wore an apron. Maybe, for all Herman Marshall knew, she wore the goddamn apron to bed. She always was talking about her late husband. He had been a martyr to the banks, she said. He had been a *good* man, she said, and he had given candy to poor children there in that St Louis neighborhood where his pharmacy had been. Mrs. Stillman had a way of drawing back her shoulders and taking a large breath and sort of *warming up* for one of her speeches. And she made so many of them. Maybe she made so many of them because her late husband had made so many of them. Maybe she was trying to catch up. Her beloved Carl had had such a *wit*, she said, and he had been such a . . . such a *martyr* to the moneygrabbers, and most of the moneygrabbers were Semites, seeing as how so many Semites were involved in the drugstore business, which maybe Herman Mar-

[89]

shall and Edna already *knew*, but it didn't hurt to remind them, did it? And Mrs Stillman spoke of how gently she had been courted by her Carl; she spoke of picnics and dancing moths. She spoke of Japanese lanterns, of canoes, of ukeleles and ruffled bosoms. She sat at the front window of that tworoom flat over the Spot Café, and she kept rubbing her hands against her apron, and one hot florid lifeless Sunday afternoon she kept blinking out that window and talking, talking, and she said: *He needs a headstone. He needs respect. Where'll we get the money for the headstone? How come the world got no respect for US? Corinne was harder for me an Edna was. When Corinne was born, Carl was in the room with me an the doctor an the woman from the midwife place, an when it was done I was all sweatin an Carl was all sweatin an he said to me: It's a wonder you didn't blow out the walls, young lady. An at was 19 an 05, an the two of us laughed, an I held Corinne, an the woman from the midwife place had weighed her, an she was ten pounds. Exactly. She had button eyes. You know what button eyes are? Well, she had button eyes. A person could of polished them with a soft cloth. She needed eleven hours, though, but Edna here . . . well, Edna came in an hour an a half; she just sort of slid out, an it was 19 an 14, an the doctor was the same doctor, man name of Hufford, an he said air now, this one surely is an improvement, wouldn't you say? An I told him I agreed with him, an Edna weighed seven pounds one ounce, an Carl wasn't air, since it was the middle of the afternoon an he was workin in the store with his mortar an his pestle an his patent-medicines an his pills. I am an educated woman. I went for a year to the Galesburg Normal School up in Illinois, an I remember readin things bout Plato an a cave, an I think it was people walkin around in the cave. Where will the money come for Carl's headstone? He came rushin to me from the store an he said to me: Mary, oh Mary my love, I thought it would take longer. Otherwise, I would of closed the store. I mean, the thing is, Corinne took so much longer. An I nodded. An I told Carl to*

*hush himself; I wasn't aggravated with him. An I told him to hold the
baby. An the baby smiled. Such a GOOD baby. Always a good baby.
Never gave me a smidge of trouble. Ate when she was supposed to. Went
to the potty when she was supposed to. Didn't hardly ever throw up.
Didn't hardly ever even bawl. Some baby. Some perfect baby.* And Mrs
Stillman smiled across the room at Edna, who was sitting on a
rattan loveseat and mending something, maybe the hem of a slip.
Edna shifted her buttocks and cleared her throat, but she did not
look up at her mother. Rusty the cocker lay asleep at Mrs Stillman's feet. Herman Marshall, who was sitting at a cardtable and
digging at his fingernails with a paringknife (this always had been
his way of cleaning his nails, even though it made Edna shudder),
tried to concentrate on what he was doing, but Mrs Stillman's voice
kept tearing at his ears and his skull. He'd had to put up with more
than six months of her stupid horseshit prattling. He wondered
how Rusty could just lay there and fucking *sleep*. There was a new
word in the language. It had been brought to the world by the late
President Harding, who may or may not have been a nigger, folks
said. The new word was *bloviate*, and it meant a lot of blahblah
that arrived at no particular point. And that was Mrs Stillman for
you, a bloviator (bloviatress?) of goddamn fucking championship
proportions, ha ha. And Mrs Stillman said: *Corinne always was a
little impudent for my taste, an I expect she ran around a little too much,
if you know what I mean, an maybe her husband had himself a teenyweeny surprise air weddin night, an remember how she just let Baby
Alexander holler an carry on at day you two got married? What sort of
mother lets her baby holler an carry on at way? Why, she just bout
ruined your weddin, an don't contradict me on it. I know what's the
truth. I . . . oh, I miss Carl, do you know that? He was good when it
came to calmin me down. He would . . . kiss me . . . an touch me . . .
the man with the woman . . . an the man is bein kind . . . an the man's*

got a voice at's deep an rich . . . an it says comfort comfort comfort, like maybe it's all pillows an warm kittycats an the breath of sweet obedient children . . . oh yes, the man comfortin the woman is a precious thing . . . it's what us women read bout sometimes . . . it's what sometimes we see when we're girls an our daddies are comfortin our mamas, holdin our mamas on air laps an whisperin to em all the proper words of soft endearment . . . Carl was at way with me . . . even after we came down here an he had his cough, an maybe he even figured he was dyin . . . even EN was he my big fine noble comfortin prince . . . touchin my hair an kissin it . . . oh, Lord . . . dear Lord Jesus, how'll we find the money for his headstone? Didnt't he earn AT much? And Mrs Stillman's eyes began to leak, and she lifted her apron and pressed it against her eyes. And Herman Marshall jabbed himself in the right indexfinger with the goddamn paringknife. His blood came like syrup. It almost was gummy. He frowned at it. He sucked the finger and swallowed some of the blood, and then he said: *Shit.* Edna looked at him, but Mrs Stillman didn't. Mrs Stillman kept bloviating away. The apron came down from her face, and she twisted the apron, and she wadded the apron, and she bloviated like a fucking unattended teakettle, and Herman Marshall sucked his bloody finger, and Edna said something to him to the effect that she'd *told* him he would hurt himself with that dumb old paringknife, and he looked away from her, and Mrs Stillman kept dancing and skipping back to the subject of that fucking headstone for her fucking husband, the saint of saints, and finally Herman Marshall stood up and muttered something about having a need to go outside for a walk and maybe a breath or scrap of fresh air, and did Edna care to join him? Mrs Stillman paid no attention to him at all. She simply bloviated. She simply put her apron through its agony. And Edna looked up from her crocheting and said: *I'm goin real good at this, an I expect I'll keep at it. Maybe you can bring us a quart of ice cream. Chocolate. You know how Mama an myself are bout chocolate ice cream. It surely would be appreciated. An mind your finger now. You want me to fix you a bandage?* Herman Marshall shook his head. He allowed as how it wasn't as though he'd been wounded while fighting in the goddamn Argonne Forest. Edna frowned. She told him she didn't know what the Argonne Forest was. She asked him whether the Argonne Forest had been before her time. Herman Marshall sighed, shrugged. *Well,* he said, *air oncet was a war, you see, an air was this place called the Argonne Forest, an our boys . . . well, it's a long story, an it don't matter none no more . . . an me, I wasn't but a little boy when it happened . . . an you wasn't but a bitty BABY . . . so, look, I'll bring you back the ice cream, all right?* And Herman Marshall walked out of that place, and he kept sucking his finger (he carried the wound's scar all the rest of his life). And he thought of Mrs Stillman and her infernal torrent of *words,* her relentless screechy jawboning of those words, her insistence that not anything, not the Depression, not murders, not wars, not the birthing of children, not practical jokes, not fireworks displays, not any goddamn thing anyone would care to name, took precedence over the mighty question: *HOW WILL A HEADSTONE FOR CARL THE SAINT BE OBTAINED?* And Herman Marshall was full up to his neck with that question. And full up to the neck with trying to make a living by doing other people's yard work, with paying part of the rent by washing dishes in the Spot Café, with struggling to make fifty cents whipping the ass off some ignorant jasper in a game of checkers, with borrowing a dollar here and two dollars there from his skinny old dad, who himself didn't hardly have but two nickels to rub together. It had been more than a year and half since the glory days of Mr W. E. Omarr's sawmill and Mr W. E. Omarr's baseball team, and wasn't it about time something broke *good* for Herman

[93]

Marshall? He figured yes, it was about time, but the Lord helped those who helped themselves (and Lord help those who were caught helping themselves, hee hee), and so he bought a penny postcard and dropped a note to Elroy Catchings down in Houston: *Im at the end of my rope my friend, and anything you can do for me I sure wood aprecciate. I got me a motherinlaw who aint werth the powder to blow her up and she talks al the time and I got to get away from the rackett. Her and Edna can come down to Houston sooner or later when the times rite, but at least maybe Ill have some piece and quiet on the open road. I thank you.* A reply came from Elroy Catchings about a week later, and yes, there was work for Herman Marshall, but only as a mechanic and general cleanup man. Herman Marshall would have to wait until one of the drivers quit or died or was fired, and that could be a long time, and did he have the patience to tough out the situation? Wrote Herman Marshall: *Does a polecat fart in the woods?* So Herman Marshall made one last visit to Leo's Barber Shop and won eleven dollars in a marathon session of checkerplaying (it was the most money he'd ever won at one sitting), packed a cardboard suitcase, told a tearful Edna she—and her mother as well, if that was what she wanted—would be following him down to Houston as soon as he'd gathered a little money together and they had a halfway decent place to stay. Herman Marshall hitchhiked to Houston. His father and mother and wife and motherinlaw bade him farewell on the sidewalk in front of the Spot Café. Edna kissed him smack on the mouth and rubbed herself against him. His father said nothing. His mother's eyes glistened. Mrs Stillman spoke of a tombstone for her good old Carl. Herman Marshall slowly walked away from them. He felt a little like an actor in a picture show. Maybe he could have been Tom Mix, slowly ambling out of town astride the mighty Tony. (He didn't think all that often about Tom Mix anymore. Tom Mix was on the radio now, but his program was aimed at little kids, and Herman Marshall paid no mind to it.) Herman Marshall walked six miles down the Texarkana road, but he barely broke a sweat; he still had his big firstbaseman's frame, and the walk was kind of nice; it sort of cleared out his bones and his vessels. He smiled. He was beyond the sound of human voices, and so it was meet and right to smile. His first ride was with a young couple headed for Dallas; the man—harelipped, plump, cheerful—had a promise of a job in a factory that manufactured transformers for toy trains. The man's wife—quiet, dark, with maybe a little Mex or nigger in her—bounced herself against Herman Marshall's thigh every time the car hit a bumpy place on the highway. A thin fellow with a truckload of hogs gave Herman Marshall a lift all the way down to a wide spot in the road near Conroe. The thin fellow had talked (hollered, rather, what with the grunts of the pigs and the irritated clatterings of the truck) all night of women who gave blowjobs and liked to take it up the ass. Herman Marshall, who'd received only two blowjobs in his whole entire life, who never had known a woman or girl who had liked to take it up the ass, had such a hardon when that skinny fellow let him off at the wide spot in the road near Conroe that . . . well, he was unable to stand straight. He grimaced, and he laughed a little, and he told himself the Lord no doubt had reached down and had twisted his spine. A gesture of Divine Displeasure. Something like that. His final ride came form two men who were in their forties and drove a Buick roadster and said they were in the Romance Languages department at Rice University. They were slender and perfumed and spiffy, and they trilled and ululated, and one of them shyly asked Herman Marshall how openminded and compassionate he was. Herman Marshall coughed into a hand, and his asshole tightened. He supposed these here old fairyboys wanted to drape him over a barrel. Or maybe they wanted *him* to drape *them* over a barrel. It was turning out to be quite a hitchhike. One of the fairyboys touched Herman Marshall's crotch, and Herman Marshall brought down a fist in a brisk chop to the fairyboy's pale fragrant neck. The fairyboy gagged and wept. Herman Marshall told the two fairyboys he sure enough was sorry, but he was just a young fellow making his way in the world, and he didn't have no time for no pervert shit, okay? And both the fairyboys snuffled and mewled. And that was how Herman Marshall rode into Houston, and the next day he was rotating tires and greasing transmissions. And within six months he was a driver for the Gulfway Trucking Lines.

CHAPTER EIGHT

A ND HE WAS A MAN, MORE OR LESS. Or at least he was as
much of a man as he ever would be. Which meant he came to
understand the simple snaggled truth that hardly anything worked
out as it should. For instance, he had been a legendary checkerplayer, and so folks had given him credit for having a great talent
when it came to figuring ahead. Well, that all turned out to be a
lot of horse cock. He and Edna were husband and wife for damn
near fifty years, and hardly anything worked out as it should have
worked out, which meant his *great talent* for *figuring ahead* was nothing more than dreams and words. Edna came down to Houston,
and of course she brought along her mother and good old Rusty
the cocker, and her mother spoke of how deeply she missed being
able to see her husband's grave, and the old piece of shit kept asking about her fucking Carl's fucking headstone, and fucking Rusty
left fucking hairs all over the fucking furniture and the fucking
rugs, and Herman Marshall kept having to take deep breaths and
dig his fingers into the palms of his hands. But at least he had work,
and his brothers envied him. Eldred Junior sold shoes for three
consecutive stores that went bankrupt in the years between 1931
and 1936. Lute worked on a State of Arkansas road gang—when
he did work. Usually he preferred to sit in the back room of a blind
pig in Hot Springs and drink lemon gin and speak with his buddies of pussy. And Jackson eventually wound up as a barker for
the fat lady in a carnival. And the fat lady was his wife. And she
had a teenyweeny voice that reminded everyone of Betty Boop.
Every so often the carnival would pass through Houston, and Jack-

son and his immense wife (her name was Noreen, and she weighed five hundred forty pounds, and her hair was all spangled with henna, and she had a substantial moustache) always managed to squeeze in a visit to Herman Marshall and Edna and Mrs Stillman and Rusty the cocker, the whole happy group. And they brought along a special reinforced steel chair for Noreen. After all, they didn't want her to damage any of the regular furniture, now did they? And she sat in that chair, and she was like a frog, and she always wore flowered print dresses, and her legs were as thick as the average person's waist, and she always carried a timid odor of suppressed flatulence. And she was, of all the goddamned things, a Republican . . . and one night she even tried to talk all of them into voting for Alf Landon. The suggestion was met with a good deal of laughter, and she pouted. She died in McAllen in August of 1938 on a night when the official temperature was listed as ninetyeight. It was a heart attack that did her in, and she fell against a tentpole, causing the tent to collapse, trapping several dozen persons, who sued the carnival and drove it out of business. Her age, as recorded on the death cerfificate, was twentysix. Edna and Mrs Stillman were astonished at how young Noreen had been, and by golly Edna for one could not believe it. Jackson had Noreen cremated. A coffin would have cost too much. No one from Jackson's family showed up for the memorial service, and so the grieving Jackson wrote identical letters to his mother and father, to Eldred Junior, to Lute and to Herman Marshall: *You shure enuf hurd me. Whatd she ever do to YALL that you ain god the dessensy to pay your respests????? She wouldnt of hurd a flie if her live had depend-ded on it. Shame on yall. JACKSON E. MARSHALL.* That was the last anyone heard of Jackson until March of 1943 when he was killed in a train wreck near Ardmore, Oklahoma. Papers in his billfold provided identification, and it turned out he had been selling bathroom tile in Tulsa. His parents and his brothers all attended his funeral, which was held in Hope. Herman Marshall never had any trouble remembering March of 1943. Not only was Jackson killed, but Rusty the cocker finally died—at the age of at least twenty. As closely as Herman Marshall could tell, Rusty choked to death on puke, which was pretty damn close to the way Mr Stillman had died, and it almost was enough to make a fellow wonder, wasn't it? Mrs Stillman wanted to have Rusty buried in a pet cemetery out near Pearland, but Herman Marshall would have none of *that* shit. He wrapped Rusty's pukey corpse in newspapers and threw the whole mess out with the garbage. At the same time, Edna vacuumed the apartment, and Mrs Stillman (a) wept, (b) kneaded her apron and (c) spoke in a tragic quaver of grief and headstones. And there was a third major event in that March of 1943; at the age of thirtythree, Herman Marshall was drafted into the United States Army. Actually, to be fucking pissant technical about it, he was taken in by the Army of the United States, which was what the Army called itself as far as draftees were concerned. Herman Marshall never quite understood why the Army called itself one thing for the people who enlisted and another thing for the people who were drafted, but he figured it probably had something to do with fucking snobby pride, and he and the other draftees all laughed and called that sort of fucking snobby pride a real comfort to a man when his balls were shot off and a Jap bayonet was jammed up his ass. He didn't really want to be drafted into the Army of the United States, or whatever the fuck it was called, but he and Edna had no children, and his truckdriving job was essential, sure, but it wasn't all *that* essential, and so he and about a hundred other guys were loaded aboard a couple of T&NO daycoaches one gray morning in that benighted March of 1943 and taken to Camp Polk, Louisiana, where they received infantry basic training, and a lot of guys called him Niggerlips, and he damn near busted his ass trying to survive the obstacle courses and the twenty-mile marches and KP, not to goddamn mention the whores who had flocked to the town of Leesville, which was just outside Camp Polk and was known to everyone as Diseaseville, ha ha, hee hee. One night Herman Marshall was given a blowjob by a woman who had no teeth. She blanketed his cock with spit, and it was kind of warm and nice. Another night he was fucked by a tiny blonde who insisted her father was a brigadier general. She poked a thumb up Herman Marshall's asshole just as he was coming, and he screamed the way rabbits scream when they are dying. Basic training lasted thirteen weeks, and then he was granted a week's furlough. He rode in a passenger train down to Houston, and Edna met him at the depot, and it was June and hotter than Billybe-damned, and she hugged him and told him *my*, he'd really lost a good deal of weight, but he looked real *good*, if he wanted *her* opinion, you know. They rode home in a streetcar, and Edna fanned herself with a lace handkerchief, and she allowed as how her mother still was in mourning for poor Rusty the cocker. *All she does is talk an eat*, said Edna, *an it's a wonder she stops the talkin long nough to do the eatin*. And Edna offered a tired and regretful little laugh. And said: *But I expect you don't want to talk bout HER, do you?* And again Edna laughed, but this time with a bit more force. And she patted one of Herman Marshall's knees. And said: *I ain't never seen you in the shape like you're in right now, you know what I mean? I mean, what I REALLY mean?* And she giggled, and Herman Marshall told her she was a goddamn sketch and a caution, and the rest of the way home the two of them whispered of mouths and of juices, of reacquaintance, of true love. The streetcar had straw seats, and the straw gave Herman Marshall a soft timid erection, and he kept licking his enormous lips. He was shipped to

England a month later, and he was transferred into the Transportation Corps. He was stationed for a time at a motor pool in East Anglia, and he was able to visit pubs and drink beer and every so often cop a feel and find an occasional fuck from an English girl. He figured he had a pretty good deal. It surely beat the hell out of the goddamn infantry. Edna wrote to him nearly every day, and she told him oh how she did miss him, and hell, *he* missed *her*, but a man still had to cop an occasional feel and find an occasional fuck, else he would go kablooey, with parts of him flying off into the goddamn wild blue yonder. (Most of the British girls lived in tiny flats that were prissily cluttered with china bricabrac, little lions and pugdogs and potbellied gentlemen, and the British girls had rigid legs and spoke of the Nazis as Nawzis and said they felt so *helpless* because they weren't *doing* enough to help *win* the bloody *war* and make the world safe for bloody *fucking*, are you with me on *that* one, love? And Herman Marshall was smart enough to laugh when one of his occasional English girls spoke that way, and he made do, even with their rigid legs.) He was sent to France in November of 1944, and his unit was trapped in the Ardennes the next month when the Germans began their final offensive. He fought alongside a jackleg collection of cooks, mail clerks, graves registration men, bakers and a few MPs, and his only weapon was a .45 automatic he pried loose from the frozen fingers of a dead major he'd found lying in a headless sprawl at a windy snowblind highway junction. Herman Marshall never drove a truck again for the rest of the war. He killed a German lieutenant from a distance of no more than twenty feet. It required two slugs from the .45, and the thing kicked like a sonofabitch, but at the same time the German lieutenant's chest and throat vanished in a brilliant red spray. And Herman Marshall laughed. He couldn't think of anything else to do. This was more fun than killing animals ever had been, and no shit. He and his jackleg companions walked into Germany in the spring of 1945. Three old men tried to defend a village from behind a pile of mattresses. A bazooka was summoned, but Herman Marshall didn't want to wait for the bazooka. There was no sense incinerating those old men when they could be killed real neat and decent. Herman Marshall ran forward and climbed over the mattresses, and the old men screamed. They turned ass and tried to run away. Herman Marshall chased them. He caught them, one by one. They shrieked in German, and he told them he was surely sorry, but he didn't speak the Deutsch, and he blew off their heads, each with a single shot. He was sprayed with blood and fragments of bone, but what the hell; the blood and the fragments of bone went with the job, didn't they? It turned out one of the old men had been the village's mayor and a member of the National Socialist Party. An infantry colonel rode into the village in a Jeep and shook Herman Marshall's hand. The colonel had his driver write down Herman Marshall's name, rank and serial number—he wanted to see to it that Herman Marshall received at least a Bronze Star. Herman Marshall grinned. Herman Marshall shook his head and flicked blood off his eyebrows. He saluted the colonel, and the salute was crisp. Nothing came of that Bronze Star bullshit. Herman Marshall's name never was put in. He tossed the .45 into a highway ditch the day the Germans surrendered. He spent that night in a roofless barn with two fat blond sisters, one nineteen, the other seventeen, whose daddy had been an SS officer and who wanted to do anything they could to please Herman Marshall, because they didn't want Herman Marshall to kill them, because their father never had spoken of his duties, because they themselves were innocent of any transgressions, because they had *known* the *Führer* had been insane, but what could they . . . two innocent girls . . . have done about it? And Herman Marshall said to them:

[102]

Shut up, you two. Which one of you wants to suck my cock first? And the girls crawled to him, but he came before they could touch him. He'd never known such a feeling, and he supposed he never again would know it. He was sent home in August of '45. The majestic and awful Houston heat caused him to breathe with his mouth open and his tongue protruding. He and Edna fell upon one another, and he grimaced and gasped, but he couldn't do anything. She kissed his belly. She told him *air, air, my darlin; it ain't all at bad; you're just TIRED, at's all, an a little rest'll do you up real fine.* She nuzzled his chest. He wept a little, but he kept it silent. He told her he would make it up to her. He told her he'd wanted it to be better for her than it ever had been. *I'm thirtyfive years of age now,* he said, *an we got to move AWN, you know what I mean? We got to make EVERTHIN better. The war . . . well, it's the only war I've knowed, an I don't want to know no other war. It made me . . . peculiar. An I don't want to be peculiar. I want to, like they say, get back on the old track.* And Herman Marshall turned his face away from Edna and closed his warm wet eyes. He eventually slept, and he dreamed the same dreams he'd been dreaming ever since that brutal day, that day all aswirl with snow, that ugly crossroads day when he'd pried the .45 loose from the frozen fingers of the dead major. The dreams all concerned themselves with people who knelt before him and begged him to spare their goddamn Nawzi lives, and those people had blond hair, and they all spoke nothing but German, and he grinned at them and told them *listen, yall, I don't understand what you're sayin,* and he squeezed off the necessary rounds, and all the people exploded. An eyelid here. A toe there. A torn and flattened testicle somewhere else, maybe over the rainbow, ha ha. And Herman Marshall groaned in his sleep, and Edna awakened him, and he howled into a fist. And a little later he said to her: *I don't understand none of it. I got to get back to work real quick. I got to get back to bein with people who ain't all the time got killin on air minds.* He coughed. Then: *I . . . the thing is, I kind of liked it, an at don't make no sense. When I was a boy, I mean, an we went huntin, an I shot this an at an the other thing, it didn't none of it make me want to clap my hands an throw my hat in the air, you know? I even . . . well, air was times I maybe even felt sorry for the animals. Oh, not that I said a word bout it. My brothers would of beat the tar out of me, an they would of called me a sissy, an ain't no boy in the world wants to let himself in for AT. So I went along—but in this here I more an went along. I kilt people an sometimes I laughed bout it, an at's the truth, an I don't like to think bout it, but I DO think bout it, so maybe you can understand why I got to get me real quick back into a situation where God damn it air's nothin but YOU an THIS PLACE an the ROAD an me now an again settin around with the boys an drinkin Shiner an tradin bullshit stories an jokes.* And Herman Marshall blinked. He even groaned a little. He and Edna were sitting up in bed, and he had been whispering to her. They hadn't wanted to awaken her mother, who was asleep in the next room and who at supper had snickered and had said something about being quiet as a mouse so Herman Marshall and her daughter wouldn't be distracted, tee hee, from whatever it was they planned to *do* in the privacy of their bedroom. Herman Marshall had tried not to listen to the old bat, who still was wearing her goddamn aprons and talking all the time about her husband's tombstone and the death of poor cocksucking Rusty the cocksucking cocker. Herman Marshall spoke to Edna that night for maybe an hour, but he never did specify his memories and his terrors. Not then and not ever. He didn't want to make her throw up, and he didn't want to make her hate him. So finally he simply fell asleep, and his face was pressed against her breasts, and her breasts were naked, and he slept that way for the rest of the night. The following Monday he reported for work at the Gulfway

Trucking Lines, and all the old boys came to him and cracked him on the spine and told him shit, the conquering hero was home, and hot damn, and good enough, and glad to have you back, and let's go drink beer and talk about it . . . the sort of things he had expected. And he grinned. And his buddies took him out and got him drunk. His friends—George McLean, loud, knobby, with bad teeth; Phil Romero, the only Mex on the payroll, handsome and quiet, a chaser who had more good tight firstrate pussy in a week than most of the other drivers for Gulfway Trucking had in a year; John Dean West, jowled and paunchy, a former cowboy who had turned to trucking when the war had come along because trucking was where the money was; Freddie Weaver, a Marine veteran of Guadalcanal who had lost both his little fingers when a grenade had exploded damn near in his face—were good old boys for certain, and Herman Marshall broke down a little when he tried to tell them how much they meant to him. He pressed an empty sweaty Shiner longneck against a cheek and spoke of loyalty, of memories, of how goddamn homesick he'd been. And he shook his head and dabbed at his eyes, and again his buddies cracked him on the spine, and he said: *Godalmighty*. Two mornings later he settled behind the wheel of a tough little Mack tenwheeler and grinned at the Mack bulldog on the hood and did a quick run up to Beaumont with a load of oil drilling parts. He fought the US 90 traffic well, and he told himself it was as though he'd never been away. He stopped twice for burgers and fries, and he belched and farted, and he kept grinning, and the little Mack bulldog snouted through the wet shimmering heat. Herman Marshall patted his belly. Everything would be just fine. He would take out a GI loan, and he and Edna would buy a house, just as soon as they figured out what the hell to do with her mother. And then the loving Hand of the Great Lord Jehova descended from Paradise and stroked Herman Marshall's soul. One morning in January of 1946 Mrs Stillman became so feverish in talking about Carl the Martyr that she abruptly pulled her apron over her head, bit her apron, then made a gagging sound and died of a stroke. She was buried in Hope, smack next to Carl the Martyr, and now he really *was* a martyr, seeing as how he would have to await the Doomsday Trump while lying next to *her*. No doubt she would have a great deal to say. Such a little old nibby thing as death wasn't about to silence *that* woman, no *sir*. Herman Marshall and his Edna moved into a brandnew tract house in southeast Houston in November of that same year, 1946. Edna told him she hadn't given up on having a baby, and Herman Marshall said: *We'll do it, sweetmeat. Don't you worry none.* And Herman Marshall smiled and nodded, and he and Edna proceeded to have a good fierce little fuck right there on the bare floor of that tract house's front room even before the movers had brought the furniture, and Edna drooled a little and trembled a whole goddamn lot. And she and Herman Marshall laughed, and she kept telling him she was only thirtytwo years of age, which meant she was in the *prime* of her *life*, and did he understand what she was trying to tell him? And Herman Marshall said: *Yes ma'am. Yes ma'am I sure nough DO.* And Edna tugged up her panties and tugged down her skirt and buttoned her blouse and said: *The future . . . well, I mean, it's all goin to work out pretty, an I hope the first one's a boy, on account of at's what YOU want, ain't it?* And Herman Marshall said: *Yes MA'AM. You got me figured out real good.* And he lounged in a corner of that bare room and said: *I loved you the first moment I seen you . . . air by God at day your daddy's car broke down . . . an the cold it popped your nipples . . . made em into nice little old buttons . . . an now, by God, her . . . at girl, I mean, at girl with the buttons . . . her an me is layin around an workin at makin a baby . . . an, ma'am, I tell you, it sure do beat fightin in a war.* And Edna smiled a little, but not too awful much. She crept to him and said: *We been married twelve years.* She rubbed her face against one of his shoulders. This time, when she spoke, she would not let him see her face. *The prime of life don't last forever,* she said, *an pretty don't last forever, an the days are gettin shorter, an you're too smart in the head not to be knowin I'm tellin you the truth. I want a baby, Herman. Two or three. As many as I can have. I don't know what I'll do if . . . no, no, don't pay no attention to at.* And her face abruptly moved from side to side against Herman Marshall's shoulder. *I . . . things don't always work out,* she said. *I'm talkin dumb when I say WANT an GOT TO. I love you. Whatever happens, happens. It's all right. An anyway, it's this sort of thing . . . the not knowin . . . at makes the world go round, ain't it?* And Herman Marshall nodded. He shrugged a little. He didn't know what else to do. That night, even though he wasn't scheduled for a run until the next afternoon, he drove all the way across town to Gulfway Trucking and bumped into Phil Romero, and they went to Phil's apartment over on McGowen, and they drank Mex beer and listened to Mex records, and the walls were decorated with pinup photos of Mex movie actresses named Dolores and Maria and such, and the Mex movie actresses all had glittery eyes and large easy tits, and Phil Romero said: *My frien, maybe you think I got the worl by the ass, me an my girlfriens an all, an all I do is set aroun an drink beer an let some girlfrien or the other diddle my nuts an tell me I got the greatest cock this side of the goddamn Yucatan, you know? But YOU'RE the one who's got the worl by the ass, my frien. You Anglos with your Anglo wives an your Anglo money . . . you go wherever you fuckin want to go, an you talk an scratch an laugh with WHOEVER an WHEREVER . . . an you don't never walk down no street with people lookin at you an sayin to themselfs hey lookit the busboy or lookit the pimp or lookit the fuckin greazzy pickpocket or even maybe he's a fairy an he rubs his balls with Camay soap,*

[107]

you know? An so all right, maybe you Anglos got ittybitty pricks, an maybe you don't know how to relax an fuck when it's time for fuckin an work when it's time for workin an take you a snooze when it's time to take you a snooze, but you got it all over us, amigo. *You don't never got to think on the fact at you can go only so far in this here life an no farther. That's some fact,* amigo. *My daddy is the personal valet to Mr E. E. Rischer, an Mr E. E. Rischer is the president of Gulfway Truckin Lines, Ink, an you already know at, an I already know at, but I got to keep tellin myself a thing I already know because I got to keep remindin myself, on account I'm the only Mex drivin for Gulfway Truckin, an at's because my daddy is the personal valet to Mr. E. E. Rischer, an my daddy gets to throw Mr E. E. Rischer's dirty shorts into the hamper two, three times a day, because Mr E. E. Rischer don't wipe his ass go good like he ought to, you know?* And Phil Romero fired up a Camel. *You got the worl by the ass,* he said to Herman Marshall. He did not inhale, and the smoke curled from his nostrils in thick and gentle arcs and blots. *At air wife of yours is pretty, real pretty, an now you got you a little house, an you was in the Anglo army an fought in the Anglo war, an . . . an, well, air's em who thinks at's important, an they tell me I should of gone over air an had my greazzer ass shot off. Well, fuck em. An fuck air war. You know what I'm sayin to you? Sure you do. You may be ugly but you ain't stupid, right? So come on now. A little Tecate. I get limes. Let us celebrate whatever it is we're celebratin, an I'll speak to you of . . . what? Of cunts? Yes. Cunts. A good cunt tastes like anchovy, did you know at? An all cunts do not taste alike. An all cunts are not the same in the dark.* Laughter, and Phil Romero swiped at his nostrils with a dark and hairy knuckle. Herman Marshall didn't get back to the apartment until five o'clock in the morning, and he never had any clear idea of how he'd managed the drive. He liked Phil Romero. For a Mex, Phil Romero was an honest man. For a Mex. And Herman Marshall was pleased that Phil Romero was impressed by Edna's looks. There sure enough still was life in the old girl, and hot shit. And in March of 1947 Herman Marshall's brother Lute came down with liver cancer. He was dead within a month, and he was buried next to Jackson. Lute left behind a skinny wife and two skinny daughters, and Herman Marshall contributed to their support for a good ten years or so. Birds sang and preened the day Lute was buried, and Herman Marshall's mother took him aside and said to him: *Your daddy ain't doin so good neither. It's his bloodpressure an his heart, you know. An all the years of the hard times.* She nodded toward her husband, who was standing a few dozen yards away and staring down at Lute's coffin. *Air's been a lot of dyin*, said Hannah Marshall to her son, *an air's goin to be more. I mean, air always is, ain't air? An even me, I ain't been feelin all at terrific here lately* . . . She allowed her voice mournfully to trail away. She turned from Herman Marshall and walked to her husband and embraced her husband. Herman Marshall and Edna drove down to Houston the next morning. His brother Eldred Junior lounged in the back seat. Eldred Junior was close to fortysix years of age, as closely as Herman Marshall could figure, and Eldred Junior always had been the bestlooking of the four brothers. Except for the mysterious loss of his coon bitch Elsie, his boyhood hadn't provided him with an awful lot of pain—but his adult years sure enough had made up for that. He had been married twice and divorced twice, and each of his wives had given him a son, but then (according to him) those bitches had poisoned the sons' minds against him, just because some of the time he was broke and was late with the alimony and childsupport payments. And Eldred Junior's good looks had caved in. His nose was pocked, and his chin was stubbled, and he alternated wearing two suits, and one of them was gray and the other was brown, and they both were shiny. He'd always been a salesman . . . selling everything from shoes to coffins to tobacco to switch frogs . . . but in that year of 1947 he was sure God down on his luck, and would it be too much trouble for Herman Marshall and Edna to put him up for a few months down air in Houston until he found a proper job for himself? And Herman Marshall said all right, fine. Maybe this was because of what had happened to Elsie. Or maybe it was because of a belief that blood was thicker than even goddamn cement. For whatever reason, Eldred Junior moved in with them, and he smoked cheap cigars, and the cheap cigars stank, and Edna made faces, but what the hell; blood was blood. One warm cottony evening in September of 1948 (Eldred Junior still was living with them, but he'd gone out to the movies), Edna took Herman Marshall by the hand and led him into the kitchen and seated him at the table and opened a Shiner longneck and handed it to him and told him she was pregnant.

CHAPTER NINE

HERMAN MARSHALL DID EVERYTHING he should have done, and perhaps more. Why, he even passed out El Productos to all the old boys at Gulfway Trucking, and his friend Phil Romero laughed and told him he's done real good for a puny Anglo who no doubt had a puny prick. And Herman Marshall even managed a laugh of his own. And he said to Phil Romero: *It ain't the size of the dog in the fight, Pancho; it's the size of the fight in the dog.* And Phil Romero displayed a sudden explosion of teeth. And everyone laughed. And the drinks were on Herman Marshall. A dispatcher named Red Cubbedge became so drunk he stood on the bar and sang all the verses of *Home on the Range*. While burping and hiccuping. He was a regular goddamn Roy Rogers, or maybe even as good as an Ernest Tubb, and someone suggested they take up a collection to send him to the Grand Old Opry. But cooler heads carried the day, and nothing came of the suggestion, especially after Red Cubbedge puked in the lap of Freddie Weaver, the former Marine who had only eight fingers. The little boy weighed eight pounds at birth, and Edna was in labor for nine hours. *He wasn't really fixin to come out,* said Edna, who lay pale and fragrant in her hospital bed. The baby was next to her, and she made a clucking sound and said to it: *Bad baby. Bad William.* And Herman Marshall, who was sitting next to the bed and had duded himself up in a gray flecked suit and was twisting the brim of his only hat, which lay in his lap like a chicken about to be plucked, said to his beautiful Edna: *He didn't want to come out on account of he knowed a good place. All warm an all, I mean.* And Herman Marshall laughed a

little. And, blushing, Edna laughed a little. And, gurgling, grinning, sticking out its tongue, the baby released a mighty fart and
filled its diaper. Edna had wanted to name the little fellow Herman
Junior, but Herman Marshall would have none of *that*. He told
Edna he'd never liked his given name. It always had sounded too
German. Herman the German . . . who wanted to be known as
that? All right, it was March of 1949, and the war had been over for
nearly four years, but that didn't cut no fucking mustard with
Herman Marshall. The boy's name would be William, not Herman Junior. William was a solid name; it carried quiet authority; it
stood tall and dignified; it was a Gary Cooper sort of name; it
always had put Herman Marshall in mind of millionaires and
straightshooting cowboys and men who made their living hitting
home runs. Eldred Junior, who was working now as a salesman for
a wholesale lumber yard but who still hadn't found a place of his
own to live, told Herman Marshall he sure enough did envy the
stability of Herman Marshall's life. He and Herman Marshall batched
together for five days while Edna and the baby were in the hospital, and one evening Eldred Junior brought home a fifth of gin and
told Herman Marshall shit, there was more to life than Shiner beer,
and gin was a gentleman's beverage, and tonight they would be
gentlemen or die in the attempt. And the two of them sat in the
kitchen, and Eldred Junior took off his jacket and loosened his tie,
and it was Eldred Junior who did most of the drinking, and after a
time he said to Herman Marshall: *You was the youngest, an I expect
you figure you got the short end of the stick, with myself an Lute an
Jackson pickin on you ever now an again, right? Well, it turned out you
got the LONG end of the stick, ain't at a fact though? I mean, Jackson
ain't with us no more, an Lute ain't with us no more, an as for Yours
Truly here—me, myself an I—the thing is, I'm your real ordinary downhome fuckup. I used to be sort of goodlookin, they tell me, but now I'm*

like a string of dogshit floatin in a swamp. I used to get fucked all the time, but nowadays I go for six months without gettin no nooky, an then like as not I got to pay for it. Now en, brother of mine, contrast what you got with what I ain't got. You got a house, an you got a beautiful wife who's goodhearted an so sweet it brings an ache to my dirty old heart, an now you got you a SON. Me, I got two sons, only they hate me on account of air mamas told em I was no good, an so it's like I got no sons at all, all right? But YOU, you lucky shit you, you got it all made in the shade, an I hope you appreciate what it is you lay down with ever night, an I hope you appreciate at boy of yours, an . . . listen, I'll be movin out of here any day now, on account of I've overstayed my welcome an en some, an I KNOW at . . . but it's been such a good time for me . . . you an Edna, you're so damn DECENT an STRAIGHT, an I been a stranger to all at for I don't know how long . . . so I been just sort of hangin round, the goddamn Uninvited Guest, good old Uncle Squat. An you an Edna, neither one of you, you ain't complained, an you ain't told me get out, you nogood bum, you fuckin . . . SALESMAN you. And then Eldred Junior shrugged. *I surely do wish I would of found somebody like at Edna of yours,* he said. *It might of made a world an all of difference, you know?* And Eldred Junior's mouth was lax. He spoke of the rewards of virtue. He wept a little. He rested his palms flat against the kitchen table's flowered oilcloth surface. He shook his head. He spoke of how pretty the baby was, but he didn't mean pretty like a sissy; he meant pretty like . . . beauty. *The girls are goin to go for him,* said Eldred Junior, *like they was poleaxed. He'll have to wade his way through em. He'll have to push em aside with a heavy stick, an I ain't just whistlin Dixie, boy. No SIR.* Exhalations. Grunts. Half an hour or so later, Eldred Junior passed out. His forehead struck the tabletop and bounced a little. Herman Marshall stood up and turned out the lights and went upstairs to bed. There was no sense trying to carry Eldred Junior upstairs to the guest bedroom where he slept. When Eldred Junior passed out after a drunk, he was dead weight to end dead weight. He was enough to make the goddamn stairs and floors give way. So Herman Marshall left his brother to sleep it off in the kitchen, and the next morning Eldred Junior sheepishly complained of a series of real awful cricks in his back. And both he and Herman Marshall smiled. He wasn't half bad, was old Eldred Junior. Herman Marshall never told him what had happened to Elsie; he didn't see the sense to it—not after the passage of so many years. And besides, he didn't want to do anything to damage whatever had been built up between them. Filial devotion. Whatever. Eldred Junior moved to Wichita Falls in the summer of '49, where he sold kitchen fixtures. He died of bone cancer in August of 1966, which was the same month Billy died. The two funerals were held a week apart. Eldred Junior was buried with the others up in Hope, and neither of his sons attended the services. Herman Marshall was taken aside by his mother, who pointed toward his father, who was standing next to the grave and talking and smiling with one of the undertakers. *Your poor old daddy*, said Hannah Marshall. *When he wakes up each mornin, I call it a miracle. He's eighty years of age, do you know at? Eighty but LOOKIN a hunnert an ten, an he don't hardly eat enough to keep a bedbug from fallin over, an maybe do you think he WANTS to pass on?* Hannah Marshall sucked at her false teeth and shook her head. Her face was solemn, sweetly profound. Her eyes were altogether too bright. Billy died three days later. He died after giving his father that final red vexed hot astonished glare, and he was as dead as he ever would be, and no one was deader. And the preacher spoke of ashes. And the preacher spoke of dust. And Edna, all black and veiled, throat scratchy from her weeping, stood next to Herman Marshall at the cemetery, and she wobbled and gasped, and he tried to remember when the last time was she had worn hairribbons. It was a blazing

[114]

August morning, and the cemetery grass was a pale tired brown. Two men leaned against some sort of trenching machine that was parked on an access road maybe a hundred yards away. The men were smoking. They probably were the goddamn gravediggers. The trenching machine carried the word *ILES* on its neck. Herman Marshall kept looking at the fucking thing. Edna's jaws clacked, and the preacher's voice was murmurous and bland, and Herman Marshall embraced Edna, and people had brought them pies, cakes, a turkey, a meatloaf, two chickens, a standing rib roast, cole slaw, several Jell-O salads and three plates of brownies, and that night Herman Marshall and Edna and perhaps fifty other people milled around the house, and all his friends from Gulfway Trucking were there, and Phil Romero told him *we all of us got to go on, my frien,* and John Dean West told him *the poor kid's better off,* and George McLean told him *at air preacher gave a fine sermon,* and Freddie Weaver told him *dyin's bad, but maybe sometimes other things is worse.* And Herman Marshall nodded, moistened his lips. He shook hands with everyone, and someone brought him a standing rib sandwich, and he kissed several of the women on their cheeks. Edna remained in bed for nearly a month after Billy's funeral. She only got out of bed in order to go to the toilet. She did not bathe, though. Herman Marshall carried the television set upstairs to the bedroom because she wanted to watch all the soap operas. She said little. He slept downstairs on the sofa. There still was a residual stink of Billy in the house, and the airconditioning didn't really do away with it. The spinal meningitis had gone to work on Billy in 1957, when he'd been only eight. Herman Marshall remembered that year pretty damn good. It had been the year of Orval Faubus and Little Rock Central High School and Sputnik and the Braves beating the Yankees in the World Series, four games to three. Herman Marshall earned something in the neighborhood of twelve thousand dollars that year, and he and Edna were missing no mortgage payments, not on your life. But then Billy began to bend, and within a year he had forgotten how to laugh. And every so often Edna would say something about it all being a Judgment, and Herman Marshall kept asking her what had they ever *done*, but she simply turned away from him and said no more. Sometimes she leaned against windowsills. Sometimes she rushed into the bathroom. But she said no more. Her eyes hardened, and her steps were brisk as she hurried back and forth, fetching and carrying for Billy, who writhed, who bared his teeth, who puked and who screamed through his puking, choking on it, gurgling, coughing, and he drenched the house with a stink of Sick, a yellow stink, an intimate and embarrassing stink. And there were special sheets for him because sometimes he shit the bed. And Herman Marshall and Edna took turns turning him so he would not have bedsores. And he hollered at them. He was a bitty and bent little *boy*, and he *hollered at them*. He called them terrible names. He said they never would know what he was going through, and he filled the room with farts and slobberings. And he turned in on himself, staring up from a crouch, every so often allowing himself to be carried to a wheelchair, and he would sit in the wheelchair and glare out the front window and curse the birds, the cicadas, and curse children, automobiles, stray poking dogs, the mailman, the man who came to the house from time to time to repair the airconditioner, working buddies of Herman Marshall's who every so often stopped by to play cards and drink beer. He hated Christmas. He said Christmas was for the living, and what did *he* have to do with the living? And Edna said to Herman Marshall: *I'd just about gave up.* And Herman Marshall said: *What?* And Edna said: *You an me, we'd BOTH just about gave up, ain't at right?* And Herman Marshall said: *Gave up on WHAT?* And Edna said: *On havin a baby. An I guess we was right, the way things turned out.* And Herman Marshall said: *No. He's our boy. He's goin to be all right.* And Edna said: *At ain't true, an you know it ain't true, and I'd appreciate it if you'd stop lyin bout it.* And Herman Marshall said: *What do you want me to say? Do you want me to say at air son of ours ought to be sent off to the trash yard?* And Edna said: *You don't know.* And Herman Marshall said: *Don't know WHAT?* And Edna said: *You're off in your truck so much of the time, an I don't know what you're doin, an I don't know too exact where you are on any given night of the week, what with maybe sometimes the roads are bad, an I want to KNOW where you are, on account of a whole lot of the time when he hollers at me it's like sayin we done WRONG bringin him into the world, an . . . an can't you figure out how at FEELS to me? An I want you with me, but you ain't air. An . . . an it's all a Judgment. He shouldn't of come along. We'd just about gave up, an you know at's true. An we should of gave up, the way things turned out. WE SHOULD OF GAVE UP. WE SHOULD OF MADE DO WITH WHAT WE HAD.* And Herman Marshall said: *Sh. You'll wake him.* And Edna said: *He won't wake. He took his pill tonight. The pain was real bad. It made him . . . squeak.* And Edna looked away from Herman Marshall. *The prime of life,* she said. *I recollect I oncet told you I was in the prime of life. I recollect I oncet told you I hadn't gave up. Well, I, oh, Lord, I SHOULD OF gave up. I'm tellin you it ain't worked out, an I'm tellin you it ain't worked out A TALL. I'm tellin you he might as well be dead. I'm tellin you what's the . . . what's the use.* And Edna embraced her husband. And Edna wept. Edna shook and Edna soaked her husband's neck with hot brutal tears. Edna made fists and pounded them against her husband's shoulders. She and her husband were sitting up in bed, and Herman Marshall blinked at the ceiling, and some of the paint was peeling up there, and some of the paint had blistered up there. He thought of the Change of Life. Maybe Edna had entered it. She wore a white cotton nightgown, and it was buttoned to the neck, and her plump body was too warm. Her armpits were sopping. As a young fellow, he'd never thought of Edna in terms of sopping armpits. Farmers had sopping armpits; Edna didn't. Jesus, the ways life had of reducing people to helpless flesh and fluids. Billy's screamings and his stink pursued Herman Marshall and Edna for nine years. Then he was Gone, and the cemetery was so fucking *flat*, and those men lounged around and smoked their cigarettes, and Billy's coffin was covered by shitty spattery cemetery dirt dropped on it by the machine that was known as the *ILES*, and the mourners stood around the house and ate sandwiches made from the standing rib roast, and then the mourners dispersed, and the world had not missed a beat, and old men laughed over a joke about a woman who believed her elderly lover no longer loved her because he was unable to shit in her face. And Herman Marshall . . . well, Herman Marshall drove for Gulf-way Trucking for ten more years before he retired, and the Inter-states sprang up, and the old boys in their pickup trucks passed on the right and brandished bottles of beer and smashed themselves to death against bridge abutments, and Herman Marshall's bladder fell apart from all the speed and all the pounding and all the jounc-ing, and he and his friends sat at the counters in every bitty truck-stop between Houston and New Orleans and New Orleans and Chicago and Chicago and Atlanta and Atlanta and New Orleans, and around and around they went, and they laughed with all the waitresses in all the bitty truckstops, and most of the waitresses had seen better days along about the time Harry Truman had been President, and Herman Marshall's nickname was changed from Nig the Lover to Papa Nig, and every time he came home Edna would insist on speaking of that thing she called a Judgment. She never had learned to drive, and so each Sunday (when he was home) she had him take her out to the cemetery so she could pull

[118]

weeds from Billy's grave and make sure Billy's headstone hadn't been spattered by birdshit (she always referred to the birdshit as Calling Cards from Our Feathered Friends), and every so often Herman Marshall glimpsed the *ILES* machine, and its neck always was twisted, coiled, poised. And Edna never wore hairribbons. And there were nights when she would embrace him and ask him please, oh pretty please, to spank her, which he did . . . lightly, reluctantly, grimacing at her fat pink bare bottom. He asked her why she wanted him to spank her, and she told him she had been bad, and that was why the Judgment had come thundering down upon them . . . the Judgment that had cost them their Billy. *Their* Billy. Not *her* Billy. She always referred to him as *their* Billy. Until near the end. When she knew she was dying. When she knew Dr Moomaw spoke the truth. And then she named Phil Romero, and she said: *I was lonely, an it all was slippin away, an he came to the house an said nice things. Oily things, I suppose. Mex things. But they was better an nothin. An it was better to be with him an to set around the house all day an feelin the fat on my belly an wonderin where you was. Listen. It was better to be with him an to set around night and day.* She spoke quickly. Herman Marshall supposed she didn't want him to interrupt. Well, he would have interrupted anyway, if he'd been of a mind, but what could he have said? Billy had been *their* Billy, and the stink of him never really had mattered, and his anger hadn't pushed them away, and Edna had dreamed of miracles, and Herman Marshall's skull had filled with a vision of a boy who stood tall and straight as an exclamation point, and now allofasudden he was *her* boy and no longer *their* boy. Well, bullshit. And Herman Marshall embraced Edna and told her *it don't matter none— not no more.* And told her *he lived with us an died with us an at's all at matters.* And later Herman Marshall did a lot of thinking that had to do with Phil Romero. He had believed Phil Romero to be an

[119]

honest man, an honest man who had stood up to honest truths. He remembered the night he and Phil Romero had put away so much Tecate with limes in Phil's apartment with all the Mexican movie stars lining the wall and thrusting out their fine Mexican tits. He remembered Phil's talk of the Anglo war and the shit on Mr. E. E. Rischer's shorts. And this straightforward Phil Romero had turned around and had fucked Herman Marshall's wife and had fathered Herman Marshall's son. And Herman Marshall said to himself: Well, I guess an honest man has to be judged by more an he says. I mean, I suppose it goes to show you brave talk ain't worth a nickel. And Herman Marshall mewled. He was sitting in a motel room in Pasadena. He had been drinking in the Top of the World, and he was too drunk to drive home, and Harry Munger had fixed him up with the room. He could have telephoned for a woman (there was a skinny fiftyish woman named Marva who liked him and had skinny legs and never was reluctant to say nice things about his cock, old as it was, old as *he* was), but a woman wouldn't have cut the old mustard for him that night. He wished he knew where his precious *book* was. Oh, he would *memorize* that book, and no mistake. That stinking Mex. Who talked straight to Herman Marshall's face, straightarrow honest, and then snuck over to Herman Marshall's house when Herman Marshall wasn't there and threw a quick jump, maybe ten jumps, maybe a hundred jumps, into Herman Marshall's wife, and did Phil Romero cause Edna to go all soppy and crazy and then cause her to come and kick and scratch, to plead for mercy, God's sake, Phil, take it out before I blow up all over the place? (Herman Marshall had no trouble imagining the things they must have said together, and had they laughed at him? Maybe so. Probably so. A wife who fucked another man probably stopped at nothing. She probably tongued the other man's ears. She probably did other things that Herman Marshall didn't want to think about, for fear he'd jam a fork into his balls and let himself goddamn good and well bleed to death.) He linked his fingers. He cracked his knuckles. He was seventyone years of age when Edna made her confession, and maybe it shouldn't have mattered. But it did matter. He had loved Billy, and he still did love Billy. Billy's death hadn't mattered a fucking bit as far as *that* had been concerned. Herman Marshall always remembered the Billy of the time before the spinal meningitis, the Billy who had played with the Lionel trains and had gone choo choo choo in time with the little trains' wheels, the Billy who had sat erectly on a porch glider in Cleveland, Ohio, the Billy who sometimes had crawled into bed with his parents and had slept with them and had made sure his body touched theirs all the night long, the Billy who had worn a cowboy hat that had said *HOUSTON TEXAS* and had displayed a cowboy with a lariat, the Billy who had been the best and the brightest and the future and all good things. Yessir, *that* Billy. The one who had represented such hope. And he had died. Which was one thing. But now it had been revealed to Herman Marshall that Billy had carried no blood of Herman Marshall's blood. And that was another thing. A worse thing. An intolerable thing. But what could be done about this intolerable thing? Would it do any good to punish Edna any more than she'd punished herself? At her age, would maybe a *spanking* have meant anything? Jesus Lord Almighty, what a thought. Herman Marshall shook his head. The motel room was stuffy, and he should have switched on the airconditioning, but fuck it. Fuck everything. Herman Marshall lay back and wept. And, hell, he couldn't even go after Phil Romero. Old as Herman Marshall was, he probably *would* have gone after that stinking greazzer wetback shit, but Phil Romero had died in 1972 when his rig had skidded off a bridge near Alexandria, Louisiana, and Phil had been trapped in the cab and had drowned. Everyone had chipped in for flowers. The funeral had been held down in Matamoras or some such godforsaken place, and no one from the company had attended. Phil had been buried, though, someplace in Houston. His father, the bigdeal valet to bigdeal Mr E. E. Rischer, had insisted the body be brought north after the funeral. No one from Gulfway Trucking had attended the graveside service, or at least no one Herman Marshall knew. What the hell, one less Mex more or less wasn't about to change the good old course of good old history, correct? And anyway, death was as much a part of trucking as was diesel fuel or flat tires. Herman Marshall's old friend Elroy Catchings had been wiped out away back in 1937 when *his* rig had skidded into a cattle truck on old US 90 west of Beaumont, and both trucks had exploded, and both drivers had been roasted, and the cattle had been roasted, and people who lived there said the stink had traveled for miles. And so much for Elroy Catchings, who had found the Gulfway Trucking job for Herman Marshall. So much for a lot of old boys who drove trucks. Herman Marshall retired in 1975, and it wasn't a fucking moment too soon. Everything was Interstates, Interstates. Squashed babies. Drunken old boys who would careen across four lanes without using their turn signals. Automobiles stripped and chopped like spaghetti. (You go to pass somebody, and you're seen as a big bully in a big truck, and so you receive the finger, and your hands tighten on the wheel, and soundless words are hollered at you.) The trucks labored, and Herman Marshall labored, running up to Little Rock, across to New Orleans, north to Chicago and west to San Antonio and El Paso and maybe all the way to Albuquerque, and yes, sure, *all right*, the waitresses opened themselves for him, and he lay in the waitresses' beds and drank Four Roses with Coke chasers, and sometimes a plastic Jesus was nailed to the wall at the head of the bed, and sometimes a photograph of John F. Kennedy was nailed to the wall at the head of the bed, and the expression on John F. Kennedy's face invariably was uncomfortable, prissy, constrained, and the waitresses licked their fingers and moistened themselves, and what the hell. A hard quick come sometimes meant a man really would be able to catch a good night's sleep and not dream of puke and stinks and meningitis. But the best of his women wasn't a waitress. The best of his women was the nervous widowed tintinnabulating schoolteacher from Beaumont, the woman who said she really loved him because he never was reluctant to jam a finger up her ass. Her name was Letitia Marlowe, and her husband had been a deputy sheriff, and that old boy had taught her to enjoy having her asshole torn open. Letitia fixed pot roasts and barbecue for Herman Marshall, and she wore sleek dresses that had bright colors and showed off her legs. She told him she was a brazen huzzy for sure, and she laughed a nervous tintinnabulating laugh, and he told her wellnow, ain't nobody perfect. And they both laughed. And he took her upstairs to a bedroom that was decorated in green and pink chintz, and the bed had a lacy canopy, and her voice trembled and danced, and she did whatever he wanted, and sometimes he used his thumb on her anxious asshole, and usually she whooped, and her elbows flapped like the silly flightless wings of a chicken. Letitia Marlowe married the owner of a TV repair business in 1968, and she told Herman Marshall she never would forget his many kindnesses. Her breasts were tiny and soft, and Herman Marshall kissed them. And drove home to Edna, who then nagged him to drive her to the graveyard where Billy was buried. *His headstone*, said Edna. *We want to wash away the Callin Cards.* And Herman Marshall nodded. And then he retired, and the company gave him a suitcase and a silver digital watch. He never had occasion to pack the suitcase. He often dreamed of highways and death and whores. He often dreamed of Billy. And finally, after Edna had told him of Phil Romero, he often dreamed of treachery, enemies, revenge, and he often dreamed of Nawzis, and the Nawzis' blood squirted and leaked. Maybe Phil Romero was to him what the Nawzis had been to him. Edna's hair fell out. Tom Mix had died in 1940, but somehow the news escaped Herman Marshall until 1980 or so, when he read an article in a newspaper, a piece having to do with Cowboy Stars of the Past. And Tom Mix stared at him from a photograph, and the Tom Mix squint was there. A lot had passed down the drain. Elsie had drowned. Nawzis had been demolished. Billy had screamed, and his poor angry life always brought a memory of the stink of shit and tangled guts. And Edna said: *Ow*. And Edna begged to be killed. And Herman Marshall's skull was rich with witless exercises in bloviation. Tom Mix was dead, and time was dead, and the television set hummed, and Harry Munger's gentle rummy customers murmured and sniggered, and Herman Marshall came down from the attic with all sorts of junk and truck and made up silly stories, and Edna always smiled, and much of the time she wept, and she always thanked him. One day he asked her whether she believed in Paradise. Frowning, she thought for a moment. Then she shrugged, tried to smile and told him why not. It was as good an answer as any. It would do until the book was written. Sweet angels with their harps and their angeltits. Not a bad thought.

CHAPTER TEN

EDNA SLIPPED INTO A COMA and died one screaming hot afternoon in August of 1984. The cicadas screamed. There was a house fire on the next block, and sirens screamed. The screams of the sirens caused the screams of the cicadas to bulge and roll. The house fire had something to do with an overheated airconditioner, and it didn't amount to much, but it surely was loud. It was Dr Moomaw who came to the house and checked out Edna and made certain she was dead. He listened to her chest and touched one of her wrists. He did whatever it was doctors did. This was the first house call he'd made in years, he said. Herman Marshall wanted to kill him. Dr Moomaw was wearing his Adidas, jeans and a sweatshirt, and the sweatshirt said: *STOLEN FROM THE TEXAS MEDICAL CENTER.* He tucked the covers around Edna's neck. "She was on her medication, wasn't she?" he said to Herman Marshall.

Herman Marshall nodded. He was sitting by the front window and trying to listen to the cicadas and nothing else. And he was trying to remember the final conversation he'd had with Edna two days earlier.

Dr Moomaw turned from the bed and said: "An the arrangements?"

"What?" said Herman Marshall.

"The funeral arrangements," said Dr Moomaw.

"Air bein made. T. C. Drucker & Sons. Jobeth Stephenson's makin em. She's real old. She's older an me. But she's . . . *spry,* you know? She lives right acrost the street, an I went an fetched her soon as I figured Edna was Gone. An Jobeth came over here, an we picked out a dress for Edna, an now Jobeth's back over to her own place, an she's makin calls on the telephone. Arrangements. T. C. Drucker & Sons."

"At's . . . well, at's fine," said Dr Moomaw. "I've . . . well, I've always heard good things bout T. C. Drucker & Sons."

"Billy was buried out of T. C. Drucker & Sons."

"Who?"

"Our son," said Herman Marshall. He nodded toward Edna's body. "Me an her. The only baby we ever had, an he's been dead since 19 an 66. She's goin to be buried next to him. It's all been planned out. The plot's bought an everthin . . ."

"Well," said Dr Moomaw, and he smiled, "at's a comfort, isn't it? Perhaps she died a little bit happy."

"Perhaps?"

". . . yes."

"Yessir," said Herman Marshall. "An *perhaps* she died all doped up an not knowin what was happenin except she didn't have no hair. *Perhaps*. Yessir. It's all a whole lot of *perhaps*, ain't it? One *perhaps* after tuther *perhaps*, an don't nothin balance out an make much sense."

Dr Moomaw cleared his throat and said: "Yes. I often think at myself."

"Surely you do," said Herman Marshall. He glanced down at Dr Moomaw's Adidas. "You're just a real old downhome country-boy runnin *fool*, ain't you?

". . . pardon?"

"But at's all right. You came all the way over here, an you don't do at sort of thing ever day, like you already done said. I'm grateful to you. A man who puts himself out is a good man."

". . . well."

[126]

"Did you *run* over here from the Medical Center or did you *drive?*"

"I drove," said Dr Moomaw. "I was in my car already. I was on my way to a late lunch with some friends. We exercise together. We pump iron together as well as run together. An then there was a beep on my beeper, an I stopped at a UtoteM an made a phone call, an the girl told me you'd called. So, well, here I am."

"Well," said Herman Marshall, "at's real nice." He dug at one of his nostrils with a thumb. He decided he no longer had to bother looking at Dr Moomaw, and so he stared out the window. Across the street, old Jobeth Stephenson was moving around in the front room of her house. Maybe he would go over there real soon and watch a dirty movie with her on her cable TV. Might as well. After all, there would be no more bedpans to empty, no more sheets to change, no more trips to the attic in search of foolish and broken things that would trigger foolish and broken madeup stories.

"I *am* sorry, you know," said Dr Moomaw, speaking to Herman Marshall's back.

Herman Marshall didn't say anything.

"When you asked me whether I *ran* over here or whether I *drove* over here, you were bein sarcastic, but it was your pain speakin, an I can understand at."

". . . at's wonderful," said Herman Marshall, choking.

"If I were to lose my Crystal, I don't know what I'd do. I can appreciate how you feel."

"Your what?"

"Crystal. My wife's name is Crystal. An she has two sisters, an air named Ivy an Charity. Very, um, Southern, if you know what I mean."

"Southern," said Herman Marshall. He frowned. Across the street, Jobeth Stephenson appeared to be patting her hips and adjusting

[127]

her brassière. "Southern. Yessir. An I expect air rich. An I expect they play golf. An I expect air joggin fools *too*, like good old Doc Moomaw, friend to mankind . . ."

"Please. I'm only tryin to—"

"I appreciate it," said Herman Marshall, almost barking the words. "But I mean maybe you can *go* now, all right? I want to be alone here in this room with her. You done your best. I give you credit. I ain't your enemy. Only now I ask you kindly leave me be. Kindly. Do her. Open the front door an haul ass out of here an don't let the flies get in, you know?"

". . . all right," said Dr Moomaw. He walked toward the front door. He hesitated. "I . . . would you like me to leave you some tranquilizers?"

". . . no . . . they don't do no good . . . I tried some of Edna's oncet or twicet, an all they done was make me feel worse . . ."

"Fine," said Dr Moomaw. "Whatever you say." And Dr Moomaw went out. Herman Marshall watched Dr Moomaw walk to his car, and the car was a Lincoln . . . a white Lincoln, with chrome that caught the screaming August afternoon in a splatter of silvery unforgiving light. Dr Moomaw stood in front of the car for a moment and jogged in place.

Herman Marshall grimaced.

Then Dr Moomaw slid inside the car and drove away. The car was silent.

Herman Marshall coughed. He did not bother to cover his mouth. After a time he stood up. He leaned for a moment against the windowsill. The cicada noise boomed and ballooned. He walked to the foot of the bed and blinked at Edna. Dr Moomaw had arranged the sheets and coverlets primly. Jobeth Stephenson had said something about buying Edna a wig for when she was laid out. Herman Marshall spoke aloud. No one was there (except Edna, and Edna didn't count, did she?), but he spoke aloud anyway, and he said: "Sure. A wig. She was a good old girl, an she used to laugh a whole lot. Her an her hairribbons an how she liked to read the funnypapers an she was real fond of animals at could talk . . ." Herman Marshall hesitated. He looked around. He nodded. Maybe he was acknowledging the silence. Maybe he was acknowledging the fact that no one was there. He seated himself next to the bed. He closed his eyes for a moment. He wondered why fucking goddamn Dr Moomaw had fucking goddamn bothered. Had Edna somehow penetrated Dr Moomaw? Little old dying *Edna*? Well, maybe so. Maybe Dr Moomaw had seen something in her. Maybe she had reminded him of something from his boyhood. At any rate, he actually had made a *house call*. But the house call was a real laugh, come to think of it. The thing was, the house call hadn't taken place until after she'd died. Herman Marshall opened his eyes. He smiled softly at his dead wife, and his nigger lips were moist. Again he spoke aloud. "Maybe you reminded him of his old mama," said Herman Marshall to the dead Edna. "Maybe you reminded him of a time when maybe he'd been a bad boy. Stealin an outhouse. Hittin a baseball through somebody's old grandmaw's window. Throwin stones at a cat. Or maybe he was tryin to make up somethin to you. Him an his Adidas an his Lincoln." Herman Marshall's eyes narrowed. It wasn't exactly a Tom Mix squint, but it would have to do. He decided there was no sense talking aloud. And anyway, he needed to bring back the talk he'd had with Edna two days earlier. Their final talk, and he'd had to lean over her to hear her words.

It's . . . I got to tell you, she'd said. Her voice was a stringy whisper, and it was wrapped in spit.

Hush now, Herman Marshall had said. *We don't want you wearin yourself out with a lot of talk. So hush. Hush up.*

[129]

YOU hush, said Edna, and she tried to sit up. But her arms gave way, and she moaned. Then, lying flat on her back, blinking at the ceiling (and her eyes were gummy, and they were without much focus), she said: *It wasn't no Phil Romero. I only used his name on account of he was dead, an you couldn't go out an try to beat up on him or nothin. A man your age, maybe it would of . . . you know, done you in . . .*

. . . what?

Phil Romero, he wasn't—

I don't CARE bout no Phil Romero, said Herman Marshall. *He ain't nothin . . . he's stones . . . he's food for the grass an the worms an a whole lot of little bugs . . . he's . . . he's . . . smoke . . . spiderwebs . . .*

You ain't listenin, said Edna.

Listenin to WHAT? said Herman Marshall. He was shaking, and he was beginning to feel another of his goddamn needs to piss.

Never mind bout Phil Romero. Mind what I'm sayin to you. Mind the truth.

Truth?

It was your brother, said Edna. She closed her foggy eyes. She shuddered.

My brother? What brother? My brother what?

Eldred Junior, said Edna. *Him an me. We made Billy. An at means a whole lot.*

Herman Marshall tightened the muscle in his prick. This was no time for him to be wetting his pants.

I didn't want to tell you Eldred Junior, said Edna, *so I picked another dead man. But now I'm thinkin different. Now I'm thinkin I'm obliged to tell the truth.* And Edna's eyes slowly fluttered open. *He . . . you got to understand . . . please understand . . . he kept tellin me what a good man you was . . . an he kept tellin me him an me was doin a bad thing . . . but I kept after him . . . an I kept tellin him I figured you was layin up with waitresses an preachers' wives all the time . . .*

You kept AFTER him? said Herman Marshall.

Yessir, said Edna. *On account of I wanted a little old baby. On account of I wanted somethin here with me when you was gone, out on the road an I didn't know what you was doin, an YOU an ME wasn't makin no babies, so I figured . . . well, I expect you can figure what I figured . . .*

Eldred Junior? When he was stayin with us? Eatin my food an all?

. . . yessir.

God damn him.

No, said Edna.

No? How come you say no? said Herman Marshall, and he was beginning to feel himself need to roar as well as piss. He supposed he probably would do both. His eyes were hot, and his nostrils had begun to clog up. He took off his glasses and rubbed them against a shirtsleeve. *I would of rather it would of been Phil Romero,* said Herman Marshall, and he rubbed his glasses, and he rubbed his glasses, and the shirtsleeve became warm.

No, said Edna. *You don't mean at.*

How do you know I don't mean it? said Herman Marshall. *How do you know what I mean an what I don't mean? Who are you to say things like at air?*

Think. Please THINK.

Think? Think bout what? You're tellin me my brother fucked my wife. My own brother. My own blood. A damn windbag who never had two nickels to rub together, an both his wives hated him, an his own sons wouldn't have nothin to do with him, an what do you want me to do? Go out an jump in the car an drive up to Hope an pin the goddamn Congressional Medal of Honor on his headstone?

You're passin right over one thing, said Edna, and her voice was flat and easy. Maybe, even though she was dying and she knew she was dying, it was calm. *You're passin over the blood thing.*

Blood? Because he was my brother? But he wasn't worth nothin. All he done all the days of his life was . . . bloviate.

What?

It's a word at means settin around an bullshittin.

Oh.

So what do I got to THINK bout? said Herman Marshall.

The blood, said Edna. *Think bout the blood. It'll come to you.*

Herman Marshall still was rubbing his glasses against the shirt-sleeve. *No,* he said. *Nothin's comin to me. Except maybe thinkin back on all the years at wasn't worth the powder to blow em up.*

The blood, said Edna. *Please. The blood.*

No, said Herman Marshall. *I can't think bout the blood. I got to think bout my brother. My brother who done fucked my wife. At air's called incest, ain't it?* And Herman Marshall put on his glasses. They gleamed. He wondered whether maybe Eldred Junior had found out about Elsie, and so Eldred Junior had worked out a hard revenge.

Now Edna's mouth hung open. She was breathing in harsh gasps.

Herman Marshall's pain sang in his chest.

. . . the blood, said Edna, wheezing. She closed her eyes and reached up and touched her eyelids. *Please don't talk bout no incest. His blood wasn't my blood. His blood was . . . it was YOUR blood . . . which meant it was Billy's blood . . . which meant your blood was Billy's blood, after all . . .*

Herman Marshall swallowed, and briefly he choked on his spit. He coughed. He embraced himself. He bent forward. His bladder was all shrieks and shredded things. He felt a drop or two of urine leak into his undershorts. *My blood was Billy's . . . blood,* he said, clearing his throat.

. . . yes, said Edna. She opened her eyes. She was trying to smile. Her naked skull was ropy and damp. *So go ahead,* she said. *Kill me for my sins. Ha. Ain't I . . . ain't I amusin though . . .*

[132]

So when they buried Billy, said Herman Marshall, *he had my blood in him.*

Edna slowly nodded.

Herman Marshall touched one of Edna's plump wrists. It no longer was all that plump. And he said: *At supposed to make ever-thin all right?*

. . . I want to hope so . . . I mean, air's a Judgment I got to face, but at least I want you to know whose blood is whose . . .

Yeah, said Herman Marshall. *Sure.* He squeezed the wrist. *It's all right, old girl. It don't matter none no more. I love you. I ain't never loved nobody else. An the blood thing . . . I thank you kindly for tellin me . . . I really do . . . it's just at . . . well, I got to keep workin it through my old skull, you know? My numb skull. Herman Marshall, he's a good old boy, but he's a numbskull . . .*

Say goodbye to me.

What?

Edna yawned. Girlishly she covered her mouth, cupping a palm. *I think this here . . . I think this here is goin to be the biggest old sleep I've ever had,* she said. *I want you to give my best to Garfield the cat. An Willie Nelson. An Harry an Beth. An at dirty old Jobeth over air acrost the street. Tell her she got my permission to take down your britches whenever she's of a mind . . . I . . . now a kiss, Herman . . . now . . . please . . . say goodbye to me real proper an nice, you know?*

Herman Marshall bent toward his wife.

She pressed a hand against his mouth for a moment. *You was the best,* she said. *You was the best, I'm tellin you. Always the best. An your blood ran in Billy's veins. Think on at. Think on it real hard.*

Herman Marshall nodded. His glasses had smeared up again.

Edna's hand came away from his mouth. She yawned, and at the same time her eyes were flooding.

Herman Marshall kissed his wife lightly on the mouth. And he

[133]

kissed away some of her tears. *I love you*, he said, *an we don't got to talk about . . . dust.*

. . . think on the blood, said Edna.

Yes ma'am, said Herman Marshall. *All right. All right. I'll do her. For you.*

Edna's eyes abruptly closed. Heavily. She never said another word.

And that had been two days earlier, and now Edna was dead, and Herman Marshall still didn't quite know what to make of what she'd told him. Maybe he was relieved. At least she hadn't laid up with no *Mex*. At least he, Herman Marshall, had been right about her to *that* extent. But the plain truth of the thing was that she'd put the horns on him, Herman Marshall, and all right, *all right*, the damn bidness had taken place like damn near forty years earlier, but surely it would work at his mind and his balls all the days and nights he had left to him. (Two days earlier, after Edna's eyes had closed for that final heavy time, he *had* made it to the bathroom, and his piss had come in a razory dribble, and he had milked his old prick, diddling the last drops from it, and then he had leaned against the commode and had stared at a can of Sani-Flush and had fought for his balance, what with the way his legs had been knocking and his knees had been giving way. And he had washed his old prick in warm water, and the warm water had put him a little in mind of saliva, and briefly he had remembered the toothless woman from Diseaseville, Louisiana, and he had sighed, and he had told himself he was a disrespectful asshole, and he had said to himself: I wish she hadn't of told me nothin bout nothin. I mean, Billy was my son. He wasn't nobody else's son. An nothin at happened to him was no Judgment. I mean, Jesus Christ, enough is enough.) And now Herman Marshall blinked at Edna's corpse. He touched her skull. Yes, a wig would be a nice thing for the viewing. What-

[134]

ever it cost, he would pay the price without complaint. He spoke to Edna's corpse. "You're goin to be pretty," he said. "You're goin to be pretty like you was the night we snuck behind at movie theayter in Shreveport." He patted one of Edna's cheeks, and it had no warmth. He drew back his hand that had done the patting. He rubbed the hand against one of his thighs. He thought of grave-yards. He thought of all the people who lay in graveyards. He wondered what had happened to all their laughter and all their ambitions and all their comes. Had the Lord gathered up all that stuff? had He placed it in storage until Judgment Day? or had it all vanished the way breath vanished? Herman Marshall spoke aloud. "I mean," he said, "it all comes down to layin in the dirt—unless you're a circus fat lady, an then maybe they cremate you, on account of the price of coffins an all." He sucked at his false teeth. "Poor old girl," he said to Edna. A hesitation, then: "Well, it ain't like I'm goin to be all at far behind . . ." And Herman Marshall shrugged a little. He told himself he should honor Edna's memory and think of blood. Well, tomorrow would be soon enough, and he—

The doorbell rang. The sound was a discreet pong, like maybe in a hospital or a department store.

Herman Marshall stood up and walked to the front door. He supposed it was Jobeth Stephenson. He opened the door.

It was Jobeth Stephenson. She was short, and she wore a striped print dress, and she had put on lipstick and mascara. "How you doin?" she said, and she managed a sort of solid ivory dentured smile.

"Real good," said Herman Marshall, and he held the door open for Jobeth.

"Me too," said Jobeth, "for an old rip." She entered the front room, and Herman Marshall closed the door and followed her. Her

skirt was too short, and her legs were knobbed. She had to be
eighty, God damn it. She probably had to be good and *past* eighty.
She walked to the bed and looked down at Edna and absently
tugged on her lower lip. Then she turned to Herman Marshall and
said: "It's all taken care of. I talked to the people at T. C. Drucker,
an they'll be right along, an a wig'd be nice on her, wouldn't it?
We . . . me an some man from T. C. Drucker . . . we talked about
a wig, an he said don't you worry, ma'am; we get a whole mess
of cancer dead people, an so we got plenty of wigs. He was a nice
man. He told me my voice sounded . . . young. It was only the telephone . . . I mean, he didn't *see* me . . . but I was pleased . . . beg-
gars can't be choosers, you know?"

"At's surely right," said Herman Marshall. He was standing at
the foot of the bed.

"You want me to go with you when you pick out the coffin?"
said Jobeth.

"I'd surely appreciate that," said Herman Marshall.

Jobeth seated herself next to the bed. She touched her hair. "I
. . . well, if tonight . . . you know, if tonight you don't want to
be alone . . . you can stay with me . . . I can fix you up with a nice
sofabed in the front room . . . I mean, it ain't at I'm tryin to suggest somethin at's . . . indecent . . ."

"No," said Herman Marshall. "I thank you kindly, but I'll be
all right here. An air's a whole lot of cleanin up I got to do."

"I'll help you," said Jobeth. "Any way I can." She was holding
a patentleather purse in her lap. She took a lace handkerchief from
the purse. She shook her head. "You should of seen me when it
was World War Two," she said. "I mean, I wasn't no chicken
even *en*, but I done all right, you know?"

"I expect I do."

Jobeth smiled. She dabbed at her eyes. "*Live friendly*—at's always been my motto."

[136]

"I can understand at," said Herman Marshall.

"Dances an all. I went to a lot of dances. I had dresses at had scoop necklines. Old Jobeth an her dances. Honkytonks."

Herman Marshall exhaled. He walked to the front window and looked outside for the ambulance or the hearse or whatever the goddamn thing would be.

CHAPTER ELEVEN

THEY CAME. SLOWLY THEY CAME. Awkward and murmurous. At their age, they probably should have been used to goddamn grief and goddamn viewings, but they weren't. Or at least Herman Marshall didn't think they were. Most of his friends came. The gentle rummies from the Top of the World. Harry and Beth Munger. People from the neighborhood. His old buddies from Gulfway Trucking. Even Marva came. Skinny Marva, who never had been reluctant to say nice things about his cock. And she wore a tight black dress that had a slit skirt. She pressed one of Herman Marshall's hands between both of hers. She embraced him. She told him to visit her if he required earnest consolation. She told him he'd always been a real favorite of hers. Herman Marshall nodded. He said he appreciated the thought. She smiled a little. She nodded. She disengaged herself from him and walked to the coffin and frowned down at Edna's corpse. This was one of the two Slumberviewing Rooms at T. C. Drucker & Sons. A quiet scattering of people stood around and chatted. Most of these people touched their noses and tugged at their chins, as though perhaps they needed to reassure themselves that they were palpable, capable of knowledge and farts and laughter and serious thought. Edna lay in a gray coffin that was banked with wreaths and sprays, and most of the wreaths and sprays were in yellows and reds. She'd always considered yellows and reds to be her best colors. The wreaths and sprays stank, or at least Herman Marshall thought so. And since he was the one who was paying for this goddamn . . . *presentation* . . . or whatever it was . . . he figured he had a *right* to call a stink a stink, if he was of a mind. He stood to one side of Edna's coffin. She was wearing a gray dress that had a lace collar and lace cuffs. The gray dress went well with the gray coffin. Jobeth Stephenson had pointed this out to Herman Marshall when they'd gone through the bidness of choosing the coffin. And he had nodded. Good old Jobeth. Edna's hands were folded over her belly, and someone . . . an undertaker or an embalmer or one of them female *cosmeticians* who worked for T. C. Drucker & Sons . . . had polished her wedding ring. It glittered and winked. It was so *alive* down there. It was like some sort of relentless and emptily cheerful fucking Christmas decoration. Herman Marshall slowly moved his head from side to side. He told himself it was necessary to think of something else. He blinked at Edna's dress. Edna had put that dress together from scratch. She always had had a gift for sewing, and she had created that dress after Dr Moomaw had told them of the cancer. She had smiled, and she had called it a proper old woman's dress. *It's all full of, um, givin up*, she'd said. And Herman Marshall had said: *What?* And Edna had said: *On account of at's the way I sewed it. Which means I've gave up. Every stitch says give up, give up. But at's all right. Everbody gives up. Sooner or later. Whenever.* And then Edna had smiled at her husband. *But don't worry none*, she'd said. *I expect, what with one thing an another, I'm sort of ready, you know?* And she had made a shushing sound, while at the same time waving off his words before he had been able to say them. And now, for the goddamn life of him, he couldn't remember what they would have been. Which meant, he supposed, they wouldn't have been much. He leaned on one leg and then on the other. Edna had asked him to think of blood, and he *had* been thinking of blood. He even had tried to talk her only remaining blood relative—Eugene Coffee, the college professor who taught now on the English faculty at the University of Pittsburgh—into

[140]

coming down for the funeral. It had taken Herman Marshall several hours to track down old Eugene through various Information operators and whatnot, and Eugene's voice had been resonant and courteous, but Eugene had said: *I really am sorry, Uncle Herman, but I am weeks behind on a paper I must write for the MLA, and I gave my word, you know.* And Herman Marshall had said: *Gave your word? GAVE YOUR WORD? You're her one an only blood relation an how many times you figure she's goin to die?* And Eugene Coffee had said: *I'm really very sorry.* And Herman Marshall had said: *Yessir. You're sorry, all right. You're sorry like puke is sorry. You gave your word. You gave your word to somethin called the BVD or whatever.* And Herman Marshall had been shaking. He couldn't understand why he'd dragged himself through such a rage. He couldn't understand why at the close of the conversation he had said to Eugene Coffee: *If you don't come, you shithead, you asshole, if you don't COME HERE AN SHOW THE WORLD SHE'S GOT BLOOD KIN, en air ain't really no way nobody's goin to know she's left more behind her an goddamn . . . goddamn . . . empty dresses . . . an maybe flowers growin in the back yard.* And Herman Marshall had wept. He had been doing a lot of weeping. He had been doing too much weeping. He remembered an old Gene Autry movie, and its title had been *Texans Don't Cry.* And there was truth to that, by God. He'd always considered himself to be more or less a real good old Texas boy, but lately he'd given way to too many tears; he'd been behaving like a weepy old steer in a slaughterhouse, and the people with the clubs and the knives were within sight. And he had hung up on Eugene Fucking Coffee without saying anything more. And he, Herman Marshall, the good old boy who still wore boots and jeans and an *ASTROS* cap and never mind his seventyfour years, had leaned against a wall and had wailed into the wallpaper. And had drooled. And had trembled. And had dropped to his knees. And

[141]

had prayed to whatever—maybe his God of Paradise, the sweet God the preachers never mentioned often ehough. And then Herman Marshall had snuffled and had stood up and had said to himself: I keep needin at goddamn *book*. We was behind that theayter, her an me, an at was the happiest night of my life, an so how come it all had to come down to this here? What the hell sort of road was it we came down? Came down. Come down. What a goddamn comedown. Sure, I had me a woman or two or six or ten or a dozen (me, Nig the Lover), an I blowed away a few Nawzis in my time, an I got to answer for Elsie an what happened to her, but did my *wife* have to go an *fuck* my *brother*? An did she have to do it on account of *blood* or whatever? How come, if blood is so important an Eugene is so smart, he ain't comin down here an doin the decent an respectful thing? And then Herman Marshall had shaken his head. And he still was shaking his head. And he swallowed. And people kept coming up to him and asking him how he was doing. In Texas, people always asked people how they were doing. Simply how they were doing. Not how they were doing *what*. People met in funeral homes, or they met at weddings, or they met in honkytonks and barbecue joints, and the call that went out was *how you doin, how you doin*. Herman Marshall wished he really could tell someone how he was doing, but he knew that was out of the question, and so he simply stood to one side and watched people walk to the coffin and thoughtfully stare down at Edna. And of course she was wearing a wig. One of the undertakers, a Mr Grizzard, had fitted her with the wig, and the wig had represented an extra hundred dollars on the Statement of Charges. Mr Grizzard had *flourished* the goddamn wig in front of Herman Marshall, and Mr Grizzard even had fluffed it out. It was a silvery blond, tight and precise as a swimming cap. It made Edna vaguely resemble a whorehouse madam. In no way did it suggest

what Edna's real hair had been like. In no way could it have ac-
commodated hairribbons. Herman Marshall figured he truly hated
that goddamn wig, and he was paying a hundred dollars for something he hated, and so why had he let that Mr Grizzard talk him
into buying it? And Jobeth had been there, and she'd gone right
along with Mr Grizzard, and there had been a smear of lipstick
on her uppers. She had nodded in time with Mr Grizzard's nods,
and she had hummed and had trilled when Mr Grizzard had fluffed
the thing. She even had pounded her dry old palms together. Good
old Jobeth, who probably had been a real good old Hot Ticket
back at the beginning of recorded time, ha ha. And now, thinking
back, all Herman Marshall could do was exhale and shrug. Then
nervous bald little Ike Sage from the Top of the World came up to
him. Ike wore a shiny black suit that was too large. His shirt was
frayed at the cuffs. It was a plaid shirt. An orange plaid. Herman
Marshall didn't recall ever having seen a man wear an orange plaid
shirt with a black suit, but what the hell. He shook hands with
Ike Sage, and Ike said: "How you doin?"

"Real fine," said Herman Marshall. "Maybe I'm a little tired . . .
but, you know . . ."

Ike touched his poor frayed cuffs. ". . . real sorry," he said.

"I thank you," said Herman Marshall. "An Edna would thank
you for bein here."

Ike glanced toward the coffin. "I seen her already. She looks real
nice."

"Not bad," said Herman Marshall.

"Pretty flowers."

"Yessir," said Herman Marshall.

"At spray we sent from the Top of the World, I think it looks
real nice. Tasteful."

"Yessir," said Herman Marshall. "A whole lot of things look

[143]

real nice. These here undertakers, they work real hard to make everthin just so, like maybe it's inspection time in basic trainin, you know?"

Ike Sage cleared his throat. He winced a little. He had a bum back, and he visited a chiropractor once a week, and he swore by the man. "I . . . well, I hear she didn't hurt too much . . ."

"She hurt a little," said Herman Marshall. Briefly he dug at the corner of an eye with a thumb. "Yessir," said Herman Marshall, blinking, "the doc done all he could, but I ain't goin to lie to you an tell you air wasn't no pain a tall. Air *was* pain, Ike. Air was *pain.*"

"Well . . ." said Ike, swallowing. He had been reaching behind himself and rubbing his sore back—but now, for some reason, he suddenly jammed his hands in his trouser pockets. Maybe he wanted to play with himself. It was hard to tell.

"Not a *whole lot* of pain," said Herman Marshall, "but *some . . .*"

"Well," said Ike, "I mean . . . well, pain ain't no fun, is it?"

"Not unless you got somethin wrong with you, like em fairies an people like at air."

"My mama died of the cancer," said Ike, "an at was all the way back in 19 an 25, an believe me, *she* was in *pain.* A good four years she had the cancer, maybe five. Cancer of the bowel. An air wasn't no drugs like they got today. Why, the way I hear it, em drugs just about make it *fun* to be sick. I hear they make you feel better than when you *ain't* sick."

". . . maybe so," said Herman Marshall.

"I mean, at's what I *hear,*" said Ike. His hands emerged from his trouser pockets. He squeezed one of Herman Marshall's arms. Weakly. Then: "Well, it's a long drive back to Pasadena, especially for an old fart like me . . ."

"Surely," said Herman Marshall. "I understand." And Herman

Marshall smiled a little. All day long he actually had been managing to smile a little. Jobeth Stephenson had told him it was necessary for him at least to *try* to smile a little. She'd told him it wouldn't be right, nor would it be manly, for folks to believe he'd fallen apart. A real man did not fall apart, Jobeth had said, and her wattled neck had flapped with an urgent tiny fierceness. And so Herman Marshall was smiling a little at everyone. He needed to stop all his goddamn bawling, and Jobeth had been correct, and maybe he'd real soon go exploring across his street and watch one of them jism and blowjob movies with her. Harry Munger once had referred to that sort of cable TV as Cornhole Theater, and everyone in the Top of the World had whinnied and had guffawed. But why was Herman Marshall thinking of that sort of thing *now*? Where was his respect? Godalmighty, what a pig he was. But he kept smiling at Ike Sage, and he displayed nothing. And Ike released Herman Marshall's arm. The squeeze of Ike's hand had been like something dead. Ike walked away. Herman Marshall noticed that the cuffs of Ike's trousers also were frayed. Herman Marshall plumped his plump nigger lips and sighed. Two of his old Gulfway Trucking pals, George McLean and Freddie Weaver, had come into this Slumberviewing Room while he'd been jawing with Ike Sage. George and Freddie were retired now, and they had been retired for years (George walked with a cane, and a detached retina had cost Freddie his left eye), but they made all the funerals, and now they were standing by Edna's coffin, and they were talking, and Herman Marshall was standing close enough to hear them. And they were talking about the goddamn weather . . .

"Hot enough for you?" said George.

"Too hot," said Freddie.

"Even for this time of the year," said George. He was squinting at Edna's face.

[145]

"I'm one of your basic native Houstonians," said Freddie, "plain an simple. But I ain't never got used to the goddamn heat. I mean, what with the goddamn bayous an all, the goddamn humidity . . ."

"Watch the old language air," said George.

"Oh," said Freddie. "Yeah. Sure."

"We got to think of respect," said George.

"Yes. Sure. Um, she don't look too bad, does she?"

"Wig an all," said George. "Even with it."

"Wig?"

"She's wearin a wig."

"Bullshit," said Freddie. "She ain't wearin no *wig*."

"I'll bet you any amount of money you'd care to name," said George. "I'll bet you a hunnert dollars, what you lost to me when you bet on Cincinnati in the Super Bowl back whenever it was. This here woman done died of cancer, an the medical people got a way of treatin cancer at takes away a person's hair. An en, when the time comes for the dyin, you got you a corpse at's like a . . . a billiard ball . . ."

Herman Marshall strode toward George and Freddie, but his steps were silent. He stood next to George and Freddie and stared down at Edna for a moment. Her face was illuminated by the white light from a tiny spot that had been fastened to the ceiling. Edna's cheeks had been stuffed with something. Maybe cotton. Certainly cotton seemed logical. Herman Marshall turned to George and nudged him sharply—twice. "George old buddy," said Herman Marshall, "you got it dead to rights." Another nudge, and George yelped a little. "She'd bald as a peeled twat. I should of let you bet old Freddie here. You'd of cleaned him out, an en maybe you would of shared some of your winnins with your old friend Herman Marshall here . . . I mean, seein as how this whole . . . *show* . . . is settin me back a whole lot . . . an seein as how I done paid to make Edna look like a movie star an all . . ."

George could not speak. He was bent forward and leaning on his cane and rubbing the places where Herman Marshall had nudged him. His breath came in strings and tatters.

Herman Marshall looked past George at Freddie Weaver.

Freddie Weaver quickly reached for Herman Marshall's hand and shook it and said: "How you doin?"

"Real good," said Herman Marshall, trembling. His jaw wobbled.

George McLean's eyebrows moved up and down, and he tried to swallow. ". . . Jesus H. Christ," he said, and he kept rubbing the places where Herman Marshall had nudged him.

"Never get a man mad at you when he's got sharp elbows," said Herman Marshall to George. And Herman Marshall patted one of George's shoulders. "It don't matter none," said Herman Marshall. "You an Freddie got a right to talk bout whatever you want to talk bout."

George stared down at the Slumberviewing Room carpeting. It was an oily green. He finally stopped rubbing himself. "I'm . . . I'm surely sorry," he said to Herman Marshall, and he held out a hand to Herman Marshall.

Herman Marshall shook hands with George.

"How you doin?" said George.

"Real good," said Herman Marshall, and most of his trembling had subsided. His eyes were warm, but otherwise he didn't feel all that terrible.

George still was staring down at the carpet, and the color of the carpet put Herman Marshall in mind of goose shit. "We was out of line, but . . . well, you know how it is, don't you?"

"Know how it is?" said Herman Marshall.

George nodded.

"Know how it *is?*" said Herman Marshall, and he leaned toward George and Freddie and hissed the words at them. "*Know* how it *is?* Who *says* I know how it is, huh? *You* two jaspers? I mean, you stand here an you talk bout her the way you just done, an *I'm* supposed to know how it *is*. Well, *shit*. I don't know how *nothin* is. All I know is she's the only wife I've ever done had, an she's dead, an she didn't die all at good, an her only blood relative ain't here on account of he can't be fuckin *bothered*, an he's blood of her blood, by God, but he's got somethin he's got to *write*, an his Aunt Edna can go piss on a stone, seein as how he don't give a fiddler's fart bout her, an so . . . well, an so *I'm* the one who's stuck with all this . . . this . . . whatever it is . . ." Now Herman Marshall was gasping, and maybe his voice had been too loud, even though he'd tried to keep it down to a hiss. He looked around. People still were chatting away. Ike Sage was talking with Jobeth, and they both were smiling, and maybe they were discussing jism movies. Hadn't Ike said something about needing to hurry home to Pasadena? Well, old Jobeth apparently had caused him to change his mind. And now he was gesticulating, and his orange shirt flared, and maybe he was telling her a joke. Or maybe he was telling her Herman Marshall was an asshole.

George spoke up. "Herman," he said, "me an Freddie, we're just plain straight out sorry." George was pale, and his face was shadowed.

"Amen . . ." said Freddie.

"People sometimes ain't got air right sense," said George.

"At's the truth," said Freddie.

Herman Marshall rubbed his enormous lips. He pinched his enormous lips. Then he abruptly took George and Freddie by their arms and steered them away from the coffin. They crossed the Slumberviewing Room to a sofa that was against a far wall. Herman Marshall sat down, and he motioned to George and Freddie to sit down with him. The two old men grunted as they sat down,

[148]

and one of George's knees cracked. Herman Marshall smiled at George and Freddie and said: "All right, you two old boogers, where's the book?"

"Book?" said George.

"What book?" said Freddie.

Herman Marshall sighed. "The *book*," he said. "The book at tells us what we're supposed to do an what we ain't supposed to do. An I don't mean no *Bible*. I mean the *book*, the *real* book. The book at spells it all out. Over air. Look over air. See at old man who's talkin an wavin his arms with at old woman? His name is Ike Sage, an I drink with him, an it's all like a big old *party* for him, ain't it? But at's all right. I know the feelin too. I've done gone to a whole lot of viewins in my day, an I done my share of talkin an carryin on. But did at mean I didn't have no respect? I don't think so. When I done talked an carried on, it was because I was *alive*, wasn't it? I'm talkin a whole lot, ain't I? But en I used to talk a whole lot. When I was a boy. But I ain't been a boy for a long time. Ha. Well, anyway, all I'm tryin to say is what the hell, the livin got a right to go on livin. I think I read at in some newspaper. *The livin got a right to go on livin*—yes *sir*. You bet your ass. Or maybe somebody oncet said at in some picture show I seen. A man never knows what things will stick with him, ain't at so? Oh, I hurt. Billy's dead, too. You member Billy? He's been dead longer an shit. Makes me hurt to think bout him. Layin out air in the graveyard, an now he's waitin for his mama, an he wasn't but seventeen when he left us, an he was blood of Edna's blood . . . an, um, blood of *my* blood . . . an where's the book at tells a person how to make even an ittybitty piece of sense out of it? If we don't leave blood behind, maybe we don't leave nothin behind. I really believe at. An so at . . . at *college professor* . . . you think he'd take the time to come down here? Bull *shit*. An so . . . I mean . . . if

[149]

you two want to talk about Edna's wig, so what? So what, huh? The livin go on livin, an they got to talk bout *somethin*, right? An it ain't so bad to talk bout Edna's wig. Air could be worse things. So don't you boys get all tore up. I was wrong to be aggravated up air when we was standin at her coffin. I was *wrong*. Nothin matters to her. Surely the *wig* don't matter. I mean, what the fuck. It's all *clocks*, boys, an the world goes around, an ain't nobody written no book tellin us *This* is *This* an *At* is *At* an layin it out all clear so even dumb peckerwood shits like *us* can parse it out. So I don't want yall to—"

"No," said George McLean and he was poking at his eyes.

"What?" said Herman Marshall. His throat was numb, swollen.

George's voice was dry, exhausted. "I never met your wife," he said to Herman Marshall. "I . . . here I am, like this . . . I don't guess I know how to figure out much of it, but I expect the life you an your missus had . . . well, it couldn't of been *too* bad . . . on account of you, Herman, you an the way you talk . . . you sure do grab holt of things, don't you?"

"I ain't so much . . ." said Herman Marshall. "Shit, I ain't hardly nothin a tall . . ."

"At's what *you* think," said George. He tugged a large red handkerchief from a hip pocket. He unfolded the handkerchief, dabbed at his eyes, blew his nose. "Hey," he said, "I sure enough been bawlin, ain't I? Some big mean old Texas boy *I* am." He shook his head. "Hoo *boy*," he said.

"An amen again," said Freddie, whose face was red and damp.

Herman Marshall didn't know what to say, and so he said nothing. He didn't really know why he'd said what he *had* said. But one thing was for sure—he'd said enough. After all, he was a Texas boy every bit as much as George was a Texas boy. The Hope, Arkansas, thing was just a little old technicality. Herman Marshall was a *Texas* boy, and Texas boys kept themselves tough and protected at all times. The thing to do was, well, think of Tom Mix. The thing to do was, well, remember *Riders of the Purple Sage* and a particular squint. The world could learn things from that squint. Maybe it even could learn how not to weep. The squint . . . the eyes . . . the annihilatingly erect torso (oh Lord, would Billy's torso have been like that if the meningitis hadn't come sashaying along?) . . . Jesus, such a man that Tom Mix had been when it had come down to the sure and unbending definition of things . . . *all* things, from horseflesh and bank robbers to the Lord's Commandments. What a way to be. Great day in the morning and little fishes, that Tom Mix had been a *man*. And Tom Mix never had wept. And Tom Mix never had bent himself out of kilter because of *blood*. Why, that would have been filth, death. So why then had Herman Marshall caved in? Why had he said so much to George and Freddie? Why these moist eyes, this swollen throat? And why had George and Freddie been so affected? What was happening to the world as Herman Marshall had been defining it for so many years? Herman Marshall stood up. He nodded briefly down to George and Freddie. There was no other information that could be exchanged between the three of them. He walked to Edna's coffin and shook hands with a neighbor named Zack Fears.

"How you doin?" said Zack Fears, who had a paralyzed left leg and stood on crutches.

"Hoo *boy*," said Herman Marshall.

"I hear you," said Zack Fears, and he teetered on his crutches.

CHAPTER TWELVE

HERMAN MARSHALL BECAME stupid pissyass drunk the night before Edna was buried, and he remained stupid pissyass drunk clear through her funeral and after. The drinking began when a few people dropped by the house. Harry and Beth. Jobeth Stephenson. Of course Jobeth Stephenson. What would that goddamn funeral have *been* without Jobeth Stephenson? And poor crippled paralyzed Zack Fears was there. And Ralph Danielson, the retired policeman from the Top of the World. He stopped in because he wanted to be goddamn sure Herman Marshall would remain tough. He told Herman Marshall he'd lost two wives of his own to the Grim Reaper (and Herman Marshall nodded; yeah, yeah, he knew all about the two wives Ralph Danielson had lost to the Grim Reaper; one of the wives had been killed in a car wreck on the Gulf Freeway; the other had succumbed to some sort of blood disorder), and Ralph Danielson allowed as how nothing was easy in this here world, but a real man never let the bastards get him down. There was a spread of ham and barbecue and potato salad and white bread on the diningroom table, and Ralph Danielson helped himself. The guests had brought whisky and beer. In deference to Herman Marshall, all the beer was Shiner. Zack Fears sat in an easychair, and his paralyzed leg was outstretched. The brass bed had been stripped by Jobeth Stephenson, and she had pushed it into a corner of the room where it wouldn't be underfoot. Harry and Beth drank J. W. Dickel sourmash. Beth still looked pretty good. The braces really had helped her mouth. She no longer appeared able to kiss a man through a bobwahr fence.

Herman Marshall wondered how old she was. She'd never told him. He supposed she had to be fiftyfive, but she appeared to be about fortyfive. Her body was trim, but it had love handles here and there, and for years Herman Marshall had speculated about her, even though she was a friend's wife and it probably wasn't decent to speculate about a friend's wife. But what the hell, a little speculating didn't do all *that* much damage, did it? He smiled a little . . . inside, where no one saw the smile. Jobeth Stephenson came to him and told him he looked all dragged out. He shrugged. He was holding a Shiner longneck, and he sucked on it. He patted one of Jobeth's shoulders and told her he *was* all dragged out. Jobeth was wearing a burgandy dress that showed the tops of her tits, and they were wrinkled. She smiled. She patted one of Herman Marshall's arms. Then she pushed past him, and one of her hands brushed against his fly. Herman Marshall sighed. He seated himself on the davenport with Harry and Beth. They asked him how he was doing. He crossed his legs. He frowned. He drank. Beth started to say something, but he held up a hand. "I'm thinkin on it," he said. He squeezed the longneck. Harry and Beth were drinking their J. W. Dickel straight, with just a little ice. And then Herman Marshall said: "I believe I'm doin real good. An I'll keep on doin real good—long as this here Shiner holds out." And Herman Marshall grunted. And Beth smiled at him and told him Edna really was better off, and could he deny that? Herman Marshall shrugged. He said he really didn't know what *life* was like when a person was *dead*, ha ha. Harry and Beth frowned. Jobeth squeezed onto the sofa with them. Her wrinkled tits flabbed. She told Herman Marshall he had held up so *well* throughout the viewing, and she was so *proud* of him. She smiled, and her lipstick moved in various directions. It was some lipstick. It appeared . . . slippery. She fetched and carried Shiner longnecks for Herman Marshall, and he made frequent staggery trips to the bathroom. The bathroom kept feeling smaller and smaller, and its lights were too bright. He sat on an arm of Zack Fears' chair, and Zack said: "You won't hear *me* sayin she's better off. None of at shit'll come from *my* mouth. I'm just an old crip, an I move like a pile of sticks, but I still get a sort of a kick out of the new day, by God. An the warmth. Even the goddamn *Houston* warmth. Folks who say other folks are better off dead, what do *they* know bout it? What do they know bout *anythin*? What do they know bout *dead*? You know, Herman, I was a car inspector for the Katy for the better part of thirtyfive years, an then I got me my nightwatchman's job —remember the nightwatchman's job, an I'd walk past this here place six nights a week with my lunch in a little old paper bag, an I got to carry a goddamn .38 Police Special? Well, at was *work*, an it was *good*, an it was a way of showin I was *alive*. An at the car inspector job . . . they made me feel like I was doin more an fillin space. An even *now* . . . now at I'm a crip an ain't worth cow flop . . . I'd rather be breathin an not breathin, you know?" And Zack Fears was gasping a little. At the same time, though, he was smiling. He was holding a glass of Corby's and Coke, and his lips and tongue worked gently at it. Herman Marshall sat for awhile in the diningroom with the food, and he breathed mustard and barbecue. He hoped all the food would be eaten. There was nothing worse than stale barbecue. Edna always had thrown stale barbecue out with the garbage, and she had been a wonderful barbecue cook. Herman Marshall breathed the barbecue and remembered Edna's barbecue, and then for a time his tongue was furry and his skull ached. He told himself not to remember Edna's barbecue. He told himself he needed to be a man. He told himself he needed to remember Jobeth's advice. He didn't want to make another scene the way he had made the scene with George McLean

[155]

and Freddie Weaver back in that Slumberviewing Room at T. C. Drucker & Sons. He stood up and wandered through the house. Several other neighbors showed up. Charlie and Harriet Newell, who originally were from Connecticut and who kept cats. The Bailey brothers, Tom and Dick, bachelors who drove Metro buses and saved every nickel they had and took annual vacations in Europe. Fred Palmer, a fat fellow, twice widowed, whose wives had been dead who knew how many years said to Herman Marshall: "Don't rush nothin. Don't accept too fast. Do whatever comes natural, an never you mind what nobody says." Herman Marshall nodded. He and Fred Palmer were standing in the diningroom, and Fred was demolishing an enormous ham sandwich, and mustard squished from it and streaked Fred Palmer's shirtfront. A little later Herman Marshall seated himself next to Harriet Newell, and she told him he needed a nice pussycat to keep him company. (Jobeth, who was standing behind Harriet's chair, grimaced.) Harry came to Herman Marshall and told him he'd better take it easy with the Shiner. "You're fixin to have you one hell of a hangover tomorrow mornin," said Harry, and he lightly punched one of Herman Marshall's arms. Then, smiling, Harry said: "It's goin to be a big day. An air's no gettin away from *at*, is air?" Herman Marshall stepped back. Herman Marshall's eyes were all hot and blurred. He brought up a hand in a chopping movement. He turned away from Harry. He wanted to say something to Harry about two suitcases and a case of mistaken identity, and ha ha, hadn't it all been a goddamn hoot though? But he didn't quite know what the point of such words would have been. What did they have to do with this funeral or whatever it was? What did they have to do with some woman's distate for stale barbecue? Ah, and what was her name again? Yes. Her name. The thing to do was concentrate on her name. Either she had sucked the cock of a Mex or she hadn't sucked the cock of a Mex. Yessir. Real smart. And either the sun rose in the east or it didn't rise in the east. Herman Marshall flopped down on the stairs that led up to the bathroom and his bedroom, and Jobeth brought him a Shiner, and he thought of his mother and his father, and he remembered how deeply his mother had worried about his father's health, and of course his father, who had died in 1973, had outlived his mother by two years, and Herman Marshall had survived *their* funerals without getting drunk, but he didn't really remember what either of them had looked like, and he blinked, and he drank, and he went upstairs to the bathroom and pissed half on the floor and half in the commode, and the bathroom lights were warm and somehow they made his flesh all watery, and his cock became entangled in his zipper, and piss dribbled, and Jobeth came into the bathroom and said there, there, lover, you just hold *on* now, and gently she freed his cock and tucked it in and zipped him up, and he tried to call her Florence Nightingale, only it came out Horance Flightingale, and she giggled. They went downstairs, and Ralph Danielson's body floated past, and Ralph Danielson's head floated past, and Ralph Danielson said: "How you doin?" And Herman Marshall said: "How *you* doin, you old fuck?" And Ralph Danielson made loose growling sounds. And Harry came to Ralph Danielson and said to him: "Hold on now . . . old Herman's got kind of a snootful, you know?" And Herman Marshall flopped on the floor in front of Zack Fears the crip and said to Zack Fears the crip: "I member you an your niwatchmn's job an your paper sack an all . . . an it was like you was on a *mission* . . . an you able made it to me I slept better all long night you good old fart you amcn an hallelujah an let the angels sing . . ." And someone seized Herman Marshall by the armpits and pulled him to his feet and led him to the kitchen and gave him a cup of black coffee, and his forehead hurt, and he

[157]

was aware of Jobeth's wrinkled tits, and she said: "You're only a man, an a man's got to get drunk ever now an again, ain't that so?" And Herman Marshall sat at the kitchen table and tried to drink the coffee but it was too hot. And then Jobeth smiled at him and handed him a Shiner and kissed him lightly on the mouth, and he drank the Shiner, and Harry and Beth came into the kitchen and told Jobeth she was a terrible old woman. And Zack Fears called out from the front room was he missing anything. Herman Marshall briefly remembered his father's funeral, and a mockingbird had been singing. He remembered nothing from his mother's funeral. He remembered a whole lot from Billy's funeral, and the name of that machine had been *ILES*. Harry and Beth stood in the kitchen and stared at Herman Marshall and sipped at their good old J. W. Dickel. The *ILES* had had a mouth, and the mouth had had fangs. Fucking *fangs*. Herman Marshall shuddered. He wanted to visit every graveyard in every country in the whole shitkicking *world* and kill every *ILES* the way he had killed Nawzis. Herman Marshall sucked Shiner. Fred Palmer sat down at the table with him, and Fred Palmer was a fat blot, and Fred Palmer said: "She had a whole lot of friends. Air's goin to be a real big turnout tomorrow. You just wait. My Shirley didn't have too many friends, but my *Marilyn* . . . well, what with her Eastern Star an all, an the VFW Auxiliary, an the Daughters of the Confederacy, old Marilyn packed em in, boy . . . packed em in . . . the undertaker told me he hadn't had to handle so many folks in three, four years . . . not since he'd buried some councilman or preacher or somebody like at air. Which made me real proud of Marilyn . . . oh, she'd been sort of a pain in the ass most of the years I'd been buried to her . . . I mean, ha ha, *married* to her . . . little slip of the tongue air, ha ha . . . she'd been, yessir, a pain in the ass most of the time, a real sort of a *hemorrhoid*, you know? But she surely did pack em in at her funeral. You'd of thought somebody was givin away pussy, ha ha. Yessir . . . pussy . . ." And Fred Palmer's eyes waggled and danced, and Jobeth Stephenson came to him and leaned over him and told him he was just *awful*. And Fred Palmer grinned loosely and said: "Too bad. I mean, in my day I was pretty *good*, the ladies used to say. Some of em, anyhow . . ." Snorting, Jobeth spoke across the table to Herman Marshall, telling him it was past midnight, and maybe it was about time he had him a little snooze. She told Herman Marshall she would draw his bath for him. She told him she would put clean sheets on his bed and turn them down for him. Herman Marshall frowned. He was thinking about what Fred Palmer had said about the Eastern Star and the VFW Auxiliary and the Daughters of the Confederacy and all *that*. Edna never had been much for the Eastern Star and the VFW Auxiliary and the Daughters of the Confederacy and all *that*. She always had preferred to stay home and sew a fine seam, or bake a birthday cake, or simply sit with her husband and talk of Hope, Arkansas, and a certain vacant lot behind a certain movie theayter in the great metropolis of Shreveport, Louisiana. Fred Palmer again was speaking, but Herman Marshall couldn't quite follow Fred Palmer's words. There was too much light. Had the Lord turned up the wattage? Was the Lord trying to seek something out? Was there truth in this kitchen? Was the book hidden in this kitchen? Herman Marshall belched. His bowels rumbled. The guests began leaving. Harry and Beth helped Zack Fears up the street to his house. Herman Marshall stood on the porch and leaned against a pillar and watched them. He waved at Harry and Beth's car when it pulled away from the curb. Beth leaned out a window and waved and grinned, and her smile was perfect. The very universe would have been proud, by God, to have had such a smile. Ralph Danielson came to Herman Marshall and nudged him and said:

"See you in the mornin. An member, boy—the thing you got to do is tough her out." And then Ralph Danielson was gone. And Fred Palmer was gone. And the Newells were gone. And the Bailey brothers were gone. And Herman Marshall collapsed on the sofa in the front room, and Jobeth primly seated herself next to him and handed him a Shiner and told him he had a whole long life ahead of him yet and she didn't want him to worry about a thing; she always would make herself available to him, and his slightest wish was her command, and the truth was she'd had a crush on him for more years than she wanted to remember, and maybe she was *old*, but it didn't mean she was *dead*, tee hee, and then she hesitated and cleared her throat and shook her head and shrugged a little and told Herman Marshall she meant no disrespect to Edna, and Herman Marshall said to her (speaking earnestly, carefully choosing his words and working up his thoughts): "You fine I yes it's clear disrespect well of never I could you no give intentions you well at you know I think sure it's true as a straight ditch on a country road an the peckers is in the air she was fat an she tried to talk us all into votin for Landrum Alf Landrum an we laughed an my daddy had a mockinbird or maybe it was my mama old dresses an purses well of no can't won't wouldn't be real smart to keep em the reminder would maybe you know sure enough be a killer yes sir I mean ma'am." And Herman Marshall drank the Shiner, and his belly was sour, and he said: "Sometimes unirate hunnerite urinate *piss* just sort of pops poppin piss you know from me." And Jobeth cuddled against Herman Marshall and said: "You dear man. This here is heaven." And Herman Marshall said: "But who what where I mean what if I go an pass my watle er water?" And Jobeth said: "Sh. Yes. Sh. You're my baby, an nothin nasty's fixin to happen, an you got my word on it." She kissed Herman Marshall's cheeks and his mouth. She tugged him to his feet. She

[160]

told him she wanted him to go across the street with her. She told him there was plenty of Shiner in her fridge, and she'd bought it for him that afternoon, and they would sit real comfy in her front room and watch a nice loving movie on her cable TV. Herman Marshall tried to shake his head no. He tried to tell Jobeth there was something wrong with watching a nice loving movie on her cable TV. He tried to tell her it maybe wasn't appropriate. But all he managed to say was: "Edna bad look no can't who would people say you know?" And Jobeth said: "Oh, bull roar, Herman Marshall." And she pulled him to his feet and more or less danced him out the front door and across the street. She told him she had been telling the truth when she'd promised to draw his bath and turn down his bedsheets, but that could wait for a little bit, couldn't it? And she helped Herman Marshall sit on her davenport, and it was a flowered davenport, and it reminded him a little of the flowered davenport he and Edna once had owned, and that flowered davenport had been important, but he couldn't quite remember why, and he figured maybe that was just as well. Jobeth squatted in front of her TV set and switched it on and fiddled with the fine tuning, and then this naked nigger was squatting over a naked white girl, and he was jacking off all over her naked tits, and she was making faces and licking his jism. "Jesus H. Golfballs," said Herman Marshall, and Jobeth giggled. She crossed the room to him and told him she didn't care *what* he thought; she was fixing to sit on his lap. Which she did. And she kissed Herman Marshall on the mouth and opened her withered tits to him. And she told him she was just as natural and human as the next person. And that nigger kept jacking off and jacking off, and he had a hose on him that could have whipped a horse to death. Jobeth forced Herman Marshall's face against her sorry tits. She told him she had been drinking gin, and gin always had put her in a real friendly mood, oh sweet baby,

Jobeth loves you. Herman Marshall nuzzled Jobeth, and his nig-
gery lips flapped, and two blond women were licking each other's
cunts on the TV, and one of the blond women was wearing a black
garterbelt, and Herman Marshall's cock swelled, and Jobeth unzipped his fly and squeezed his cock, and she set to work jacking
him off, and she told him she didn't really want anything for *herself*;
all she *really* wanted was to make *him* happy, and her palms were
callused, but at the same time they did create a certain friction, and
Herman Marshall groaned, and the two TV women went lap, lap,
lap, and music came from something that maybe was a clarinet,
and the TV women went diddle, diddle, diddle, and Herman Marshall closed his eyes and briefly saw that fine and fancy lady from
the Rice Hotel, and abruptly he released a watery little wad into
Jobeth's hand, and she smiled at him and slowly raised the hand to
her mouth and extended her tongue and licked the hand clean, and
the nigger joined the two women and fucked the garterbelted one
in the ass. Jobeth snickered and spoke of true love. She told Herman Marshall he had been such a wonderful *man* here in his hour
of personal tragedy. She sighed. Briefly she worked at her nipples
with her thumbs. Then she jammed Herman Marshall's face against
her bosom and told him to *suck* and *lick*; it was the *least* he could
do. And after a time he was home again, and he was standing naked
under the shower, and the water was hot, and he winced, and
Jobeth was standing with him, and she was embracing him, and
her body was all spotted and wrinkled and bent (her flesh had the
shape and texture of the flesh of turtles, of jowly hound dogs, of
weary politicians), and she whispered to him, and he was holding a
Shiner longneck, and he drank from it on account of he didn't
want the beer to be diluted by the showerwater. And then, blinking, he lay flat in his bed, and Jobeth was at the foot of the bed, and
she had pressed a cheek against his cock, and he said: "No always

from now on too like I say an like to be clear too old no I preciate it but well you no not no more." And he heard birds, and they were loud birds; the sound of them carried over the sound of the airconditioning, and a hot shadowed morning rolled in from the Gulf, and Jobeth kept trying to milk and diddle Herman Marshall's prick, and she said: "I ain't been so happy since maybe never." And shyly she licked his limp cock, and briefly he was reminded of that woman, that Gloria or Diana or whatever her name was, who had licked Milt Willis' balls. If you cared to believe Milt Willis. Beautiful Gloria or Diana from the Plymouth Rock. Jesus. Herman Marshall had two Shiners and a slice of burnt toast for his breakfast. Jobeth had fixed the toast for him, and she had to scrape it with a knife. "I . . . I am a real bad girl," she said. "All I ever do is run after pleasurin myself. I can't even put a piece of bread in a toaster an have it come out right. A woman my age, an all she does is try to pleasure herself. She ought to be ashamed of herself . . ." A pause, then: "But she *ain't*. No *sir* . . ." And Jobeth allowed herself a dry cackle. She laid out his funeral clothes for him. He kept lurching into the bathroom and pissing, and sometimes he pissed in the commode, and sometimes he pissed on the floor, and once he pissed in the bathtub. Jobeth dressed him and tied his tie for him. The sun rolled across the sky like a balloon, and Jobeth said: "Goin to be a nice day." And Herman Marshall said: "He was her cousin. No. He was her *nephew*. Her blood kin. Her only blood kin. But he wouldn't come down here. He was too *busy*. He was too *important*. His shit smells like per fuckin fume." And then Herman Marshall's mind and tongue again became confused and witless, and he said: "No respect ain't got he fat brat selfish who knows where nothin comes from no more where's the book tell me speak explain ahhh fuck you." Jobeth went across the street to put on a fresh dress for the funeral, and Herman Marshall sat in the bathroom and drank

[163]

Shiner and breathed the odor of his own pissing. And every so often he would stand up and try to piss in the commode, and sometimes he did, and sometimes he didn't. He leaned against the mirror that was over the washbasin, and he kept brushing his teeth because he didn't want anyone at the funeral to know he had been drinking. He leaned so heavily against the mirror that he left vivid handprints, and they picked up all the lines on his palms, and he kept looking at the handprints; he could not take his eyes off the handprints; he blinked at them and he even sort of sniffed at them. They told him as much about himself as any photograph would have. Maybe they told him more. Jobeth returned, and she was wearing a black dress and patentleather pumps, and she helped Herman Marshall downstairs, and he lurched into the kitchen and popped open a Shiner, and he and Jobeth sat in the kitchen, and noisily he sucked at the longneck, and she said: "I don't care what *nobody* says. I mean, *I* say you're *entitled*." She was painting her fingernails and holding her fingers to the light and squinting at them and blowing on them. "If a little beer gets a man through a bad day," she said, "en a little beer it ought to be—ain't at so, honey?" Harry and Beth picked them up at ten o'clock that morning, and Harry's green Camaro had been washed, and it gleamed. Herman Marshall sat in the back seat with Jobeth, and Beth frowned at Jobeth, and Jobeth's fingernails were as bright as the Camaro was. Herman Marshall belched, and trees whisked past. Beth said something about the odor of beer, and she waggled a finger in Jobeth's direction, but Herman Marshall couldn't quite figure out what was being said. It was as though Beth and Jobeth were hollering at one another at the far end of a tunnel. And hollering they were, and why did their names have to be Beth and *Jobeth*? Weren't there already enough confusions? They were met at T. C. Drucker & Sons by Mr Grizzard, the undertaker who had sold the wig to

[164]

Herman Marshall. Mr Grizzard had a flunky park the car, and Herman Marshall and Jobeth and Harry and Beth were ushered to seats in the front row of the Slumberviewing Room. Edna's coffin still was open and Herman Marshall went to it and leaned against it and vaguely he needed to piss and he studied her wig and he turned around and said to Mr Grizzard: "Pretty." He staggered from the Slumberviewing Room and had himself a substantial piss just before the funeral service began. Mr Grizzard stood in the men's room with Herman Marshall and held one of Herman Marshall's arms and Herman Marshall wished to fuck he had a Shiner. Mr Grizzard steered him back to the Slumberviewing Room and a fat man came to Herman Marshall and, whispering, said to Herman Marshall: "I'm Eugene, Uncle Herman." And squeezed Herman Marshall's right hand. And said: "I was wrong." And this Eugene's face was gray and a trifle blotched, like the face of the moon. And this Eugene tried to smile, but nothing much came of it, and so he turned away and went to a vacant chair next to Harry Munger and sat down and the chair squealed. Herman Marshall looked around, and maybe forty persons were on hand. He recognized all of them, and he tried to smile at them, and he wondered about his breath. Quiet music was playing, and the minister was large and thick, and he was some sort of jackleg Baptist who had been hired by T. C. Drucker & Sons, and Herman Marshall never had caught the name (Herman Marshall and Edna hadn't been inside a church since the day of Billy's funeral), and this here minister or windbag or whatever he was said: "In the midst of life." And: "The spirit of Edna Marshall has survived, as all spirits survive." And said: "We petition the Lord to grant her peace." And said: "May the hope of glory comfort our brother Herman Marshall." And smiled in Herman Marshall's direction. And Herman Marshall needed to piss. Next to him, *Jobeth* squeezed his hand, and *Beth* frowned. Herman

[165]

Marshall spoke rather loudly while the minister was uttering a prayer having to do with the Lamb of God, and Herman Marshall said: "Maybe she wasn't perfect, but why did she have to *hurt* so much? I mean . . . *shit*." And then a hand was clapped over Herman Marshall's mouth, and the hand was Harry's, and the minister shrugged and coughed. Ralph Danielson and Harry and Frank Lee Doubleday and George McLean and the Bailey brothers were the pallbearers, and they wheeled Edna's coffin from that place at a brisk clip. Herman Marshall and Jobeth and the fat one, the nephew whose name was Eugene, rode to the cemetery in a T. C. Drucker & Sons limousine that was personally driven by Mr Grizzard, and at one point, as the procession was arriving at the cemetery, Mr Grizzard said: "She was very lovely, an I do believe the wig was a positive factor." Herman Marshall's bladder was hot. There had been a dry spell, and the cemetery grass was a sort of babyshit brown, and sprinklers were slowly spraying water in pale languid arcs. Herman Marshall belched and wobbled when he emerged from the limousine. Mr Grizzard and Eugene braced him, and Jobeth kept patting his hands and his arms. He watched the pallbearers carry the coffin to the edge of the grave, and the grave was surrounded by artificial grass, and it was inside a tent, and the urge to piss was so strong it almost made Herman Marshall's hot old cock actually want to *sing*, and he listened to the sprinklers, and the minister spoke, and he listened to the sprinklers, and he listened to the sprinklers, the *sprinklers*, and finally he pulled himself to his feet and went careening out of that tent and he unzipped his fly and emptied himself on the headstone of someone named *LAMAR* and Mr Grizzard came pounding after him and Mr Grizzard was trying to smile and Herman Marshall said to himself: I expect air's somethin a whole lot real wrong. And maybe then Herman Marshall almost laughed.

CHAPTER THIRTEEN

THE FAT NEPHEW'S FULL NAME originally had been Alexander Eugene Coffee. He was born on July 27, 1932, and Herbert Hoover was President of the United States, and Alexander Coffee grew up to be an enthusiastic liberal, and he was a dues-paying member of Common Cause and the Americans for Democratic Action, and he did not like to be reminded that he had been born when the glum Hoover had been sitting in the White House. In 1953 Alexander had his name legally changed to Eugene Alexander Coffee because he was weary of being called Smart Alex all the time—just because he wasn't afraid of doing well in school. Ah, dear God, the cruel blundering snobbery of the ignorant . . .

Now then, this Alexander/Eugene Coffee was born fat and he lived fat. His mother was fond of telling him that as a baby he had looked like Churchill. Well, what the hell. A great many babies looked like Churchill. And a great many babies looked like Eisenhower. Everyone knew that. But then his mother always had been a great one for underscoring the obvious. In so doing, she often was able to layer away Alexander/Eugene's pride. And at the same time she kept feeding him more and more starches. Puddings and pies and . . . stuff. She told him it was her way of showing him how deeply she loved him. He sometimes thought of this when he stood in the shower and was unable to see his feet. (His mother often called him weak. She often said he was unable to resist temptation. And she told him he often displayed bad manners. She was fond of telling him of the time when he'd been two years of age and he's gotten to squalling during the wedding of his Aunt Edna and his Uncle Herman, and he'd squalled so loudly that he'd nearly disrupted the wedding. *Oh, I was so EMBARRASSED*, said Mrs Coffee. *You'll never know how embarrassed I was.* And so of course, as the proverbial night came chugging along in pursuit of the proverbial day, he had hated his mother.)

One day Eugene's second wife said to him: *You are a real case.* Her name was Beryl. She was the only Beryl he'd ever known, and of course he'd had to go and marry her. *You put it all on your mother*, said Beryl, who was a child psychologist and clearly knew about such matters. *You won't take responsibility for your own behavior. You ought to be ashamed of yourself.*

Eugene Coffee looked away from this Beryl. *But I didn't really want to eat so much*, he said. *At least not at first.* He folded his hands in his lap—what there was of it.

God, you're so WEAK, said Beryl.

Which maybe is why you married me, said Eugene Coffee.

Beryl was sucking on a Marlboro. She exhaled smoke. It appeared as though grit and cinders were swirling around her head. She snubbed out the Marlboro in a brass ashtray that was shaped like a toilet bowl. The ashtray had been a Christmas gift from a brother who drank too much and often smoked bananas. This man was the only true bananasmoker Eugene Coffee ever had met.

I wish I knew, REALLY knew, why you married me, said Eugene Coffee to Beryl.

That makes two of us, said Beryl. *It's not as though I was desperate. It's not as though I was the dog's dinner then, and it's not as though I'm the dog's dinner now. It's not as though people PUKE and SWOON just from looking at me. And, well, my breasts have been widely admired . . .*

· *Yes*, said Eugene Coffee. *I suppose so.* He blinked at Beryl's breasts. They were sharp; they were belligerently upthrust.

It wasn't desperation, said Beryl. *No. Not that. Not that at all.*

You married me, said Eugene, *because I am easy to push around.*

Beryl grinned, and the grin made her appear to be sucking broken glass. *Easy to push around?* she said. *Well, all right. But only in an abstract sense, Fatso.*

Eugene didn't say anything. That particular conversation with Beryl took place in 1974 or perhaps 1975, when Eugene was in his middle forties and weighed perhaps two hundred sixty pounds. And he was barely five feet, nine inches tall. Which meant that when he sat down he seldom missed the chair. But then so what. He'd always been that way. When he had been a kid and he had attended the Hough Elementary School in Cleveland, Ohio, his peers had called him the Human Garbage Can. He had eaten just about everything except the paint off the walls. He cadged goose-liver sandwiches. He would have tapdanced for a fig newton. He was his parents' only child, and his mother kept feeding him and *feeding* him. Maybe she believed he was in danger of being carried off into the sky by a strong wind. If he didn't put away three helpings of everything except the kitchen tablecloth, she would toss a small pinched pout in his direction and tell him he hated her cooking and accuse him of being a snotty ingrate. And Eugene's father . . . a tall and declamatory man who made his living selling insurance and resembled a jaundiced and vaguely dissolute Pat O'Brien . . . would glare at Eugene and accuse Eugene of being a stupid pig. Which didn't make an awful lot of sense to Eugene, seeing as how his mother forever just about tried to *cram* food down his throat. (This sort of treatment was of course the stuff ax murderers were made of, but Eugene never had the heart or the balls for that sort of thing, and it was a failing he wholeheartedly regretted.)

Eugene gnawed and belched his way through Hough Elementary School, Addison Junior High School and East High School, and he plumped out, one might say, and his face exploded with acne, and he even developed warts on his palms, and one night his father came home drunk and stumbled into Eugene's bedroom and said to him: *Why don't you straighten up and fly right, boy? You got to get HOLD of yourself. And I don't mean jacking off.* A laugh. Brief. Wet. Astonished. Then: *I think about you. I talk with my friends about you. I tell them you're decent. I tell them you got a good heart. I really do.*

Eugene covered his face. He squeezed his pits and his pustules. He had been dreaming about one of his teachers at East High. Her name was Miss Goldfarb, and she taught English, and she had real big globes, and sometimes her nipples popped when she walked in a draft, and she had been kneeling in front of Eugene in the dream, and gently she had been asking him whether there was anything she could do to comfort him. And she had smiled up at him. A terrific smile, quavery and subservient. A perfect smile when a fellow was having that particular sort of dream.

And then Eugene's father got to punching him about the belly. No, Eugene's father really didn't do that at all. Rather, he got to *shoving* Eugene's belly, to *kneading* it. And he grunted. And his breath made Eugene grimace. And after a time he said: *Son, you . . . why do you have to . . . oh, shit . . . I mean, I keep wondering about your . . . your . . . God damn it, your PRIDE . . .*

Eugene began to whimper. His eyes were full of knives and nails.

One of Eugene's father's palms slapped Eugene's belly, and Eugene's belly flabbed and rolled.

Eugene squeezed his face.

You make people look away, said his father.

Eugene's head moved from side to side.

You make them want to dig a hole, said his father. *You make them want to leave the room, take a powder, scram, hit the road . . . I don't know what all . . .*

Eugene drooled against his palms.

His father squeezed Eugene's belly and said: *Too bad you're not a fucking toothpaste tube. I'd tear you open and squeeze it out of you ... all the fucking fat, you fatass you ... you walk like you got a corncob stuck up your fatass ASS, you know that? You walk like you're sitting on a bicycle, only somebody stole the bicycle, you follow what I'm trying to say?*

Eugene tried to nod. Maybe he succeeded. He didn't really know.

And the thing is, said his father, hesitating. . . . *the thing IS . . . I love you. I mean, tonight when I was over at the Avon Bar and Tommy Humphries and Bill Salso and Joe O'Brien and the rest of them were asking me was it true you had to stay in the middle of the house on account of if you stood in a CORNER or OFF TO ONE SIDE, the house would tip over ... oh, it was all good clean fun, only it HURT me, you know? And the thought occurred to me: Jesus Christ, if that sort of talk hurt ME, what did it do to YOU? And so now here I am, and you got an answer for my question?*

Eugene could not speak. He was altogether too occupied with whimpering, with squeezing his face.

His father waited.

Eugene tried to shrug. Perhaps he even tried to form a syllable. That was the extent, though, of whatever it was.

His father gave Eugene's belly a final slap, but the slap was soft and defeated. It glanced off Eugene's wretched foul flesh, and there was no pain. His father grunted. His father's bones and joints seemed to crunch together. His father sighed. *Yeah,* said Eugene Coffee's father. *Yeah. Right. The only answer is no answer. Right.*

Eugene's hands came away from his face. His eyes came open. He blinked. He swiped at a patch of drool at a corner of his mouth. His eyes were open because of his father's voice. It just then had sounded as though it had been dragged through a dead place.

Now Eugene's father was standing at the door. Hands linked in front of his crotch, Eugene's father blinked down at the floor and said: *I'm sorry.* The man was whispering . . . or at least he was close to whispering, since his voice was hardly much more than a sound of sand in a flat dish. And he said: *It's all . . . bullshit. You are what you are, and if you get hurt . . . well, that's none of my goddamn beeswax, is it?*

Eugene managed to say something. He said: *Dad . . .*

Eugene's father shrugged. He unlinked his hands. He waved away the sound of Eugene's voice, dismissing Eugene's single tentative word as though he were warding off a gnat or a moth. *I'm at fault,* he said. *I'M the one.*

. . . no.

Eugene's father wrenched open the door. *What do YOU know about anything?* he said. And then he was gone, and the door slammed.

Eugene winced. Eugene rolled on his belly and created a great mound and jammed shut his eyes and tried to bring back the image of Miss Goldfarb. He was a little hungry.

He never forgot such encounters as that one. He never forgot much of anything. He liked to say he was full of knowledge and memory—as well as full of shit—but he had little wisdom, and maybe he had no wisdom at all. (After all, would a wise man have bothered to change his name—an act that beggared the question, right?) He tried to write everything down. He liked to keep lists. He had a complete list of all the women with whom he had had sex. The total came to seven, and it included three prostitutes and both his wives. (One of the prostitutes had resembled Shirley Temple, *circa* 1949, and she had had tattooed buttocks, and he often thought of her. He had been with her only once, and she had pounded him with her fists and had called him Good Old Rolypoly, and he had told her okay, fine, if it makes you happy. And she had laughed. And she had had a gold tooth that had glinted. And she had told him he was a fucking *piece* of *work*.) He also kept a journal, and here is the entry for Friday, November 22, 1963, when he still was married to his first wife, whose name was Trudy:

I forgot to pick up the cleaning this afternoon, and Trudy yelled at me. I told her the news from Dallas must have affected me. She said: "Well, it hasn't affected ME. I'm a Republican." And then she said: "We're still going to the football game Sunday, aren't we?" And I said: "Will there be a football game?" And Trudy said: "Why shouldn't there be?" She rushed out to the cleaners. The car's tires and brakes shrieked and carried on. Priss came to me, and her little bottom was wet, and she wept. The assassination bulletins had preempted Heckle & Jeckle, and Walter Cronkite's jowls were grieving. I kissed my daughter's sweet red hair. I told her the world sometimes was a terrible place, and I told her people sometimes were . . . unkind. I told her sometimes all of us had to be brave and all of us had to sacrifice things. I tried to explain what the President's sacrifice had been, but my voice gave way. Priss asked me would her mother and I be sacrificing the football game. I said no, I didn't believe so. She asked me why she had to sacrifice Heckle & Jeckle but her mother and I didn't have to sacrifice the football game. She told me that dumb old Walter Cronkite was BORING. I could say nothing to her, and a little later she wept and wept and wept and wept some more.

(Poor Priss. In 1984 she was married to an orthodontist, and she had no children, and her best friend was a woman named Eleanor LeBay. Priss was only twentynine in 1984, and Eleanor LeBay was forty or so, and the two of them liked to giggle and gossip and have their hair frosted. Priss' husband's name was Ben Lichtenstein, and he was sixty, and he often told Eugene how amused and delighted he was by sweet Priss, and sometimes he fondly referred to her as Mrs Stepford. Priss and Lichtenstein lived in Cos Cob,

Connecticut, and their home faced Long Island Sound. Each time Eugene Coffee visited them, her hair was a different color. He was reasonably certain she watched Saturday morning television cartoons. Maybe, for all he knew, Eleanor LeBay joined her, and they fluffed their hair and drank Bosco.)

The football game, incidentally, indeed was played. The Cleveland Browns defeated the Dallas Cowboys, 27-17, on Sunday, November 24, 1963, the day Ruby killed Oswald. A large crowd was on hand at Cleveland Municipal Stadium. After all, would staying home have brought back the dead? Eugene Coffee and Trudy had good seats in the upper deck. Trudy had freckled arms, and she was . . . sturdy. She preferred her steak so rare it just about screamed (her phrase), and she lifted weights, and she liked to shout. She and Eugene Coffee were divorced in 1968, and she received full custody of Priss, who was the only child by the marriage. Eugene went out and became drunk the night the decree was granted. He was an English instructor at Cleveland State in those days, and he walked into a place called Pat Joyce's and drank Chivas Regal and talked with the bartender, whose name was LaRue and who hailed from Georgia or Alabama or some such place. Eugene felt as though his chest cavity had been scooped out. He knew he should have been exultant, but he simply felt as though his chest cavity had been scooped out, and there really was nothing more to be said concerning how he goddamn *felt*. He explained this to LaRue, and LaRue said: *Shit. It ain't no worse an a bad cold. At air Chivas. It'll act like penicillin.* And Eugene said: *You think so?* And LaRue said: *I don't THINK so. I by God KNOW so.* And Eugene said: *That would be nice.* And LaRue said: *En relax, boy. Be happy. Tell me. You happy right now?* And Eugene said: *Yes. Of course.* And LaRue said: *You sure enough don't SOUND happy. You sound like you don't know what you're doin. You sound like you're here*

[174]

on account of you don't know where else to be. *An you don't even look comfortable.* And Eugene said: *What?* And LaRue said: *With at air Chivas, the way you're sort of HANGIN ONTO it. An the way you're hunched forward. You're goin to hurt your spine. Which wouldn't be NO way to celebrate a divorce.* And Eugene nodded. And he began speaking, and his voice began to balloon, and he said: *You know, what the hell, maybe it's not right to CELEBRATE a DIVORCE. Trudy and I . . . there were good times. She had a lot of energy. Still does. One night the bed collapsed. She was on top. She was riding the horsie, and the horsie was a big fat horsie named me, and Trudy and I were slipping and sliding and pounding and grunting, and then the frame went all to splinters, you know? The FRAME. The WHOLE FRAME. And the casters rolled across the room, and you want to know something?* A significant pause, and Eugene smiled. And LaRue said: *You an her, you didn't miss a stroke.* And LaRue did some smiling of his own. He had a benevolent smile. It was all blue lips and scrambled yellow teeth. And Eugene said: *How'd you know?* And LaRue said: *Man came in here last week. Told me the same story. An the endin was the same—he hadn't missed a stroke. So I just now figured, well, maybe it was the same with you.* And Eugene said: *Well, it was special to us.* And LaRue said: *Good.* And Eugene said: *I really want to get drunk.* And LaRue said: *I expect at can be arranged.* And Eugene said: *That makes me seem weak, doesn't it?* And LaRue said. *Weak, SHIT. Nothin wrong with drinkin. Keeps people like you an me off the street-corners an out of the motherfuckin poolhalls. An besides, I like listenin to my customers an air talk. I nod a whole lot when they talk. An I sort of tug at my chin. Makes me seem wise like a wise old owl. An I make real low grumbly sounds in the back of my throat. UMMMMM. UMMMMM. Makes me sound like a goddamn one of em Mills Brothers. UMMMMM. UMMMMM.* And Eugene smiled. And LaRue poured him many drinks. Eugene awakened the next morning in his own bed, and he had no idea how he had gotten there. He never returned to Pat Joyce's, and so he never spoke with LaRue. He was afraid he might have embarrassed himself.

His divorce from Trudy (the court allowed him to visit Priss twice a month, and Priss almost always was bored and sometimes downright cranky and sleepy, forever staring away from him with dull opaque eyes) gave him three years of a second bachelorhood, but in his view those three years didn't amount to much. Here is his journal entry for Friday, July 3, 1970:

> I have phonograph records and television, and I have books. But today is too hot for phonograph records and television and books. I am sitting at a cardtable in front of the airconditioner, and I am listening to traffic, and the planet is beating a path across the river and through the woods to Grandmother's place we shall go, tra la, but all I have is phonograph records, television, books. I am thinking today of my Aunt Edna and my Uncle Herman down in Texas. I seldom think of them. I see them as being unremarkable. And yet today I am thinking of them. What will they do tomorrow when there is a holiday and the world will stand back because of the sound of fireworks? Will they slaughter a calf and barbecue it and invite all the neighbors for a great feast? Will Uncle Herman slit the calf's throat? I seem to recall that he killed Germans several wars back. I've never seen Uncle Herman. I only know him from a few snapshots. Isn't that strange? Aunt Edna, yes . . . I've seen HER. I remember when she came up here with little Billy back in '50 or '51. And now he is dead of spinal meningitis, and I did not attend the funeral. God, I would settle for a funeral today. It would be something to do.

He met Beryl at a faculty party in the fall of that year, 1970, and they were married the following spring. She was lanky, and her pointed breasts indeed were admired. She had narrow hips, and she looked sensational in jeans, and she knew it. She read nothing except books on child psychology, and she never attended movies, plays, concerts. There were entire weeks when she would not speak to Eugene, and he never knew why. He wanted to ask her, but he never quite had the nerve. His mother died of a cerebral hemorrhage in August of 1972, and Aunt Edna came up from Houston for the funeral and said to Eugene: *Me an Herman, we'd sure enough like to have you come see us one of these here days.* And Beryl, who was standing next to Eugene, sighed and glanced at her fingernails. And Aunt Edna appeared to blush. Uncle Herman wasn't with her because, well, Uncle Herman every now and again had a touch of the old rheumatizz, and the old rheumatizz could be painful, especially for a man of his age. He was getting up there, and in three years he would be retiring from Gulfway Trucking, and it wouldn't be a moment too soon, what with the awful traffic and the long hauls. *He just ain't gettin his proper sleep*, said Aunt Edna, *an I sure enough worry about him a lot.* And Aunt Edna shook her head. She was short and round, and she made circular movements with her hands, and it almost was as though she were trying to make herself rise from the earth. She had remarkably beautiful hair, long and lush, almost indecent. She had it done up with pins and small tortoiseshell combs. In Eugene's view, most women twenty years younger than Aunt Edna would have killed for such hair. That night, after the services, he commented on this to Beryl, and she said: *How can you talk that way? Do you have some sort of offthewall Oedipal fixation on your poor old dumpy Texas auntie?* And Eugene didn't answer. He walked into the kitchen and fixed himself a gin and tonic, and he told himself a gin and tonic was the greatest drink in the world for a fellow who was thirsty on an August evening. He pushed away what Beryl had said. Christ's sake, he had to consider the source, didn't he? They were divorced in 1976 after he found her in bed one afternoon with an Army

[177]

recruiting sergeant who had short hair and a prominent jaw. The recruiting sergeant was fucking Beryl smack between her pointed tits, and Eugene actually said to Beryl and the sergeant as they stared up at him: *Oh, I beg your pardon.*

So much for marriage, as far as Eugene Coffee was concerned. By then he had tenure at the University of Pittsburgh, where his specialty was the Modern American Novel. He had an associate professorship in the English department, and for three years he had sex twice a week with a graduate assistant named Leora Flagg. She was a blonde, but she wore her hair in a thin Little Dutch Boy cut, and she always seemed a trifle androgynous to Eugene. She wrote dreadful poems and dedicated them to him and sent them to him by Internal Mail. Many of the poems had to do with how splendid she believed his penis to be. Finally he said to her: *For God's sake, please stop gilding a not very impressive lily.* And Leora, whose field was Spenser, said to him: *But I love you.* And she rooted at his fly. And she jerked him and sucked him, and she told him he always was so . . . courteous. She always wore heavy skirts and argyle kneesocks and lumpy shapeless sweaters, and her armpits and crotch gave off astringent odors, but any port in a storm, any port in a storm. He took her to England with him in 1978, the year of his sabbatical. They lived in a cottage in Cornwall, and he wrote a book having to do with an overview of the various generations of *New Yorker* writers, including O'Hara, Cheever, Salinger, Updike and Barthelme. It was favorably received by the *New York Times*, although the reviewer did say that Eugene's prose style often was stiff. He fucked Leora the afternoon he read the review, and he laughed and said: *Stiff? STIFF? I'll show them STIFF, God damn it!* And Leora smiled and told him he actually was being downright Falstaffian, and it became him. But Eugene quickly subsided. *No*, he said, *I don't have that much style, and it's foolish to try to create one.* Leora kept asking him to marry her, but he told her no. He told her he probably loved her, but two marriages down the drain were enough for a lifetime. She told him she would try to wear more attractive clothing. She told him she would do up her hair so it would be more sexy. She told him she would be all things to him, whenever he wanted them. And he said: *You're better off with Spenser. I don't mean to sound harsh, but you're too young for me and, well, I would be . . . taxed.* And Leora wept. She spoke about her childhood, and he already knew all *about* her childhood, but he heard her out. *They tried to be nice,* she said, *or at least some of them did. The thing about an orphanage is the luck of the draw. You can draw good people who'll try to take care of you, or you can draw bad people who either don't care or actually come after you with . . . meanness. I don't know who my parents were. I'll never know. I was found in a trash barrel. I probably was conceived in the back seat of an old Studebaker. But anyway . . . there I was, and I'd been tucked in with all the OTHER trash that God knows always has been plentiful in such a place as Scranton, Pennsylvania, which is not exactly your average hotbed of style and culture, don't you know, old chap. And this little piece of trash you see here before you was chucked off into an institution that was full of nuns. And it was full of shit. We mustn't forget the shit. We must NEVER forget the shit. And Father McGreevey said to me: You read a great deal, don't you? And I said to Father McGreevey: Yes, Father McGreevey, I like to read almost as much as I like to give myself the Finger of Love. And quickly he slapped me. And his face became all red and veiny. And he said something to the effect that he was sure I would fry in hell. And I nodded. I believe I was reading Dante. Someone passionate and therefore innocent. At any rate, I spent eighteen years in that place, and we sang Christmas carols in shopping malls, and everyone had a soft sentimental smile for us, and we all were the Little Match Girl, and for two Christmas seasons I was a bellringer instead of a singer of*

[179]

carols, which made for a neat contrast and livened up my Little Match Girl days. I ate oatmeal every morning for the first eighteen years of my life, and once a week some people would visit from the K of C and show Disney movies or maybe The Song of Bernadette, *and a few of the nuns occasionally would look at some of us with what I can only call a bizarre intensity, and MORE than a few of them really seemed to enjoy spanking us with rulers that sometimes would whine and whistle as they cut through the air. I never slept alone in a room until I was nineteen and out of that place. I lost my virginity by fucking five Phi Deke pledges in seventeen minutes. Oh, Eugene, God damn you, don't tell me what I'd be better off without. I have nothing NOW, don't you understand? You're the first person, thing or animal I've ever loved. EVER. So please don't speak to me about things you have no way of understanding. So come on now. I want you to eat my pussy.* And Leora Flagg lay back and spread her legs, and Eugene obliged her, and she was astringent. And then he held her, and they both wept, and he told her no, no, there was no future to any of this. And finally Leora nodded and got dressed. She smiled. She nodded. *Yes,* she said. *All right.* Her words were clipped. They were without moisture. The next night she wrapped a garterbelt around her neck and hanged herself from a light fixture on a wall of her apartment.

CHAPTER FOURTEEN

L EORA FLAGG LEFT NO NOTE, and of course Eugene Coffee grieved, but he also was a trifle irritated. After all, if she could write all that bad poetry about his penis, why couldn't she be bothered to write a suicide note? And he supposed there was a great deal of vulgar symbolism in the fact that she'd hanged herself with a *garterbelt*. But what had she *wanted* from him? After all, hadn't he obliged her that final time by eating her pussy? All right, so love and marriage and all that nonsense had been out of the question. Why had she felt it necessary to punish him *that* severely? She was buried in a Catholic cemetery in Scranton, and a Rev Fr Paul X. McGreevey officiated. He flung holywater this way and that, and he spoke all the prayers in English. Eugene wanted to ask this Father McGreevey if Leora really had been so snippy and impious as to speak to a *priest* of the Finger of Love, but maybe she hadn't, and Eugene liked to think she had, and so he didn't ask the question, for fear of hearing the wrong answer. He also wanted to ask Father McGreevey how she had come to be named Leora Flagg, seeing as how she'd had no name at birth. Couldn't a more graceful name have been chosen by whoever was in charge of such matters? But, again, Eugene said nothing. Maybe this Father Mc-Greevey was in charge of such matters, and maybe the fellow would have taken offense. So Eugene remained silent, and he bowed his head, and it was a chilly day for early September, and he said to himself: It's a good thing these people somehow have managed to distort the truth and make her death appear to be an accident. Catholics are skillful at that sort of thing, I suspect. There he is, the priest, all muttery and humble, and he is burying a *suicide*, and that sort of thing is beyond the pale, isn't it? I swear, most of those priests could teach us all lessons in expedient secularism. No wonder so many of them drink. And Eugene sighed, gnawed his lips, twisted the brim of his hat. Questions, questions, questions . . . an orphan who had a dumpy body and looked like the Little Dutch Boy, why should she have mattered? why should this priest have agreed to ignore her suicide? did he believe the truth would bring a bad name to his fucking orphanage with its oatmeal and its staring nuns? Eugene had no idea where the truth lay. He supposed the truth ultimately was unimportant, but his *curiosity* had some value, didn't it? Ah, shit, when push came to shove, Leora probably was nothing more than another of his tormentors, another of those people who found it amusing or gratifying to humiliate him. They had been everywhere all his life. Everywhere. They poked open the wallpaper and jumped out at him. Two of them even had married him. They stuck out their heavy booted feet and tripped him and watched old Fatso bounce on the sidewalk and listened to old Fatso's girlish weepings, and it all was an absolute *gas*, and how come he couldn't take a joke, huh? It all had begun back in Cleveland, at Hough Elementary and Addison Junior High and East High. (All three of those buildings, incidentally, eventually were razed. The neighborhood abruptly had gone black, and it hadn't been long before everything had fallen down. More or less. What was that sort of thing called? The urban imperative? Contemporary inexorability, considering the path of history? Eugene Coffee invariably snorted whenever he got to thinking along such lines. He said to himself: Christ's sake, what am I dragging through my skull? He said to himself: I am as profound as a sheep waiting to have its throat slit, and its eyes are swiveling, and its outraged bleatings and bellowings collide with the dull bloody walls of the

[182]

abbatoir, and *who gives a fuck*?) Well, anyway, back to the tormentings that were inflicted upon Eugene Alexander Coffee, who in
those days was known as Alexander Eugene Coffee, Smart Alex
the Fatass. There were plenty of the tormentings, and he remembered them all, and sometimes he would write about them in his
journal. But at the same time enormous chunks of the calendar had
vanished from his memory, even though he believed he had rather
a good memory. But what then had happened to the year 1944, for
example? He had no coherent memory of anything that had happened to him in 1944. What then *had* happened in 1944? It was the
year he had turned twelve, and he'd already entered puberty (*that*
much he did remember), but at the same time he could not recall a
single breath, laugh, odor or moment of grief from that entire
goddamned year. Oh, there was a war, and his mother received
occasional letters having to do with Uncle Herman and Uncle
Herman's service in the Army, and on the homefront people drove
rattletrap cars, and Errol Flynn was fearless, and everyone was
urged to buy War Bonds, but there were no *specifics* to 1944 for
Eugene Coffee. They'd all been gobbled up, spat out, farted, permitted to creep away and curl and die. The thing was, did Eugene
Coffee not once breathe perfume in the year 1944? Did he not once
stand at home plate and spit on his hands and seize somebody's old
cracked Louisville Slugger and smack the old pill over the center-
fielder's head and go flabbing and huffing around the bases?
Damned if he could remember. Did it matter? You bet your ass it
mattered. The thing was, what else did we have? And yet Eugene
Coffee, known then as Smart Alex Coffee, the Fatass Pillar of
Fretful Suet, ho ho, ha ha, always had to wince whenever he
tried to gather together the events that had governed his life.
Eugene Coffee, he of the precise memory, ha ha. Eugene Coffee,
he who kept a journal, ha ha and *ha*. But the *humiliations* flourished.

[183]

His memory of them. East High then, and he was a good student (his specialties were history and English; bravely he poked his way through Dickens and Poe and *Arrowsmith*; bravely he lumbered to the stage at assemblies and accepted awards for writing), but he was a complete washout when it came to gym, for example, and it was there that his tormentors really climbed all over him. They called him Tits. And one afternoon a guy named Harry Sternad came to Eugene as Eugene sat in the locker room and breathed odors of sweat and footbath and dirty socks. And Harry Sternad was holding what appeared to be a fried fish sandwich. And Harry Sternad leaned against Eugene. And he told Eugene he really admired Eugene's ability to eat so much. Harry Sternad was a tackle on the East High football team, and he jammed one of Eugene's shoulders against a locker, and Eugene could not move. Harry Sternad began eating the fish sandwich. He told Eugene he just bet Eugene would like to have a warm meal, wouldn't Eugene, good old Eugene, this hotshot Eugene who would eat dog shit if it was decorated with fucking *parsley*, and wasn't that so? And Harry Sternad chewed the fish sandwich. And spoke of good old Tits Coffee . . . yeah, good old Tits Coffee and his *food*. Ha ha ha. And several other football players appeared, and they gathered in a semicircle behind the munching Harry Sternad. Who took large bites of the fish sandwich. Who chewed on those large bites until they were a pale beige mush. Who then spat on Eugene. Who then spat on Eugene's hair. Who then spat in Eugene's face. Eugene tried to cover his head, but Harry Sternad was too strong for him. The other football players laughed and danced. Eugene began to weep and drool, and the mush from Harry Sternad's mouth made Eugene gag. Harry Sternad made an amused reference to Niagara Falls, and he compared Eugene's fucking sissy tears with Niagara Falls, and the football players got to guffawing and backslapping, and finally

Eugene fell forward and vomited, and everyone went away happy, and Eugene heard one of the football players say he had nipples like Farmer Brown's prize goddamn blueribbon cow. Eugene embraced himself. His vomit spread on the floor. One of the football players returned and kicked Eugene flat on the floor and rubbed Eugene's face in the vomit. Eugene's eyes were clotted with puke, and so he never knew which of the football players it had been. Finally Eugene was able to stand up. He waddled to the shower room. Of course he still was weeping. He turned on the *HOT* spigot, and he let the water run hot, then hotter, then hotter than hot. He never had stood under water that was so hot. It blinded him, and his flesh . . . all of it, every flaccid foot, yard, acre, mile . . . turned crimson. He held his breath. He kept splashing the hot water in his face and his hair. He shook his head. He did indeed have breasts, and he stroked them. Then he whacked them. He stood there and scalded himself and he barely could see, what with all the steam, and busily he whacked his tits. And of course he still was weeping. Of course. He squealed as well. His flesh began to pound and throb and blister from all the hot water, and finally he switched off the *HOT* spigot. He returned to the locker room, and promptly he began to shiver. He had forgotten to bring his gym towel, and so he dried himself with his underwear. It stank. His arms and his buttocks were all pink and blistered. He hoped his father never would find out about any of this. He figured he knew what his father would say, and he really didn't want to hear it. His throat stung from vomit. He glanced down at his tits and gave them a brisk and brief valedictory whacking. The following Saturday afternoon he took a regional examination, competitive as hell, for a Harvard scholarship. There were thirty participants, and they were gathered together in a musty empty classroom at John Hay High School. Most of the other guys appeared to be Jewish. Most

[185]

of them wore glasses. Most of them had large noses. Some of them appeared to be friends, and they addressed one another by their first names, and they wished one another luck. Many of them wore light sweaters that were decorated with marching deer. Eugene came in first. He beat them all. He was not Jewish, and he did not even own a sweater that was decorated with marching deer, but he beat every one of those motherfuckers. They assumed themselves to be the Future Geniuses of America, and Fatso Smart Alex Coffee had demolished them. He floated through the whole goddamned thing. Not even the Spatial Relationships section set him back. In those days, an easy school chore was known as a pipe. Well, that day the Spatial Relationships section was a pipe. Even that. And as for the Essay section . . . well, he raped it. He threw it to the floor and showed it who was Boss. It was a brief autobiography, and he sailed through it like a goddamn canoe drifting across a pond layered with lilypads. He was careful with the words, but at the same time he was relaxed. By then he was saying to himself: Fuck those Mockies with their deer sweaters. And he even sprinkled a bit of humor through his little autobiography, and he laced the humor with snippets of selfdeprecatory bullshit: *I may not be much, but I have to live with whatever I am, and so I'll not surrender.* His grammar and his punctuation were without fault, and he knew this. He wished Harry Sternad and the rest of those football players could see him *now*. This was *his* game. He grinned. He sucked his pencil. He wrote. And he flattened all the Jewboys and all the other Smart-asses in that room. He was only sixteen, and his victory was important to him beyond anything. He had skipped a year and a half in school, which meant he already was a senior at East High. His mother took him to the Hotel Statler to be interviewed by some guy from Harvard. The guy's name was Willender, and the three of them met in Willender's room. The wallpaper was decorated with brown urns from which ominous vines sprouted. Willender kept blinking in the general direction of Eugene's belly. Perhaps Willender never had seen such a belly. Eugene kept smiling at him. Eugene and Willender spoke of Whitman and the Shenandoah campaigns of T. J. Jackson. Every so often Willender would press his upper teeth with his thumbs. Eugene wanted to ask him why a Harvard representative didn't have better false teeth. Eugene's mother's flesh appeared oily. She surely wasn't getting any thinner. Maybe she was stealing from Eugene's plate, har de har har. She kept nodding. She probably would have kept nodding no matter what—even if Eugene and Willender had leapt to their feet, had stripped raw, had waved their wizzles at her and had told her in no uncertain terms that the moon was made of whale shit. Eugene received a halftuition scholarship to Harvard. It was a wonder his mother didn't send for photographers and notify the Associated Press. She settled for feeding Eugene a majestic dinner of meatloaf, mashed potatoes, lima beans and chocolate cake. She told him he was the family's hope, its beacon. Eugene chewed. Eugene gulped. Eugene nodded. His father sat loosely across the table from Eugene and thoughtfully drank Erin Brew beer from a tankard that had been a present from a police prosecutor friend. The tankard was made of heavy china, and it carried the legend: *HOLY WATER.* The police prosecutor had been Irish, and Holy Water was a rude euphemism often employed by certain of the Irish. A rude euphemism for Guinness, as an example, or Harp Lager, as another. And after a time Eugene's father said to him: *You have brought us great pride. Even I, the old tosspot, will acknowledge that. Even I. Of all people. Even I.* And Eugene's father drank dry the *HOLY WATER* tankard. And idly strolled to the refrigerator and refilled the *HOLY WATER* tankard, even though his wife said to him: *You'd better be careful, Jack. You know what the doctor says.* And Eugene's father

[187]

came strolling back to the table . . . it was a shame he didn't have a cane and a top hat . . . and said to Eugene's mother: *Frankly, my dear, I don't give a damn.* And, surprisingly, Eugene's mother briefly laughed, and then she said: *And frankly, my dear, you're not Clark Gable, and I'm not Vivien Leigh.* And then both of Eugene's parents laughed, and he laughed right along with them, seeing as how there never had been much real laughter in that family. It was such a small family, for one thing. Eugene's father had been an only child, and his mother had only the one sister, Aunt Edna, who lived down in Texas. And in that year of 1948 Aunt Edna and Uncle Herman had no children. Which meant the family, such as it was, probably wouldn't have filled a broom closet. Eugene sometimes wondered what his life would have been like if he'd had brothers and sisters. Maybe he wouldn't have been so fat. And surely he wouldn't have been such a puker and weeper. It was something to think about, all right. Eugene rode to Boston in a New York Central daycoach. All the male passengers wore hats that had large brims . . . 1948 was a good year for large brims. Eugene had enough money so that he was able to eat in the diner. He was waited on by darkies who had moist purple gums. The darkies called him *sah,* and one of them allowed as how he didn't look like the sort of young gemmums who too often, you know, missed a meal. Eugene smiled. He rubbed his belly and told the darky *yes, you speak the truth.* Briefly Eugene embraced his chest and therefore his tits, but he told himself it was necessary that he take things in stride. He said to himself: *I may not be much, but I have to live with whatever I am, and so I'll not surrender.* He covered his mouth so no one would see him smiling, and one of the darkies came along and asked him was there somethin wrong with the food, sah. And so Eugene quickly attacked the food. It was a slice of roast pork, and it was served with new parsley potatoes and applesauce. Eugene never forgot that meal. He could not remember one fucking event from the entire fucking year of 1944, but he always remembered that slice of roast pork, those new potatoes, this blot of applesauce. And he always remembered that particular brisk railroad day, and the fields and woods and little cities were smashed and battered by sunlight and unexpected whisking shadows. Well, maybe he always remembered that brisk railroad day because it marked the beginning of something he valued—namely, his Harvard years. He received his bachelor of arts degree, *summa cum laude*, in just three years. He had two majors, English literature and American history, and he wrote a number of papers that were adjudged to be excellent. He had two poems and a story published in the *Advocate*. The story had to do with the suicide of a football player who had made a crucial fumble in a crucial game, with his parents and brothers and sisters sitting in the grandstand. It was a controlled story, almost a rigid story, but the *Advocate*'s editors admired its discipline. Eugene began keeping his journal shortly after the story was published. Here is the entry for Monday, April 24, 1950:

> I despair of ever losing weight, but it occurs to me that I none-theless can command respect. People still come up to me about the story. Norm Fensterwald today told me it should be mailed to every football coach in the Big Ten. And little Lily Noonan, from Radcliffe, stopped me on Mass Avenue right in front of the Hayes Bickford's and said: "I had no idea you felt so deeply about things. A man who writes such a story is a man who has a bone to pick with Motherhood and Apple Pie, and I can admire such a man. Really I can." And, smiling, little Lily walked away from me, and she twitched and switched her ass at me, and could that mean anything? I don't suppose so, but where's the harm in hoping? Has my girth condemned me to a life circumscribed to an area occupied only by whores

and wet dreams and masturbation? (Does the previous sentence make any sense? I am using too many words. God damn it, I want to be a fat man who writes lean prose! That would be a real accomplishment, by God, and perhaps it would divert attention from my waistline.)

Eugene was correct in his assessment of little Lily Noonan's behavior. The twitching and the switching of her ass meant nothing. A week later he asked her to attend a showing of Welles' *Macbeth* with him, and she told him there was a fellow from Dartmouth, and she'd promised the fellow she wouldn't . . . well, surely Eugene understood. And of course Eugene understood. Eugene always understood. This immense Eugene, who sometimes caused chairs to collapse. So he concentrated on his studies, and he attended summer school. He continued to write well. One of his pieces, published in the *Northeastern Historical Journal*, was a witty and perceptive speculation on what might have happened at Chancellorsville if the porch pillar hadn't struck Fighting Joe Hooker on his head. Eugene received thirty dollars for the article, and he spent the money on a whore he picked up in Scollay Square. She had red hair, and she said her name was Eunice, and she complained because she said his prick was too small and his goddamn potbelly kept getting in the way, you dumb fuck you. So Eugene mostly concentrated on masturbation. He lived in a place called Hollingsworth Hall, and he had two roommates. One was an Italian; the other was a Jew. The Italian told Eugene he shouldn't jack off so much. *We don't want the building to fall off its foundation, do we?* said the Italian, whose name was Guido Cesco. *And who the hell ever will have the goddamn nerve to shake hands with you?* And Guido Cesco laughed, slugged Eugene lightly in the belly, told him it was like slugging tapioca in the belly, then danced hotly from the room, grinning and scraping. Eugene's other roommate, Murray Bernstein, the Jew, was a little guy with prematurely thinning hair, and he was from Lexington, Kentucky, and he seldom spoke of Eugene's masturbatory habits. This probably was because he whacked his whang just as often as Eugene did . . . and maybe more often. Eugene once interrupted Murray while he (Murray) was doing himself in tandem with reading aloud from *Tropic of Cancer*. He (Murray) was sprawled in an old easychair, and he had dropped his pants and his shorts, and his legs were bony and bluish, and he was muttering over the book as he jerked his prick. Eugene had been to the library, and his arms were full of books, and he dropped them. Guido Cesco became a lawyer in New York City and died in 1978 of congestive heart failure. Murray Bernstein took over his father's chain of shoe stores and still was going strong in 1984. He contributed lengthy essays to the annual classbook, and he had become a father of nine—by five wives. He and Eugene occasionally corresponded, and Eugene often congratulated him (Murray) on his (Murray's) stamina. Eugene took his master's at Harvard (his thesis was on John Dos Passos & the Trap of Omnipotence) and his PhD at Yale (his dissertation was a study of Slavery & Fiction: Prelude to Conflict), and he taught at Brown, Case Western Reserve and then Pittsburgh. He wrote a dozen or so stories that were declined by the *New Yorker*, and he submitted them noplace else. He married Trudy, and then he married Beryl, and they shared the sentiments of that Scollay Square whore—they complained about the smallness of his prick and they complained about his vast belly. He wondered why they had married him in the first place, but he was afraid to ask. He couldn't understand why they and so many other people chose to torment him. He needed someone who would *accept* him. Not even Leora Flagg had done that. Instead, she had written mendacious poetry having to do with his penis. And finally she had given way to the ultimate betrayal—suicide. His father died in 1964 of—what else?—cirrhosis of the liver. His father had been a tormentor as well. His father always had been . . . ambivalent. His father had gone waltzing away in a fog of beer, or call it *HOLY WATER*; call it by its rightful name. Jack P. Coffee, drunken dreamer of formless dreams, witness to faceless events. Such a man. Such an enigma wrapped in waxed paper and shoestrings or whatever. *I'm hearty the way a screwdriver up your nose is hearty*, he'd once said to Eugene. *All my life . . . oh, all my miserable LIFE all I've wanted was to sit by the side of the road and pick at my toenails and keep track of all the Plymouths that went past. That's been IT, Eugene. All the rest is smoke.* And Jack P. Coffee had tried to smile, but there hadn't been enough strength in the corners of his mouth. So he'd simply made a hopeless movement with a hand . . . the hand that hadn't been holding the *HOLY WATER* tankard. And he'd said nothing more. And so wasn't it fair to call him just another tormentor of Eugene Coffee, along with Eugene Coffee's mother and those football players and Trudy and Beryl and Leora Flagg and even Guido Cesco and Murray Bernstein and little Lily Noonan and that Scollay Square whore and certain of his students who picked their noses in front of Eugene Coffee or went to sleep in front of Eugene Coffee or told him his admiration of Hemingway's prose style was all a crock of shit and why the fuck didn't he get his act together and catch up with the times? And maybe even Joe DiMaggio, of all people, was one of Eugene Coffee's tormentors. After all, it was Joe DiMaggio's television commercials that had made the Mr Coffee coffeebrewer famous, and now Eugene couldn't go anywhere without being called Mr Coffee and creating indulgent smiles. *You're looking perky, Mr Coffee*, people would say. Or: *Anything exciting brewing in your life, Mr Coffee?* Or: *Has anyone ever called you a drip, Mr Coffee?* This last question had been asked of him by, among others, his daughter's best friend, Eleanor LeBay,

[192]

the fortyish woman who was Priss' neighbor in Cos Cob. He and Eleanor LeBay went to bed three times within a week in the summer of 1980. He was the house guest of Priss and her orthodontist husband, but three times he managed to couple with Eleanor Le-Bay. After all, her husband was in New York all the livelong day, and there was so little to *do* except go out and have Duane *frost* her *hair*, and, well, you know, I do believe I have a remarkably trim body for a woman of my advanced years, and I *do* admire a man who is involved with literature and the arts, and yes, yes, bite my tits; oh I love that. I don't know why, but Howard's always been afraid to bite my tits. He keeps telling me he's afraid he might draw blood, and *I* keep telling *him* I don't mind if you *do*, but it doesn't do a smidge of good. Not a smidge. Yes. Draw blood. See if Eleanor cares. Yes, Mr Coffee, dear Mr Coffee, bite them, bite them, yes, yes, you are not a drip. And Eugene Coffee was sitting up, and Eleanor was astride him, and he bit her tits, and he actually drew blood from the left one, and later she sucked all his fingers, and her bloody tit dripped, and she told him she always would adore him, and had he ever considered walking a mile or two every morning? It was great for the old muscle tone, said Eleanor LeBay, not to mention the old stamina. Eugene Coffee smiled. He told Eleanor he appreciated her concern, but . . . well, he couldn't even begin to estimate how many people had made similar suggestions to him over the previous thirty years or so, and they might as well have saved their breath. With all due respect. Yes. With all due respect. And Eleanor LeBay shrugged and touched the tip of her torn tit and told Eugene she didn't suppose it mattered, since he already was enough of a real man. Eugene didn't say anything. Leora's suicide had taken place a year earlier, and he didn't know what sort of man he was, and maybe it didn't really matter. He and Eleanor and Priss and the orthodontist played bridge that night in

Eleanor's home, and Eugene and Eleanor won by more than five thousand points. Eleanor's husband, who didn't play bridge, sat in the kitchen and did the crossword puzzle from the previous Sunday's *New York Times*. And Eleanor said: *Howard really is a whiz at that sort of thing*. And Priss said: *That must be a comfort*. And everyone at the bridge table laughed. And Eleanor reached across the table and lightly touched one of Eugene's hands. Eugene hadn't visited Cos Cob since 1980. He wasn't quite sure why he'd stayed away. Maybe he was afraid Eleanor would betray him. Or maybe he was afraid he wouldn't have the strength to repeat his great demonstration of tearing a tit. He was afraid of many things. Sometimes, if he really concentrated, he was able to smell a hint of a certain fish sandwich and a certain puddle of puke. And then one night the telephone rang in his Pittsburgh apartment, and an old man from Texas was on the line, and Aunt Edna was dead, but who was Aunt Edna to the great Eugene A. Coffee? And so the great Eugene A. Coffee made up a story about having to write a paper for the Modern Language Association, and he told the old man he had given his word to the Modern Language Association, blah blah blah. And the old man became enraged. And the old man shouted words having to do with blood kin, and the old man called Eugene a shithead and an asshole, and was the old man another tormentor, or was the old man simply righteous, or was it all bullshit, or *what*? The next morning the great Eugene A. Coffee said to himself: Well, for once in your life why not try to find out the truth of a thing? But he worked the question through his mind for the better part of two days before finally making up his mind to fly down to Houston. He read several dozen of the Pound *Cantos* in the airplane. He really didn't understand most of them.

CHAPTER FIFTEEN

Herman Marshall passed out after he pissed on the *Lamar* headstone, draping himself over it, his mouth open and leaking spittle. His fly remained undone until a grimacing Mr Grizzard zipped it up. Herman Marshall was carried to the limousine that had brought him and Mr Grizzard and Jobeth Stephenson and Eugene Coffee to the cemetery, and the sprinklers worked lazily, spraying, spraying, tapping the babyshit brown cemetery grass, trickling across the dry unyielding earth. Herman Marshall was given smellingsalts by Mr Grizzard. Herman Marshall choked, gasped. He shook his head. He was sprawled in the back seat of the limousine, and Jobeth was hugging him. He glanced out a window and saw the tent where Edna's grave was. He wept a little, but not much. His tears were like sand. Again he shook his head, and his nephew—Eddie? Edgar? Eustace? Eugene?—smiled back at him from the front seat and told him everything would be all right. Hey, the nephew's name was Eugene . . . no longer Alex . . . and this Eugene was a fat tub of shit, all right, and where had he come from? What had happened to the paper he'd been writing for the BVD or whatever? Herman Marshall wriggled a little. Jobeth was clinging to him too tightly, and she was kissing his cheeks and his ears. Harry and Beth leaned in one of the windows, and Beth asked whether everything was all right. She frowned at Jobeth, but Jobeth apparently didn't notice. Eugene spoke. His voice was a comforting baritone. Jesus Christ, he could have been an undertaker. Speaking to Beth, he said: "Uncle Herman simply was . . . overcome. He'll be fine. Time can be miraculous."

"Say at again?" said Beth, and she still was frowning.

"We must give him time," said Eugene. "That's all I'm trying to say. I'll go to his home with him, and we'll—"

"I'll go to his home with him," said Jobeth, "an him an me'll have us a nice little talk." Jobeth patted her hair. "Him an me been friends a whole real long time, an I been a comfort to him here in his hour of need, an ain't nobody goin to say I ain't been . . ."

"Perhaps we both can go to his home with him," said Eugene to Jobeth.

"God save him," said Beth, almost whispering.

"What?" said Jobeth.

"Never mind . . ." said Beth.

"You ain't never liked me," said Jobeth. "You think I'm trash."

"It don't matter . . ." said Beth.

"Well, it sure enough do matter to *me*," said Jobeth, and now she had released Herman Marshall, and she was sitting erectly, and her hands were in fists.

Beth and Harry backed away from the limousine's window. Beth made a hissing sound and looked away from the limousine. Harry shrugged in the general direction of Herman Marshall.

Herman Marshall called out to Harry. "I'm . . . it's goin to be fine!"

"Surely," said Harry, nodding.

The limousine pulled away. Herman Marshall winced every time the limousine struck a bump or a pothole. He didn't really know how drunk he was now. He had said something at the funeral, hadn't he? He had interrupted that jackleg Baptist minister, hadn't he? He had registered some sort of complaint about Edna's pain, hadn't he? Yessir, the things a man did when he was drunk. Still, what was wrong with registering a complaint about Edna's pain? At least Herman Marshall's words had diverted attention from the minister's horseshit comments and prayers. Herman Marshall leaned back and closed his eyes. Next to him, Jobeth patted his knee. He told himself he no doubt always would be ashamed of himself for the way he had behaved today. He wanted to know what sort of man it was who became drunk at his wife's funeral and interrupted the formal words and then pissed on a stranger's headstone. His belly gurgled. He opened his eyes and glanced toward the front seat, and the back of his fat nephew's neck was red and spotted. His miserable stupid mealymouthed fat nephew, the *college professor* who for some reason had changed his goddamn lardass *name*. Oh, Lord have mercy on the youth of the nation. Abruptly Herman Marshall inhaled, and he listened to his breath agitate the snot in his nostrils. Jobeth murmured and cooed. She had done things to him, hadn't she? And she had done things *for* him. Why, the old bag of turkey turds, clearly she still found that sort of thing worthwhile. Herman Marshall touched his temples. He wondered when he would begin really weeping for Edna. Maybe he never would. Maybe he should have killed himself. Hadn't the ancient Egyptians done something like that? No. Not quite. The ancient Egyptians had killed pet dogs and cats, and sometimes they even had killed wives, so that the Dear Departed would have company in the Sweet Bye & Bye. Not a bad idea. Who said you couldn't take it with you? A person could take his whole world with him, if he was of a mind and if he was strong enough. Those ancient Egyptians must really have had balls. Maybe they even had written a book, and the book had contained nothing but truth and wisdom. But what had *happened* to that book? Now there was a real secret of the ages, and it aggravated Herman Marshall no end. The limousine hummed, and its tires made heavy flupping sounds, and Mr Grizzard kept asking Herman Marshall are you all right? are you sure you're all right? are you sure you don't want to stop at a doctor's office or an emer-

[197]

gency room? And Mr Grizzard allowed as how it was a good thing T. C. Drucker & Sons held to an ongoing policy of always having smellingsalts and other basic firstaid materials on hand in order to assist those whose funereal grief became overpowering. And Herman Marshall said: "Yessir. Between your wigs an your smellinsalts, you kind of got the world by the ass, ain't you? Yessir."

"*Herman* . . ." said Jobeth, clucking.

In the front seat, Eugene cleared his throat and rubbed his mouth.

Herman Marshall looked out a window. Houston roared with the golden heat. Sidewalks shimmered. Pickup trucks passed on the right, and signs advertised Budweiser and Ninfa's and *TOTALLY NUDE GIRLS*. Houses crouched, and housewives bent over their flowergardens, and the housewives were wearing shorts, and most of the housewives had veiny legs. Joggers beat their way through the heat, and many of the joggers wore sweatshirts, and the sweatshirts were black with moisture. Mr Grizzard hummed through the openings between his teeth. He said something to the effect that the service really had been quite lovely, and hadn't the *flowers* been pretty though? Flowers really were such an *eloquent* acknowledgment of loss, weren't they? And then Mr Grizzard said: "She received a fine sendoff, Mr Marshall. She really did. An as for your . . . your *outbreak of grief* . . . well, it was perfectly human, an it's happened to others, an I don't want you blamin yourself for a perfectly human thing over which you had no control . . . you hear me?" And now Mr Grizzard's voice was full of a fake Dutch Uncle severity, and his face perhaps even twinkled a little . . . as much as an undertaker's face *could* twinkle.

Herman Marshall didn't know what to say to any of that shit, and so he said nothing. He kept looking out the window, and he watched a barechested fellow unload a Coke truck that was parked next to a Kroger's. Women pushed shoppingcarts across the parking lot, and some of the women were pretty, and he saw several who wore only halters and exhibited their bare bellies for an admiring world to see. These women walked with their hips swaying, and they were young, and they were not bloated, and they didn't have chicken necks, and Herman Marshall wished it was maybe 1940 again. Oh, how did he wish that little thing, ha ha. And then he was home, and Jobeth and Eugene and Mr Grizzard were helping him up the front steps, and still he nearly stumbled and fell, and he was thinking of Shiner, and surely there would be Shiner in the fridge. Jobeth unlocked the front door for him, and he was greeted with a stink of stale barbecue. He made a face and held his nose. Apparently Jobeth hadn't cleared away all the stink. Well, maybe that was why he had married Edna and not Jobeth. But that was stupid. He hadn't had a choice. He hadn't even *known* Jobeth. He was stupid to be thinking that way. He insisted on going to the fridge and popping open a Shiner. He sat at the kitchen table and drank the Shiner, and it made him feel better. Oh, there was too much light, but at least he had wet his whistle. Mr Grizzard stood at the kitchen door for a few minutes and made small-talk with Jobeth and Eugene. Herman Marshall breathed the stink of the stale barbecue, and god *damn*. Then Mr Grizzard said something about having to return to the funeral home and help prepare a Mrs Ashurst who had died after falling from a horse. "She suffered terrible head injuries," said Mr Grizzard, "not to mention a whole passel of severe facial lacerations, an so we have our work cut out for us, if you know what I mean . . ."

"Oh, yessir . . ." said Jobeth, smiling.

And Eugene said: "I believe we know what you mean, sir."

And Herman Marshall said: "Well, Mr Grizzard, I sure do appreciate your kindness." And Herman Marshall stood up and extended a hand toward Mr Grizzard. "An I'm sorry I made such a

[199]

fool of myself. I guess . . . well, maybe I don't know *what's* the matter with me. But I ain't drunk now. I guarantee you at. An I ain't even got to piss. An at's the truth."

"Good," said Mr Grizzard, shaking Herman Marshall's hand. "You're goin to be just fine an dandy, Mr Marshall. All you got to do is give it time. Like they say, ha ha, time wounds all heels." And Mr Grizzard then shook hands with Jobeth and Eugene, and Jobeth showed him to the door.

Herman Marshall seated himself and nodded toward the fridge. "Help yourself," he said to Eugene. "Air's plenty of Shiner in at air fridge. Maybe you've never had no Shiner. Well, you're in for a treat."

Eugene smiled. He went to the fridge, opened it and extracted a Shiner longneck. He popped it open and looked around. "Glass?" he said.

"Never mind bout no glass," said Herman Marshall. "Just set down here at the table an drink your Shiner from the bottle, the way the Lord intended."

Eugene nodded, shrugged. He seated himself at the table and drank from the Shiner longneck. He swallowed, shuddered. His jowls sweated.

"Takes a little gettin used to," said Herman Marshall.

"Mm . . ." said Eugene, nodding.

"I was . . . well, I sure enough was surprised to see you at the funeral," said Herman Marshall. "I mean, after the way I done hollered at you over the telephone . . ."

"I was wrong," said Eugene. "I was being selfish. It's not the first time, and I don't imagine it'll be the last. I'm afraid I'm not a really rare bargain, Uncle Herman."

"An *I* ain't no picnic at the beach neither," said Herman Marshall. "I mean, lookit the way I was today. Drunk an carryin on

[200]

at my wife's funeral. Actin like a . . . like a what . . . like maybe a baby . . . I don't know . . . I keep wantin to go up to the attic . . ."

"Pardon?"

"I used to go up air just about ever day an *find* things for her. For Edna. Old things. Find em an bring em downstairs an tell her stories about em. Madeup stories, an the more outlandish they was, the better. They took her mind off the hard truth, you know? Old me, I'd come scamperin downstairs, fast as I could, what with my bad joints, an I'd clown around an wave some *thing* at her . . . some *old* thing that maybe onceuponatime had meant a little somethin to us back when we'd been at least a little bit happy an—"

Jobeth came into the kitchen and said: "Why, look at you two. Both of you with your Shiners." And Jobeth smiled. "Men an air beer. Men doin the things men do best. At's the way Jobeth likes her men, an no mistake. All her life she's been—"

It was Herman Marshall's turn to interrupt. "Jobeth . . ."

Jobeth's eyes enlarged. "Huh?"

"Well," said Herman Marshall, "me an . . ." He hesitated.

"Eugene," said Eugene.

Herman Marshall smiled. "Yessir," he said to Eugene, "your name sure enough is Eugene. I'm sorry, but I keep remembering when it was Alexander. You changed it a whole long time ago, though, didn't you? An now your first name's the same as my middle name. Eugene. Herman Eugene Marshall—at's my name, all right. My full name." Then Herman Marshall directed his smile toward Jobeth, who was standing in the doorway and leaning against the frame. "Jobeth," he said, "me an Eugene here, we're kin, an we got things to talk about, you know?"

"Alone?" said Jobeth, stiffening.

"Yes ma'am," said Herman Marshall.

[201]

"You want me to go home?"

"Well . . . you put it at way . . . yes ma'am."

"After all I done for you?"

". . . I sure enough have appreciated it."

"After *last night* an all?"

". . . just for a little while is all I ask. En you can come back, an maybe you can fix us somethin to eat . . ."

"Well, I *never*," said Jobeth, and she pushed herself away from the frame. "Talk about your *ingrates* . . ."

Herman Marshall and Eugene sat and listened to Jobeth go storming through the front of the house and out the door. She slammed it, and the sound echoed. Herman Marshall and Eugene both flinched, and then Herman Marshall said: "I don't member last night all at good."

"Perhaps something happened," said Eugene.

"I think she jacked me off," said Herman Marshall.

"Oh?"

"Yessir. An I gave her a wad, I think. A little bitty wad, but it was a *wad*. She was bein Christian or somethin. Comfortin me or somethin. Lovin me or somethin. She's eighty I don't know what if she's a day, an I think she's sort of all worked up. At her age. All worked up. Jesus H. Christmastrees."

"Women," said Eugene.

"Women," said Herman Marshall. "Um, tell me somethin, all right?"

"Tell you what?"

"My lips . . ."

"What about them?"

"You think I got nigger lips?"

"My God, no. What kind of a question is that?"

"I don't know," said Herman Marshall. He stood up and went to the fridge and grabbed two more Shiner longnecks and popped them open. He returned to the table and handed one of the long-necks to Eugene. "Drink your joy juice," he said.

"My dad called it holy water," said Eugene.

"Well, maybe he had a point," said Herman Marshall.

"Why did you ask me that question about your lips?"

"I worry about em."

"That's silly," said Eugene.

"Maybe so," said Herman Marshall, "but people worry about the goddamnedest things, don't they? With me, it's nigger lips. I was called Nig when I drove for Gulfway Truckin. I guess I don't *know* anythin, Eugene. How much do *you* know? I mean, you're a *college professor* an all, an at *means* somethin, right? I came down from the attic with this an at an tuther thing, an I told stories to Edna, an all her hair fell out, an at the end she kept after me bout *blood* . . . blood *this* blood *at* . . . an so at was why I hollered at you . . . you're blood of her blood, an I wanted you down here . . . to make it so it wasn't like she wasn't leavin nothin behind. Your Cousin Billy, you remember him? Him an his mama came visitin you an your folks up in Cleveland in I think it was 19 an 50, an you member em?"

"Yes," said Eugene. "I enjoyed listening to the soft southern way Aunt Edna talked. It indeed was the summer of 1950, and I was home from college for the summer. It was the only summer I didn't attend summer school. I worked that summer as a baker's helper at Hough Bakery. I ate a lot of free pie and cake. Ha. Billy was a good little boy. I'm sorry about what happened to him. I should have come down here for his funeral. *Someone* should have."

"You're blood of her blood. Blood of Edna's blood. At was important to her. At the end, whenever she talked, I swear it was blood an blood an blood."

"A lot of people feel that way. I think I feel that way about my daughter."

"Daughter?"

"Yes. Her name is Priscilla, and she is married to an orthodontist, and they live in Cos Cob, Connecticut."

"Where?"

"Cos Cob. It's not too far from New York City. It's on Long Island Sound."

"Oh," said Herman Marshall. He drank. He licked the bottle. He frowned. He had a whole mess of thoughts he wanted to lay out on this here kitchen table, but he didn't quite know where to begin. Many of them were questions rather than thoughts. And a few were questions he'd never even considered before. "Can I talk?" he said.

"Of course," said Eugene.

"Maybe I'll scare you."

"Maybe you will."

"But that'll be all right?"

"Until I start screaming," said Eugene, and he smiled. And he swiped sweat off his jowls. "And if I start clawing at the door, well, lay off me a little, fair enough?"

"Fair nough," said Herman Marshall.

"She really did jack you off?"

"I think so," said Herman Marshall.

"Well, fair enough," said Eugene.

"I want to talk," said Herman Marshall.

"All right," said Eugene.

"My brother Eldred Junior had a dog," said Herman Marshall, "but one day Eldred Junior was real mean to me. Him an my two other brothers was real mean to me, far as *at* goes. But I couldn't do nothin to *all* of em, so I picked out Eldred Junior. An I drownded his dog. She was a good old dog, was old Elsie, but I held her in the water until she died, an en I buried her, an I ain't

[204]

said nothin bout it to nobody from then until just now. You're
the first person who's ever knowed about it. Not even Eldred
Junior ever found out, an he's dead now. But the *thing* is . . . the
thing I can't *understand* is . . . I kilt old Elsie without hardly givin
it much of a second thought, but years later, when your Grandma
Stillman was livin with us, an your Grandma Stillman had a little
cocker name of Rusty, an that Rusty was a pain in the ass, an I
could of kilt him so quick it would of made your head spin, but
I never did do nothin. Rusty lived a full life. He lived until he died,
an I never done *nothin* to him. I mean, I was in the war, an I kilt
Germans, an I didn't mind killin Germans, an I hadn't much minded
killin Elsie, an I'd gone huntin with my daddy an my brothers an
I'd bagged my share of deer an rabbit an whatnot, but Rusty didn't
get drownded or nothin. *I let him live.* How do you figure at one,
huh? Me, I'll tell you—when I'm of a mind, I can be rough as a
cob stickin out of a chicken's asshole. You can ask anybody who
knows me. *But I never kilt that old goodfornothin Rusty.* An your
Grandma Stillman sure enough did love at dog. Do you figure
maybe at's why I didn't kill him? But Eldred Junior loved *his* dog,
an I sure enough kilt *her.* Your Grandma Stillman . . . I'm real
sorry to say this, but she talked too much, an she got on my goddamn nerves, with the blah blah here an the blah blah air, here
a blah, air a blah, everywhere a blah blah, an always she wadded
up her apron and twisted it an fussed at it like maybe all her troubles
was *its* fault . . . an where's the sense in any of *at*? How come folks
can't be . . . consistent?"

Eugene shrugged. "You expect me to answer that?"

"Can you?" said Herman Marshall.

"Of course not," said Eugene.

"Drink your beer."

"That won't help me answer the question," said Eugene.

[205]

"Don't matter none," said Herman Marshall. "I just don't want you to go thirsty. I'm tryin to be a real good host."

"You're a fine host."

"No. This here place got a stink of stale barbecue."

"It'll go away."

"I got lots of questions. Maybe I ought to die, an en the questions won't matter."

"That's true enough," said Eugene.

"I think maybe I feel sorry for a lot of people."

"Oh?"

"Most of em are old people," said Herman Marshall, "an it ain't no fun bein old, an either you hurt or you ain't got no answers or you feel dirty an you want to make yourself feel clean like you was on the day you was borned. I worry bout why I didn't kill Rusty. Sure God I do. I kilt Germans, but I didn't kill Rusty. Your mama ever tell you how you bawled an carried on the day me an Edna got married?"

"Yes."

"Edna. Poor Edna. I don't know what happened."

"What?"

"Her an me, we met one cold day when she was wearin a blouse that made her nipples stand up . . . an she was so *pretty* . . . an now she's Gone, an she was bald as ice air in her coffin under her god-damn *wig*, an it's like we all get torned down an sold for scrap, ain't it? A man can be a big old Texas boy for fair, an his boots can kick shit a hunnert miles, an he can holler an drink, an he can dance with the bestlookin women an feel air rear ends an squeeze air tits, an he sweats real sweat, an he don't take nothin from nobody, but at the end he's just like everbody else; he's layin flat in some graveyard, an some preacher is sayin words over him, an the words don't mean *nothin*, on account of he's all *alone* . . . an the dirt he's

[206]

layin in is maybe kind of a reflection of the dirt he's passed through all the goddamn mornins an afternoons an evenins of his life, an maybe oncet he dreamed of bein a cowboy hero like your straight–shootin Tom Mix, only he didn't hardly have no time to *breathe* but what it all was over, an it's the ashcan for you, oldtimer, an don't forget to pull the lid down tight."

"Am I supposed to say something to that?" said Eugene, sucking on his second Shiner.

"I don't know," said Herman Marshall.

"*I've* known things, too."

"Things?" said Herman Marshall.

"Things," said Eugene. "Pain. My daughter's husband is sixty. How many children do you think she'll have? To date, she has zero. Her husband is a nice man. For that matter, perhaps even I am a nice man, although a few years ago I ate a young woman's pussy and then she went home and killed herself. I ask you—does the one follow the other? I ask you."

Herman Marshall spread his hands on the table. He spread them palms up, and there was altogether too much light.

CHAPTER SIXTEEN

Aᴌᴌ ᴛʜɪɴɢꜱ ᴄᴏɴꜱɪᴅᴇʀᴇᴅ, Herman Marshall emerged from his pissyass drunk in pretty solid shape. He and fat Eugene sat in the kitchen and talked for hours, and a somewhat sullen Jobeth returned and fixed them ham sandwiches and a crock of homemade baked beans. Herman Marshall talked about the end of the world, and he talked about being old. He told fat Eugene he believed the end of the world would come in a bright explosion, but he also told fat Eugene he believed in the possibility of Paradise. He even spoke of angeltits peeking through the strings of heavenly harps, and Eugene smiled. The kitchen whirred and clacked with sounds of the fridge and the airconditioner. Jobeth sat at the table with Herman Marshall and fat Eugene and what the hell, they indulged her. She said she had been married four times, but Stephenson was her maiden name, since her last married name had been Schmittlapp, and who wanted to be stuck with *that*? She should have known enough not to have married a man named Schmittlapp, and that was the truth. Fat Eugene snorted and snickered. Jobeth appeared pleased. She patted one of Eugene's hands and told him he was the sort of fellow who *grew* on a girl, if he followed her meaning. And Eugene said something lame and academic, something having to do with better to grow on a girl than to grow on a tree, ha ha, or on a grapevine, ho ho. And Jobeth joined fat Eugene in a scattering of laughter, but Herman Marshall frowned at them: he told them he didn't know what the joke was, and he was real awful sorry, but would they kindly explain it to him? And they did, and he shook his head and told

[209]

Eugene *shame* on *you* for stretchin so far. And Eugene reminded Herman Marshall that he (Eugene) was an academic, and academics weren't exactly your standup comics in your Catskill nightclubs. Herman Marshall didn't know what a Catskill nightclub was, and he didn't ask. He didn't want Eugene to think he was all *that* much of a dimwit. Eugene spent the night in the guest room, and Jobeth slept with Herman Marshall. She and Herman Marshall lay in bed and listened to Eugene take a bath in the next room, and Eugene farted in the bathtub, *bloop* and *balubb*, and Jobeth pressed her face against Herman Marshall's chest and sniggered. He didn't know whether this was right. He supposed he knew damn well it *wasn't* right. He supposed he should have been thinking of Edna's bald head and the *LAMAR* headstone. He supposed he should go to the telephone and get in touch with Mr Grizzard and thank Mr Grizzard for supplying such a terrific wig. At the same time, he wanted to kill the world. He wanted to do away with all kindness and sentiment; he wanted to take all the the angels and skewer them and tear off their angeltits. He wanted to club the universe with a particular book that would reveal the flaws of God and the sky. He wondered what the gentle rummies at the Top of the World would say about all this. He decided he would take Eugene for a little ride the next day and show Eugene what the real Houston was like. And they would visit the light-bulbed nighttime Houston with its skyscrapers that grimaced and loomed. Yeah, good old Houston. The traffic never stopped hissing. Herman Marshall knew all about Houston and its goddamn traffic. He had made his living out there on those Houston streets and those Houston roads. As a young man, he'd been able to drive a rig all the way to New Orleans—and on old US 90, at that—without once having to stop and piss. And he had liked working the gears, grunting over the gears and sucking his lips. He'd been a married man, sure, but every now and then there were temptations *no* sort of man could resist. Even a man who had nigger lips. Why had Herman Marshall asked Eugene about the nigger lips? What could Eugene have said? *How* could Eugene have said anything other than the proper polite and astonished words? Lord, no wonder Eugene had farted in the bathtub. And Herman Marshall embraced Jobeth and said to himself: I don't expect none of this here is right, but I think we're lost, an a fart in the bathtub makes about as much sense as anythin else does. Jobeth wriggled against him and sighed. Her flesh had an odor of a neglected sachet, and maybe it was a forgotten sachet; it was all dusty, and it caught at his eyes, and he blinked. He fell asleep, and in the middle of the night she tried to awaken him by diddling his cock, but he groaned and rolled away from her. She made angry little sounds, but she didn't pursue the matter any further. Herman Marshall dreamed of how it had been to kill Nawzis, and he saw the mattresses and the old men, and had the mayor been wearing a sash of office? Maybe so. Such a detail was difficult to remember, but maybe so. Herman Marshall had lost a whole mess of details from his life. In a manner of speaking, maybe he'd pissed them away. It went right along with being old, with sitting at a dying woman's bedside and making up stories that had nothing to do with nothing, on account of that was a way to give the illusion that she was moving through her days as though her days goddamn *meant* something. Herman Marhsall squinted at the Nawzis, and they were spraying blood the way those sprinklers had sprayed water, and his .45 roared and leapt, and he told himself he amounted to something, and a gaggle of English girls stood in the snow and applauded him, but they were wearing mittens, and so the sound of their applause didn't carry very well. Herman Marshall came awake at the first slice and hint of dawn, and he had to piss, but he lay mo-

[211]

tionless so as not to disturb Jobeth. He didn't want to awaken her, because maybe then she again would try to diddle his cock or do something else that maybe would annoy him. There was a dresser at the foot of the bed, and the dresser had a cracked marble top, and Edna always had considered that dresser to be of considerable monetary value. She had bought it at an auction involving a neighbor family that had died off, and she had allowed as how it was a sad and terrible thing when a family died off. The dresser had cost her three dollars, and Harry had helped Herman Marshall load it into his (Harry's) little old Dodge pickup truck, and Edna and Beth had chatted of the hidden value of certain antiques, if you held onto them long enough. Maybe today Herman Marshall really would grieve for Edna. He needed to roll on the floor. He needed to be *real* about his goddamn grief. He thought of his nephew, fat Eugene. He didn't know how much he liked fat Eugene, and he was surprised he even liked fat Eugene a little bit. He'd never known a college professor, and he'd never figured he would have any use for one, and fat Eugene seemed a little weak, a little too easy with the words, a little too anxious to please, but surely Herman Marshall had known worse people than fat Eugene. Certain truckers. Certain farmers and merchants from Hope, Arkansas. Certain nigger drivers who would tailgate a man just because they didn't have nothing better to do and they were mean and ornery and niggers to boot. That made for a bad combination, and it was best to stay away from such niggers. Herman Marshall took fat Eugene for a drive around Houston that day. He drove fat Eugene's rented Chevvy, and it made comfortable sounds on the hot swelling Houston pavements. They passed supermarkets that said *RICE* and *KROGER*, and they tooled along Westheimer Avenue where the modeling studios and the fairy bars and the dirtybook emporiums were, and a lipsticked boy of no more than fifteen pranced across the street in front of the car and called to them that he simply *adored* old men and fat men, and wouldn't they just *love* for him to pull their grizzled poopy old bellropes? And Herman Marshall and fat Eugene drove downtown, and no one was outdoors in the heat, and new glass buildings stood in an arbitrary tumble, and they glinted, and they were all angles and panels, and the angles stabbed the clouds, and fat Eugene spoke of what he called downtown's *rage*, its . . . its *belligerence*, its *silent* and *hateful* insistence on creating a skyline that was like no other skyline in the world, and fat Eugene said yes, he had *read* about the Houston skyline, and he had *seen photographs* of the Houston skyline, but words and photographs captured little. "It's something," said fat Eugene, "where you have to *be* there." And Herman Marshall said: "I seen it spring up. I swear, one day it wasn't air an the next day it was, an the rich folks put on air soup an fish an had em air parties, an the next night somethin else was openin, an air soup an fish got a workout, I tell you." And fat Eugene said: "I can imagine. I have students who think they want to major in architecture at Carnegie-Mellon or some such place. They ought to visit Houston first. I seem to recall reading somewhere that Houston's downtown represents the Architecture of Cruelty. Maybe that's a bit extreme, but I think I know at least a little of what the writer was trying to say." And Eugene blinked at all the glass and all the light. He shaded his eyes. His tongue tapped the roof of his mouth. Other cars passed on the right. Horns seldom were honked, though, and Eugene said something about this, and Herman Marshall said: "If you honk your horn in this here town, it ain't considered polite, an you just might get shot. I ain't foolin. I'm talkin *shot* . . . like in bang, bang; you're dead. I'm tellin you these here old boys may drive like maniacs, but God spare the man who . . . well, who tries to pass along the information." And Herman Marshall chuckled. Eugene

[213]

stared at him. They had lunch in a place called the Ragin Cajun, on Richmond by the SP tracks. They ate red beans and rice, and Eugene had two helpings, and the place was decorated with business cards and bumper stickers and such, and one of the bumper stickers said

IF YOU AIN'T DONE IT WITH A COONASS YOU AIN'T DONE IT

and Cajun music scraped and rambled on a PA system, and Herman Marshall belched over his red beans and rice, and he and Eugene washed down their lunch with three bottles apiece of good old Shiner, and all the customers sat at spindly little tables and munched on poboy sandwiches and slugged down beer and spoke of hog futures and football and tits and the ohl bidness and the music was loud but the talk wasn't, and there was a table loaded with old yearbooks from various Louisiana colleges and universities, and Eugene asked Herman Marshall about those yearbooks, and Herman Marshall said: "Well, now an again some old boy comes in an he says he's Tulane Class of '75 or whatever, an maybe somebody don't believe him, an so he grabs the Tulane Class of '75 yearbook an damn if he don't look up his picture, an it's right *air* in the *book*, an he shows it to em who don't believe he went to Tulane, an at's the end of the argument, you see what I mean?" And Eugene smiled and nodded. And Herman Marshall said: "At air's *important*." And Eugene continued to smile and nod, and he scarfed down his second helping of red beans and rice with just as much energy as he'd shown when he'd scarfed down his first helping of red beans and rice, and he said: "I've never had this kind of

[214]

food before, and I really like it." And Herman Marshall said: "From the looks of you, you like just about everthin, don't you?" And Eugene said: "I do believe you have me there, Uncle Herman." In the afternoon they drove out on I-45 toward Pasadena, and Herman Marshall showed all the oil storage tanks, and then they cut north toward Galena Park and the Turning Basin and the ships that lay in the Turning Basin, and the air was slick with an odor of oil, and Herman Marshall said: "These here towns may not be pretty, but they make the world go round, you know? Good old ohl. Without ohl, you an me'd be in a horse an wagon right now. So don't knock Pasadena, an don't knock Galena Park. They got air place in the world, too." And Eugene said: "I am knocking nothing, Uncle Herman. I am your guest, and I find this little tour very interesting. Last night, when I said you were a fine host, I wasn't just beating my teeth together to hear what sort of sounds they made. I am fiftytwo years old, Uncle Herman, and please believe me when I say the things I say. My age sort of demands it." And Herman Marshall said: "Age ain't got nothin to do with nothin. But I believe you. Maybe because I want to, but at don't matter. All at matters is we're sneakin through another day, ain't we?" And Eugene said: "Well, that's one way to put it." And Eugene smiled. Then they drove north, back to Houston, and Herman Marshall showed his nephew the posh River Oaks section where the rich people lived. He showed his nephew the River Oaks Country Club, and he showed his nephew the grand homes where Jesse Jones and Leon Jaworski had lived. And said: "Muhammad Ali, the nigger fighter, they wouldn't let him in River Oaks. He didn't have enough of the old moolah. Somethin like at. Or leastaways at's how *I* heard it. Or maybe I read it in the paper. I can't quite member. But anyway, he ain't livin air, an maybe the proof's in the puddin, you think?" And Herman Marshall

[215]

chuckled. He told Eugene he supposed he sometimes behaved a little . . . peculiar. He drove slowly up and down the silent humid streets of River Oaks, and here and there some skinny Mex was clipping a hedge or digging in a flowerbed, and after a time he said: "People . . . air all supposed to be borned with the same chances, ain't at so? All the people who live here in old River Oaks, they wasn't all *borned* rich, *was* they? I mean, some of em have to of came from . . . well, where the old boys stand around on Saturday night an kick shit on account of air ain't nothin else to do except maybe fuck the Town Pump an likely as not she's got the clap or maybe scabs or runnin sores, haw haw, you know? So em old boys, em old boys who's now livin in these here houses in River Oaks, I guess they sort of took holt of emselves by air balls an squeezed real hard an *got goin*, you know? Me, I never got goin. I wouldn't even be here in Houston if it wasn't for a friend of mine from high school, an he found me a job rotatin tires at Gulfway Truckin back more years ago an I expect right now I can member. He's dead now, an he's been dead for a long time, an his name was Elroy Catchins, an he pitched for the Hope High School baseball team, an he was one of em whatchacall south-paws, an he had as good a curve ball as I ever seen. So, I got the job at Gulfway Truckin, an then I was *drivin* for Gulfway Truckin, but nothin went nowhere after at. The Army was a break in the old routine, an your Cousin Billy came along, blood of your blood an, um, blood of *my* blood, but everthin got real sort of . . . scaly, you know? Everthin scabbed up, an your Aunt Edna an me, after we lost Billy, well, all the days was like soup, an I couldn't tell one from tuther, an I wonder how come I never squeezed my balls, you hear me?" And Eugene said: "A great many of us don't squeeze our balls. After all, when a man squeezes his balls, it hurts." And Herman Marshall said: "Yessir. At air's sure enough true, but

[216]

maybe ain't the hurt a *good* hurt?" Said Eugene: "I suppose that has to do with how much tolerance a man has." Said Herman Marshall: "What's tolerance?" Said Eugene, and he looked out a window so Herman Marshall wouldn't be able to see his face: "I think it might be bravery. I think it might be a way of facing the real world and not blaming your troubles on other people. My father drank himself to death, did you know that? He did so while keeping his own counsel, and his liver fell apart, and I never heard a peep out of him that could have served as an explanation. Perhaps he said something to my mother, but she never passed anything along to me. I think she might have been tormenting me. I think she was one of a large group. I suppose you think I'm a whiner, but *I have been tormented*. I mean that. I am in earnest." And Herman Marshall reached out and twisted one of Eugene's doughy shoulders and forced Eugene to look at him and then said to Eugene: "You're her blood. I don't want to hear you talk like at. You're desecratin her memory, you fat sonofabitch, an I won't *hear* of it. I loved her. Love her. Whatever. An she told me you was important. Blood of blood, whatever at meant. Blood of blood. Her, she was blood. Me, I expect I always been water. I . . . well, I don't know . . . I think I got a right to ask you to *act* like you was blood." Said Eugene: "I'm not sure I know what you're talking about." Said Herman Marshall: "I'm talkin about . . . family." Said Eugene: "Oh." Said Herman Marshall: "Nobody ought to be alone." Said Eugene, and now he was sniffling, and now he was poking at his nostrils with his little fingers: "I don't want to feel guilt. It's neither reasonable nor intelligent to feel guilt. But Leora . . . Leora . . . I ate her pussy and then she did away with herself. I had told her there was no way I could marry her. She was from an orphanage. She needed me, didn't she? *Me*. The battlescarred veteran of two bad marriages. Whose wives had considered him to be as exciting as shit in a teapot. And yet Leora, Leora the orphanage girl, Leora didn't want to be alone either, did she? And she concluded that it was better to be dead than to be alone. I . . . sometimes even *I* feel that way . . . I, well, the thing is, I have had sex with my daughter's best friend . . . I don't know why . . . all the woman did was plead with me to bite her tits until they bled . . . what sort of practice is *that*? I have a partial upper bridge, and it kept slipping as I tried to bite her tits. But I finally did draw blood, and what do you think of *that*, Uncle Herman? Doesn't it just make you balloon up with pride because you're a member of the human race? You . . . what are we talking about? We're talking about being alone, aren't we? Leora preferred death. She hanged herself with her fucking *garterbelt*. Oh, listen to me. I said *hanged*. Most people say *hung*, but *hanged* is correct. Listen to the learned Herr Professor of English. *Jawohl*, such a brilliant fellow . . ." And Eugene covered his eyes. Eugene, fat Eugene, trembled. His shirt and jacket sang with sweat. It was August in Houston, and he should have had more sense than to have worn a shirt and jacket. Herman Marshall sighed. He drove home, and the traffic on the Gulf Freeway was clogged and jumbled, and the old boys in their pickup trucks . . . the Fast Lane old boys with their gun racks and their tengallon hats and their heavy kicker boots . . . all passed on the right and swerved across lanes of traffic and made left turns where they should have made right turns, and a skim of clouds was rolling up from Galveston, and the bright sky was clotted, and then came a quick pale rain that made Herman Marshall want to piss, but he tightened his prick and chewed his tongue and told himself he'd by God control himself, and he did. He lurched from the car as soon as it had pulled into the driveway. He unlocked the front door and stumbled inside the house and made it to the kitchen, where he pissed hotly into the sink. Eugene followed along and said nothing. Eugene still was sniffling, and he kept trying to clear phlegm from his throat. Jobeth brought over a fried chicken for supper, and Eugene ate most of it. He and Herman Marshall drank more Shiner, and they said little. Herman Marshall was wondering, though. He was wondering about what he supposed was the end of his world. He was wondering about what those Nawzis had felt when he had killed them. He had been such a goddamn *terror* in those days, and it all had felt so fucking *good*. Jobeth kept smiling at him, but Jobeth was no Edna, and it didn't matter how many times Jobeth jacked him off and licked his prick. And it didn't matter how many times she showed him movies where a nigger gave it to a white woman up the ass. Herman Marshall wondered how people could place much stock in sunflowers and kittens and peach pie and Scrabble and marriage vows and Mickey Mouse. He wondered how people could believe in religions that kept insisting a virgin was capable of popping a baby. He wanted to be in Paradise, and surely Edna was in Paradise, and maybe they would have a grand reunion there in that celestial forest of harps. But there was more. What had happened to the Nawzis he had killed? What had happened to Elsie? What had happened to Eldred Junior, who had fucked Herman Marshall's wife? What had happened to all the useless come juice Herman Marshall had planted inside Edna? Edna and her goddamned funnypapers. Edna and those people and animals that had talked in balloons. Edna and her quiet laughter. Edna and her *hair* and her *combs* and her *hairribbons*. Edna and her fucking *wig*. Where was the logic to any of this? Where was the scheme? Things had to have schemes. Diesel engines had schemes. Insurance policies had schemes. Computers and television sets had schemes. Even all those goddamn Houston freeways were *supposed* to have schemes. And even the music of cicadas had its own horny scheme.

[219]

But the behavior of people wasn't a *thing*. It was more an *accident*, a series of completed possibilities. Herman Marshall mused on all this, and Eugene went upstairs and fetched a notebook and sat across the table and wrote in the notebook. "You keepin some sort of record of things?" said Herman Marshall. Said Eugene, looking up from the notebook: "Yes. But please don't think I've acquired any sort of wisdom. That would be . . . unwise." And Eugene smiled and returned to his writing. Herman Marshall looked away from Eugene and the notebook. What did Herman Marshall care about some goddamn notebook? It wasn't *the* book, and that was for sure. No such a person as fat Eugene would have been able to write *the* book, and no, you don't want to chain me to at tree, you boogers you. No. No. Don't do at. An don't leave me no watermelon. No. No. I mean, not *watermelon*. Never mind my nigger lips, you fuckfaces. You'll go to hell. At's what'll happen. You'll go to hell, an Satan'll set your pricks on fahr. Herman Marshall decided he needed to do something strong and brave, and never mind what the neighbors thought. And it could not be made up. It could not be created from some artifact rescued from the attic. It would have to be straightforward, and it would have to be good. Maybe there would be pain, but only if it were inflicted in a good cause. You say you both want to suck my cock first, girls? You say you didn't know about all at Nawzi shit, an anyway, you're too young? Well, fuck you, girls. Show your Uncle Herman a little cunt and a little mouth, haw haw. Herman Marshall made fists. Four empty Shiner bottles were on the table before him. Fat Eugene scribbled. Fat Eugene bit his pen and every so often blinked at the ceiling. Jobeth hovered and smiled, and surely she would have to go. Herman Marshall wondered how long her cunt had been in use . . . since maybe 1910 or so? He wished he knew how to conjure up peach pie and Mickey Mouse.

[220]

He wished he knew how to weep when certain music was played. Maybe he even wished the deaths of President Roosevelt and President Kennedy and Grace Kelly had meant more to him. Maybe all the juice had been squeezed from him, but had it really been within him in the first place? He and Eugene would visit the Top of the World tomorrow, and what would happen to the gentle rummies? For that matter, what would happen to Eugene? Why had Herman Marshall been deprived of *blood*, of *continuation*? What did a person do for company? Edna, Edna . . . I love you . . . it won't hurt none . . . just . . . at's it . . . your bloomers . . . it was a good picture show, wasn't it? Oh, Edna, Edna, I ain't never goin to feel bout nobody the way I feel bout you . . . yes, yes . . . *down with em* . . . you won't be sorry. And Herman Marshall blinked. He was feeling strange, and the edges of his vision were blurred and warm, but he didn't believe anyone else would notice. He coughed, and Eugene glanced up for a moment, but there was nothing on Eugene's face that showed any sort of alarm. Eugene had tiny eyes, and they were encased in fat, and they didn't even blink. Herman Marshall was delighted. He thought of the two holdup men Harry Munger had killed in the Top of the World. It all could be done quickly, and John Law wouldn't be able to act until it was too late. (Would Tom Mix have understood this? Maybe. You just never knew about Tom Mix, him and his squint and his courage and his righteousness.) Trains stabbed through the night, and the cicadas rubbed and howled. Traffic hissed over on the Gulf Freeway, and a car roared past, and its radio was playing too loudly. The jeweled Houston skyline loomed over treetops, and Herman Marshall said to himself: It's all a crock, so what difference it make if I change things a little? Or a whole lot, dependin on how you think on it. Herman Marshall sent Jobeth home for the night. She complained. She told him he still was in a state of

[221]

terrible grief. He told her he wanted to be alone with his terrible grief. He thanked her for her kind attentions, and he told her he never would forget all the fine things she'd done for him, but tonight he wanted to be alone with his thoughts (and his pecker, although he didn't say *that*), and couldn't she understand? Quickly Jobeth nodded. She told Herman Marshall she'd never intended to be a *bother*. She swiped at an eye with a sleeve. She told him she would be over in the morning to fix breakfast . . . eggs and bacon, grits and gravy, biscuits. Herman Marshall nodded. He told Jobeth fine, that would be real nice, and he'd surely appreciate it. He lay awake most of the night. He worked at a scheme. He needed a scheme. He thought ahead. He planned. He hadn't been an ace checker player for nothing. It was 1928 again, and the checkers clicked, and he would defeat the world. Hell, he wouldn't only defeat the world. He would god damn you bet your fucking ass end it.

CHAPTER SEVENTEEN

THAT NIGHT, which was the night of Thursday, August 23, 1984, Eugene wrote this entry in his journal as he sat at the kitchen table with Herman Marshall:

It has been a strange day, and Uncle Herman is a strange man. I believe I am frightened. Oh, there's nothing particularly new about that, but perhaps this time my fear has taken on a new dimension. Do I talk as though I am an actor in a *Twilight Zone* episode? Probably so, but I feel as though I am naked in a forest of axes and razorblades. He called me a fat sonofabitch, and he kept making references to blood. And I confessed to him about Eleanor LeBay, aka Our Lady of the Bleeding Tit. I am wandering barefoot in vomit and nerve ends. It is reasonably clear he sees no purpose to his life, and I believe there is a great deal of danger involved. My plane for Pittsburgh doesn't leave until tomorrow night, and I wonder whether I'll be aboard it. I hope so. There are many more of the Pound *Cantos* I need to read and try to understand. (We toured the city today, and the city is every bit as frightening as Uncle Herman is. There are altogether too many skyscrapers and freeways and oil refining facilities, and it is as though everyone is on a perpetual restless stroll, like whores shaking their rear ends for the world to see. But the strolling takes place inside cars and pickup trucks, and sometimes dogs ride in the back of the pickup trucks, and the dogs dance and balance, and the dogs' tongues protrude, and that way maybe a rush of air won't suck them out into the road. What's all this talk of blood?)

That old woman, Jobeth Stephenson, came to Uncle Herman's house at 7:30 the next morning. As advertised, she fixed a breakfast of eggs and bacon, grits and gravy, biscuits. She kept touching Uncle Herman whenever she had the opportunity, and maybe Eugene should have been amused. She touched Uncle Herman on his chin, on a cheek. She patted Uncle Herman's temples. Uncle Herman said little. His expression appeared . . . well, paralyzed. He paid no attention to Jobeth Stephenson when she touched him. His flesh gave him the appearance of an old dead lizard. He drove Eugene out to the Top of the World late that morning. He drove steadily, easily. He drove almost as though he understood the future. Or at least he drove as though he wasn't particularly afraid of it. The rented car's airconditioner sucked and rattled. Eugene didn't understand the rattle. Oh well, what did anyone have a right to expect from a Chevvy? And he said: "It's a peculiar sound, isn't it?"

"Sound?" said Uncle Herman. "What sound?"

"The airconditioner. There's something wrong with the airconditioner, isn't there?"

"Well," said Uncle Herman, "maybe it'll break down."

"I hope not. I'll melt."

"Maybe at air's what you're supposed to do."

"Pardon?"

"Melt. Melt in the fires. Melt on account of it don't none of it matter."

"Pardon?"

"The light's too bright," said Uncle Herman. "It's like my eyeballs is being layered away, you know? Like maybe the peelin of a grape."

"I don't . . . well, I'm sorry, but I'm afraid I don't quite understand . . ."

"What was it you done told me yesterday? Somethin about eatin some girl's pussy an then she went an kilt herself? An didn't we . . . both of us . . . talk about lonely?"

[224]

". . . yes," said Eugene. He was carrying a packet of Kleenex. He opened the packet of Kleenex and mopped his forehead, his cheeks. "I do believe . . . yes, I do believe I could use a beer when we arrive at our destination . . ."

"Yessir," said Uncle Herman. "Sounds good." And then Uncle Herman again was silent. The Chevvy clamored and bounced along the Gulf Freeway, past the *EXXON* signs and the *PLYMOUTH* and *TOYOTA* signs, and Eugene watched a German shepherd slide and skitter in the back of a pickup truck, and once or twice he glanced back at the harsh unexpected skyline and told himself he didn't *care* about the Recession . . . he preferred the poor weathered bankrupt Northeast to all this frantic boomtown noise and stress. He wondered what the German shepherd was thinking. Maybe the German shepherd was thinking along the same lines. Uncle Herman rubbed his mouth. Maybe Uncle Herman was trying not to drool. But why would Uncle Herman have felt a need to drool? What in the name of God was Uncle Herman working through his mind, and would Eugene be harmed by it? Eugene touched his knees and squeezed them. He didn't want to be harmed by anything. Oh, he knew he should have paid more attention to whatever it had been Leora had sought from him. And he knew it wasn't proper to bite his daughter's best friend's tit until the damn thing gave up little smeary blots of blood. And he knew it did no good to curse his tormentors and whack his bosom and wonder what his father's sad purpose had been. But did any of this mean Eugene had to be *harmed*? He almost wished he could jump from this car. Almost. All his life had been a succession of almosts. There even were times when he wished he could stride into a Freshman Composition class with one of those Vietnam Era M16s cradled in an arm and cut down all those little buggers who lounged there in their fucking Jordache jeans and chewed their fucking gum and didn't know Edith Wharton from goddamn Jen-

[225]

nifer Beals. He could see the little buggers flying in all directions. He could see them spouting blood as though they were background extras in a Sam Peckinpah movie. The thought almost always made him smile. That was the thing about violence and abrupt carnage. It was attractive even to an utter sissy such as your basic Eugene Coffee. And Eugene Coffee used Kleenex after Kleenex on his face. He used them until they were sopping. And then the Chevvy was gliding onto one of the Gulf Freeway feeder roads, and it made a left turn, and a little later it was on the Stevens Highway, and then it was bouncing across the parking lot in front of a building that had a neon sign on the roof, and the neon sign said: *TOP OF THE WORLD*. The roof was corrugated, and heat wiggled up from it in steady blurry waves. Eugene and his Uncle Herman hurried inside the place, and they were met by a heavy rush of cold air, and Eugene recognized the man who stood behind the bar. The fellow's name was Harry or Harold or something like that, and Eugene remembered him from Aunt Edna's funeral. Two men were sitting at the bar. One of them looked up. The other didn't. The one who looked up also had been at the funeral. He was beefy, and he introduced himself as Ralph Danielson, and he said he was a retired member of the Pasadena, Texas, cops. The other man, the one who did *not* look up, was real deef, according to Ralph Danielson, and it surely was a shame about poor old Rollie, the way he seemed to be falling apart so fast. The bartender introduced himself as Harry Munger, and he and Eugene shook hands. Eugene and his Uncle Herman bellied up to the bar and ordered Shiners. There was a clatter in the back of the place, and Harry Munger said his wife was washing last night's supper dishes. They served a nice barbecue in the evening, said Harry Munger, and it hadn't killed anyone in oh maybe three or four weeks now, ha ha. And then Uncle Herman made an attempt at a smile. At least it caused a corner of his mouth to move around in a sort of flutter. And he said to Harry Munger: "I had to bring my nephew here. I mean, this here's a real tourist attraction. A regular Gilley's."

"Now you're talkin," said Harry. "Now you got it. A regular Gilley's, all right. Like a pile of sheep dip is your regular sirloin steak." And Harry snorted. The morning *Post* was open on the bar in front of him. He brought Eugene and Uncle Herman their Shiner longnecks, and then he seated himself on a high stool and sucked on a pencil and went to work on the crossword puzzle.

"What a lot of shit," said Uncle Herman, swigging at his Shiner.

Harry Munger looked up.

"The bartender an the crossword puzzle," said Uncle Herman. "You seen at in some picture show, didn't you? The wise old bartender with his wise old pencil an his wise old crossword puzzle, an any minute now you're goin to ask me what's a fourletter word for screwin, ain't you?"

"Hey," said Harry. "Hold on, boy. I mean, I know Edna ain't been in the ground but less an two days, but at don't mean you got to . . . well, you know, come after me like I was some sort of maybe your enemy . . ."

Uncle Herman began to choke and wheeze.

"Hold on with at," said Ralph Danielson. "Don't give way, God damn you."

The old deaf man did not look up.

Harry Munger set down his pencil and said to Ralph Danielson: "If he wants to give way, at's okay."

Uncle Herman nodded.

Eugene touched Uncle Herman's shoulder.

Uncle Herman flinched.

The old deaf man looked around. He blinked. "Someone say

[227]

my name?" he said. He was leaning forward, and his arms more or less were curled around a can of Budweiser.

Uncle Herman looked at the old deaf man and hollered: "*How you doin, Rollie?*"

"Real good," said Rollie Beecham.

"*They hangin tight an strong?*"

". . . yessir," said Rollie Beecham.

Uncle Herman blinked at Harry Munger. "I . . . I'm sorry. I didn't mean to holler at you. If you like crossword puzzles, at's your business. I mean, it probably beats rapin little babies, don't it?"

Harry Munger nodded. "Forget it," he said. "These here been tough days." He hesitated for a moment, then: "At air Stephenson woman, she still stayin with you? Me an Beth, well, you know, we don't think she's the best sort of person to be movin in with you. No offense, but she's sort of—"

"I know what she is," said Uncle Herman.

"You can do better," said Harry.

"I wonder . . ."

"Look at Milt."

"What?"

"Milt an his Diana, the old girl from the Plymouth Rock? Remember when he told us about her? Well, he brought her in here last night, an she ain't bad, an she was all over him, and she even got to him to dance to at air jukebox. Kenny Rogers an Willie Nelson an I don't know who all. An we all sort of stood around an watched, an he was grinnin an clappin an havin the time of his life. Today's her day off, an I believe they said they was comin back today. Wait until you catch her. You'll know why he bragged on her so loud."

"Well," said Uncle Herman, "good for Milt. Now he ain't goin to be lonely, ain't at so?"

"It surely is so," said Harry. "Why, you should of seen Beth. She was jealous fit to be tied. She thinks she's the queen bee round here, you know? I mean, ever since she had her teeth fixed, a man can't hardly live with her. But last night . . . well, she had to take a back seat to at old girl from the Plymouth Rock . . . the way at old girl danced an all . . . tits flappin ever whichaway . . . big smile on her face . . . an she's hangin onto old Milt like he's the earth an the stars an the sea . . ."

Uncle Herman nodded. "Good enough. I'd like to see her. I'd like to see everbody. I want to see people with other people. I want to see what it means like when people talk about blood. I want to know what all the sunshine means."

"Say again?"

"Never mind," said Uncle Herman.

"You all right?" said Harry.

"I'm just fine," said Uncle Herman. But then he looked around, and he got to frowning. "He comin here?"

"Who?" said Harry.

"Milt. Him an at woman of his."

"I expect so," said Harry.

"Good," said Uncle Herman. "The more, the merrier . . ."

"What?" said Harry.

"Nothin," said Uncle Herman, but he still was frowning. "An what bout old Ike Sage? Where's he at?"

"This is his chiropractor day," said Harry. "The highspot of his week, member? The only day his back feels good, member?"

"Oh," said Uncle Herman. "Well, lucky him."

"What?" said Harry.

"Nothin . . ." said Uncle Herman.

Harry Munger frowned. Then, shrugging, he returned to his crossword puzzle. People came and went. A retired schoolteacher named Frank Lee Doubleday was introduced to Eugene, and they

[229]

shook hands. Frank Lee Doubleday spoke of the deplorable state of contemporary education, and Eugene agreed. Eugene did not mention the M16, though. Perhaps this Frank Lee Doubleday wouldn't have understood. Frank Lee Doubleday bought Eugene and Uncle Herman a drink. Frank Lee had been one of Edna's pallbearers, and he told Uncle Herman he wouldn't soon be forgetting her. He told Uncle Herman her barbecue always had been a work of art. He told Uncle Herman her sweet disposition had been enough to render the heavens mute. He touched one of Uncle Herman's arms and squeezed it and said nothing more, but his eyes were wet, and from time to time he would nod, as though he were listening to a silent voice that was ticking off Edna's gentle attributes. Milt Willis came in with his Diana, and she was wearing a black dress, and maybe she was overdressed for so early in the day, but no one really gave much of a whoop. Harry Munger whistled, and Beth came out from the kitchen and frowned at him. But he'd had a right to whistle. Diana, whose last name was Epps, was tall and leggy, and she still had her figure. Her hair was ashy, and she probably was sixty, but she carried herself with slow grace, as though maybe at one time she'd been a fashion model or some such thing. She went to Uncle Herman and told him how sorry she was about his wife. She told him she would have attended Edna's funeral with Milt, but she'd had to work. She was real sorry about that, and she hoped Uncle Herman forgave her. Uncle Herman nodded. He looked away from her. She shook hands with Eugene, and her fingers were tight. Eugene swallowed. Milt elbowed next to Uncle Herman and said something to the effect that she surely was a good old girl, wasn't she? In Eugene's view, this Milt was too big, too slobby. He was nearly as big and as slobby as Eugene himself was. And Eugene sighed. And Eugene breathed Diana's perfume. It had a greenish cast, and it was interesting. Harry Munger looked up from his crossword puzzle and announced that he had finished it. Everyone applauded. Everyone except the old deaf man, who did not look up. Harry Munger bought drinks for the house. Beth made loud abrupt sounds in the kitchen. Milt began speaking to Diana of Harry Munger. He spoke of how Harry Munger had killed two holdup men. He spoke of the gun Harry kept in the cash register. It was a .38 Smith & Wesson revolver, said Milt, and it had killed two men, or at least one and a half, haw haw, seeing as how the second one had been a nigger. Diana gasped and covered her mouth. Harry Munger looked away and said nothing. The uproar persisted in the kitchen. And finally Harry Munger looked at Diana and smiled and said: "I didn't do nothin. Not really. I mean, a man's got a right to protect his property, an at's all air is to it. I mean, I didn't have nothin personal gainst em old boys. A little old gun's like a little old insurance policy, you follow what I'm tryin to say?"

Diana nodded. "Of course I do," she said. "But I know *I* wouldn't have the nerve to do what you done. If somebody came into the Plymouth Rock, why, I'd give him whatever he wanted, an no questions asked." She smiled at Milt Willis. "Right, honey? No questions asked, ain't at so?"

Milt stared down at his knuckles.

Ralph Danielson laughed, and so did Frank Lee Doubleday.

Milt glared at both of them.

Diana looked around. "Did I say somethin?"

"You didn't say nothin at all," said Milt. "You're a good girl, an you're good to me, an I love you."

Uncle Herman suddenly smiled. It was an ideal smile, a genuine smile. He spoke to Diana. "*Love*," he said. "Good old *love*. It'll mean you ain't goin to be lonely. It'll mean you can go on. Everbody wants to go on. One way or tuther. Love beats dyin, don't it?"

Diana blinked. "What . . . you're talkin about your wife, ain't you? I'm sure sorry about her. I guess maybe she hurt a little, didn't she?"

". . . somethin like at," said Uncle Herman.

"At's a real shame," said Diana.

"We all feel at way," said Frank Lee Doubleday to Uncle Herman. "Myself, I helped carry her to the grave. As you know. I mean, you chose me for at . . . honor. An I'm proud to have been chosen. An I *was* aware, an I *am* aware, of what she went through."

Uncle Herman was wearing a cap that said *AS TROS*. He touched its bill. "You expect you could go through it?"

Frank Lee Doubleday's mouth opened, but he said nothing.

"I think maybe nobody ought to have to go through it," said Uncle Herman. "I think maybe her an me, we didn't live all at much. You take your average person, your average person sleeps eight hours a night, correct? I read at all the time in the papers, so it must be true. An all right, just you suppose a person lives to the age of seventyfive . . . what do *at* mean? It means he's done slept *twentyfive years*. So he ain't seventyfive a tall; he's only fifty. But he *feels* seventyfive, don't he? Only he been cheated. He been cheated. He been cheated out of a third of his life, an you call at *livin*? Well, fuck all of you, an fuck your dogs an your canary-birds an the worms wigglin in the earth. Me an Edna, it all got away from us, an Billy . . . Billy . . . you should of heard him . . . all of you . . . the way he flang out dirty words an screamed an carried on . . . an at the end Edna called it a Judgment . . . an I expect a person's got to ask *why me*? Ah, shit, here I am, talkin away. Not since I was a boy did I talk so much as I'm talkin these here days. In *em* days, yessir, I talked a whole lot, an I used to make up stories for Edna, stories bout folks in MKT Pullman cars

[232]

an daycoaches, stories maybe bout animals or old folks or movie stars or the President, whose name was Hoover an then whose name was Roosevelt, an anybody here member em old boys? Well, all I'm tryin to say is at at one time I blabbed away an blabbed away like maybe somebody was payin me for it. But em days is gone, an so I know I ought to shut up now, but I keep wonderin about em twentyfive years, an Billy made too much *noise,* you know, an he was in too much *pain,* you know, an I ain't exactly feelin on top of *my* game, you know?"

Everyone was looking at Uncle Herman. Even Rollie Beecham was looking at Uncle Herman.

Uncle Herman glanced around. His ideal and genuine smile had not gone away. It was precise and unmoving; it was solidly dentured. "Maybe we all ought to go together," he said. "The light's too bright, an I can't seem to find no book."

"What?" said Harry.

Uncle Herman cleared his throat .His ideal and genuine smile went away. ". . . nothin," he said. "I just been . . . bloviatin . . . which means sort of blowin off hot air . . ."

"That came from President Harding, didn't it?" said Eugene, speaking quickly.

"Yessir," said Uncle Herman.

"And I believe it meant simply doing nothing at all," said Eugene.

"At so?" said Uncle Herman.

"I believe so," said Eugene.

"Well, I wouldn't want to argue with no college professor," said Uncle Herman.

"To bloviate," said Eugene, "is not necessarily to bullshit."

"Well, kiss my ass an call me a liar an a fool," said Uncle Herman. He snickered.

[233]

Rollie Beecham, who was looking at him, smiled.

No one else particularly did anything.

"What's goin on?" said Milt Willis. He chewed his lips, and then he said to Uncle Herman: "We all of us sure enough feel bad on account of Edna, but at don't mean we got to listen to a lot of talk at don't make hardly no sense."

"We're all *old*," said Uncle Herman. Then, nodding toward Eugene: "Even him, nephew or no nephew. Old Old. *Old*. Old as the hills, an we ain't really lived but twothirds of the time we been on the earth. An me, all the years I battled highways an freeways an fuckin jackass stupid drivers an greazzy burgers an dirty waitresses an dronk old boys who wanted to fight me because maybe my shoelaces was untied or my earwax was the wrong color . . . well, at's all a good quick way of gettin old. An with nothin much to show for it." And Uncle Herman again summoned the ideal and genuine smile, and he directed it toward Harry Munger, and he said to Harry Munger: "You. You and Beth. Lucky you. At least you got kids, an air good kids, an at means *somethin*, don't it? But it don't stop the *old* none, ain't at so? It don't stop Rollie goin deef, an it don't stop Ike Sage's back miseries. An it didn't stop my Edna's cancer. Am I correct or am I correct? An the people on the TV, all they got to do to get a big laugh is to say old This an old At, an like old is flabby, an old is leakin from your asshole, an old is bein so stupid you want to open a door for a lady, an old is not likin it when all the pain comes crowdin around, an old is not likin it on account of air ain't enough time for the livin of it, an 19 an 37 was the day before yesterday, an we all of us was eatin the same greazzy burgers, an I . . . well, I don't know but what I—"

"No," said Harry.

". . . what?" said Uncle Herman, still smiling the ideal and genuine smile.

[234]

"It don't do no good."

". . . what don't do no good?"

"Talkin this way. Relax, Herman. Have another Shiner. Have all the Shiners you want."

Uncle Herman looked at Eugene and said: "You're Edna's blood. Don't *you* believe me?"

Eugene's mouth was furry. He didn't know much, but he did know this was leading somewhere, and probably somewhere dark. "Uncle Herman," he said, "it's your . . . well, it's your grief that's speaking. We all can understand that . . ."

"Sure enough . . ." said Diana, exhaling.

The ideal and genuine smile again went away, and Uncle Herman said to Eugene: "These here is all good people, but they hurt, an they oughtn't to have to hurt. I mean, if *I* hurt, *they* hurt. An if *I'm* dirty an tired, *air* dirty an tired. I know I'm talkin the —"

"Hold on," said Frank Lee Doubleday.

"Just a goddamn minute," said Milt Willis.

"—truth," said Uncle Herman. "We need to get clean. We need to wash our feet an pray for a better day. She . . . my Edna . . . she wasn't perfect, but at didn't mean no *Judgment* had to come crashin down on her like maybe lightnin or thunder or the final flood on the Last Day . . . an what did *Billy* ever do? Now you take me, all right, I been a sinner. Other women an all. An I done sinned in the mind more an old Jimmy Carter ever would of dreamed of. But even *me* . . . I don't think I was all *at* bad. *But it don't matter. The thing is—we all die. The thing is—nothin's been worth all at much to begin with. Which means—all we can hope for is good old Paradise. The Sweet Bye & Bye. Where we all can set around an drink beer an maybe tune our harps . . .*" And Uncle Herman's ideal and genuine smile again returned, and it was perfect. He smiled as though he were the inventor of the smile. He smiled as though he were the inventor of goodness and mercy.

Eugene reached up and gnawed on a knuckle, and Eugene wasn't particularly breathing.

Smiling, smiling, smiling, Uncle Herman walked to the far end of the bar. No one moved. Harry Munger's mouth opened, but he said nothing. Uncle Herman walked behind the bar. He walked to the cash register. It was an oldfashioned cash register with a large drawer. He rang up *NO SALE.*

Harry was standing perhaps ten feet away. "Hey now," he said.

The cash register's bell echoed. Uncle Herman reached deep inside the drawer and came up with the .38 Smith & Wesson that had killed the two holdup men. "I kilt people in Germany," said Uncle Herman, "an it ain't no big trick." He hefted the .38. "Loaded," he said. "A gun at ain't loaded ain't worth much of a shit, is it?"

Diana squealed a little.

Harry moved toward Uncle Herman.

Smiling, oh and how splendid it was, Uncle Herman shot Harry squarely between the eyes, and most of Harry's skull blew away.

CHAPTER EIGHTEEN

SCREAMING AND CLATTERING, Beth came rushing in from the kitchen, and Herman Marshall shot her twice in the belly. She was slammed back against the kitchen door, and she sat down. She bled from her belly, and she bled from her perfect mouth. Ralph Danielson tried to climb over the bar after Herman Marshall, but Herman Marshall shot Ralph Danielson in the neck, and Ralph Danielson collapsed in a sprawl across the bar, and he knocked over several bottles of beer. No one else moved. Diana from the Plymouth Rock was shaking and chattering. There was a box of shells in the cash register. Herman Marshall's ideal and genuine smile was as perfect as Beth's mouth had been. He took the box of shells and reloaded the Smith & Wesson. "Ain't nothin to it," he said to no one in particular, and he was thinking of Nawzis. Diana and Milt tried to make a run for the front door, and Herman Marshall shot Diana in a leg, and he shot Milt in the buttocks. The two of them were supposed to be in love, and maybe Herman Marshall should have spared them, but he didn't believe they really were in love. Just because she had licked Milt's balls, what did *that* prove? Diana and Milt lay squirming on the floor. Beth made gagging sounds over by the kitchen door. Herman Marshall went to Beth and blew away her head the way he had blown away her husband's head. He didn't suppose their kids ever would understand, ha ha. He came around the bar, and Eugene was motionless, and Frank Lee Doubleday was leaning against the bar and weeping into his hands, and Rollie Beecham appeared to be paying no attention to anything. Herman Marshall squatted over Diana and

[237]

Milt. They tried to crawl. He told Diana she could lick Milt's balls until hell froze over, and she whimpered, and her skirt was hiked up, and the backs of her legs were altogether too veiny, and he shot away the back of her neck. Blood flew, spattering his face, and he flinched, and his ideal and genuine smile was interrupted for a moment. He swiped at his face with a sleeve. Milt was pissing his pants and moaning and farting, and Herman Marshall wanted to tell Milt there was nothing special Milt would be leaving. He shot Milt in the small of the back, and he shot Milt in a temple, and so much for Milt. He turned and shot Frank Lee Doubleday from a distance of perhaps fifteen feet, and the bullet struck Frank Lee in a shoulder. Frank Lee yowled. A second shot blew away most of Frank Lee's throat, and he slid to the floor, and he gasped and bubbled, and so much for Frank Lee. Eugene was blubbering, and he had pressed his hands over his skull. Old Rollie Beecham drank Budweiser and didn't appear to know what was happening. Herman Marshall reloaded the Smith & Wesson. He walked to the blubbering Eugene and lightly embraced the blubbering Eugene and said: "Never you mind now. You're blood is what you are." Then he moved down the bar to Rollie Beecham, and Rollie Beecham looked up at him and smiled. "Drink up," said Herman Marshall to old Rollie Beecham. Nodding, old Rollie Beecham lifted his can of Budweiser to his mouth. "Have a nice trip," said Herman Marshall to Rollie Beecham, and he shot Rollie Beecham in the face, the chest, the belly. Eugene screamed. Ralph Danielson's body slid off the bar. Blinking, Herman Marshall looked around, and his ideal and genuine smile had returned. So far, so good. So far, and his scheme had worked. So far, and there had been no resistance at all. So far, and they all were better off. Herman Marshall stepped over various corpses and went to Eugene, and Eugene still was screaming, and Herman Marshall told Eugene to fucking good and well start behaving like a man. Herman Marshall had an odor of beer. Rollie Beecham's can of Budweiser more or less had exploded. Eugene dropped to his knees and tried to embrace Herman Marshall's legs. Herman Marshall began beating Eugene on the head, and Eugene fell back on the floor. Herman Marshall briefly pressed the Smith & Wesson's warm barrel to his cheek. He sighed. He glanced at Ralph Danielson's corpse, and he saw that Ralph Danielson had shit. Poor old tough Ralph Danielson. And Herman Marshall looked around at all the corpses and said: "Poor old all of em." Then he squatted over Eugene and said: "You're blood of her blood. You think I'd kill you? Shit, at wouldn't make no sense. I'm only killin the ones at are goin anyway. On account of it don't make no matter. On account of now they'll be all together where the whole damn bidness'll be explained." And Herman Marshall jammed the Smith & Wesson inside his belt and began tugging at Eugene's armpits. He barely was able to budge the big fat sonofabitch, and so he finally said to Eugene: "If you don't stand up, I'm goin to go back on my word an shoot your fuckin ass off . . . an then I'll go to work on your damn *balls*, you understand me?" And Eugene twitched. And Eugene shuddered. Herman Marshall backed away from him and pulled out the Smith & Wesson and said: "I ain't funnin around with you, Eugene old boy." And Eugene nodded. And Eugene was bleating. And Eugene sat up and hugged his knees for a moment. Then he struggled to his feet, and he flailed, and he bumped against the bar. He looked around at the corpses and he began to puke all over the front of his jacket. "Yessir," said Herman Marshall. "At's the ticket. It's what I seen a whole lot of old boys do durin the war an we'd had to kill Nawzis. Not at these here folks is *Nawzis*, but the principle's the same, ain't it? The principle of what it's like to be dead an layin in your own fuckin mess. Look

[239]

over air at Diana from the fuckin Plymouth Rock. Maybe this mornin she was lickin old Milt's balls. *Now* look at her. We all go real easy, don't we? Remember old JFK in Dallas; he was *President of the United States,* but he wasn't nothin when it came to dyin, ain't at so? *Nothin.* Ain't nobody is nothin, an so it's real easy, don't you see?" And now Herman Marshall's ideal and genuine smile was breaking up, and this time it probably wouldn't return. At least for awhile. He pushed Eugene toward the door. "I got more work to do," he said, "an I want you to be my witness. You're a college professor an all, an you keep a journal, an maybe you'll write it all down." And Eugene was shoved out the front door of the Top of the World, and sunlight briefly blinded both Herman Marshall and Eugene, and briefly they groped, and the heat caused Herman Marshall to grimace and bare his dentures. He held Eugene by a wrist and shoved him toward the car. "We're goin home now," said Herman Marshall, "but air's still work to do. A man who's a real man . . . when he sets out to do a thing, he does her through an through until air ain't nothin left . . ." And Eugene nodded. And Eugene still was puking a little. He glanced across the Stevens Highway, but nothing was there except a little old Burger Chef place, and so Herman Marshall said to him: "You hungry or somethin? Why don't you eat what's on the front of you? It's real warm an all." And Herman Marshall touched the corner of an eye. "Edna used to preach to me bout havin a warm meal at least oncet a day . . . especially when I was out on the road an pushin some rig or tuther. A warm meal, she said. A warm meal will keep my Herman healthy an wealthy an wise, ha ha." Herman Marshall yanked open the car door on the passenger's side. He shoved Eugene inside the car. Then he hurried around the car and slid in on the driver's side. He started the car, and it bumped across the Top of the World parking lot. "This here is a worse parkin lot an the Gilley's parkin lot," said Herman Marshall, "an I be goddamn if I know why Harry ain't fixed it up." A hesitation. Then: "But I expect now it don't matter none, ain't at so?"

Eugene was huddled against the door on the passenger's side.

The car skidded across Stevens Highway and turned west, back toward the freeway. Herman Marshall sucked saliva through the openings between his teeth. The car's airconditioner still was making peculiar sounds, but who gave a shit? He knew of at least seven dead people who didn't. "Seven of em," he said aloud. "Seven."

Eugene shuddered and gagged.

"An it would of been eight, only Ike Sage was lucky, the old fart."

Eugene's eyes squinted. He drooled.

"Life in the real world, Eugene," said Herman Marshall.

Eugene's head moved from side to side in fat spasms. He carried a sharp stink of puke, but the airconditioner did away with much of it, and thank the Lord for the airconditioner, peculiar sounds and all. ". . . no," said Eugene, choking. ". . . no . . . what why I don't understand you there they were and they hadn't done anything I could see to you you were their friend and they gave you their condolences my God they were there one moment and gone the next no explanation you give no explanation I want I need you see explanation otherwise no sense you got to understand what I mean don't you . . ."

"Think on it," said Herman Marshall.

". . . what?"

"Just think on it."

". . . on *what*?"

"*It*," said Herman Marshall, and then he was silent. He kept sucking the saliva. He listened to the traffic, and he listened to the

[241]

airconditioner. He had all their faces memorized. The faces of the dead ones. And the faces of the ones who would be dead. At least four more people would be dead. Ralph Danielson's face always had been heavy, a police officer's face. And Beth and that Diana had been pretty, considering their ages and all. And poor little Rollie Beecham had been such a good old driedup little fucking toad. And the face of Milt Willis had been coarse. And the face of Harry Munger had been intelligent, with sharp features. And the face of Frank Lee Doubleday had been rimless, thoughtful. Herman Marshall sighed. Maybe, if it had been brought to a vote, those people wouldn't have chosen to die. But maybe he understood more than they did. Maybe he knew more about loneliness and cancer and age and betrayals and disappointments. Grunting, he placed the Smith & Wesson on top of the dashboard. Eugene blinked at the Smith & Wesson and began to snivel. "Christ," said Herman Marshall. "Christ, Eugene, *stop* at shit. An while you're at it take some of at air Kleenex of yours an try to clean off some of at air puke. Jesus."

Eugene shrugged, gasped, fumbled for the Kleenex.

"At a boy," said Herman Marshall.

Eugene nodded. Eugene wadded Kleenex and rubbed and rubbed.

The Smith & Wesson bounced a little on the dashboard. Herman Marshall drove carefully on the freeway. He drove in the curb lane, and he didn't care how many cars and trucks passed this here rented Chevvy. He wasn't in all that much of a hurry. There was no sense being in a hurry. People who were in a hurry most of the time fucked things up. All of this here city of Houston was in a hurry, and it wanted to be the first and the best and the most and the biggest, but what about one final ultimate question? What about the possibility that none of it mattered? What about the possibility that only *people* mattered, even up to and including *old* people? Because right now they didn't matter. Because right now they had been scrapped. Because right now an old woman licked an old man's balls and then the old woman and the old man spoke of love. Because the old people of this life were seen as foolish, and so why didn't they vanish? Well, Herman Marshall had made a start. There now were seven fewer old people than there had been half an hour ago, and maybe Herman Marshall would be awarded a medal. It all made perfectly good sense to *him*, by God, and it wasn't as though he didn't know what it meant to kill things. Animals . . . people . . . boyish ambitions . . . what the fuck. Killing was killing, and maybe there was something worse than killing. Maybe living was worse than killing. Maybe pissing on a stranger's headstone was worse than killing. Maybe—

"I'm . . . I'm better now," said Eugene. His voice was thin, reedy, a child's voice. (It reminded Herman Marshall of what Billy's voice had been like when Billy had been, oh, maybe four years of age.)

"Better?" said Herman Marshall.

". . . yes," said Eugene. He rolled down the window on his side. He tossed out maybe a dozen wadded Kleenexes. He rolled up the window. "I've been good," he said. He patted his jacket. "I've disposed of as much as I can. I've been good, haven't I? You won't hurt me, will you?"

"*No*, God damn you. I already done *told* you at. I ain't goin to *hurt* you. You're *blood*, an Edna told me blood was important, an I'm takin her word for it. An anyway, I want you to give all this a good writeup in your notebook."

". . . I'll do that, Uncle Herman . . . I promise you I'll do that . . ."

"You'll do just about anythin I want you to do, won't you?"

". . . yes."

[243]

"On account of you're so scared your shit feels like canal water, right?"

Eugene cleared his throat. He shrugged, spread his hands. ". . . yes."

"It's important to stay alive, right?"

". . . I think so . . . *yes*."

"So how come at little old girl strung herself up?"

". . . I don't know."

"You probably never even gave it much of a think, did you?"

". . . maybe not."

"You're a pig," said Herman Marshall, "but it really pisses you off when folks *call* you a pig, don't it? It hurts your fuckin *feelins*, don't it? You say to yourself: Why is everybody pickin on me? Oh, you're a goddamn *load*, you are. It's a good thing you're blood, or you'd be layin back air with the rest of em . . ."

". . . I still don't understand."

"For a college professor, you're pretty fuckin stupid. I've already done explained it, an if you don't know the why of it *now*, you never will. An keep this in mind, Sunny Jim—*I liked those folks, an so doin what I done wasn't no fun for me, an it didn't get me all hot an bothered an excited, you hear what I'm sayin?* I only done what *had* to be done, on account of I wanted to get rid of hurt an bullshit . . ." And Herman Marshall took the Smith & Wesson and sniffed it. He exhaled. He pressed the muzzle against a nostril. The Chevvy was moving along at about fifty. "I . . . for a long time now, I've wanted to get clean. Like a calf or a new lamb. Whenever I see rain, I want to run outside an, well, take me a bath in the soft rainwater, on account of the soft rainwater is the best water air is, by God." And Herman Marshall twisted the muzzle of the Smith & Wesson against the nostril. He twisted it as though he were twisting a screwdriver. And then he said: "I got a whole lot to answer for, an I ain't just talkin bout today an at air mess back at the Top of the World. Today ain't no *accident*, Eugene. It ain't no unexpected thing. It's happened on account of everthin that happened *before* it led *up* to it . . . the life of *me*, Herman Eugene Marshall, all the days an the nights an the laughin an the bawlin an all the sick times with Billy an all the sick times with Edna an all the times I kilt Nawzis back when it was all right to kill all the Nawzis you could get your goddamn craw full of . . . or, haw, your *nose* full of . . ." And Herman Marshall jerked the Smith & Wesson away from the nostril. He drove with one hand and he hefted the Smith & Wesson with the other. He abruptly switched on the radio, and a nigger was singing a song that had to do with highways and Cadillacs. He switched off the radio. "Shit," he said. He reached across the front seat and pressed the muzzle of the Smith & Wesson against Eugene's fat sweating neck.

". . . my God," said Eugene.

"Try not to shake too much," said Herman Marshall.

". . . what?"

"You might make it go off."

". . . no," said Eugene.

"You goin to be a good boy?"

". . . yes."

"You want a second piece of pie for your supper?"

". . . yes."

"En you got to be a *real* good boy. You got to listen to what I say, an you got to stop pickin at me with your goddamn questions, on account of I've done *answered* all your questions before you fuckin *ask* them . . . you sad sack of shit you . . ."

". . . yes."

"Well," said Herman Marshall, "it's real nice to hear you agreein with me like at." And he pulled the Smith & Wesson away from

Eugene's neck. "People like you," said Herman Marshall, "got to work out a way of understandin what's real. I got talked into buyin a wig for Edna so at she wouldn't look bald when she was laid out. I don't like to think bout at. I don't like to think bout how . . . how stupidass dumb she looked layin down air an wearin at . . . thing. It wasn't no way *real*, you see. It *hid* the real, an what's the sense in *at*? At old girl Beth Munger, the one who came out of the kitchen an I shot her down, she used to have buck teeth, but she spent umptyump hunnerts of dollars on braces for herself, an so her buck teeth went away, but en she wasn't *real* no more, all right? Which means she might as well of been Dead an Gone, ain't at so? Oh, it's all fuckin *smoke*, an at's a fact . . ."

Eugene nodded. His fingers moved like worms.

"Blood is family," said Herman Marshall, and he returned the Smith & Wesson to the dashboard. "An blood is blood. It's like you an Edna, the connection you got. An it's like me killin Nawzis. We all of us got to be real careful when we talk bout blood. We don't want to get the one meanin all mixed up with the other meanin. If we was to do *at*, a whole big serious *mistake* could be made . . ."

Eugene nodded and mewled.

"At's easy for *you* to say," said Herman Marshall, and the ideal and genuine smile returned for a moment. At the same time, Herman Marshall was squinting at the sun, and he wondered whether maybe his squint came close to being a Tom Mix squint. Close, though, was all he could hope for, and he knew that. He exited the Gulf Freeway at the 610 Loop and drove home. Eugene mewled all the way. Herman Marshall parked the car in front of the home of old Zack Fears, the crip with the paralyzed leg. "Old Zack is a good old boy," said Herman Marshall to Eugene. Herman Marshall leaned against the steeringwheel for a moment, and then he took the Smith & Wesson off the dashboard. He flipped open the Smith & Wesson and loaded it. He blew on the chambers. He didn't know why. Maybe it would appear to be a competent thing to do. He nudged Eugene and said: "We're goin in air."

". . . no," said Eugene.

"Fuck we *ain't*," said Herman Marshall, and he pressed the Smith & Wesson's muzzle against Eugene's mouth.

Eugene began to gag.

"Well?" said Herman Marshall.

Eugene's eyes were all flooded and raw.

"*Well?*" said Herman Marshall, and he moved the muzzle from side to side across Eugene's mouth.

Eugene nodded.

"Good for you," said Herman Marshall, and he pulled the Smith & Wesson away from Eugene's mouth. He got out of the car and went around and opened the door on Eugene's side. Eugene came out in a sort of splayed stagger, and Herman Marshall had to help him with his balance. The street was shady, but no leaves were moving. A spattering of blood had dried on Herman Marshall's shirtfront, and he genuinely regretted that. Maybe, if he had the time, he would go home and change his shirt. Did his scheme allow for such time? He believed it did. After all, an expert checkerplayer always was ready to take care of unforseen things; an expert checkerplayer foresaw the unforseen, ha ha. Herman Marshall glanced around at all the trees and their motionless leaves. The trees had been baby trees when he and Edna had moved into this neighborhood thanks to his good old GI Loan. Edna had been fond of touching the baby trees and speculating on how tall they would grow. That fondness had become lost somewhere within all the years, but it had been a sweet fondness while it had lasted. Herman Marshall steered Eugene onto Zack Fears' porch and opened the front door without knocking. Zack always kept the front door unlocked. That way, he didn't have to hobble all the way to it whenever someone came calling. He simply could yell to the visitor to come on in. He was sitting in the front room when Herman Marshall and Eugene entered the house. He frowned at them. Herman Marshall supposed they were a sight, what with the puke and the blood. Zack Fears saw the Smith & Wesson and raised his crutch. The first shot from the Smith & Wesson shattered the crutch, and Eugene wailed. Zack Fears tried to crawl from his chair. The second shot from the Smith & Wesson penetrated Zack Fears' chest just below the collarbone. He reached toward Herman Marshall and called him a motherfucking cocksucker. Herman Marshall released a sad regretful sigh and shot Zack Fears in the groin, and Zack Fears flew backwards, overturning the chair, and Zack Fears was dead, and there was a painting of wild geese on a far wall, and a glass of beer was on a table next to the overturned chair. Herman Marshall suddenly felt thirsty, so he crossed to the table and emptied the glass of beer. Eugene was kneeling, and Eugene was saying something about how everyone picked on him, and what had he ever *done*? Herman Marshall told him to stop being such a goddamn sissy. He pointed the Smith & Wesson at him and told him to stand up. Eugene scrambled and scrabbled on the floor, but he did manage finally to stand up. Herman Marshall unleashed the ideal and genuine grin and told Eugene he was a brave little trooper. He steered Eugene out of Zack Fears' place and across the street. Jobeth Stephenson was standing on her front porch. She was shading her eyes. Herman Marshall was holding the Smith & Wesson, but Jobeth's eyesight wasn't all that good. She shouted to Herman Marshall and Eugene. Had they heard shots too? "*What shots?*" shouted Herman Marshall. Now he and Eugene were close enough so that Jobeth could see the Smith &

[248]

Wesson. She backed against a porch pillar. She began muttering to herself. She turned and went inside her house. Herman Marshall sprinted after her, and he dragged Eugene with him. Eugene's free arm moved in stupid arcs. Herman Marshall and Eugene were inside the house before Jobeth Stephenson could lock the front door. She knelt in her front room. She wept. She told Herman Marshall there was absolutely nothing on this earth she would not do for him. Briefly she spoke of him of diddlings and dirty movies. Her television set was blind and white against a far wall. Eugene flopped down on the sofa and closed his eyes and howled. Jobeth crawled toward Herman Marshall, and he allowed her to do that. She touched his fly, and he allowed her to do that as well. She told him she had been so good *to* him and *for* him. She told him she was a marvel for someone of her age, wasn't she? "Yes ma'am," said Herman Marshall, and he fired a shot that entered her skull through her left ear. Briefly he was blinded by bone fragments and blood. Eugene jerked and puked. How could he have so much puke in him? Herman Marshall wiped blood from his eyes and walked to the television set and shot it, and it sparked, and he shot it again, and smoke emerged from its fucking bowels or whatever. Jobeth's corpse lay in a sort of spraddle, and Herman Marshall said to himself: Good old Jobeth. She done died the way she lived. And the ideal and genuine smile illuminated the room. And then Herman Marshall led his nephew across the street, and they took showers and changed into clean clothes.

CHAPTER NINETEEN

HERMAN MARSHALL, in *extremis*. Herman Marshall, showering. Herman Marshall, scrubbing himself as blood bubbles down the drain, trickling from his face and his eyelids and his nose and his hair. Eugene is sitting on the bathroom floor. Herman Marshall has tied Eugene to the commode in such a way that Eugene is embracing the commode, and Eugene is naked, and Eugene's forehead rests against the lip of the commode. Eugene's hands are tied with a pillowcase, and the knots are cruelly tight, and Eugene is whimpering, but the sound of the water does away with the sound of Eugene's whimpering, and this is just as well. For here it is not Eugene who is significant. It is Herman Marshall who is significant, for Herman Marshall has killed nine persons this day, and he intends to kill more. There is more blood than he expected, and it swirls, and the water makes it as pink as a little girl's summer dress. He figures he will feel better when he towels himself dry and puts on clean clothes. He even will have to wear another cap. His *ASTROS* cap is altogether too bloody. He only has one other cap, and it says *LONE STAR*. He wishes it said *SHINER*, but then life never is perfect. Small inaccuracies forever creep in and lie down and take up permanent residence. This sort of thing can gnaw away a man's nuts. If he permits it entrance. And Herman Marshall has permitted entrance to just about any little old thing. His wife wanted him to kill her, and so she said she had sucked the cock of a Mex. But Herman Marshall did not kill his wife. That would have been simple, and his rage would have been quick, and it all would have been over. Instead, he brought this & that down from the attic and made up stories about princesses and she rewarded him with laughter and tears. He sees himself as a quiet and easy countryboy, and his overalls have been baked in sunlight, and he can play checkers with the best of them, and he didn't *want* to drown his brother's dog, but a young fellow has to do *something*. A young fellow needs to tell the world it shouldn't mess with him simply because he has nigger lips. He cannot *really* remember the details of his parents' features. Nor can he remember how fat the fat lady had been, and hadn't she tried to talk him and Edna into voting for Willkie maybe, or Dewey? He summons the face of Tom Mix, and Tom Mix has been dead since 1940, and why can he summon the face of Tom Mix and not the faces of his parents? They haven't been dead anywhere near that long, and yet they are without form, and void. Doesn't Holy Scripture begin that way? Ah, but Holy Scripture is the wrong book. There needs to be another book. It should be an unsparing book; it should be truth the way sunshine and blood are truth. Herman Marshall, in *extremis*, and he soaps his underarms. He tickles himself a little, and he giggles. Herman Marshall, in *extremis*, and maybe he should have discussed the fucking situation with a preacher. But the preacher only would have been shocked. What can a preacher possibly say to a man who seeks to end the world? Whatever I have to pay, says Herman Marshall to himself, I'll pay it. An maybe I won't pay nothin. Maybe I'll go straight to Paradise, an they'll all be waitin for me, an Harry'll chew on his pencil an ask me for a fourletter word meanin great affection. An at Diana's tits'll peek through the strings of her harp. Peek an wink an flirt, oh you bet your ass. If a man goes to Paradise, can he fix it so his balls get licked? I mean, do you got to get a permit, like for a dog or a car? Herman Marshall smiles. It is a smile of lesser intensity than his ideal and genuine smile, but it will do. Like they say, ha ha, any smile in a storm. And his brother fucked his wife, and so Billy was blood of Herman Marshall's blood, and this is supposed to be important. Well, it is keeping that puling sonofabitch of a Eugene alive, and so it surely is important to *him*. Killing is not important, though. Killing is too easy to be important. Kennedy's skull probably was like the shell of an egg that had lain too long in the goddamn hot sun. And the Nawzis had died every bit that easily. Herman Marshall gasps, shakes his jowls, adds more water from the *HOT* spigot. It is good to take a hotter than hot shower in Houston in August. That way, when you step out from under the water, you almost feel cool for a minute or so. Herman Marshall, in *extremis*, philosophizing on Houston's goddamn heat. He loved her. He loved his Edna. It doesn't matter that she fucked his brother. Herman Marshall looks down at his pecker and recalls the weak wad he'd presented to Jobeth Stephenson, and he is able to see her licking her hand, and her tongue is languid, and he shakes his head and tells himself no wonder Edna found it necessary to fuck poor old bloviating Eldred Junior, who had eaten at Herman Marshall's table, who had slept in Herman Marshall's home, whose own sons wouldn't even talk to him, oh the shitfaced peckerwood asshole. Herman Marshall dances and shudders in the hot water. He needs to piss, and so he pisses right there in the shower, and who ever will be the wiser? He pisses hotly, and he winces. But it's the first time he's pissed since early in the morning, and what does this mean? He recalls Beth's wrecked mouth. He recalls old Rollie Beecham's final smile. He recalls drinking dead Zack's glass of beer. He doesn't know why he was so thirsty right then. Maybe he'd found it necessary to take something more of Zack's. Something beyond Zack's life. Herman Marshall, in *extremis*, sees everything real clear, though, and he knows his scheme is not crazy. He hopes Eugene will come to understand this, but Eugene is such a goddamn sissy that . . . well, there's a good chance he'll get the whole thing all fucked up. Herman Marshall figures he, Herman Marshall, just a little old countryboy at heart, a little old countryboy who hoisted Tom Mix onto a pedestal and later sought a book as he passed through his years and busted his bladder in this truck and the next truck and the truck down the road, will be famous, however briefly, and *why don't Eugene pay attention so it all can be explained by him without no guessin an without no bullshit?* Air just might be money in it for Eugene, if he pays attention an uses his goddamn collegeprofessor brain. Herman Marshall, in *extremis*, is too tired to do any more explaining. His brain is too cluttered. Broken plates here. A torn innertube there. Shattered locomotives. Piles of chicken bones. A bloody *ASTROS* cap. *If You Ain't Done It With A COONASS You Ain't Done It.* Save your Confederate money, boys; the South will rise again. Herman Marshall rests his forehead against the shower wall. He closes his eyes. He never has understood why he didn't kill Rusty the cocksucking cocker. He should have done it smack in front of his motherinlaw, that goddamn blabby old bitch with her goddamn apron. He should have whacked Rusty to death with an ax. Hell, the old cunt probably would have choked on her apron. Herman Marshall groans. He is aware that if he is not in *extremis*, then no one ever has been in *extremis*. Some of his Coonass buddies from Louisiana every so often would use that word in his presence, and sometimes they even would cross themselves, for whatever the fuck good *that* did. Herman Marshall shudders as the hot water leaks down his spine. He is sorry he has killed so many people, and he is not sorry. He wonders how many of them already have picked out their harps. He wonders if any of them knows he loved them and loves them. They now are on top of the world. All of them, unless he misses his guess. Even Jobeth, and maybe she has a new television set up there, and maybe she is being entertained by happy niggers whose dorks are big enough to get an elephant in the old family way. This is a good thought, and it is as good a thought as Herman Marshall can summon. His eyes remain closed, and he sees an old night sky and ancient highways, and a Greyhound bus is churning along one of the ancient highways, and its destination sign says *TEXARKANA*, and Herman Marshall is riding alone, lounging in the back of the bus and taking advantage of the darkness by reaching inside his fly and flicking his dick in a brisk highway rhythm, and he is on his way to visit goddamn roundheeled Ethel Mae Kelleher, who had been his Edna's best friend, and sometimes it really is confusing when an Ethel Mae and an Edna are best friends, seeing as how their names are kind of similar, but what the hell, life seldom is a bowl of cherries, and anyway, the talk is that Ethel Mae is the best fuck in either the Texas or the Arkansas part of Texarkana, and Herman Marshall wants to rush and stagger to the front of the bus and urge the driver to lean hard on at air gas pedal, buddy; a good time is waitin to happen. But that's all bullshit. Herman Marshall never fucked Ethel Mae; he only *wanted* to fuck Ethel Mae. For how many years? Twenty? Yessir, a good twenty. At least. And he squeezes his eyes. And there is no way he can understand why he is thinking of Ethel Mae Kelleher. Shit, he says to himself, a man probably could of drove an Oldsmobile 88 inside her an lost his fuckin way. And Herman Marshall soaps his sorry old crotch. Again he remembers the timid wad he gave to Jobeth, and he is ashamed of himself. He says to himself: How come so much always comes down to fuckin? He says to himself: How did I get brung up? He says to himself: Why did I just now dream up somethin at never happened? He says a great many things to himself, and he encounters tangles and eruptions, and old Rollie Beecham's sweet smile hangs around the edges and maybe blesses the proceedings, and words flop, and images clamor and recede, and Herman Marshall, in *extremis* and beyond *extremis*, looms over Billy and tries to hold one of Billy's hands and Billy calls him a cocksucker and Billy's taut flesh is yellow, yellow, yellow, and Billy's sheets stink with that fragile hopeless stink of a sickness that will prevail, that *must* prevail, and *He was a Judgment, Herman,* she said weeping hugging coughing, and the bright phony funeral grass was like the sort of paper grass that lines Easter baskets, and Billy lay in a slender brown coffin since there wasn't all that much of him to bury, and Herman Marshall wondered Judgment on account of *what*? He wondered if the Judgment had anything to do with the mythic *TEXARKANA* bus he had imagined—and more than once. He wondered if it had anything to do with his whores and his waitresses and a certain tintinnabulating schoolteacher who'd been trained to treasure a good stiff finger up her sweet Hershey tunnel. Those women had been *real*, and he had happily worked them over and under and around and fucking *through*, and he figured hell, they were the real Judgment. But why had *Edna* been made to suffer? What had *she* done? It was a long time later that she told him she had fucked Phil Romero, and then she finally told him she had sucked Phil Romero's cock, and she had begged him all right, all right, fine; now you got a real reason to kill me. But Herman Marshall didn't kill his wife. The cancer killed his wife . . . and it took away all her hair. He opens his eyes. He pushes himself away from the shower wall. He isn't quite sure what any of this has to do with all the people he's killed this day. There is a reason, but it keeps losing focus. Too much brightness crowds in on him. He switches off the shower, and abruptly he hears Eugene's whimpering. "Shit," he says, and he steps from the shower. He leans over Eugene's enormous pale flabby body and says: "What the fuck's the matter with you? *You* ain't done nothin. You're innocent like a baby. So try to act like a man. Lord God, what must they think of you back at at air place where you teach?" And Herman Marshall squats over Eugene and unties him and pulls him to his feet. The two men stand naked and facing one another, and Eugene's prick is tiny and retracted, and hardly any hair surrounds it. "You look like a baby, you know at?" says Herman Marshall. "A baby at's got somethin wrong with it. A baby with a weeny prick an big tits." And Herman Marshall grabs Eugene and pushes him into the shower and turns on the water and the water is too hot and Eugene squeals. And Herman Marshall again unleashes the ideal and genuine smile. "*Go* for it," he says. "Rub a dub dub, one fat man in a tub at's also a shower. Rub a dub dub." And Herman Marshall towels himself and gets dressed . . . shorts, a T-shirt, overalls, boots, the cap that says *LONE STAR*. The Smith & Wesson and the cartridges are on the dresser. Herman Marshall stuffs them into a pocket of the overalls. Now Eugene finishes his shower. Herman Marshall crosses the hall to the bathroom, and Eugene is swallowing a handful of pills. Mouth trembling, Eugene says the pills will help him through the day. He says the pills are known as Valiums, and they help a great many people through the day. Herman Marshall has heard of these Valiums only in passing. He never has known much about pills. Oh, he was familiar with Edna's pain pills, but they hadn't been Valiums. Their name had been . . . well, he'd never learned to pronounce it, and so what? Would pronouncing that goddamn name have made her pain any easier to fucking endure? Herman Marshall stands in the bathroom and wipes steam from the mirror and combs his hair. "I think I'm going to be better now," says Eugene, waddling down the hall to the guest room. "I think I'm going to be a real surprise to you." Herman Marshall stares after his nephew and shrugs. The guest room door closes, and Herman Marshall

[257]

can't imagine what the hell Eugene is talking about. Since when does a handful of pills have the power to turn a pig into a man? Oh, well, there is nothing wrong with hoping for such a fine miracle. Herman Marshall figures it has about as much chance of coming to pass as Edna has of coming back to life. He walks downstairs and seats himself on the davenport. Eugene comes downstairs no more than ten minutes later, and he has done himself over from head to foot. All his clothes are fresh. He is wearing a gray suit, and it is crisp, and his black shoes are brilliantly polished. He turns this way and that, and he is smiling a little. "See what I mean?" he says. Then he allows as how he is hungry. Herman Marshall blinks. He escorts Eugene into the kitchen, and Eugene raids the fridge. Herman Marshall tells Eugene they have to be on their way. He tells Eugene there still is unfinished business. Eugene nods. He says fine, he won't take up much time. He fixes himself three ham sandwiches and wraps them in foil. He will eat them in the car, he says. He roots in a cupboard for a paper bag. He finds a paper bag and drops the sandwiches into it. Herman Marshall frowns. Herman Marshall can understand nothing. "It's the Valium," says Eugene. "It has a very decided effect on me. I'll not be giving you any more trouble, Uncle Herman." Eugene tucks the bag of sandwiches under an arm. "Whatever you have in mind, I want to see it. I should have taken the Valium this morning, do you know that? I mean, if I am to be the Recording Angel, the least I can do is have my wits about me. I'm sorry for all my blubbering and vomiting, but I'm just not . . . well, I'm just not *used* to this sort of thing . . ." And Eugene nods toward the front of the house. "Well," he says, "shall we be on our merry way?" And Herman Marshall says: "Yessir." And he and Eugene walk out of the house, and they both walk briskly, and their heels clap purposefully against the sidewalk. The sound of their heels does not carry too well. The air is too heavy. Nonetheless, the uncle and the nephew have purpose in their stride. Clearly the game is not yet concluded. Herman Marshall, *extremis* or no, works at his ideal and genuine smile, and it emerges nicely. He drives the rented Chevvy to T. C. Drucker & Sons. "Oh?" says Eugene. "Yessir," says Herman Marshall. He waits for Eugene to ask for specifics, but Eugene says nothing. The T. C. Drucker & Sons building is enormous. It is supposed to be a replica of Tara, from *Gone With the Wind*. But it is larger than Tara. After all, this is Houston, and Houston is in Texas, ha ha, and so it is *mandatory* that this place be larger than Tara, ho ho. Herman Marshall and Eugene stride across the front gallery. Eugene is carrying the remnants of his first ham sandwich, and he is chewing thoughtfully. "Whatever you have in mind," he says to Herman Marshall, "I'm sure it will be . . . interesting." Eugene chews and swallows the last of the ham sandwich as he and Herman Marshall walk into a reception room that has drapes decorated with what appear to be orchids. The room is empty, and so Herman Marshall leads Eugene down a narrow hallway. "Air's got to be somebody here somewheres," says Herman Marshall. He has removed his *LONE STAR* cap. He figures this is the least he can do. He pushes open a heavy steel door. There is a sign on the heavy steel door, and the sign says *NO ADMIT-TANCE*, but fuck the sign. Eugene wipes crumbs from a corner of his mouth. At the same time, he yawns a little. Now he and Herman Marshall are in a room that has an odor of chemicals. Maybe the chemicals are mostly formaldehyde, although Herman Marshall doesn't recall ever having breathed formaldehyde. Mr Grizzard and a colored fellow are standing at a table, and the table has a sort of trough, and no doubt the trough is for the body fluids of the Dear Departed. Mr Grizzard is wearing a leather apron, and the colored fellow is wearing a prim white smock. A thin girl lies naked on the table, and Mr Grizzard is about to press something (a pump maybe?) against her belly. The thin girl has long black hair. Perhaps she is fifteen. The room is chilly, and so her nipples . . . and they are tiny nipples . . . are erect. Again Eugene yawns, and he peevishly shakes his head. Mr Grizzard and the colored fellow advance on Herman Marshall and Eugene, and Herman Marshall shows the Smith & Wesson. "Godalmighty *shit*," says the colored fellow. He is thin and bald. He freezes. He wraps his arms around his chest. "I don't want no trouble with you, boy," says Herman Marshall to the colored fellow. Nodding toward Mr Grizzard, Herman Marshall says: "It's *him* I got bidness with." And Mr Grizzard, who also hesitated, and almost in midstride, says: "Mr Marshall, what . . . .what . . . why are you . . . is air . . . well, is air somethin we can do for you?" Says Herman Marshall: "I won't mess around bout it. I'm here because of the wig." Says Mr Grizzard: "Wig?" Says Herman Marshall: "I want you to take it off of her an give me my fuckin money back, you greedy sonofabitch." Says Mr Grizzard: "You mean your wife?" Says Herman Marshall: "No, you asshole. I mean fuckin goddamn Eleanor Roosevelt." Says Mr Grizzard: "But your wife has been buried, an the wig was buried with her. An it was quite an attractive—" Herman Marshall interrupts Mr Grizzard. He interrupts Mr Grizzard by smacking Mr Grizzard across the jaw with the Smith & Wesson. "My," says Eugene. Mr. Grizzard drops to his knees. The colored fellow's head moves from side to side and he says to Herman Marshall: "Can I go? Can I get out of here?" Says Herman Marshall: "Stop bein such a pain in the ass, boy. You stay right where you are." Herman Marshall walks to the table and seizes the dead girl's hair and lifts her head. She might have been pretty if there had been more meat on her poor little bones. Herman Marshall shakes her head up and down and he says: "She's got a real good head of hair. At's what I like to see. A real good head of hair. Not no goddamn *wig*." And Herman Marshall releases the girl's hair. Her head falls back, and it bounces. Mr Grizzard, down there on his knees, is shaking his head and hugging the pump or whatever it is. It has a sort of plunger. He is bleeding from a corner of his mouth, and one of his cheeks is beginning to puff up. Herman Marshall blinks at the girl. "Now *at's* what *I* call goddamn *skinny*," he says. Quickly the colored fellow speaks up: "Anorexia nervosa. She . . . at means she starved herself to death. She's fourteen. Her name is Emily Doolittle, an her daddy used to be a member of the Texas Railroad Commission." Says Herman Marshall: "Well, kiss my ass." He begins prodding Mr Grizzard with a boot. "Stand up, you fucker," he says to Mr Grizzard. He waves the Smith & Wesson, and Mr Grizzard stands up, and Mr Grizzard still is hugging the pump. "I want my money back for at wig," says Herman Marshall, and he presses the Smith & Wesson's muzzle against the tip of Mr Grizzard's chin. A stink of piss comes up, and Herman Marshall says to Mr Grizzard: "You havin you a little problem?" And he rubs Mr Grizzard's chin with the muzzle of the Smith & Wesson. Eugene speaks up. "Nine people are dead today," he says to Mr Grizzard. He nods at Mr Grizzard. "Nine," he says. "The number is nine, and I propose to write all about it. My uncle here is quite a man. Give him his money back. Do yourself a favor." And Mr Grizzard says: "But I'm not authorized to—" And Herman Marshall squeezes off two quick rounds, and Mr Grizzard is effectively beheaded. Blood erupts in a geyser, and the girl's fleshless corpse is soaked. Blood is spattered all over Herman Marshall's face. He turns to the colored fellow, and the colored fellow says: "You want you a nice clean towel, Mister?" Herman Marshall smiles his ideal and genuine smile at the colored fellow. "At would be real nice," he says. The

[261]

colored fellow hurries to a cabinet and fetches a towel for Herman
Marshall. He hands it to Herman Marshall, and Herman Marshall
says to him: "This is gettin to be fun, you know at? Maybe it's
like fuckin. Maybe the more you do, the more you want to do."
And now the colored fellow is shaking and moaning, and Herman
Marshall fires three shots into the colored fellow's chest. A tall and
slender middleaged woman comes highheeling into the room, and
briefly she screams, and Herman Marshall kills her with a single
shot to the jugular. The colored fellow has fallen across the girl
who died of anorexia nervosa, and his face is pressed against her
bush. Herman Marshall reloads the Smith & Wesson, and he and
Eugene hurry out into the parking lot. Herman Marshall starts
the car on the first turn of the key. Herman Marshall's hands are
unsteady on the wheel. He didn't mean any harm to the colored
fellow and the middleaged woman, and yet he'd enjoyed killing
them (he even is feeling maybe the beginnings of a hardon), and
it all reminds him of the way he'd grinned and had carried on
back in '45 when those old men had tried to set up that roadblock
behind those goddamn mattresses. He shakes his head and puts
the car in gear and drives out of the parking lot. Talk about your
extremis. Talk about your fucking end of the world. Eugene opens
the bag and removes another ham sandwich. He tears away the
foil and begins to eat the ham sandwich. Again he yawns. His
eyes are vague, and his mouth hangs loosely. He chews with his
mouth open, and his tongue slurps. He asks Herman Marshall
what's next on the agenda. Herman Marshall tells him only one
more thing is on the agenda, and then this whole goddamn bidness
will be over and done with for good and forever. "An en you
can write about it," says Herman Marshall. "Oh, I will," says Eugene. "An maybe it'll be the book," says Herman Marshall. "What
book?" says Eugene. "The book at tells the truth," says Herman

Marshall. "Oh," says Eugene. "The book at comes down like the sun, an don't nothin hide from it. I ain't talkin bout no *fantasy*, an I ain't talkin bout no *dreams*. I'm talkin bout the *truth*." And the windshield is spangled by shadows. They whisk over the car. Herman Marshall drives north on Kirby, and the Chevvy weaves from lane to lane. And then the airconditioner spits, farts and gives out. "God damn it," says Eugene, and he reaches in a jacket pocket for Kleenex. The car turns off Kirby just north of Bissonet and heads toward Dr Moomaw's office, which is in a brick building that has fake Tudor trim. Herman Marshall and Eugene don't have to visit Dr Moomaw's office, however. Eugene, of course, wouldn't know Dr Moomaw from a bag of coal. Eugene is swallowing the last of his second ham sandwich, and he is humming and snapping his fingers. But Herman Marshall knows who Dr. Moomaw is, and he smiles his ideal and genuine smile when he sees Dr Moomaw jogging along the street, and Dr Moomaw's calves are pumping, and Dr Moomaw's Adidas are slapping the pavement, and Dr Moomaw's arms are churning, and the sun and the moon and the heavens are applauding Dr Moomaw, a doctor who once made a fucking house call *after* one of his patients had died, and Herman Marshall leans out of the window on his side and shouts: "*Look at the runnin fool!*" And Dr Moomaw glances back. Eugene begins to wheeze and chuckle. He belches. Herman Marshall's first two shots miss Dr Moomaw altogether, and Dr Moomaw sprints into a woods next to a supermarket parking lot. Herman Marshall brakes the car to a skidding stop and trots into the woods after Dr Moomaw. He wings Dr Moomaw just before Dr Moomaw ducks behind a tree. Shrieking, Dr Moomaw tries to push himself away from the tree. The earth is hard, and Herman Marshall's feet begin to hurt a little. Dr Moomaw is bleeding on the trunk of the tree. Herman Marshall shoots away both of

Dr Moomaw's kneecaps, and Dr Moomaw falls unconscious, and Herman Marshall kneels next to the sorry bullshitting greedy heartless cocksucking sonofabitch and puts him out of his misery with a final shot that penetrates the adamsapple. Herman Marshall walks back to the car, and he is all asparkle with blood, and he slides into the front seat, and Eugene is working on the third ham sandwich.

CHAPTER TWENTY

SOPPING AND COATLESS, Eugene lounged on the dirty brown gravcyard grass and said to his uncle: "It's been a remarkable experience, and I thank you for it. You may have changed my life, do you realize that?"

Herman Marshall shrugged. He was sitting on the *LAMAR* headstone. His cheeks and his chin were splotched with other people's blood. He had been sweating. Of course he had been sweating. It was August in Houston, and nearly everyone sweated in August in Houston. And he still *was* sweating, for that matter. And his sweat had caused the splotches of blood to run.

"Please don't be so modest," said Eugene. He fingered a blot of sweat off his forehead.

"I don't know what I'm bein modest bout," said Herman Marshall. "You're sort of talkin in riddles, you know?"

Eugene sighed. "I never thought . . . well, I'd never thought I'd be able to get *into* this sort of thing. The way I was at the beginning, when I wept and vomited and all the rest of it, *that* could have been expected. But *now* . . . the way I am *now* . . . I'm not being the naturally lilylivered Eugene Coffee. If my wives could only see me now . . ."

"Well, write bout it."

"I shall."

"Tell the people old Herman Marshall was all fucked up."

"*Was?*" said Eugene.

"Yessir," said Herman Marshall. "Was. On account of I ain't *nothin* no more. On account of just bout all my friends is gone an

[265]

all my enemies is gone, an a nigger an a woman are gone whose names I don't even know. At's sort of scary, ain't it? I mean, I just sort of got carried away."

"Perhaps that's what people mean when they speak of blood lust."

"*No*," said Herman Marshall, and he smacked his palms together. "No *sir*." The Smith & Wesson lay in his lap. He lifted the Smith & Wesson and frowned at it. "I always been a peaceful man. I kilt people when air was a war, but at was a *war*, an killin people is what a man is supposed to do. But I ain't no . . . murderer."

"You'll be perceived as one," said Eugene.

"Well, you got to write me up so I come out better an at."

"I don't know whether I'll be able to."

"Eugene, you want to know somethin?"

"What's that?"

"I think I liked you better when you was pulin an pukin. At least en I could understand you."

Eugene shook his head from side to side. "No," he said, "I'm the same Eugene. It's just that I gave myself some helpful medication. And you were right in what you said about killing."

"Right in what I said? What did I say?"

"You said it was easy. You said there was nothing to it. You spoke of Kennedy, and you said it had been easy to kill him, and I think you said it always was easy to kill people. Something like that. Well, I took your words to heart. I had myself a nice shower, and then I popped a handful of dear old Vitamin V, and so you see a changed man here before you."

"You understand what this all has got to do with your Aunt Edna?"

"Yes, I believe so."

"She didn't get no respect."

". . . like Rodney Dangerfield," said Eugene.

"Who?"

"Never mind," said Eugene.

Herman Marshall nodded. He hefted the Smith & Wesson. "An en," he said, "it came clear to me at . . . well . . ." A frown, "It came clear to me at hardly none of us gets no respect. An so I kind of said to myself: They can go with her like Egyptian cats. An so I *also* kind of said to myself: Air old, an they ain't gettin no younger, an people'll laugh at em. People always laugh at old people. Old women with bad tits. Old men with limp peckers. It's all supposed to be in a spirit of good clean fun, I been told, but I don't see nothin good about it, an I don't see nothin clean bout it. The only thing is, I'm sorry bout the nigger, an I'm sorry about at woman. I shouldn't of kilt them. I guess it's just too fuckin easy to get carried away. I guess it just ain't somethin you'd want every jasper in off the street to be doin. An me, I'm a jasper myself. If I wasn't, the nigger an the woman would be alive . . ."

"Do you know what set you off?"

"Set me off?"said Herman Marshall, and he drew up his knees and leaned his chin on them. "Set me *off*?Do I *know* what set me fuckin *off*? Why, it *all* set me off. The pain set me off. Losin Edna an nobody givin a real honest shit set me off. Not havin no kid to stand by her coffin set me off. People lookin down at her an talkin bout her *wig* set me off. Flowers set me off. They *stink*. Havin old Jobeth fuss over me set me off. I'm sayin it *all* set me off. *You* set me off. Dreams at fell apart in the night. Layin up with English girls, an they most of em couldn't relax, an they talked about Nawzis . . . *at* set me off. Knowin I'd cheated on Edna set me off. I mean, it's all promises at the beginnin, ain't it? Words an smiles an hope. But nothin's said bout your fuckin teeth fallin out. An nothin's

[267]

said bout wigs at are uglier an cat shit. An nothin's said bout the glory of the open road an all the noise an all the bouncin an your kidneys blowin up. All you *get* from this here life is words that promise you good things in the Sweet Bye & Bye if you mind your P's an your Q's an stay in your place, an at the end you can bring stuff down from the attic an make up stories on account of the stories mean more an the truth does. What set me *off*? Shit, why don't you ask me what *didn't* set me off?"

Eugene glanced over a shoulder. He glanced at Edna's grave, and it was raw with mounded earth. "The police will catch you sooner or later. Do you want them to catch you here?"

"Why not?" said Herman Marshall.

"So you're staying here?"

"Yessir."

"I could go get them. Maybe you're tired."

"You can do whatever you want to do," said Herman Marshall. "It don't matter now." His chin came off his knees. He straightened.

"If I go get them, will you promise not to do anything to yourself?"

"No."

Slowly Eugene nodded. "Well . . ." he said, and he shrugged.

"You don't give a fiddler's fart one way or tuther, do you?"

". . . I don't know what to say to that."

"How about the truth?"

"The truth?" said Eugene. "I don't believe it's . . . well, I don't believe there's anything simple about any of this."

"Now you're talkin like a professor, all right. You're real calm bout all this, ain't you? One minute you're a naked bawlin fat man layin on the floor of my bathroom. The next minute you're a regular fuckin cucumber."

"But hasn't the change been for the better? I had seen enough,

[268]

you see. I had seen more than enough. I took the pills and I put on fresh clothes, and it then occurred to me that everything I'd seen no longer mattered. And so four *more* people—four? yes, four— have died, and I was able to stand around and eat ham sandwiches, and you don't have to tell me I was behaving like an insensitive grotesque, but we all have to defend ourselves however we can, isn't that so?"

"What are you tryin to tell me?"

"Nothing in particular."

"You're tryin to tell me it's all been bullshit."

"Oh, I wouldn't go *that* far . . ."

"It ain't goin to last. You're goin to forget me."

"No," said Eugene, and he sat up and embraced his chest and his tits. "I'll not be forgetting you."

"I don't believe at," said Herman Marshall. He glared up at the sun. "You're lyin. You're lyin in the sight of God." His gaze shifted to Eugene. "I'm givin you the chance to *write* the *book*. I'm givin you the chance to walk back to the car an go fetch the cops an tell em all bout the fuckin mass murderer who's settin in this here cemetery, an en you can *write* bout it, only you got to write bout it *good*, on account of I want it to be nothin but the truth. All my life I been lookin for a book like at. An without one fuckin *word* bout virgin birth an Lazarus an the Partin of the Red Sea. An if at book comes out of all this, en today's been a good day an a right an proper day."

"I'll do my best. That's all I can say."

"Do better an at," said Herman Marshall. He pointed the Smith & Wesson toward Eugene.

"Hey now," said Eugene, and he tried to push himself to his feet, but he sprawled forward on his belly.

Herman Marshall walked to Eugene and stood over him and

said: "Don't make light of this, you fucker. I got it all figured out, you understand? Air all dead on account of the world's got to be told a thing or two . . ."

Eugene clawed at the terrible dead grass. He began to whimper.

"Lord God . . ." said Herman Marshall.

". . . don't kill me . . . please don't kill me . . . I'm your . . . your Recording Angel . . . don't you remember?"

"Don't talk to me like I'm crazy," said Herman Marshall to his whimpering nephew. He kicked Eugene in the ass and the ribs.

Eugene screamed.

"Jesus, you're changin *back*," said Herman Marshall.

Eugene clawed and flapped and flailed, and finally he managed to sit up. ". . . no," he said, wheezing. "I'm the new . . . the new Eugene . . ."

"An you'll remember me?"

Quickly Eugene nodded.

"I wonder . . ." said Herman Marshall.

Eugene struggled to his feet. "I'll go now. I'll drive with the windows open because the airconditioner's on the fritz, and maybe the air, even this Houston air, will do me some good. It will be healthy to be out of an artificial environment, and I'll be a better—"

"What the fuck are you talkin bout?" said Herman Marshall.

"I was just—"

"You ain't goin to member me," said Herman Marshall. "Not for long anyways. You're not a serious man, are you? Well, maybe I can give you a fuckin reminder." And Herman Marshall fired the Smith & Wesson at Eugene's left hand and shot off two fingers.

The stumps bled. Eugene wrapped them in his good hand. He blinked at Herman Marshall. His legs gave way a little, and he lurched from side to side like a prizefighter who has been whacked in the belly.

[270]

"Go," said Herman Marshall. "Get out of here. Go peddle your fish."

Tears smeared Eugene's face. "I'll . . . ow, it hurts . . ." And he squeezed the place where the fingers had been. "I'll . . . I'll write the book . . ."

"You'll write *a* book," said Herman Marshall. "You won't write *the* book. Now go away, you bullshit sonofabitch . . ." And Herman Marshall leveled the Smith & Wesson at Eugene's head.

Eugene retreated. The car was parked on a service road just beyond a line of trees. He stumbled and nearly fell, but he kept retreating. "I'll do it," he said. "I'll . . . I'll remember you . . ."

"I'm dyin," said Herman Marshall.

". . . yes," said Eugene.

"Go," said Herman Marshall. "Go away."

Eugene nodded. Eugene's tears were loud, but they were blotted by the humidity. This was just as well, at least as far as Herman Marshall was concerned. His gaze followed Eugene all the way to the car, and he watched the car lurch down the service road toward the cemetery's main gate.

"I'm dyin," said Herman Marshall to nothing. Or maybe he said the words to the sky. He'd never known a sky to be so bright. "Dyin," said Herman Marshall. "Dyin. Dyin." He walked to Edna's grave. Next to it, Billy's grave was flat, It had settled within a year, as closely as Herman Marshall could recall. Edna had worked so very hard on Billy's grave. She often had spoken of how deeply at peace Billy was. No more screams. No more pain. No more dirty words. Herman Marshall stood at the foot of Edna's raw new grave and wished he could open it and remove that fucking wig. But that would have been improper. What sort of man was it who would rob his own wife's grave? Well, at least he hadn't killed Eugene. He supposed blood was thicker than bullets. Something like that. And he had to keep reminding himself how important blood had been to Edna. Ah, such a plain and sweet name: Edna. Would she have approved of all that had happened this day? Not fucking likely. It was quite a roll, though . . . Harry and Beth, Ralph Danielson, Milt Willis and his Diana, the licker of balls. Frank Lee Doubleday. Poor old Rollie Beecham. Poor old Zack Fears, the crip. Jobeth Stephenson, the old harpy who would fuck a polecat. Mr Grizzard, the undertaker and wig man. A nigger in a prim white smock. A highheeled woman in a black dress. And finally that real prince, Dr Moomaw. A total of thirteen. An unlucky total. Well, Herman Marshall could change that, and he would. His grave plot was next to Edna's grave. This meant she forever would rest between him and Billy. Well, that was all right, what with the truth of Billy's origins. Herman Marshall lay down where his grave would be. He lay with his hands folded on his chest, and the Smith & Wesson was held between his hands. He said to himself: Air was good times, an I don't want to say air wasn't. One time she saved up her money an bought a white blouse at had black buttons down the front because I'd told her I'd seen Claudette Colbert in at sort of blouse an it had sure enough got me in a fair state, on account of all my life I sure enough been your good old average countryboy tit man. I sure enough am sorry bout Elsie. I should of let her live an kilt Rusty instead. I feel bad bout em as who I kilt, but air was a point to it, an air goin to be better off in the long run. How come we're never told enough bout Paradise? And Herman Marshall blinked at the merciless sun. Maybe the sun always was merciless, at least in Houston. It was an unforgiving sun, and it took no sass, and it listened to no excuses, and so therefore it had little use for eloquence and wit. Surely then it was merciless. Herman Marshall breathed the Smith & Wesson, and its odor was like wisps of powdered coal. Loop 610 was behind a distant row of tract houses, and he listened to the traffic. It was an unrelenting hiss the way Niagara Falls no doubt was an unrelenting hiss. It was a perfect and endless sound of fear and danger that had been created by the human race because everyone said Progress, and hip, hip, hooray, kiss my ass, let's all bow down in the face of good old Progress. Herman Marshall grunted. He wondered whether the police cars would use their sirens. He hoped so. He didn't want to keep checking that service road. Instead he wanted to remember whatever dribs and drabs of his life that came wandering across his mind. Arkadelphia Savings & Loan had had a southpaw pitcher named George (Frosty) Higgins, so named because his hair was prematurely white, and one Sunday afternoon in 1930 Herman Marshall hit a Frosty Higgins blue darter at least five hundred feet, or so the Arkadelphia paper later reported, and after the game Frosty Higgins came to Herman Marshall and said: *You sure made a fastball out of my fastball, you sonofabitch.* And then he and Herman Marshall went to the best blind pig in Arkadelphia and drank expensive imported Mexican beer, and all the beers were on Frosty Higgins and the Arkadelphia manager, a fellow named Fritz Blatt, who once had played briefly as an infielder for the Brooklyn Dodgers back in the Wilbert Robinson days. And Herman Marshall spoke aloud. And he said: "So this is the end of the world." He couldn't quite understand the whys and twists of the path that had taken him from that blind pig in Arkadelphia, Arkansas, to this graveyard in Houston, Texas, and an event that no doubt was the end of the world, but maybe he wasn't supposed to wonder about such a thing; maybe this was why he'd never been able to learn very much about Paradise. And yet he still believed in Paradise. It was such a pretty thing to believe in. One time in 1941 or so he was laying up with a waitress named Sunny Bunn, who was small and dark and very nearly titless, and she said the damnedest thing to him. She said: *I always wanted to have a snake crawl inside me.* That was all she said. Simply: *I always wanted to have a snake crawl inside me.* She was a Coonass, was that Sunny Bunn, and she was a fine little old piece of twat, but Herman Marshall never again had anything to do with her. He was afraid she might want him to bring her a snake so the three of them could go at it, haw haw. Now Herman Marshall was rubbing his cheeks, and blood came off with his sweat. He supposed he was glad about Phil Romero's exoneration. He'd always liked Phil back in the old days. Phil always had appeared to be straight, and he never had tried to be something he wasn't. *I ain't no Anglo*, he would say, *an at's just fine with me. It means I don't have to eat no GRITS an GRAVY, you unerstan?* And then Phil Romero would laugh, and his laughter was large; it boomed out like a sunrise in an open place. And he'd never shoved his cock in Edna's mouth. Good old Phil Romero. Surely he had a harp, and surely he was enjoying an eternity of lovely women. Which was what Paradise was all about, wasn't it? Herman Marshall smiled his ideal and genuine smile. Blinking, he directed it at the sun. He tried to give the sun the Tom Mix squint, but he didn't know how successful he was. He sniffed the barrel of the Smith & Wesson. Nothing like a good old revolver. If he'd had a revolver instead of that .45 automatic back in Belgium and Germany in '44 and '45, only God knew how many more Nawzis he would have killed. A revolver had a better heft to it. Which meant you had more confidence when you squeezed off a round. Oh, well, the goddamned .45 had done its work well, and so Herman Marshall wasn't really complaining. A dozen roses were waiting in the bedroom when Edna came home from the hospital with the baby. Red roses. A skinny little sissy with curly red hair had helped Herman Marshall pick them out. Edna gasped over them, and Herman Marshall told her she was beautiful. She held him, and then she pulled him to the bed, and they lay on the bed with the baby, and

[274]

the baby made fists, and Herman Marshall honest to God wept, and who really gave a damn that Texans weren't supposed to weep? He wondered whether he should have done something about his fragile abilities as a teller of fanciful stories. No, that wouldn't have been consistent. A teller of fanciful stories couldn't on the other hand turn around and demand a book that communicated only the truth. Maybe Herman Marshall was stupid, but that didn't mean he was illogical, ha ha. A fellow is driving past a loonybin and he sees an inmate standing at the side of the road. The driver stops his car and asks the inmate what is the cube root of seven hundred twentynine. And the inmate promptly says: *Nine*. And the driver says: *Hey, good for you*. And the inmate says: *I may be crazy, but at don't mean I'm stupid*. And, remembering the story, Herman Marshall nearly laughed aloud. That was the thing about a good joke. It often had meaning in whatever passed for real life. Herman sucked the barrel of the Smith & Wesson, and it was warm, perhaps even a little salty. He removed the barrel from his mouth and swiped at his lips with the back of a hand. It would not be an easy time for him. Oh, not that he wanted to stay alive, but he wasn't too sure about the pain. There had been so much pain involved in Edna's dying, and maybe he had no more room for pain. But, hell, dying was easy. Certainly it hadn't been much of a struggle for most of the people Herman Marshall had sent across that day. Harry Munger, for instance. Poor old Rollie Beecham. The woman who had come highheeling into that embalming chamber, or whatever it had been. Hell, for that matter, how much could Kennedy have felt? One moment a brain, the next moment a rotten and broken eggshell. No, there was nothing to killing. Which meant that those who did the killing had to make themselves believe that dying was just as simple. A matter of velocity and tension and the strength of various bones and masses of tissue. Herman Marshall glanced over at Edna's grave and said:

[275]

"Maybe we done the best we could. Maybe it wasn't our fault nobody gave a shit. Maybe it ain't *nobody's* fault when nobody gives a shit. They polished your weddin ring before they done planted you. Maybe it's helpin you see in the dark. You expect I got a point?" And Herman Marshall shook his head. He was hearing sirens. Good old Eugene had gotten out the word, and now good old Eugene probably was in a hospital and weeping over the pain of his lost fingers. Well, at least there would be a reminder. Jesus, nothing *cruel* had been intended. Herman Marshall certainly didn't want anyone to think *that*. He grimaced into the sunlight. He supposed the cops would advance on him with their guns drawn. Houston cops were much taken with advancing with their guns drawn. And Herman Marshall didn't suppose Houston cops very often wept. It occurred to him that he hadn't pissed but the one time all day long. Briefly he sat up and watched the police cars, and the lights on their roofs put him in mind of whirling jellybeans. He looked around. His mouth opened. A big yellow Thing had emerged from the row of trees. It had jaws, and the jaws had teeth, and it had a long neck, and the word *ILES* was displayed on the neck. Herman Marshall stood up and got off three quick rounds at the Thing. The driver jumped out of the Thing and scrambled toward the gathering police cars with their nervous jellybean lights. The cops opened fire on Herman Marshall from behind their cars. He paid them no attention. He kept firing at the Thing, the *ILES* Thing, and he smiled his ideal and genuine smile whenever one of his bullets clanged off the Thing. The cops advanced, and they were crouching. Herman Marshall fired all but one of his bullets at the Thing. Then he seated himself where his grave would be. Quickly he patted the mounded dirt on Edna's grave. He crossed his legs like the Brave Little Tailor. He sucked the Smith & Wesson and closed his eyes and saw everything and saw nothing, and all of it was white.